MONSTER IN MY SHADOW

RAVENSWOOD

BOOK ONE

LANA SKY

Monster in My Shadow

Monster in My Shadow By Lana Sky

ACKNOWLEDGMENTS

Thanks so much to everyone who supported this draft along the way, including the many beta readers who provided encouragement! Please keep in mind that this story includes dark, graphic, and explicit content matter that may not be suitable for readers under the age of 18—or for readers who are uncomfortable with the following subject matter: age-gap relationships, explicit sex, mentions of abuse, and graphic depictions of violence.

So what if I had a stalker? As one of three female servers under fifty, I was used to unwelcome attention—though this man didn't ogle me like the other men past puberty did. His expression was different, more nuanced.

There was no outright anger, per se.

No desire, either.

Every night for the past two months, he sat at the bar, ordered a beer, and observed me until closing, his lips tilted in a slight frown. Stuck in a town like Kittywatt, I'd glower at the locals too. To be fair, I couldn't stop staring at him either, though for an admittedly shallow reason.

He stood out like a sore thumb. The only bar in Kittywatt and the third largest employer, Bardee's, was mostly frequented by truckers. *He*, on the other hand, lived nearby but kept to himself.

I knew of him around town. Every single woman did. I think his name was Levi. *Levi-something-or-other* worked at the Ravenswood gas station and was one of the most handsome things walking around on two legs. Sometimes, while filling up my car, I'd see him hauling boxes around the yard or washing the windows of the cashier booth.

I might have imagined him without his shirt on once or twice—not that I'd ever act on the attraction. The way he carried himself made him seem older than my meager twenty-two, and I was far too shy to approach him.

For the past few years, my innocent crush had been a harmless distraction considering that I'd rarely seen him in town, let alone the bar. In fact, we had never talked outside of the gas station. So why could I feel his eyes on the back of my neck at that very moment?

Breathe, Kaydee. All I could do was fiddle with a dishrag and pretend I didn't notice. What if he wanted me to? Should I have said something? Looked at him in return?

Instead, like a good little waitress, I plastered on a fake smile, tapped my cowboy boots in tune to whatever tired country song was playing, and attempted to survive my shift without cracking. I managed to keep up the innocent act for most of the night until my boss Mari nudged me with her elbow on her way from the kitchen.

"Kaydee, honey…" Her eyes met mine from over a mountain of wings she carried piled on a platter. "I'm swamped. Would you mind manning the bar solo for a bit? That damned football team won again."

She rolled her eyes in exasperation toward a table in the corner where a rowdy crowd whooped and hollered around the bar's only television.

"Oh. That thing was tonight?" I sighed in sympathy. The men in this town sure could get excited whenever the team of their choosing put a ball in a hole. "No problem."

Squaring my shoulders, I took stock of the remaining customers. Overall, it was a pretty slow shift, minus the raucous celebration. Only five people sat at the bar—two of whom had already reached their limit and were in danger of needing to be escorted outside. As for the man in the corner…

I tried to play it cool. What if he wasn't here for me? After all, he was on Mari's usual side of the bar, and even though his beer was running low, she could top him off when she got back…right?

Right. But that didn't mean I couldn't sneak glances at him from the corner of my eye. As always, I stared for much longer than necessary. He was so abnormally pretty. Jet-black hair formed a ponytail longer than mine, and his dark eyes were set in a face that would have made any woman's head turn twice. The most striking feature of all, however, was the color of his skin—a deep russet shade unlike any I'd ever seen. In a town like Kittywatt, where the population was ninety percent Caucasian—with the other ten percent being *mostly* Caucasian mixed with a little something else— my stalker stood out like a gold coin on white paper.

And for the past five minutes, his gaze had remained fixated on me alone. Or not. In reality, the poor man probably just wanted another beer. Nodding to that logic, I dug into the cooler beneath the counter for a fresh one. Then I spun to face him for what had to be the first time since his mysterious appearance.

"Hey there," I chirped in my friendly waitress voice.

He didn't grin in return. Instead, his eyes coolly observed my approach. About a yard from him, I cleared my throat and raised my offering in a trembling fist.

"C-Can I get you another?"

He swiped the near-empty bottle aside, allowing me to set the new one down in its place, and…

He *didn't* jump over the counter to ravish me. Go figure. As truth would have it, he was nursing a burgeoning drinking problem rather than a fascination with me. The smart thing to do would have been to turn around, right then and there, with my head held high and my pride still intact—but as Mama liked to say, *"Damn us Blanchetts and our inability to know when to leave things clean and dry."*

So, I stood there like a brain-dead idiot until something goaded me to speak—a strange and overpowering urge to fill the air between us with anything at all. "So, d-do you come here often? It seems…it seems like you come here often. I mean, I've seen you here a lot…lately."

Way to answer your own question there, Kaydee. Ugh, just stop while you're ahead.

"I'm Kaydee," I blurted next, though the quick flick of his eyes toward my name tag told me he already knew that. "You're…Levi, right?" A muscle in his jaw twitched. I figured he had clenched his teeth, anxious for me to take a hint. *Go away.* "I'm just gonna…go…back…over there. Yeah, um. Okay. If you need anything, you know where to find me."

As if that wasn't obvious already. Like a wounded bird, I scrambled back to my corner anyway. No reply ever came from behind me. Not even a "Sayonara, sweetheart, don't you ever bother me again."

To survive the crippling shame, I hunted for a distraction and settled on someone sitting just a few stools away. He looked around my age and sported a head of strawberry-blond curls that fell carelessly in his eyes. When he noticed me, he smiled and lifted his half-empty beer in a silent request for more. A surge of relief rushed through me. *Thank God.* Someone normal.

"Hi, there! What can I get you?" I called while heading in his direction.

His smile grew even wider. "Kaydee. Don't ya remember me?"

The twang of his voice seemed familiar, and a name slowly came to mind to go along with his crooked grin.

"B…Boyd? Boyd Thomson?"

The last time I'd seen him, he'd had a face full of acne and a mouth encased in braces. These past four years out of high school had done him some good apparently—the baby fat in his cheeks had hollowed out, revealing a handsome, chiseled jawline, and his straightened teeth formed a beautiful smile.

"In the flesh," he said with a wink. "I'm in town on a break from school. Before heading back, I thought I'd stop at the old haunt for one last drink. I picked Delville, by the way —" He pointed to his sweatshirt, which sported the name of a nearby college. "It's not exactly Harvard, but it's not the community college either."

A twinge ripped through my chest. I might have been a little jealous. "Wow," I croaked. "So, what do you study?"

"Astronomy with a minor in Natural Sciences. Senior year," Boyd replied. I remembered something about him having been head of the science club in high school.

"Senior year," I repeated absently. "That's really great." Only fifteen people in our class had actually gone to college, and apparently, Boyd was one of the even fewer who hadn't already dropped out.

"Thanks." He grinned, and before I could react, he was leaning over the bar, dragging me in close for an impromptu hug. "I've missed you, my old lab partner—"

Clink! I whirled around just in time to witness a bottle of beer fall from the opposite end of the bar, sloshing dark liquid all over the floor.

"Oh crap!" I started forward, reaching for the washcloth I'd left by the sink. "I'll get that for you—"

When I glanced up, I realized the bottle had come from my stalker's corner. He must have dropped it, but he didn't seem alarmed. His gaze met mine, and for the first time, he held it without turning away. *Zap*! It was silly, but it felt as though an electric current shot through me then and there. I found myself frozen mid-lunge, unable to move even as the rag slipped from my fingers.

The look in his eyes wasn't blank for once. His brows were furrowed, lips pursed. A terrifying explanation crossed my mind—he was angry, though I couldn't begin to guess why. Had I offended him somehow?

"Kaydee?" Boyd cleared his throat to regain my attention, but it took me way too long to turn back to him.

"Huh?" Only then did I realize my cheeks were flaming.

"I was saying that I was in town scouting out a spot to watch the lunar eclipse next month," Boyd went on. "The moon turns red. It's a hell of a sight. Maybe you could join me if you're into that sort of thing. What have *you* been up to, anyway?"

"Up to?" I could feel my smile start to slip as I struggled to regain my bearings. *Focus, Kaydee.* Liquid dripped steadily onto the floor amid the eerie sound of what might have been teeth grinding together. I should have rushed to clean it up before the beer could damage the wood, but for some reason, I couldn't seem to move. I didn't want to.

"What college do you go to?" Boyd asked next. "I remember you getting into almost every one you applied to. Did you pick that fancy private university? Journalism major, I'm guessing. I remember how you used to scribble all the time in those notebooks of yours."

"Oh." It was the question I dreaded the most. Rather than beat around the bush, I just released the truth with a sigh. "I didn't go to college."

"What?" It was Boyd's turn to blink in shock. "Really? But you were the smartest girl in the whole—"

"Another beer?" I interjected. Without waiting for a reply, I snatched one from the cooler beside the sink. The icy surface sent a shock through my system, making it easier to focus. *Keep it together, Kaydee.* After a steadying inhale, I faced Boyd again.

"Here ya go!" I placed the beer on the counter a little too eagerly and tried to maintain my cheerful bartender façade, but my gaze kept straying to the front of his sweatshirt. He would probably graduate in the spring. Earn a degree. Buy a plane ticket straight out of Kittywatt.

In the meantime, I would have been lucky to cajole a dollar raise out of Mari. While Boyd merrily went off into the wider world, I would be here, withering away before a shelf filled with liquor that I don't even get to enjoy for myself.

"Thank you," Boyd said with a gallant nod. "So, you've just been working…here, then?"

I nodded and forced a playful laugh. "It puts food on the table."

I didn't miss the way Boyd's friendly expression wavered. "Right. I remember the fries were decent here."

"Don't forget the milkshakes," I quipped. Honestly, Bardee's wasn't as much of a "shithole" as everyone liked to make it out to be. Mari and her husband, Mark, went out of their way to make it seem as homey and inviting as possible. There were posters of famous baseball players on the walls and a second-hand pool table scavenged from the junkyard. They tried their best—but booze and beer only attracted a certain type of folk regularly and well…

I couldn't count the number of times I'd been hit on by some punk too drunk to know when to quit, and rarely did a night go by without a drunken fight needing to be broken up with force. As if on cue, a cacophony of sound burst from the corner—smashing glass and angry shouts. I glanced over just in time to find a rush of bodies racing toward my end of the bar, including a frantic Mari.

"Kaydee, I need that bat!" she screeched, and I automatically snatched the old Louisville Slugger from underneath the counter and tossed it in her direction. With honed reflexes, Mari caught it one-handed and hefted it into the air with a look that claimed she meant business.

"Deacon! Miller!" She shouted in the general direction of the commotion. "Y'all, stop this right now!"

Miller—a trucker in his mid-forties who sported a rather formidable beer gut—lunged at Deacon. "I don't owe anybody here a damn dime! And especially not you, you cheating bastard! Wasn't it enough you slept with my wife? Now you want my money too?"

Deacon threw a punch that landed squarely between Miller's eyes, staggering the larger man, but not for long. Howling in rage, the trucker then tackled the younger man to the ground.

"Damn hicks," Boyd hissed.

Ignoring him, I braced myself for what might happen next. Usually, I'd wait for Mari to do her thing and bust up the brewing slugfest until Bubba came back from his smoke break to toss both hotheads out on their rears.

Tonight, however, Mr. Miller had come prepared. Before anyone could touch him, he yanked something from the waistband of his beer-stained jeans.

"Mari! Look out!" I stumbled for the door, ready to go grab Bubba myself, and that's when everything went straight to hell.

"You son of a bitch!" A rush of movement caught my attention from the corner of my eye. Whether empowered by beer or just plain stupidity, Deacon had charged forward. "You think you can pull that shit on me? I oughta kill you—"

Bang! The sound roared through my ears, and I jumped, thinking that, in the chaos, someone had knocked over a heavy case of beer. But even shattering glass didn't sound so sharp. So violent. And suddenly, I couldn't feel anything anymore.

Not my arms.

My legs...

"Kaydee!" The sound came from a billion directions, drawn out as if in exaggerated, slow motion. *Kaaay-deee!*

I tried to speak. Say something, anything.

Move.

But the next thing I knew…

I was staring at the ceiling while a pair of watchful eyes chased me into the darkness.

"Not yet… Not yet. Come back, Kaydence." That deep voice sank into me like a hook and wouldn't let go, long after everything else had faded. "Come back!"

I tried to remember which muscles controlled my throat so that I could ask where the hell I was.

"That's it," the voice urged, when I mustered up a groan instead. "That's it. Now open your eyes. Look at me."

Look. The command seemed laughable, considering that the world had gone dark and…quiet—though I wasn't afraid. For once, no one was there nagging about my dead-end job or wondering why I, the class valedictorian, had never left this shitty town on a bus headed straight for academia.

I was so damn tired. All I wanted was to sink into the tempting blackness that surrounded me. *Sleep.* And I could've had it, if it weren't for him.

"Damn it, Kaydence, look at me! Now!"

Obediently, my eyes flew open. Indistinguishable details wove in and out as if seen through a faulty camera lens—I must not have been wearing my glasses. Thankfully, the figure hovering above was close enough that I didn't need them.

He was too beautiful for my nearsightedness to obscure, an angel with golden skin. Strands of raven hair fell across a face that could have been sculpted—it seemed so perfect. Only a few flaws ruined the façade—namely, a frown that tugged at a pink mouth and haunting brown eyes narrowed with concern.

"Focus on the sound of my voice," he demanded. "Stay with me—"

"Oh, God!"

That was Mari's voice. The groggy realization tugged at something in the pit of my stomach, making it a little easier to resist the tempting darkness—it wasn't like Mari to take the Lord's name in vain. Something bad must have happened.

Once again, I tried to speak. "What...what's going on..."

Above me, the man frowned and leaned in close enough for me to make out everything from the ridge of his cheekbones down to the gentle curve of his nose.

"Get everyone out of here," he called to someone beyond me. "She hit her head. Call an ambulance!"

I tried to find the helpless victim he spoke of, but my body felt weighted to the floor, and all I could do was stare at him. He looked familiar, and I tried my hardest to come up with a name. Something beautiful. *Lee…*

"Look at me," he commanded. "Stay with me. Focus!" The force of the shout rocketed through me like a jolt of electricity. "Talk to me, Kaydence. Say something."

One coherent word finally slipped from my throat without me understanding how. "Hurts…"

It was only then that I actually noticed the pain, sharp and aching—harsher than anything I had ever felt. I breathed, and it hurt. Blinked, and it hurt.

What the hell happened to me?

"I know it hurts, but you can't give in to the pain. Look at me, Kaydence," the man urged before any fear could truly set in. God, he had such pretty eyes. They were incredibly dark. Endless… "Look at me."

Suddenly, he reached down. Yanked, and something gave way with a violent sound. My sweater?

"Focus," he ordered as my eyes drifted down. "Hear my voice, nothing else. I won't let you go. It'll be okay. Trust me."

I went limp at his tone. Even Pastor Wallace didn't sound as heartfelt during one of his Sunday sermons. Genuine. I had no idea why he seemed so afraid for me, or why he even cared, but I believed him.

I'll be okay.

I trust you.

As if reading my mind, his arm shifted, and warm fingers softly traced the—surprisingly bare—flesh of my belly. I gasped as, all at once, the pain flooded back. It seized my body, and then everything went white…

Like the moon. I could actually see it. Not like a faulty view from the streets of Kittywatt, where it was dimmed by the glow of streetlamps, but a vibrant ball of power in an indigo sky.

This was…

Real.

The type of unfiltered glimpse of nature that only came from seeing the sky through the branches of a forest while you raced underneath them. While you felt the wind on your bare skin and tasted the hint of salt in the air that promised a heavy rain. No longer was it just the *moon*—some distant chunk of rock in the sky—but a confidant and protector, imparting a strength that made my muscles hum from the force of it.

I was unstoppable. Feral. Driven solely by the musky scent of prey poised at the back of my throat and the metallic hint of blood.

The thoughts were terrifying in their honesty. Raw. Beautiful, even.

And…

They weren't mine.

I had rarely ventured further than old Mr. McCoy's farm in all twenty-two years of my life. I had never run through the slick wet earth as a spring storm set in, each raindrop so cool and fresh that I longed to taste it.

In fact, I had a sudden desire to taste a lot of things.

Honey and steak. Sweet and savory. Such a strange combination.

Fish. Beer.

Her... I ached to taste her in every way imaginable. Her kiss. Her skin. Her pleasure—

Wait.

I was pretty sure that I was interested only in the male persuasion—but the thought, no...*longing* for her was so strong, I couldn't ignore it. It was a primal need. Instinctive. Hungry. A rush of sentiments assaulted me all at once, making my head spin.

God, she was beautiful. Red hair, wild and untamed. Bright blue eyes clouded over with pain. I needed to stay back. Let the inevitable happen, but... She can't go. Not yet. Damn it!

Stay with me...

"Kaydence, stay with me."

Warmth broke through the dizzying cocoon of images, inching from my hand, up my wrist, and into my chest. I felt a gentle, rhythmic heat on my fingers—almost like breath. Then a sharp pain lanced through the pad of one.

I winced and weakly tried to pull my arm back. *Snap!* Just as quickly as they came, the memories vanished, and I was left blinking up at the peeling ceiling of Bardee's. Lucidity returned like a punch, and a million sounds blared in my ears as though a nearby television had been flipped to maximum volume—shouting, yelling...*screaming*.

"Did you call 911 already? Oh, God...Kaydee!"

Uh-oh. The usually stone-cold Mari sounded frantic. Distant, too, as though she were outside.

Why wasn't she at the counter? What the hell was going on?

More importantly...why was I lying on the floor while a stranger had his hands up the front of my shirt? Technically, they were against my stomach, applying gentle pressure—but they were too warm. Too hard. Too real.

"Get off me!" Fear drove my reaction, and I reached for the tiny mace keychain I kept clipped to my skirt. "Get off—"

"Wait."

I blinked as everything came into focus. Namely, the man hovering above me—not some random perv, but my stalker. He was on his knees, his hands held out cautiously in front of him. For once, he wasn't looking through me, or beyond me, but right *at* me. That fact alone overrode everything else, and I almost forgot that I was sprawled out over the floor until I happened to tear my gaze away from his long enough to glance down. I could see my belly button, peeking from underneath the rising hem of my sweater. At least…it *looked* like my belly button, barely visible beneath a scarlet smear so vibrant it could have been paint.

The same liquid was all over my hands, and…

A drop clung to *his* mouth as if perfectly placed to highlight the fullness of his lips. Strange, but for some reason, my brain didn't associate the sight with utter horror. If anything, the garish red highlighted the concern in those fathomless eyes.

"Don't move," he warned the second I attempted to. My body felt too heavy, and all I could manage was to let my hand fall to my side.

Still, I attempted to choke out a question. "What…what happened—"

"You got dizzy and fainted," he said over me. "You must have gotten a splinter when you grabbed the counter. Your hand is bleeding—" he nodded to the throbbing digit on my left hand. Sure enough, the index finger was coated in fresh, glistening red. A splinter? It sounded plausible, though I couldn't take my eyes off his mouth, still moving. "Or you cut yourself on glass."

Without warning, he stood and snatched a bottle from the counter. Deftly, he ripped off the cap and overturned it, pouring a stream of lukewarm beer over my abdomen. I was too stunned to speak as the liquid seeped into the fabric of my green sweater—along with something else. Something red. Something wet.

It looked as though someone had also spilled wine down my shirt. The fabric felt heavy. Sticky, too—but the smell in the air wasn't the sweet stench of sour grapes. It was pungent, salty, and metallic. Almost like...

Crash! I glanced up, just as the man above me smashed the bottle against the counter, sending glass spraying in sporadic directions. Before I could fully process what I had seen, he came at me with the jagged end, and fear rendered me breathless. *Oh, God...*

All he did was sprinkle the larger shards over the floor, before forcing what was left of the bottle into my hand. I sucked in a breath as thick fingers brushed my own. He was warm. Almost *too* warm, but when he pulled away, the resulting chill ached worse than frostbite.

"You tripped into the beer case and fell," he grunted as he headed for the door. A musical sound ate at his words. Sirens? "That's all."

I'd only finished processing the words when the door slammed shut behind him.

THEY SAID that strange things happened on the night of a full moon—*they* being Dee, who blamed the lunar cycle for her fluctuating libido, and my mama, who blamed it for anything strange that happened. Ironically, I didn't even realize, until I staggered outside while holding the edges of my sweater together, that the beautiful hunk of cosmic rock in the distance was round tonight. Watchful. I could only wonder what it thought of me as I hobbled over to my shitty blue Beetle and climbed into the driver's seat.

A bottle fell... Unsurprisingly, no one had bought that eloquent explanation at face value.

"Bullshit," Mari had snapped the second she heard my story. Sheriff Michaels had seemed just as unconvinced, no matter how many times I insisted on the false version of events. *I just spilled beer on myself, silly Kaydee, haha.*

"Beer isn't *red*," Mari had pointed out. "Next, you'll tell me that you pitched over some wine too? And that cut looks nasty. I doubt a splinter did that, but I'll make Bubba sand the bar down. You should go get it checked out, just in case."

I'd felt tempted at that point to just come clean—*Well, you see, this weird guy who I think hates me broke a bottle and pelted me with glass. He might have bitten me too, but that's beside the point. A hospital is a good idea...* Whenever I opened my mouth to blurt out those words, though, I'd see his face. See those eyes. Then, that tired old lie would just tumble out.

"I fell. Got a splinter. A bottle broke. Besides all the blood, I'm okay."

Apart from my finger—which sported a single stinging cut —there wasn't a mark on my body to prove otherwise. Beneath my soaked sweater was just plain, pale skin. Boyd must have been too far back to see much because, even though he looked doubtful, he didn't dispute my story either.

Despite the general consensus, I had passed the neuro checks by the paramedics with flying colors—though that hadn't stopped Mari from trying to shove me into the back of the ambulance anyway. For all intents and purposes, I was physically fine…

But *something* was broken.

I ached. A residual pain lingered within my pores like poison. I had felt it—something had torn right through my body. Right there in the pit of my stomach.

Knock it off, I told myself while my hands clutched the steering wheel. They trembled, and it took me a good minute of trying to reverse, to no avail, before I realized I needed to start the darn car first. With a sigh, I reached into my apron pocket and pulled out my keys, but I couldn't fit them into the ignition. My brain was too busy trying to discern the truth from the lie.

What had happened? I'd been working the bar like always. Mari needed help. I could remember Deacon and Miller fighting. Shouting. A *bang!*

And…

The keys slipped through my fingers and landed on my lap as the memory unfolded.

Think Kaydee. What happened next? You know there's more. Think.

All I remembered after that was *him*. Those fathomless russet eyes. That voice calling me back from some distant, dark place. Fingers so warm that I could feel them even now, hot on my bare skin.

Anything other than that was a total blank. Just the same phrase over and over. *You fell...a bottle broke...that's all.*

Which made sense, and I was grasping at straws for no reason. On that morbid note, I finally managed to start the car. The loud, mechanical purr of the engine coming to life didn't elicit the usual cheer from me—normally, I celebrated anytime the damn thing turned on.

I almost wished it hadn't so I would have had an excuse to go crawling back into Bardee's and remain under Mari's watchful eye. As if on cue, my phone buzzed at my hip. I reached for it and stepped on the gas pedal while flicking the answer button.

"Hello?"

"You home yet?"

"Almost," I lied as I pulled out of the gravel-filled parking lot and onto Main Street. I could only hope that she wasn't watching from the window.

"You get some rest now," Mari commanded without challenging my lie. "They arrested those two assholes but want to do some more questioning at the station. And don't worry about coming in tomorrow night. They want to run 'forensics' or whatever the hell it's called to find out where the bullet went. I'll be out of business for the next few days," she hissed. "Damn those bastards. I just hope the police find every shred of evidence they need."

"Oh, yeah?" I gulped, though I had no damn idea why the thought made me so uneasy. My mind kept replaying the sound of the gunshot on a morbid loop. *Bang, bang, BANG!* "W-What are they going to do when they find it? The bullet, I mean."

"I dunno. Use it as evidence, I guess. I'm just glad that drunken fool didn't hit anyone. Hopefully, the insurance company will be able to take both Deacon's and Miller's asses to the cleaners. Although, if I look on the bright side, maybe now we can finally afford a new beer tap?"

"Yes, I hope so," I murmured, though I was worried for an entirely different reason. Mari sounded way too calm for someone who'd just broken up a gunfight in her bar. My guess was that Bubba was handling the police stuff while she helped herself to her own merchandise—not that I could blame her when the sheriff had given me explicit instructions to call him once I "had some rest and had a clear head."

Neither option seemed possible right about now. No matter how much my lungs heaved, I couldn't seem to suck in enough air. The world kept spinning. I almost pulled over just to keep from crashing into a ditch. To distract myself, I readjusted the phone against my ear and blurted the first thing that came to mind.

"So...um, that Levi guy, do you know him?"

"Who?"

"The uh, gas station guy that comes in all the time," I stammered. "You know. The one who helped me tonight."

"Oh! You mean *Liwai*. Liwai Raven," Mari said, giving the name a musical pronunciation. "Interesting name, right? He's a nice guy, though he bailed without talking to the police—not that I blame him, given the rumors about that family of his," she added under her breath. "There's no love lost between him and Sheriff Michaels, that's for darn sure."

"Rumors?"

"Oh, nothing a good girl like you should concern yourself with," Mari said with a sigh. "Just forget I said anything."

"Well, he helped me out tonight. I wanted to say thanks. You wouldn't happen to know where he lives, would you?"

I cringed at my gross lack of tact. *Who's stalking whom now, Kaydee?*

"I might," Mari said after a distinct pause. Her voice took on a teasing tone as she asked, "But you could just send him a card, honey. Why *else* do you want to know?"

"No reason," I said a little too quickly. I didn't miss the sneaky edge to Mari's tone—she could be like a fox when it came to gossip. "I just think I should thank him in person—"

"That's my Kaydee Marie," Mari boasted with a laugh. "Our sweet, if klutzy, resident bartender. You plan on giving him some of your famous Kaydee Blanchett cookies?"

Something told me that she wasn't just talking about the dessert variety. "Mari!"

"Hey, he is one gorgeous specimen," Mari countered with a chuckle. "And you need some fun after tonight. I swear to God, if you get a concussion or something, you better join me in suing the shit out of Miller's sorry ass."

"Sure thing," I replied, only half listening. My thoughts had already turned back to Liwai. "And that address?"

"For Liwai? He lives on Hooser Lane if that's what you were after. All the way at the end of the road, near the creek. Battered white house."

"Thanks."

After enduring another command to "get some sleep," I hung up and tried to focus on exactly where the hell I'd been driving during the entire phone conversation. I knew of Hooser Lane—a road that stretched to the outskirts of town. According to the rumors, it was Kittywatt's version of the wrong side of the tracks—where all the addicts and delinquents lived. I had never really driven down that long, gravel road before, yet I wasn't surprised when a glance out of my window revealed a landscape of desolate yards and rickety dwellings. At the end of the proverbial road, the loneliest house loomed on a hill.

Mari had called it battered and white. It was more like silver —the color that old wood turned after the paint had been all but stripped off by years of wear and tear. In the moonlight, it looked ancient. Foreboding. The type of place you certainly didn't want to go skipping up to in the middle of the damn night.

Biting my lip, I eyed the clock on the dashboard—it was way past polite visiting hours. I couldn't resist the impulse that had me snapping off my seat belt anyway and reaching into the back seat for the jacket I kept in case of rain. Once I was somewhat sure that no one was watching from behind dusty windows, I shed my filthy, wet sweater and zipped up the jacket over my bra.

To go or to stay? I mentally wrestled with the options. What could I possibly say to him anyway, without sounding insane? To my credit, even in a place like Kittywatt, shootouts weren't a normal occurrence.

In a barroom full of people, it was a miracle that no one had gotten hurt. *Yeah,* I insisted to myself as I shivered beneath a layer of polyester. *A freakin' miracle.*

I hadn't quite decided whether to wander up to confront a complete stranger in the middle of the night, when a burst of commotion drew my attention—the white screen door of the house flew open, and a barrage of people exploded from it.

Four of them—three brawny boys in various stages of adolescence took the lead. Whooping and hollering, they leaped off the porch, wearing jeans, sneakers, and little else. Trailing behind them was a girl who looked no older than fourteen, swathed in a delicate white nightgown. I could tell —even from this distance—that she was beautiful. They *all* were. Like Liwai, they shared the same golden skin and jet-black hair that seemed to shine brighter than the moon.

As I watched, the boys bolted across the yard, laughing and doing cartwheels on the brown grass, heedless of any neighbors who might be sleeping. Though, I had to admit, as I glanced around the desolate driveway, they might not have had any neighbors in the first place.

Tearing my gaze from them for a second, I scanned the house, searching for a sign of the man I had come to see, but there was no movement inside, no lights flickering. Just darkness and moonlight. Gradually, my attention returned to the four teenagers while I mulled over what the absence meant. Could they be Liwai's siblings—in any case, who in their right mind would let their children run loose this time of night?

In any case, they didn't seem to have any qualms about being up so late. Taking a deep breath, I undid my apron and tossed it onto the dash. Then I climbed out of my car, just as the strange group headed toward the cluster of trees behind the white house.

Approaching them, I strained my voice to carry across yards of gravel and dried grass. "Um, excuse me."

All at once, the four froze in unison. Given the cover of shadows that draped their bodies, it was hard to tell where the forest ended, and they began. I could only make out slivers of tan limbs and black hair amid the backdrop of emerald and ebony. An even eerier thought crossed my mind as I inched closer—they almost didn't look human.

Their limbs were too long. Their eyes were too bright, and their teeth looked…sharp?

Or I was just going insane. With a mental command to "*knock it off*," I shook my head to clear it.

"Uh, hi…sorry," I stammered before I could lose the nerve and jump back into my car. "Could you tell me where I could find Liwai—"

"Why the hell do you want to know?" The smallest of the boys—and that wasn't saying too much because they all towered over me—whirled around. His eyes bore into mine from across the field, so sharp in the moonlight that they reminded me of a hawk's. Or maybe something more dangerous…but a fitting comparison didn't come to mind quick enough. In only a few strides, he crossed the distance between us. "Because of that piece of shit sheriff? If he has a problem with us, he can come say it to our fucking faces—"

"Cody! Back off—" The largest of the three caught up to the smaller one and seized his shoulder, stopping him in his tracks before he could come any closer. "Liwai's not here," he grunted in my direction. "You should go."

They were less than a yard away from me now, and the remainder of the adrenaline still in my system from the events at the bar warned me to back away. Get in my car. Run.

"Yeah, he's not here," Cody snapped from behind his two comrades. As silent as a shadow, the third boy had appeared beside the taller one. "What do you want anyway? Is that sheriff of yours too chicken shit to do his own dirty work?"

What?

"No, I…I just…"

Weakly, I trailed off. He had a pretty good point. What the hell did I want? The wind tore at my hair while I grappled for a reason. "I…"

"Look, whatever you're after, he's not here," the nicer one grumbled before turning for the woods.

"Yeah," Cody snapped, following suit. "So, you go head on back to that piece of shit town and leave us all alone."

I swallowed hard. It wasn't a secret that Kittywatt wasn't exactly the most welcoming of places to outsiders, and I knew that Liwai hadn't grown up there—or gone to our high school with a rousing graduating class of fifty-five. Apparently, his family hadn't received the customary fruit basket and cherry pie that we dished out to all newcomers, either. Nonetheless, the blatant hostility threw me off. Stung even. After a night like I'd just had, I couldn't climb into my car fast enough.

By the time I slid into the driver's seat, the kids had already disappeared through the trees. I could no longer hear them, which didn't comfort me in the slightest.

Shrugging, I reached for the gearshift. Just as my foot connected with the gas pedal, I glanced up only to catch sight of someone watching me through the windshield… standing right in the middle of the road.

"Jesus!" I barely managed to slam my foot on the brake in time, narrowly avoiding the young girl in white, her dark hair flying out behind her. She didn't move, even when I hastily put the car in park and clambered out, nearly tripping over myself to reach her.

"Are you okay—"

"It's you." Her voice made me freeze—a haunting, melodic whisper. Paired with her doll-like features and ethereal dress, I only had the way her chest rose and fell to determine that she wasn't a ghost. "He's finally found you."

"Are you okay?" I continued in her direction, but the moment I came close enough, she reached out and snagged my wrist in her bony grip.

"He's found you," she repeated, her icy fingers tightening their hold. "But you're still alive…"

For the first time, she met my gaze, and I sucked in a breath. The look in her eyes cut right through me, as wise and ancient as an owl's. She had such delicate features that her eyes nearly overpowered her face altogether.

"He hasn't done it yet," she added, her voice hoarse.

"Who hasn't done *what* yet?" I croaked.

"He hasn't—"

"Renae!" The shout came from the woods, and the girl flinched. "Hurry up. We won't save you anything this time if you can't keep up."

"Done what?" I asked again, uneasy though I had no idea why. Her grip was tight, but I didn't feel the urge to yank my hand away just yet. There was something frantic in her touch. It almost reminded me of a grandmother trying to soothe a child and assure them that everything would be *alright* even though they knew that shit was about to hit the fan.

"Forget it." Renae shook her head. "You can't come back here." Suddenly she released me and turned in the direction the boys had gone. "*Please*. Don't come back. Maybe if you stay away, he'll…" She looked over her shoulder and met my gaze one last time. "Just don't come back. Stay away from him. Stay away from all of us."

In a flurry of white, she was gone, disappearing through the trees, and then there was nothing left but silence.

Liwai Raven haunted my nightmares. Namely, his eyes, so dark they mimicked the deep, endless black he had called me back from. Scattered in-between glimpses of him were disjointed images of a forest. The moon. Wet, muddied earth. Then a smell, sweet and feminine. Perfume? No, just her natural scent. So damn perfect. Eyes like the sky…

I couldn't let her go.

Like a soundtrack to the strange, disjointed thoughts was a voice, low and rumbling.

Tell no one.

You only fell.

Only fell.

I only fell…

"I thought you grew out of that?" The honeyed drawl was a stark contrast to the masculine tones I couldn't seem to escape. With a groan, I peeled one eye open to find a blurry shape hovering somewhere over my bed.

"Dee?" I croaked. The human-sized blob shrugged in response. "Grew out of what?"

"Talking in your sleep," Dee replied. "I didn't know you were into Liwai Raven."

I groaned, cursing the habit of mine that made it damn near impossible for me to keep a steady boyfriend. After all, it was hard to move forward in a relationship when after a night of platonic cuddling, I'd often wake up to angry demands of, "So you just want to be friends?" "You're not looking for anything 'serious' right now?" "You only went out with me because you don't want people to think you're a lesbian?"

I'd been blabbering in my sleep since childhood—which made any type of rebellion futile because Mama only had to wait until bedtime for me to spill the beans on my own.

"It's rude to barge in on someone, you know," I sighed, while fumbling for my glasses, which rested somewhere on the nightstand.

"Oh, come on! I let you sleep in till *noon* today, little Miss Prude. I heard about what happened at the bar and thought you might need some rest."

"What happened at the bar?" I wondered innocently as I settled my glasses on the bridge of my nose. I was surprised by how calm I sounded—as though I hadn't been reliving every second of the previous night since leaving Liwai Raven's.

"What *happened?*" Dee just raised one blood-red eyebrow as I blinked to bring her features into focus. "Nothing…other than Robert Miller going all ape-shit and firing off a gun in the place."

It was barely noon, but I wasn't surprised that Dee had already gotten the full scoop on what had happened. "Oh, that."

"Yeah, that!" Dee's narrowed eyes skimmed me from my ratted-out hair down to my blanket-covered toes. "You okay, Kaydee-pie?"

I did my best to muster a nonchalant shrug. "No one was hurt."

"Thank the Lord," Dee exclaimed. "And to think that I ever slept with that idiot Miller." She ruffled her cherry-colored curls in disgust.

"To be fair," I countered as I pushed back the blankets and planted my feet on the floor, "he's not the only man in town you've slept with."

Dee blinked and slapped a hand over her ample chest, which was shamelessly displayed by her low-cut blouse. "Why, you little tart! You better learn to respect your elders."

I laughed while I bent down for a sweater lying on the floor and pulled it on over my tank top. "Point one out to me, *Aunt Deanna*, and I'd be glad to."

The truth was that at thirty, Aunt Dee was only a few years older than I was. She was Granddaddy's illegitimate mistake, and damn proud of the fact. We were more like sisters than anything else.

"Oh, you sweetie-pie," she crooned, flashing me a red-lipped smile. "You always say the cutest little things."

She simpered beneath the veiled compliment while I hunted for a pair of jeans tossed casually into a corner. I could sense Dee watching as I slipped them on before heading for the dresser to swipe a brush through my hair.

"You got plans today?"

"Just more questioning down at the station," I lied. "I'm meeting Mari down there around one—"

"She can't wait for you to take a shower first?"

I flinched when I noticed that her eyes were on my hands. My crusty, stained, *rust-colored* hands. I managed to shove them into my pockets, but it was already too late.

"What the hell is that? You go playing in mud last night?"

Dee's talon-like fingers snatched my wrist, grazing the skin with her bright-red nails. "God, Kaydee…Is that blood?"

"No!" I wrenched my hand away before she could wake up the whole damn town with her screeching. "Just beer. I spilled some on myself."

"Oh." Her face fell, and suddenly she was my overly caring Aunt Dee again. "You sure you're okay, honey? That must have been terrifying, being in the middle of all that bullshit…"

"I'm fine." But even I didn't miss the hoarse edge to my own voice. "You know what? On second thought, I will take that shower." With a sigh, I pulled open my drawer for a fresh shirt and a pair of jeans, holding them up for her benefit. "Happy?"

Dee shrugged. "You take it easy today, ya hear? No wandering off to the library to read or whatever it is you do there so much. After the questioning, I want you to come right back here and lounge around in front of the TV like a normal person. Understood?"

I rolled my eyes but nodded anyway. "Whatever you say."

"Great…so why were you dreaming about Liwai Raven?"

Damn. True to form, Dee never forgot anything dealing with the opposite sex. If I wanted to be brutally honest with myself, the fact that I'd uttered a man's name in my sleep probably interested her more than any damn shooting.

"I wasn't." Tucking my clothing under one arm, I made my way into the hall with Dee hot on my heels.

"It has to be serious if you mentioned him during one of your sleepy-talk nonsense blathers. So, what's going on between you two?"

I staggered into the bathroom and wrestled the door shut behind me.

"Oh, come on!" she exclaimed from the other side. "I know who he is. He's that fine, sexy piece of ass working over at the gas station."

Deanna probably kept a list of every eligible man in town under her pillow. With a groan, I pulled back the shower curtain and turned the water on full blast to drown her out.

"Can't hear you!" I shouted. "I'm in the shower."

Praying to God that she took the hint, I stripped off my jeans and top and clambered inside—but not before getting a good look at myself in the mirror.

I looked terrible. Or, as Mama would have said, *"Death warmed over and slathered on a cracker."* My hair was a mess. My eyes were bloodshot—probably the result of drifting in and out of sleep all damn night. Of course, the crowning glory of my haggard appearance consisted of the dark substance smeared all over my stomach. It looked as though I'd rolled around in rust-colored paint. Some of it was beer, from what I could tell, but the rest…

Don't think about it, Kaydee.

I doused myself beneath the shower spray and scrubbed until the last drops of reddish water circled the drain. When I finally got dressed, wrapped my finger in a Band-Aid, and peeked into the hallway, Dee was nowhere in sight, and I took advantage of her absence by darting into my bedroom for my keys.

My floor was a mess of dirty clothes and stray books strewn everywhere. Last night, I'd been too tired to even hang up my uniform—what was left of it, anyway. Looking at my bed now, I realized my folly the night before—darkly-colored ick stained my sheets and comforter. I quickly bundled the set and threw them in the washer before returning to my room. Then, I stooped for my apron, but as I lifted it, something small bounced off to roll across the floor.

Confused, I chased it to the edge of my bed and tried to feel along the floor for it. I didn't remember wearing any earrings last night. Maybe it was a piece of the broken bottle from the bar? Whatever it was felt small when I finally brushed my fingers over it. Round. Crusty.

I captured it in my hand, but when I finally viewed it in the daylight streaming through my window, my blood ran cold.

I had only seen a bullet a handful of times—mainly when my grandfather cleaned his rifle during hunting season. Those bullets had been long and tapered to a point, but when he shot at targets on his property, became smushed. Like a crushed tin can.

Liwai Raven said I'd gotten a splinter and knocked over a bottle.

So why the hell was there a bullet in my hand?

There wasn't time to think about it. In a daze, I tucked the object into my pocket and headed for the front door.

Someone had taped a sticky note just above the doorknob: *Kaydee-pie, I have a lunch date, but as soon as you're done with that questioning, you better get your ass back in this house. No library!—BTW, someone left a gift for you on the porch. Move over Liwai. Who is Boyd?*

I balled the note in a fist. So was the curse of living with someone like Dee, who couldn't imagine a life outside of parties and sex. To her, a book was nothing more than an interestingly-shaped doorstop. She probably thought she was doing me a favor—though, come to think of it, she most likely only wanted to prod me for more answers. I made a mental note to lock my door that night, just in case she decided to come sneaking in. After all, if anyone was entitled to more information about Liwai Raven, it was me...

I had all but forgotten about the second half of her note when I staggered outside and nearly tripped over something left near the edge of the welcome mat. A beautiful, albeit simple, arrangement of peonies—my favorite flower. The note attached to the bouquet simply read, "Thinking of you. Boyd."

I couldn't hide the small smile that the simple gesture brought to my lips. I had almost forgotten all about Liwai Raven by the time I climbed into my car, placed the flowers on my passenger seat, and headed down Main Street, driving right past the police station. As I watched the building shrink in my rearview mirror, a growing dread quickly erased the previous sense of normalcy. Mari was probably waiting for me in the sheriff's office, but I couldn't seem to stop.

At least not until *after* I took a back road and pulled into the Ravenswood gas station. It was a small, old-fashioned place. There were only three rusty gas pumps and a sign out front that proclaimed *full service*. Not many people came here—most preferred to frequent the nicer, more modern one on the other side of town—but I liked the simplicity of it.

Liar, a part of me hissed. *You only started coming here when you found out who pumped the gas…*

But for the first time in weeks, he wasn't there. Instead, Barney, the balding guy who owned the place, was the one to greet me as I pulled up to the nearest pump.

"Morning, Miss Blanchett," he said when I rolled down my window. "What can I help you with?"

I made a show of pointing out how I was running low on gas, though I had more than half a tank left. Then, as Barney approached, I peeked around the yard, looking for Liwai.

Was he inside the attendant's station? I couldn't tell. He definitely wasn't by his usual spot, leaning against the rickety old sign, waiting for cars to pull in.

I hated how frantic I felt. Restless. I couldn't stop scanning the same area over and over, searching for a glimpse of dark hair or brown eyes…

"It's about damn time!" I turned as Barney shouted at someone approaching from behind the station. "I know you're always on time, Liwai, so I won't make a big deal about it today. Just don't let it happen again."

His teasing smile kept the words from seeming too harsh, and Liwai smiled in response, flashing straight, white teeth...

Then he saw me, and all the color drained from his face.

"Hey. Give me a hand, why don't you?" Barney said, jerking his head toward my battered car. "Finish taking care of Miss Blanchett while I go tend the station. All this 'fresh air' isn't good for my lungs."

Chuckling, he scampered back beneath the safety of the small building, leaving me alone with a man who looked as though he wanted nothing more than to disappear as well. For a long time, he stood there, watching me from across the parking lot, and I was sure that at any moment, he would bolt, heedless of what Barney had said. Then, without a single word, he came closer. I tensed as his gaze raked over me, but I didn't hold his interest as much as something beside me did. I looked over and only saw my wilting flowers and nothing else.

When I turned back to Liwai, he was jerking the cap off my gas tank.

"Regular?" He had such a deep, clear voice. His accent was crisp, too—he had to be from up North. The sound reminded me of snow and ice and wild, feral things like the animals they kept on national preserves. He wore those stained overalls again, with nothing but a black T-shirt underneath while his hair hung down his shoulders, as sleek as an ebony cape.

"Do you want Regular gas?" I jumped when I realized that I'd been staring.

"T-That'd be fine," I stammered, feeling my cheeks catch fire.

Liwai reached for the pump and slid it into the tank. I could tell from the set of his shoulders that he would have rather been anywhere else, *with* anyone else. I was tempted to clam up like my usual, timid self—but then I caught sight of my stained, green sweater on my back seat.

I needed to know.

"Can I ask you something?"

He froze. If it were possible for a human being to turn to stone in the blink of an eye, then call me Medusa.

He didn't move an inch. Say a word.

But he wasn't running away, either.

"It's about last night," I soldiered on. "Did you…see anything? Or h-hear anything strange—"

"I heard a gunshot," he insisted, cutting over me. "I heard glass shatter. I saw you fall."

"But that's not all, is it?"

I didn't know what the hell was wrong with me. One minute I was sitting in my car, and the next, I was climbing out to stand beside him. He smelled good up this close— like spice and earth. It was a stupid thing to notice, all things considered, but I couldn't seem to ignore even the tiniest detail when it came to him. Like the way he stiffened at my presence, for example.

"I think you did something to me," I blurted on one long exhale. At the same time, I reached into my pocket and withdrew the tiny cube of metal. "And this morning, I found this in my apron. So, I know *something* happened."

My hand shook with that tiny object balanced on my palm. In the harsh daylight, it looked so small. So delicate.

Suddenly, Liwai reached over and took it before I could react—he was so fast. As he shoved it into his pocket, he didn't say a word, but it was already too late to keep my mouth shut.

"I was shot…wasn't I?"

Glunk!

His hand jerked, and gasoline went everywhere. In a violent arch, it sprayed onto the asphalt below, and the blue paint of my car.

"Shit." Sighing, Liwai wrestled the nozzle back into the pump. Then he turned, swiping at his hands with a cloth pulled from his back pocket.

"Everything alright out here?" Barney poked his head through the doorway of the station, his eyes darting between the two of us.

"Fine," Liwai snapped while he swiped at the side of my car with his rag. With every wiping motion, the muscles in his arm tensed, coiled, rippled…

"Thirteen, ninety-nine."

"Huh?" I blinked, unsure if I had even heard him—he spoke so low.

His eyes were unreadable as he finally turned to face me. "For the gas."

"Oh!" Feeling like an idiot, I scrambled into my pocket for a wad of bills. But even as I curled them in a fist, something kept me from reaching out to him.

I could still feel the imprint of his fingers pressing against my skin. "You did something to me," I repeated, aware of Barney watching us. For some reason, nothing else seemed to matter but *this,* hearing the truth. "Just tell me what it was. CPR? First Aid?"

As if those methods alone could heal someone who'd been shot. Rather than answer, Liwai stared past my head as if just ignoring me might make me disappear. The scary part? An internal part of me flinched as if it were a possibility.

Fading away just because he withdrew any notice.

Which was just plain silly. Obviously, last night's event had affected me more than I realized.

"Look," I said, trying a different tactic. I even inched closer to him, aiming to come off friendly. "I'm not accusing you of anything. I just want to know what happened to me—"

"Don't touch me."

The warning came as I reached out for his forearm. Stunned, I let my hand fall to my side. "I'm sorry, I just…"

Was going crazy. Maybe I *had* just fallen and broken a bottle and nothing else?

Maybe Dee was right, and I read too much, and an overactive imagination led me to exaggerate?

Or maybe…he was lying through his teeth.

"I'm supposed to go down for questioning later," I added, sounding much braver than I felt. "Maybe I should tell them everything, huh? And even if you took the bullet, I'm sure they could get a subpoena or something if I tell them about it—"

"Barney." I jumped as he spoke, but once again, he seemed to be seeing right through my body toward some distant spot.

"Yeah?" Barney called from the direction of the cashier's booth.

"Miss Blanchett thinks that her engine's been making strange noises. I'll take it around the block to check it out."

"Um…okay?" Barney sounded confused, but Liwai didn't hesitate to open my driver's side door and climb onto the seat. A pointed look in my direction made his intentions clear—*Get in.*

The moment I opened the passenger-side door, he snatched my flowers in his fist and tossed them out of my still-open window.

"Hey! Those were mine," I blurted, but he didn't even look my way.

Instead, he took the wheel, and gestured to the seat. "Do you want to talk or not?"

The question weighed on me with more significance than I think it should have. Finally sitting down felt like a monumental decision that I didn't have long to process. The next second, Liwai pulled out of the parking lot. He drove about half a mile down the road, and with every passing yard, I felt more weightless. Breathless. I supposed I should have been afraid. After all, he could have been taking me anywhere.

A shack to rape me.

A ditch to bury my body in.

In an ironic twist, my mother had spent nearly every waking moment while she was alive warning me about the dangers of strangers, but despite how hard I tried to muster up the emotion…I wasn't scared one bit.

For one, he didn't seem eager to talk to me, let alone hurt me. He went out of his way to angle his body as far from me as the cramped confines of my Beetle allowed. Because of the low roof, he had to hunch over the dashboard, and he resembled a giant squeezed inside of a clown car. It was a wonder that he could even move the steering wheel, though he had to balance it between both knees. The sight would have been comical, if it weren't for his stern expression.

That look alone kept me from trying to speak until he finally pulled onto the shoulder. Only then did I face him, with the barrage of questions poised on the tip of my tongue—namely, *Did you save my life?*—but he beat me to the punch.

"Get out."

His tone was deep enough to send a foreboding shudder through me. I blinked, still reaching for my seat belt. "E-Excuse me?"

Suddenly, all those little murder scenarios didn't seem so far-fetched, and a new one came to mind—me, with my throat slit, dumped on the side of the road.

Liwai stiffened as if sensing the thought, but with a heavy sigh, he put my Beetle into park and nudged open the door. "Get out," he insisted, though his tone was markedly softer. "Please."

I peeked out of the window and decided that where we were now—beside an empty field near the McCoy farm—wasn't *too* far out of earshot, in case I needed to scream. Just as long as old man McCoy had his hearing aids in and was close enough to his telephone.

Cautiously, I eased myself out onto the pavement and turned around. My little Beetle sat between Liwai and me, a poor shield against those piercing eyes. For the first time that afternoon, they met mine head-on, peering deep down like lasers.

"I'm only going to tell you one more time," he began in a voice laced with unquestionable authority. "Nothing happened last night. You fell. You hit your head. That's it. End of story."

My heart skipped a beat at his intensity. I almost believed him—until his gaze abruptly cut away from me. He was lying, and damn it, I just couldn't understand *why.* Though, more importantly, why the hell did it matter so much to me if he was?

I was alive. Uninjured. I could safely wear a bikini without a nasty scar—if I truly believed for a second that I had really been shot. I had nothing to worry about.

In theory.

The reality was some rabid part of me couldn't leave it alone. Couldn't leave *him* alone. *Dig deeper*, it said. In those haunting eyes, I saw only shadow and mystery and guarded secrets—but that same nosy little voice kept whispering…*you need to learn more.* And, God help me, I *wanted* to know more, almost as badly as I wanted to run far away.

"Do you understand?" he prompted when I didn't reply. Both of his hands palmed the roof of my car, dark tan over baby blue, rippling with tension.

"I understand," I stammered once I remembered how to speak. "But…but I don't believe you."

I stepped from around my side of the car, and he shifted his weight to the balls of his feet. The response reminded me of when a horse got "spooked" on Granddaddy's farm. The look in his eyes was the same—wary, watchful, mistrusting.

And while not the size of a horse, he definitely had the upper hand against me when it came to strength.

"If you won't tell me the truth, then answer this." I felt like a child pleading for a cookie. *Just one, please?* "Why did my apron have a bullet in it?"

His reply came like a slap. "Glass."

I fought to keep from rolling my eyes. Instead, I swallowed and cautiously took another step while sneaking a peek at him through my lashes. With that hair streaming down his shoulders, he almost didn't seem human—*God-like*, if that was even a word. An ancestral spirit standing before me in a ratty pair of overalls.

My sneakers crunched over the gravel as I tiptoed closer, as if I really were dealing with a startled horse. He held firm, but I knew that he noticed every little move I made. I wondered if he could also hear how my heart pounded louder than the local high school's marching band—I sure could. The sound echoed eerily in my mind, worse than the suspenseful music in a thriller movie.

He let me come close enough to touch him before he finally took a step backward.

"I have another question," I stammered as I pulled open the door to my back seat and snatched up a wad of torn wool. It looked even worse in the daylight. At least now, it was all too obvious that the glaring, crusty stains were way too dark to have been made by any damn beer. "Why did you rip my sweater if I had only a splinter? On my *finger?*"

Without warning, Liwai snatched the sweater from me and tossed it to the side of the road, where it mingled with the rocks and weeds. "It was *glass,*" he insisted.

I stared down at his feet, encased within a muddy pair of boots, and for the first time, I think I fully appreciated just how enormous he was…

He towered above me, and there I stood, confronting him on the side of the road, utterly alone. He could have crushed me in an instant and returned to the gas station without even breaking a sweat.

"Glass," I repeated, as if I had finally accepted his version of events. "So, if I only fell and nothing else happened as you keep insisting…then why do I keep hearing *your* voice in my head?"

Admitting it out loud made me feel stripped naked. There was no going back—I had really been to that dark, quiet place. I had almost given up…

Died.

And he really *had* brought me back… Deep down, I'd known all along that it had felt way too real to have been a dream. I waited for him to insinuate as much anyway or respond with the obvious. *Because you're nuts.*

I waited…

But the seconds passed, and he only stood there impassively until I gathered enough courage for one final question. "Why are you lying to me?"

He whirled on me, and I shrank inside myself. Anger on Liwai Raven was like witnessing a thunderstorm in the middle of an empty field with nothing around for the lightning to inevitably strike but your body. "Why can't *you* just leave it alone?"

With him so close, finding enough air to even form words was a struggle. "There's a bullet hole in my sweater, which you practically tore off of me..."

He flinched and cut his eyes over to where the garment in question lay in the grass.

"And," I added, taking a step toward him though I had no idea why, "blood. So much blood that I had to scrub it off my hands and stomach this morning. I didn't cut my finger on a splinter, did I? You... You bit it."

I sounded so incredibly calm about that. So serene. *I found a bullet hole and blood on my clothing, but I'm still alive.*

"I don't have time for this," he grumbled, turning on his heel—and in response, I did something so impulsive and out of character that I reckon I would never understand the full reasons why. I reached for his hand...and when my fingers came into contact with his, it was like an explosion went off inside me. Warmth seared through my veins. I couldn't think. I could only breathe as his scent hit me with all the strength of a speeding truck—spice, wilderness, and musk. All inherently *male*. My eyes fluttered shut as I inhaled him—and I knew...he was doing the same to me. Every low, ragged breath of his rasped against my ear, and when my eyes opened again, I found him standing even closer.

Pulling away would have been the right course of action. Running. Not stepping closer. Not meeting his gaze directly and sensing a torrent of emotion that nearly barreled me over—hurt, pain, regret…longing. It was the longing that had my heart surging in my chest more fiercely than it had even the night of the shooting. Strangers didn't *long* for me.

And I certainly didn't long for them. I didn't try to shift against them, drawn forward by some dark impulse running through my skin, too uncertain to name.

And girls like me certainly didn't kiss said strangers without so much as an invitation.

FOUR

The good girl in me could only watch in horror as I pressed my mouth to Liwai's—and he didn't recoil. Instead, he remained almost stubbornly within my reach, and just a single word at the recesses of my psyche could name the impulse surging through me like an electric current—*need*.

As a result, my movements were jerky. Automatic. Wild. Our lips met—collided. His teeth carelessly caught my lower lip, but the pain wasn't enough to combat the wave of emotion that threatened to consume me in the aftermath.

More. I needed more of him.

I had only been kissed three times in my whole life. Once on the playground by a regretful Bobby Fisher, who did it on a dare. Then again, by my two short-lived boyfriends. All could have been described with a few, short adjectives— wet, sloppy, and gross. Frankly, I had never understood the hype.

But this…

This wasn't a kiss. Liwai stiffened as though his first impulse was to pull away after all. Then, before embarrassment could set in, his mouth opened, inhaling me—drawing me in—and nothing else mattered.

Mindless, I clung to him, snagging fistfuls of black cotton and denim to pull him closer, closer, *closer.* It wasn't close enough, but I was too distracted by other observations to care. He tasted good—like warmth and the slightest hint of honey that had me plunging my tongue unashamedly into his mouth.

This is right, a part of me urged as lips softer than anything I'd ever felt flexed against mine. *Taste him. Take him.*

He's mine, and I'm his…

His arm went around my waist, crushing me close as his other hand coiled in my hair, holding me in place while his mouth expertly overpowered mine. He was so damn hot. I was drowning in heat. Fire.

It sparked to life in parts of me I'd barely explored on my own—but now I ached for him to touch me there. Everywhere. In my right mind, the thought would have scared me. Right?

Yes. When his mouth left mine, I could think clearly again. I struggled to take in air, only to feel his lips trail across my lower jaw, tracing my skin.

"I've waited so damn long for this…" His voice was so guttural my belly lurched in response, and I was frozen. At the same time, his hand left my waist and slid down to the clasp on the front of my jeans. One flick of his thumb and the denim was being tugged down my legs.

And my mind went blank again.

"To touch you. Taste you."

The longing echoed those strange thoughts I'd had ever since the night of the shooting. *Touching. Tasting. I need her so fucking much. The instinct is unbearable…*

I shivered beneath the onslaught of new thoughts, as his lips inched toward my earlobe. Was I going insane?

"No," Liwai told me out loud as if reading my mind. "You're just finally waking up to the connection that was always there. Always."

As he spoke, his hand caressed my thigh, raising goose-bumps in its wake. No one had ever touched me so intimately, but the gravity of the situation didn't seem to register. He was a stranger, but I arched into him anyway, guiding the descent of his fingers until my pants were bunched around my ankles. I could feel his gaze on the bare skin of my legs, traveling up to my frilly, pink panties.

When he trailed a finger along the lacy hem, I couldn't silence the groan that broke loose. I reached for his forearm, digging my nails into the coiling muscle beneath—but I didn't make him pull away. I couldn't.

The pad of his index finger brushed me through the fabric, sowing devious friction. Sparks flew. It was the most intense reaction I'd ever felt in my entire life. A sound I had never heard a human being make before welled up in my throat as his touch traveled back and forth. Back…

I twisted my hips, chasing the contact. Suddenly, the barrier of my panties was a hindrance. I needed them off. Needed more of him. I needed—

"Damn it—*No*. I'm not…" Liwai jerked away, shaking his head, leaving me swaying for balance. "No. We're not doing this. You need to go—what the hell?"

I blinked, struggling to take in several occurrences at once.

One, my pants were on the ground.

Two, someone stood on the other side of the road, watching us. I recognized her instantly from last night—that tall, willowy girl in the nightdress. *Renae.* Wild, black hair partially obscured her face, hanging down over the hem of her ratty T-shirt—but even from paces away, I could clearly make out the bruise clashing with the russet skin on her right cheek.

Apparently, so could Liwai. An animalistic sound tore from his throat, and he was across the road in five seconds. When he reached Renae, his hands went to her shoulders, turning her to face him.

"*Son of a bitch*," he bellowed when he saw her face up close. "What the hell happened?"

"They're fighting again," Renae said in a flat, monotone voice. Her owl-like eyes were empty, staring at nothing. "I tried to stop them, and…"

If she said anything else, I couldn't hear her over Liwai's growl of rage—but the next second, before I could even grasp what was happening, both had turned and headed for the woods. They moved so fast… It seemed as though they had just vanished into thin air, rather than beneath the trees.

And there I was, alone on the side of the road, with my pants around my ankles.

"Holy, freakin' hell," I croaked, just as it all began to sink in, but there was nothing in the world that could explain what had just happened.

Nothing.

I was Kaydee Blanchett. I didn't throw myself at strangers—and I certainly didn't allow said strangers to pin me up against the side of a car, ready to do anything and everything in broad, fucking daylight.

I was still a virgin, for Christ's sake—

You better be. The thought wasn't mine, but it was in my head, ripping through every other thought, growled and unmistakable. *Better be.* More images flooded my mind without warning—me with Boyd the other night. My laugh. His flowers.

With every disjointed memory, I swayed, infected with so much rage it felt like my skin was boiling.

Mine!

The thoughts dissipated just as quickly as they came, and I was left panting on trembling legs.

What in the world? Gradually, reality came back to me. I was still standing on the side of the road. The wind blew, whipping my hair around and chilling my bare skin. In the distance, the trees swayed as if shooing me away. My fingers had grown numb by the time I finally had the sense of mind to pull my jeans back up. A whimper broke loose from my throat when I realized that the clasp was broken, snapped off by careless fingers.

I dug through my back seat until I found a spare work apron and looped it around my waist like a makeshift belt. Then, I climbed into the driver's seat and tried to regain some sense of clarity.

Maybe Liwai was right—maybe I really had hit my head? I could have had a concussion—a dangerous, life-threatening concussion—with symptoms that could explain away impulsive, reckless behavior. At least then, I could *begin* to put everything that had happened since the previous night into perspective.

I tried to feel sorry for myself, but I could only picture Renae…

Something told me that Liwai had been more irritated by the sight of that mark on her face than surprised—as though her winding up injured was a regular, if unwelcome, occurrence.

My mama had been a nurse. Sometimes she'd come home with stories about the battered women around town who were treated in the emergency room for "falls" and "accidents." One, in particular, was Daisy Mae Willcott, who "slipped and fell" at least once a month, breaking some bone or another. Renae reminded me of Daisy Mae—thin, pale, and scrawny with those big, haunted eyes.

Had one of those boys hit her? And if they had, should I have called the police?

My cell phone was in my bag, right there at the foot of the passenger's seat—but I couldn't describe what stopped me from reaching for it. Maybe it was the thought of how a certain stranger might react if I did? Would he be furious? Feel betrayed?

Yes, no police. The thought seemed like mine…but it wasn't. The tone was too stern. Masculine. *Trust me*—him, I corrected. God, I was going insane.

In the end, the only move I made was to shove my key into the ignition. *Police station,* I insisted as I drove back into town. Glancing at the clock on the dash, I realized there was still enough time to give a statement. I had promised Mari…but I just kept driving until I reached the one place in town where I spent more time than I did, even at Bardee's.

The Kittywatt Free Public Library was—ironically enough —housed within an old fire station. It didn't even have a public computer, and the "current" selection was about ten years behind whatever was selling in the bookstores these days.

But it was my haven. Growing up, I had spent so much time there that I had my own area—a nice, yellow armchair near the second-floor window. The librarian, Melinda Pearson, even knew me by name. Like the drug dealer of an addict, she also knew when I desperately needed my fix of something heavy and literature related.

Breakups. Failed tests. Bad hair days—you name it, Melinda always supplied the right medicine. One look at my face, and she darted from her seat behind the front desk, adjusting her glasses.

"What can I do you for today, Kaydee?"

I swallowed, trying to displace the sob I could feel threatening to break loose from the back of my throat. "Can… can you show me the mental health section?"

Melinda raised an eyebrow, but without a word, she turned and led the way, up a flight of stairs and past two rows of shelves until we reached a small section of books in the far corner.

"Here ya go, darlin'."

"Thanks."

Melinda left me to my misery, and I proceeded to swipe every book dealing with mental illness into my arms. Deanna was going to be pissed at me for disobeying her orders, but frankly, I didn't care. I couldn't seem to reach my spot fast enough, and once I was comfortably settled within my chair, I sucked in a deep breath and popped open a book on schizophrenia.

Two hours and ten books later, I was no closer to discovering anything that might have been able to explain my reaction to Liwai Raven than I was to answering how I could have been shot without a scratch.

I didn't have the auditory hallucinations associated with schizophrenia.

According to the literature, I was too "functional" to be depressed.

Strangely, none of the books seemed to mention anything about throwing yourself at a complete stranger *after* convincing yourself that he had saved your life. Go figure. Though, there was one promising passage about sexual promiscuity and bipolar disorder...

Maybe that was it?

I certainly felt torn between two polar opposites. One minute, I had been myself—normal, good ol' Kaydee—and the next, I had been no better than Deanna, who took her dates to the back of the bowling alley for more than just bowling.

Though, self-diagnosing yourself was just as dangerous as letting one stranger shape your entire mindset, in any case.

My finger darted to my lips, absently tracing the path where Liwai's had wandered earlier. Every little nerve there felt sensitive. Overstimulated. *Alive.*

God, what was wrong with me? For the first time in my life, I was alarmed to discover that the answer couldn't be found in a book. Jane Austen and her flowery prose didn't appear to be enough to soothe these newer mental wounds. I felt no desire to disappear into a fantasy or—God forbid—a steamy romance.

I felt numb, and that was how I found myself leaving the sanctity of my spot to wander aimlessly through a section of the library that even I had never ventured before. One wrong turn, and I was in that dark, shadowy corner near the back where the Goth kids from the high school were known to lurk. At random, I read the title of a book on a nearby shelf—*The Occult and Unexplainable Phenomenon.* I reached for it and snatched a nearby *Guide to Wicca* for good measure. Maybe someone had put a spell on me?

I knew that Dee had dated a guy who claimed to practice voodoo once. I wouldn't have put it past her to have chanted some weird incantation she found on the internet in her misguided attempt to finally "catch me a man." God, I hoped it was as simple as that—a crazy spell gone wrong. Voodoo.

With a sigh, I turned, ready to add the books to my collection, when another one caught the corner of my eye. It was an old, tattered volume on a nearby shelf, and I grabbed it without thinking. When I returned to the safety of my chair by the window, I glanced down at the title—*Lycanthropy, Vampirism, and the Allure of Animal Magnetism.*

In the end, I fell asleep before I could read a single line. By the time I woke up, curled in my chair, Melinda was all but ready to kick me out of the door. She gave me an odd look as I rushed past her, books bundled in my arms. God only knew what I had mumbled in my sleep this time.

I was in such a rush that I nearly ran into someone standing by the entrance.

"Sorry!" I choked out before promptly dropping everything onto the poor person's feet. I stooped to grab them, realizing that the figure rushing to help me sounded awfully familiar.

"It's okay, Kaydee. I'm the one who should be apologizing."

"Boyd?" I looked up, horrified to find that he was in the process of dusting off the cover of my text on the occult. Too panicked to think through the consequences, I snatched for it and tucked it under my arm. "What are you doing here? I was just… Getting some books for my Aunt. She's into this weird occult stuff."

Boyd cracked a wry grin, and I couldn't tell if he bought the lie or not. "I decided to stick around for another day," he said. "Mainly to check up on you, but you weren't home. Then I remembered where you liked to spend most of your time when we were younger. Seems I was right."

I felt my cheeks flame, and I rushed to my feet before I could do something stupid. Like, ask if he'd seen someone shove a bullet from my body. Or bite my finger.

"Well, I should be going—"

"Wait!" He grabbed my forearm and stood as well. "I don't have class until tomorrow. We could grab something to eat if you want? My car's not far."

Dinner with an old friend—it sounded harmless enough on its face. So why did some part of me hesitate at the prospect? Boyd had always been nice enough, but… A pair of piercing, watchful eyes snuck into my skull and wouldn't leave. *Mine.*

No. I shook my head to banish the unwelcome sentiment. Liwai Raven wasn't a factor—finding answers was. Besides, I doubted I could eat anything without getting to the bottom of what happened last night.

"I can't," I blurted before bolting for the parking lot. "Maybe some other time!"

I was racing down the block before poor Boyd could even reply. As I climbed into my car, I was shaking so badly I couldn't think straight. Getting the key into the ignition took three tries. By the time I finally looked up, a dark shape drew my notice, and I choked on a scream.

Someone was watching me from a nearby alley. I could see them. Their long dark hair whipped in the wind, their eyes cold and observant. *Mine,* a voice hissed through my skull.

But when I blinked, the image vanished. No one was there.

For a second, I considered going to the hospital—I had to have a concussion or something. Maybe post-traumatic stress? Instead, I made it home just as darkness was falling. Dee's red Miata was already in the driveway, and I steeled myself for one of her good-hearted lectures as I climbed the porch steps.

True to form, she certainly didn't disappoint, greeting me with an indignant, "I thought I told you not to visit that damn library today?" the moment I walked through the front door.

For the first time in years, I didn't respond to her ribbing with a quip of my own. I couldn't even look at her, sprawled out on the couch watching reruns of *Dallas*.

Instead, I raced up the stairs to the confines of my bedroom. "You're welcome, by the way," Dee called after me. "I made your bed for you. Your room was a mess, kiddo. You're usually neater than that."

"Um, thanks," I croaked back.

Closing the door behind me, I locked it and tossed my books into the corner near my bed. Then, breathing heavily, I finally turned to the mirror and faced my reflection with wide, accusatory eyes.

The girl staring back at me didn't look any different. She was pale and—despite the fact that she wore an apron around her waist—seemed normal. One might have never known that she had thrown herself at a virtual stranger for no reason other than, *it felt right.*

"You're a slut," I hissed at my reflection. "What in the hell is wrong with you?"

I couldn't come up with a reply. Trembling from head to toe, I sank down on my bed and buried my face in my hands.

Liwai. Liwai. Liwai!

He dominated my mind—my thoughts. I couldn't stop thinking about him. Worrying about him.

Was Renae okay? Why on earth had Liwai sounded so damn angry? Why was he lying to me?

Why? Why? Why?

The questions circled my brain, but as night fell around me, I couldn't find the answer to a single one.

And this tiny voice in my head warned that if I wanted to preserve what little sanity I had left…

I should stop looking.

I had locked my door that night so that Deanna couldn't barge in and listen to my sleep-talk theater—but she was there, nonetheless, knocking away at what felt like the very moment dawn broke across the sky.

"Kaydee? Kaydee! Rise and shine, sweetie pie!"

I groaned and snatched my glasses from the nightstand. Somehow, I managed to stagger to the door without tripping over my own two feet and pulled it open. "What the hell?"

Deanna greeted me from the other side with a beaming smile. "How ya feeling today?"

I frowned as I mulled over the question. I felt horrible. Mentally, emotionally, physically—though, if anything, the sight of my misery made my aunt's grin widen.

"I made you breakfast," she chirped a little too sweetly for my liking.

I raised an eyebrow. "Breakfast? *You?*" The Aunt Dee I knew and loved couldn't even successfully operate a microwave without setting something on fire—let alone the equipment necessary to prepare a whole meal.

She shrugged. "Well…it's more like toast and coffee, but it's the thought that counts, right? I'm sure you're hungry anyway."

I couldn't argue with that. After the night I'd had—one spent tossing and turning with thoughts of Liwai Raven plaguing my mind—coffee was a welcome drug. Sensing the break in my resolve, Dee ushered me down the hall with a wave of her hand.

"Well, come on, then."

I followed her into the kitchen, where, as promised, a steaming mug of coffee awaited me beside a plate of partially burnt toast. I took a seat and slid my hand around the handle of the mug but paused right before taking a sip. I couldn't help the way my gaze suspiciously darted to Dee, who had leaned against the counter.

"This doesn't have poison in it, does it?"

She gave me the sweetest little smile that instantly set me on edge. "What makes you say that?"

I hesitated, breathing in the rich aroma of fresh coffee. In the end, pure exhaustion won out, and I took a gulp, pleased to find that it had been perfectly brewed to my preference of blacker than black. A shudder ran through me as the caffeine churned through my veins.

I had even begun to relax a little when Deanna finally blurted what I figured she'd been dying to say since I'd woken up. "So, I heard about you and Liwai Raven yesterday."

I choked, spraying coffee across the table. "W-What?"

Dee blinked innocently. "Leroy McCoy, you know him? Well, while putting his horses out to pasture, he swore that he saw you speaking 'rather intently' with Liwai Raven—" She even made air quotes. "So naturally, Nadine, the nursing aide that checks up on him, told Susan at the Mini-Mart, who told me."

Damn. I inwardly winced at the thought of what else poor old Mr. McCoy might have seen. Wasn't it bad enough that I had already scarred an innocent teenage girl for life?

Which reminded me… Turning to face Dee fully, I squared my shoulders. "What do you know about Renae Raven?"

Dee raised a blood-red eyebrow. "Huh?"

"Well, she goes to the school, right?"

Dee, surprisingly, worked as a secretary down at Kittywatt Senior High. Everyone knew that she had only gotten the job on account of being rather *close* to the principal, Mr. Edwards. I was also pretty sure that she would be fired any day now due to the correlation between her wardrobe and the sudden spike in male students purposefully getting sent to the principal's office.

"Yeah," Dee said while twirling a blood-red curl around her pinky finger. "She's a quiet, shy little thing. Though that whole family of hers is rather strange, so you can't really blame her."

"Strange? How?" I asked. Though as I recalled that battered, white house on Hooser Lane, I didn't have much difficulty coming up with suspicions.

"Well, Sheriff Michaels had to all but threaten to go after them for truancy if they didn't put that girl in school. There are some older boys in the house," Dee added, "but they're all over the age of eighteen, so he couldn't do a thing about them."

I frowned, thinking of Renae's bruise. *They're fighting again,* she'd said. With that many men cooped up in one house, it was no wonder. Had one of those boys—men—hit her? Cody?

"Why do you care?" It wasn't until she cleared her throat that I realized Dee was talking to me.

"Oh, no reason." I gulped down some more coffee to hide the tremor in my voice and took my time swallowing, hoping that she didn't notice.

"Mari called you last night," she said, surprising me by changing the subject. It wasn't like Dee to pick up on social cues. "She said you never showed up at the station."

Oh, that. I forced down another sip of scalding coffee and then choked out the first excuse that came to mind. "I got…distracted."

"Hmmm." Dee's smile alone should have put me on guard, even before she added in a knowing tone, "Distracted by thoughts of *Liwai Raven*?"

I lurched to my feet and snatched my piece of toast from the table before hurrying into the hall. "You know what?" I called as I darted up the stairs. "I think I will go see the sheriff now."

"You have time to eat some more, at least," Dee scolded after me. "I know you didn't eat anything last night. I'll leave some snacks in your car."

I winced at the offer. Dee only brought up food when she was worried. Just how wretched had I looked?

Despite the rude wake-up call, I was alarmed to find that Dee had let me sleep in again. By the time I managed to drag a brush through my hair and rush out of the door, dressed in a sweatshirt and a pair of jeans, it was already past one o'clock. Regardless, I climbed into my Beetle, fully prepared to meet the sheriff and give him my statement... only to drive right past the station again.

I didn't go to the Ravenswood gas station, surprisingly enough. Something told me that Liwai wouldn't talk to me, even if I did, though I fully intended to apologize—eventually. I merely had to come up with a decent line first—*I'm sorry for kissing you impulsively. It will never happen again.*

But whenever I unintentionally recalled the feeling of his lips on mine, heat coursed through my body. I drove around town aimlessly in an attempt to lessen the reaction I almost went to the clinic, just in case I really did have a concussion—but in the end, I somehow found myself pulling into the parking lot of Kittywatt Senior High.

School had already let out, and aimless teenagers milled in the parking lot, bemoaning homework and sharing jokes.

All but one. She lingered on the edge of the crowd, dark hair flying as she cut, alone, around the side of the school, heading toward the woods. I couldn't explain what made me follow her, driving along the curb. For all she knew, I could have been a deranged psychopath out searching for my next victim. But when I pulled up beside her and rolled down my window, she stopped.

"Hey! Renae, right?"

She turned, confusion flashing through those massive eyes —but she didn't run away. If anything, she didn't seem surprised to see me there. She merely tilted her head to take me in fully, appearing more owl-like than ever.

The bruise on her cheek had deepened to deep violet and stretched from the corner of her right eye down to her jaw. It looked painful. Not that her face revealed any hint of it. She held a pile of textbooks in her arms, but I couldn't see a bag dangling from her shoulder or even a backpack. I supposed that I should have left it at "hello" and driven away, but I blamed the suspected concussion for what I did next.

"Want a ride?"

I tried my hardest to sound friendly. Innocent.

"I was just passing by, and I saw you walking. It's a long way to the other side of town. And it looks like it might rain," I added, piling on as many excuses as I could so that I didn't seem quite the sick pervert I felt like on the inside.

This was *wrong*. Renae Raven was a child. Hell, I didn't even know Liwai or her relation to him. For all I knew, she could have been his daughter—though the thought made me flinch for some reason. How old was he anyway?

"I don't mind," I insisted as the seconds passed while Renae just stared at me. I nearly jumped out of my skin when she finally crept forward with all the caution of a wild doe. As she pulled open the passenger's-side door, a gust of wind blew her scent in my face—soap and strawberry shampoo.

Today she wore a long, burgundy dress that had probably been in fashion when Dee had gone to high school. Unbound, her hair pooled on the seat beneath her, thick and untamed.

"Hi," I said, only to ease the tension.

It really did look like it was about to rain, and Renae didn't even have a jacket, let alone anything to keep her books from getting wet. The only thing she seemed to be wearing besides that dress and a pair of boots was a small, golden necklace that spelled out a name. *Laurie.*

Her mother? A sister?

I was too chicken to ask, and she didn't seem inclined to answer anyway. She sat on the seat, hunched over and silent. Awkwardly, I started to drive off, trying to ignore the desperate questions circling my brain, dying to be asked. *Who hit you? Why did you tell me to "never come back" the other night? What can you tell me about Liwai?*

It was only when I finally gathered the nerve to glance in her direction, a few minutes into the drive, that I realized she had a notebook open and seemed to be absently doodling on one of the pages. I snuck a peek and felt my mouth fall open.

"That's beautiful!" She had painstakingly drawn a grove of trees. Every little leaf had been etched with careful, precise detail. It looked as though a wind could blow through the branches and lift the image right off the page. "I wish I could draw like that."

She glanced up at me then and smiled. The expression transformed her face. She almost looked her age for once—around fourteen, I guessed—but just as quickly as it had appeared, the look was gone. Her eyes darted away from me, settling on the storage box between our seats. Someone —Dee most likely—had stuffed it full of chips and snack cakes, upholding her earlier promise.

"You can help yourself," I said, nodding to the haul.

Renae went so still that I bit my lip, sure I'd insulted her somehow. Then her tiny hand darted for a bag of chips, and she tucked it into her pocket.

"So… Have you and your family been in Kittywatt long?" I asked, unnerved by the display. She didn't even have a lunch bag, from what I could tell. Had she eaten breakfast?

I didn't receive an answer.

"It's cold out," I said, nodding toward her bare arms. "Do you not have a coat?"

More silence.

I fidgeted, driven to keep talking just to avoid the awkward quiet. "I have some old clothes I could give you. They aren't very fancy, but they should probably fit you."

Her head shot up, though she kept those pink lips firmly sealed. While she'd taken a ride from me, Renae didn't seem inclined to do anything more than sit. *Serves you right*, I thought while eyeing the road. The only time she spoke up at all was right before I would have turned onto Hooser Lane.

"Here's fine," she rasped and climbed out of the car before I even had the chance to park.

"Wait!—" I took a handful of Dee's snack offerings and held them out. With a glance over her shoulder, Renae lunged for them all, stuffing them into the pocket of her dress.

"Thank you," she chirped before taking off down the street just as the first few rain drops fell.

"I'll bring you those clothes later tonight," I called out. Unsurprised when she didn't respond, I watched her go, oddly uneasy. It was nice to know that Liwai wasn't the only one who seemed to want nothing to do with me.

I sighed, adjusting my grip on the steering wheel—but just as I was about to turn, I noticed something on the passenger's seat—a single piece of paper. Renae had forgotten her drawing. I reached for it while glancing out the window, but she was already gone. When I looked down again, I promptly felt all the color drain away from my face.

Taken out of context, it was a breathtaking drawing. In pencil, she had sketched a woman wearing wire-rimmed glasses whose frizzy curls had been tied back into a ponytail. The detail was astounding, right down to the little name tag on the collar of her sweater that read *Kaydee B.*

I knew, without a doubt, that the woman was meant to be *me*, working on what would have been any average night at Bardee's. Renae had even drawn my cowboy boots. Everything, down to that loose curl that always slipped out of my ponytail by the end of my shift, was the same.

Everything…

Except for the neatly drawn hole, right over the sketched-Kaydee's abdomen, where a series of darker, heavier strokes slashed through her sweater…

Like splotches of blood.

THE FACT that my delusions were the subject of creepy sketches drawn by a teenage girl somehow made it all sink in—I was insane.

And apparently, Liwai was making light of that fact by gossiping about me. I pictured them, all gathered in that battered white house, snickering about the crazy girl convinced that she'd been brought back to life.

God. That shame was what finally made me drag my sorry ass into the sheriff's station. Shaking in my sneakers, I shuffled up to the front desk, where the receptionist didn't seem surprised to see me.

"Burt!" she called to someone lurking in the depths of the station. "She's here."

A second later, the sheriff poked his head from the doorway of his office.

"Kaydence," he greeted with a nod of his head.

I had to fight down a rush of nerves. "Hello, Burt."

The relationship between Sheriff Michaels and I had always been…

Strange.

He used to date my mama before she'd married Daddy—and when I say dated, I mean "dated."

They had been the high school power couple—the kind that everyone swore would get married one day. He had been the jock hero/class president, and she, the head cheerleader. Some of the more ancient teachers still told stories about their legendary courtship. In their words, Burt and Marie had been destined to last…

At least until Burt went through his alcoholism and Mama met Daddy—the born-again once-upon-a-time rebel with an artist's soul.

Yes, things were strange between Burt Michaels and me. In some ways, I think he saw me as his almost-daughter more than I would have liked—especially after my mother died. All throughout high school, he'd been unusually strict with enforcing the town curfew when it came to me, always tattling to Dee if I stayed out even a second after eleven— but he was also rather lenient about any speeding tickets that I might have incurred once upon a time, so I wasn't complaining.

Now, his blue eyes took me in, full of gruff concern. "You didn't have to come in today, Kaydence," he said, crossing the room. That was another thing about Burt Michaels—he was the only person in town who called me by my full name. In addition to Liwai Raven, it seemed. "I was going to tell Mari to give you until next week if you needed it."

"Thanks." I swallowed hard. "But I think I just need to get this all off my chest…"

Renae Raven's drawing was in my bag, and Liwai Raven's words were racing through my mind as Sheriff Michaels ushered me into his office.

"Well, you're here now," he said, closing the door behind me. "So, we might as well make use of it."

I nodded and sat down in the chair in front of his desk.

"Now," he began after taking the seat across from me. "I just need your statement to help tidy up the case between Deacon and Miller. All you have to do is tell me, in your own words, exactly what happened."

I nodded as my purse—containing Renae's cryptic drawing—weighed heavily on my lap like a ton of bricks.

"Okay," I said, trying to ignore the part of me that wondered if I could ever begin to explain it all. "What happened is…"

Taking a deep breath, I ignored the doubt, and started talking.

Half an hour later, I found myself slumped in the chair across from Sheriff Michaels, exhausted. It was as though I'd spent the entire day running a marathon rather than answering a few simple questions.

You saw nothing?

Are you sure, Kaydence?

And this is your God-honest recollection?

You don't remember anything else?

After a while, my voice had faded to a monotonous murmur, much like that of an automated machine—*Kaydee's not here right now, but if you want her to say "yes," press 1. For "no," press 2. If you want her to repeat the same statement five times in a row, press 3.*

Beep.

By the time I finally trailed off, I wasn't sure what Sheriff Michaels believed. He was a tough old codger with an uncanny knack for sniffing out trouble. I couldn't help the nervous twist in my stomach as I mentally went over my statement. Had I or had I not mentioned potentially being shot?

"I guess that's it, then," the sheriff said with a sigh, sitting back in his chair. "Thank you for coming in today—" Relieved, I nodded and started to stand, slipping my bag over my shoulder. "But there is one more thing I wanted to talk to you about…"

Uh-oh. I froze, facing him with what I knew was a blank expression. "Sir?"

He nodded toward my chair. "Sit down, Kaydence."

I did, subconsciously keeping my purse between us as though it were a magic shield against any more prying questions. "I gave you my statement. Is there anything else you want to go over?"

"No." Burt shook his head. "This isn't about the shooting. This is about you…and Liwai Raven."

"There is no '*me and Liwai Raven*,'" I blurted, even as my cheeks flushed red with shame. First Dee. Now him. The last thing I needed was to have the entire damn town gossiping about my love life.

"I heard you were talking to him yesterday," the sheriff admitted, seeming even more stern than usual.

Damn that Leroy McCoy and that nosy nurse of his. Who knew the old man was such a gossip?

"That was nothing," I insisted through gritted teeth. "He was answering a question about my car. That's all."

At least, that was my story unless the whole "heated kiss" aspect of our meeting came out.

"I don't like you being near him," Sheriff Michaels warned, once again forgetting that he wasn't my father. "He's dangerous. He and that whole family of his."

I thought of Liwai with those shadowed eyes and jet-black hair. Alarming, yes, but dangerous?

"He's just a guy from the bar. He shows up sometimes," I stammered with what I hoped was a dismissive attitude. *No one special…who most definitely did not (maybe) save my life.*

"They're drifters, Kaydence. Damn near Gypsies, and they're criminals. He's been questioned in connection to a murder, you know."

"Oh, that's nice—" Wait a second. The words *murder* and *connection* seemed to take longer to register in my brain, but once they did, I nearly fell out of my chair. "Liwai Raven? You think he killed someone?"

"He has a record, Kaydence." Burt's eyes were a cold, no-nonsense shade of navy. "Fourteen years ago, a girl was found dead in Chambersburg, just over the county line. Liwai was a suspect, but there was never enough evidence to prove it. It was the strangest thing. I'm friends with one of the detectives on the case, and he swore that the body looked mauled. Like by a stray dog or something. Several witnesses, however, named Liwai as being near the scene and no one—and nothing—else. That's just the start of the list. That whole family is trouble, going back decades."

Weakly, I shook my head. "You can't believe that Liwai would actually kill someone—"

"The Chambersburg police sure did," the sheriff countered. "As I said, other crimes in the area were tied to him and the Raven family. They're dangerous, Kaydence—and if he really did kill that woman…she had a little baby girl who's had to grow up without a mother. You know better than anyone what that's like."

I flinched and scrambled to my feet before he could dredge up any more of the past. "I appreciate your concern, Sheriff Michaels, but I can take care of myself."

Albeit, dealing with a man suspected of murder fourteen years ago was not exactly what I had bargained for. Was it utterly pathetic that I did the math within my head and realized that he had to be around ten years older than me? He looked way too young to be in his thirties. No wonder the thought of us together had gotten everyone's tongues wagging—though for very different reasons, considering Sheriff Michaels' reaction.

"I promised your mother that I would watch out for you," he said as if reading my mind. "I've been known to keep my promises."

"And I appreciate it," I insisted. Like the well-meaning Dee, I knew he was only obsessive out of genuine concern.

"You're a good woman, Kaydence. I wouldn't like to see you get caught up with the wrong people."

"Me neither, to be honest."

Once we said our customary goodbyes, I tore out of there like a bat out of hell. As overbearing as he was, Sheriff Michaels was right. Today was a brand-new day. I was putting Liwai and his strange family and all of the weirdness of the shooting out of my mind. It was time to return to my old life, living with my aunt and working at a bar like any normal, rudderless twenty-two-year-old.

I headed toward my Beetle with a bull's eye sense of determination. After fumbling through my bag, I withdrew my keys, but just as I prepared to insert them into the car door, a dark shape came out of nowhere to bat my hand away.

"What did you tell him?"

My first instinct was to panic and reach for my mace keychain, but something else—stupidity, maybe?—made me glance over my shoulder to meet a pair of watchful brown eyes instead.

"Why, Liwai Raven," I croaked as though I didn't have a care in the world, even as the words *murder suspect* raced through my mind. "Fancy meeting you here. But I really need to go now—" I turned and tried to jimmy my key into the lock again—only this time, his hand fell over my shoulder, too firm to be ignored. Before I could shrug him off, he spun me around, and my keys slipped through my fingers to land on the pavement.

"What did you say?" His voice was neutral enough, but his posture was too stiff—as if he preferred to yell. Dominate.

My stomach flipped, and I could barely speak in response, "I told him what you *told* me to say," I replied. "Though—" I dug into my bag with trembling fingers. "Maybe I should go back in there and tell him what *really* happened. And maybe, I should show him this?"

I shoved Renae's picture into his hand, perhaps a little more violently than necessary. Nonetheless, he drew back when he saw it, his eyes narrowing into slits.

"Where did you get this?"

I pulled myself up to full height, trying my hardest not to flinch at his tone. "Do you want to tell me why your little sister has a creepy drawing of me with a gunshot wound?"

It all sounded so crazy when said out loud. I half expected Liwai to burst out laughing. *Haha! You fell for it.* But the joke was on him, apparently, because all the color drained from his face.

Wham! The next second, I was pressed between a wall of metal and a body formed of pure, coiled muscle. He held both of my hands trapped in a single fist, and his eyes raged worse than the storm clouds once again rolling across the sky. *He's dangerous,* Sheriff Michael's warning echoed in my brain. When up this close to him, I had to agree.

"You went to Renae?" he asked in a lethal tone, his eyes sparkling like dying embers. "*Alone?*"

"Yes." I forced down a swallow as I swayed on my feet. "I just...I..." There wasn't any way to spin it. I had all but stalked a teenage girl for no reason other than this irrational need to get close to him—any way I could.

It was pathetic, but there it was.

"If you didn't believe me, all you had to do was just say so," I blurted, conveniently forgetting for a second that he *had* —multiple times. "You didn't have to tell your sister so that she could draw some creepy little picture—"

"She's not my sister," he snapped through clenched teeth. "And don't bring her into this. Renae drew that two months ago."

I recoiled from him, smacking my head on the roof of my car in the process. *Two months.* His eyes quickly narrowed as if he hadn't meant to say that last bit. The next second, he balled the picture in a fist and shoved the remains into his pocket. "Listen—"

I flinched as a rumble of thunder sounded in the distance— only to realize, glancing up, that Liwai had made the sound himself as he released a heavy sigh.

"Tonight," he said, meeting my gaze directly. "Come to this address."

As I watched, he dug into his pocket for what seemed to be an old receipt and scribbled something onto the back of it with a pencil pulled from the same place. He wasn't wearing his customary overalls today—just a black T-shirt and jeans.

"If you see anyone out front who isn't me...leave."

I blinked as he shoved the slip of paper into my hand.

"W-Why?"

He frowned, almost as though he were trying to reason that out for himself. Eventually, he settled on one answer. "You want to talk or not?"

I didn't have a chance to respond before he was moving down the street with that dark hair flying out behind him.

A smart woman would have marched back into the sheriff's station and filed a restraining order against the entire Raven family. My arm ached from how tightly Liwai had grabbed me. I wouldn't be able to sleep tonight without seeing Renae's creepy little drawing every time I closed my eyes.

Me.

Gunshot wound.

Blood.

Liwai said that she had drawn it months ago…

It just didn't make sense, and maybe sheer desperation for answers was why I found myself creeping out of the house, long after Dee had gone to bed, with that crumpled receipt clutched in my fist. What I carried in my other hand was a bag of old clothes I couldn't fit anymore. Renae may have been part of a family of murderers and prone to drawing creepy things, but I couldn't blame her. I knew what it was like to be overlooked by everyone else in your life, too wrapped up in their own problems to notice yours.

And maybe, I wanted to prove a point to Liwai Raven as well—he couldn't boss me around. We would talk, but on my terms.

Only, the address he gave me wasn't on Hooser Lane.

Once my car finally stopped, I found myself parked outside of a small trailer, partially hidden behind a grove of trees on the outskirts of town. A battered red truck was parked on a gravel driveway a few feet away from it and light spilled through a screen door.

The place had a vibe that just read *male* down to the overgrown lawn and mismatched curtains shielding the small windows.

Did Liwai live here alone?

Armed with my bag of clothes, I reached for the door handle, only to freeze as a slender figure drifted from the woods before I could even pull it open.

I knew who it was in an instant. Renae's long hair streamed behind her, gleaming in the moonlight. She was underdressed again—wearing only an oversized man's T-shirt that stopped below her knees and a pair of pink flip-flops.

I watched as she crossed the small clearing and entered the trailer after knocking once.

Liwai had claimed that she wasn't his sister. His daughter, then? There weren't a lot of reasons that could explain why a girl that young would casually stroll into the home of a grown man wearing little to no clothing.

Bad! My conscious hissed, and I glanced down to realize that my hand was still on the door, already easing it open.

Liwai had told me to leave if I saw anyone else there.

But she's a child, I told myself to rationalize my potential eavesdropping.

In the end, even common sense couldn't hold me back. Before I could talk myself out of it, I pushed open the door and followed her. With every step, I felt more desperate, unable to rationalize why I was aiming for stealth. Or why —when I came close enough to the door—I strained my ears to listen.

I needed to know…

Something.

Anything.

The inside of the trailer was lit by a single, artificial light bulb. I couldn't make out much through the screen door besides a few pieces of furniture. Renae had taken a seat at a small table pushed up against the wall of what I guessed to be the kitchen. I couldn't see Liwai, but going off the sounds of cupboards opening and closing, I assumed that he was at the counter.

"What are you doing out so late, Rae?" he asked with a sigh.

"You didn't come home," Renae said, ignoring the question. "We went hunting without you."

She stared at her hands while absently kicking her feet underneath the table. The simple act made her seem so young. Something ached inside my chest at the contrast against the sullen girl who walked home in the rain.

"I was busy," Liwai grumbled without elaborating. "But I *should* have been there… Did you eat?"

Renae bowed so that her face was hidden behind a curtain of dark hair. "A little."

If Liwai noticed the slight tremble in her voice, he didn't mention it. Instead, he appeared behind her like a shadow and slid a plate of food onto the table.

My breath caught at the sight of him. He wasn't wearing a shirt, revealing thick, coiled muscle. I tried to lower my gaze, but that only gave me an uncanny view of how low his jeans rode over his hips. As Deanna would purr, they were *deliciously* low.

Crap! As if feeling my attention on him, I swear he cocked his head my way, before turning his attention back to Renae.

Only when he spoke to her did I remember how to breathe. "Leftovers," he grumbled. I cut my eyes to the food he offered—a sandwich and a small bag of potato chips. "Help yourself."

"Thanks."

Renae gingerly lifted a sandwich in both hands and took several greedy bites. Her savoring moans made me suspect that it was her first substantial meal in a long while. Her frail body certainly bolstered that suspicion, and it broke my heart. I'd seen rabbits with more meat on their bones.

I made a mental note to ask Dee for more snacks.

"I thought you said they took you hunting," Liwai murmured from the other end of the trailer. His tone was accusatory.

Hunting. I hoped that was slang for eating at a restaurant or something. The alternative—she got her meals while scavenging with a pack of wild teenage boys in the middle of the night—was way too strange to consider. Not even the most rural residents of Kittywatt were *that* hick.

"They didn't wait for me. I trailed behind again, so Cody only gave me the entrails this time—" Renae admitted in between bites of her sandwich. "And I threw it all up. On his *shoes.*"

"That's not funny," Liwai scolded, though even he chuckled once in response to Renae's impish grin, but the next second, his tone hardened. "I'll kill him—"

"No, you won't," Renae replied, as she rummaged through a pile of chips. "He's always worse when you confront him. I'm fine. At least he took me hunting this time."

"Fine. But I'll be the one to take you out tomorrow."

Anger still smoldered in his tone, which was obvious in the way he stomped to the other side of the trailer—but *I* was still stuck on entrails.

Guts, blood, gore. I blinked, hoping that I had just imagined the wording, but I knew in the pit of my soul that I hadn't. They had made her eat entrails…

What kind of sick prick was this Cody?

And why the hell wasn't Liwai reaching for the phone right then and there to dial 911?

I scanned Renae's face, looking for traces of blood, but from there, I couldn't see anything but golden skin.

"When you finish eating, go get some sleep in the back," Liwai said, snapping me from the thought. "I'll camp out in the truck."

"Okay." Renae nodded, and I sensed that this was a regular occurrence.

For a moment, Liwai let her eat in silence, but I could sense a tension between them, filled with unspoken words itching to be said. Finally, with a heavy sigh, Liwai broached a subject I figured he'd wanted to the moment she entered the trailer. "Rae…why did you give that woman your drawing?"

"I…"

"You *terrified* her," Liwai continued. "I had to talk her out of going to the police."

"Good."

I blinked, shocked by the hard, rebellious edge in Renae's soft voice. Apparently, so was Liwai.

"Renae—"

"Good," she repeated, cutting over him. Her hands were clenched into fists, her large eyes glaring down at the table. "I *wanted* to scare her. I wanted her to be so afraid that she'd run far, far away from here and never come back. I wanted her to stay the hell away from *you!*"

Liwai was silent, apparently just as stunned by her outburst as I was—but it only took him seconds to recover.

"Rae—"

"You don't have to do it!" Suddenly, the girl lurched to her feet, her eyes shining. She whirled to face where I assumed he stood, just beyond the door, out of sight. "We could just leave. You shouldn't *have* to do it!"

"*Renae.*" Liwai's tone held a note of exhaustion that made me suspect they had played out this conversation multiple times. "You know the law."

"But you're not like *them!* You're good. I know you don't want to—"

"Renae!" There was a sudden *bang!* as though someone had slammed their fist against a solid surface. "We are not having this conversation."

"What about her, huh?" Renae went on, her voice rising in pitch. "She…she's nice. She gave me a *ride*—" The awe in her tone made it sound synonymous with "a pot of gold." "She talked to me. She's a good person. She doesn't deserve to…"

Whatever *it* was, she couldn't say. Instead, she stood there, tears spilling from her eyes.

"Renae," Liwai's voice was softer this time. "Honey—"

"This isn't just about her—I know you want to join the clan," she went on, shaking her head. "I know you miss it, but if you leave…then I'll have no one else."

She broke down. Huge, wracking sobs shook her small body, and I could only stare, feeling like a creepy voyeur as I watched through the screen door.

Liwai was beside her in an instant, folding her into his arms. His hair shielded them both like a cloak as his mouth settled against her ear, growling words that made me shudder beneath their intensity. "I will *never* leave you. Do you hear me? As long as I have any breath left in me, no matter what happens, I'm not going anywhere. *Ever.*"

"Then don't do it," she mumbled against his shoulder. "Please don't do it. Don't kill her—"

CHAPTER

SEVEN

Those two words held the intensity of a sucker punch—*kill her*—but the only thought to cross my mind was, *If I die, Mari won't have anyone to cover Friday night's shift.*

I didn't think after that, let alone try to come up with any rational excuses to explain away what I'd just heard. For once, I tossed logic and reason right out the window, turned on my heel, and ran like hell.

My Beetle was still parked on the side of the road. The keys were in the ignition. All I had to do was climb into the seat and slam my foot on the gas. I came close to doing that, too. Close enough to have lunged for the handle and been home free, but without warning, a sound like a gunshot echoed behind me. I knew the culprit without even having to look back—the screen door flying open to smash against the metal siding of the trailer.

Run! Pure instinct took over—that kind of terror so intense that you could *taste* it. My body tensed as I dropped my bag and turned on my heel, forsaking my car altogether. Panting, I made a break for the woods. It was a stupid move in hindsight—but, against a pounding rush of adrenaline, nothing made sense other than the urge to just run and keep running.

I sprinted, convinced that Liwai was every flicker of shadow. Every rustle and crunch of the underbrush was him gaining on me by the second.

It was so dark. I couldn't see a damn thing. The moon hung up above, casting everything in silvery shadow, and I had to throw a hand out in front of my face just to keep from careening head-first into a tree—but each wasted second just brought him closer. I swore I could feel his breath on the back of my neck, heavy and thick on the night air. *In and out. Out and in. Closer, closer, closer…*

Eventually, I had the sense to scream. My mouth opened, and I sucked in air, but just as I prepared to let it loose, something rammed into me from behind, and I went sprawling. My chin smacked off the icy ground as blood welled on my tongue. My glasses slid down the bridge of my nose, and it was all I could do to weakly flail out my hand for a makeshift weapon—a heavy branch that I could barely lift.

"Kaydence, wait—"

"Stay away from me!" I turned, swinging the stick blindly and kicking out with my legs.

"Easy—" The hulking shadow I knew to be Liwai Raven drew back. His hands were held out passively in front of him, but his eyes… They practically *glowed* in the waning light of the moon—two pools of earthy brown threatening to swallow me whole.

He reached for me again, and I swung my stick up, spraying dirt through the air. "Stay away!"

To my shock, he hesitated. "Listen—"

"Help!" I shrieked over him, clutching my branch so tightly I was surprised the damn thing didn't snap in half. "Stay the hell away from me! Help!"

He took a step forward. Then another. That dark hair fluttered over his shoulders like a demonic cloak, whipped up by a sudden breeze. "Listen to me."

I sucked in a breath, prepared to scream again and… I never even saw him move. I figured I *smelled* him instead—a primal scent hit me with all the force of his weight pinning me down. My scream stuck in my throat as his hand covered my mouth.

I kicked. Flailed. Bit the thick, calloused palm attempting to seal my lips shut—but he was too heavy. Too strong. Too powerful. There was no way in hell I would ever be able to push him off alone.

This is it, I thought with a chilling sense of finality. I was going to die here, strangled in the middle of the woods. My vision blurred. My lungs screamed for air—but just as my heart began to surge with panic, Liwai growled something into my ear.

"Don't move. Don't speak. Don't even *breathe*."

Before I could react, he was gone, and I could finally suck in a few precious breaths of air—but I didn't have the chance to savor the freedom long before my ears caught wind of something crunching through the underbrush. Footsteps.

My first thought was that the intruder was someone just taking a leisurely night stroll who might have been able to help me. Until they spoke…

That low, husky tone was all too familiar, and my heart sank with every word.

"Come out, come out, little owl…"

Snap! Leaves and twigs crunched underfoot—this time, so close that I could hear the erratic pattern of the intruder's breathing as they crept along, like an animal hunting prey. Liwai's silhouette turned toward the sound. His entire body tensed in an instant, ready to spring. Attack.

"Cody," he called before the other man came into view. "Looking for someone?"

There was a sharp intake of breath—but if anyone had expected Cody to sound guilty at being caught doing… God, I didn't even want to consider what he was doing.

"Where is she?" That husky voice had to belong to the younger man, but it held not one ounce of shame.

"None of your damn business." If possible, Liwai's tone was even colder. I couldn't see his face—his back was turned to me as he stood only a few feet away. "I heard about what you did to Renae, you little prick," he hissed. "Pull something like that again, and I'll give you a taste of your *own* insides."

An optimistic part of me wanted to believe that he was joking…but there wasn't a shred of humor in his tone.

"She's lying," Cody said dismissively. "Besides, it's not like she's *your* problem. Rank. Familial ties. Ability. None of that matters out here, remember?"

Even I could sense the subtle threat in those words, but they didn't make sense.

Whether he was her brother or not, Liwai was older—if anyone could have taken responsibility for Renae, it was him—but Cody sounded too smug to have been bluffing.

"You know I'm right," he added, "Besides. Once you rejoin the pack, that little mutt will be on her own—"

A slight rustle was the only warning. The next second Liwai disappeared, and a violent sound echoed through the woods —*bang!*—as if something or someone very heavy had just been slammed against a solid surface.

"Call her that again," Liwai's voice caught the air, sounding slightly farther away, "and you'll regret it."

"Will I?" Cody's reply came somewhat muffled—and I pictured a pair of thick hands wrapped tightly around his throat. "You won't always be around to protect her. Sooner or later, you'll return to the clan, and she'll be…"

He let the statement hang in the air, and I shuddered to imagine what words might have filled in the blanks.

"Something tells me that you'll find your mate before I find mine," Liwai countered. "And like a good little soldier, you'll do what needs to be done and take your 'rightful place' among the pack—whatever the hell that means."

"I will," Cody spat. "Because I'm *proud* of what I am. I'm not ashamed of our ways, and I don't feel responsible for some stupid, little half-breed—"

Bang! The sharp crack resonated throughout the clearing, and I had a grim suspicion that it was Cody's head meeting the unforgiving surface of a tree. Repeatedly.

"Get out of here—*now*, before I do something that I won't regret," Liwai warned.

"Fine. But don't you think it's strange how it's taken you this long? No one else has stayed on the outside even half as—"

"Go."

"You don't think they've realized? Even before we left, there were rumors about the great Liwai Raven, who turned out to be a fucking disappointment. The others think you're just a freak, but I know better. After years on your own, you would have had to come across her by now. Seen *her*."

I didn't like the emphasis he put on that single word. *Her.* He might as well have said, "the bane of your existence."

"And yet, you still haven't taken your place in the clan. One might start to wonder… Especially when strange women come looking for you in the middle of the night."

I felt as though someone had drenched me in ice water. I knew instantly just who Cody was referring to. *Me.*

"She's no one," Liwai snarled over him. "Now leave."

"You can't escape what you are, Liwai," Cody said. "Though —if *she* really is just 'no one'—maybe I should pay that little redhead a visit myself. It can't be too hard to find her…"

The words lingered in the air as retreating footsteps echoed throughout the clearing.

I was too stunned to move. The branch was still in my grasp, held so tightly that my nails dug into the bark. Terrified, I could only wait, counting every breath that left my chest.

One.

Two.

Three.

I trembled as someone pushed their way through the brush at my right and a familiar pair of eyes met mine through the darkness. "Are you afraid?"

I could only cling to my branch for dear life.

"Then run," Liwai replied as if my silence alone had answered his question. "Go home. Stay away from me. Stay away from Renae. We never met. *This* never happened."

Then he turned, leaving me panting on the forest floor, and I could only watch him fade through the trees...

It took me nearly a whole minute to remember how to move. Breathe. An hour could have passed before I finally got up and ran like hell.

A smart woman would have called the police, I supposed. An even smarter woman might have gone straight to the sheriff's station—or maybe just gotten her daddy's gun from the safe stashed in the hall closet and sought out her own Southern Justice?

Apparently, my I.Q. had plummeted drastically all in the span of three days.

I drove in a series of jerky stop-and-starts until I somehow pulled into the driveway of the house I shared with Dee. There, I sat trembling in the driver's seat, unable to open the door without picturing a pair of haunting eyes watching from the shadows. Liwai's or Renae's...it didn't matter.

You heard it wrong, a part of me insisted. Why would they want to hurt me? I had never done anything remarkable outside of winning the eighth-grade county science fair. I rarely went anywhere beyond the bar or the library. Hell, my closest companions were my aunt, our town's librarian, and my middle-aged boss. Girls like me didn't tend to wind up on many hit lists.

Though, to be honest, the whole Raven family seemed to have a few screws loose. All those boys living together like a lawless frat house. Liwai living almost on the other side of town, and Renae seemingly trapped in the middle.

For all I knew, I was just one of many who had crossed their path. I shuddered, thinking of the dead girl from fourteen years ago and the police's interest in Liwai. Everything had the makings of some creepy urban legend—and something told me that if I stuck around for too long, I would find myself right in the middle of it all.

And I doubted such a tale had a happy ending.

EIGHT

I always got this weird feeling when my life got out of control—as if I'd exploded, and all the gory, nasty bits of me were spilling out for the world to see. I would bleed emotion like blood, staining the ground with every step, but the funny thing was that no matter how twisted and raw I felt inside, no one around me seemed to notice. It was as though my own personal hell was contained within a neat, invisible box. All anyone else saw was the perfect, cardboard cut-out of Kaydee Blanchett they were all used to seeing.

Dee didn't even seem fazed when I stumbled in a little after dawn as she was getting ready for work.

"Early morning jog?" she asked, while slipping a sandwich into a paper bag.

What looked like the entire contents of our fridge were spread out along the counter. I didn't know what was more shocking—her being awake that early without my help or her putting a meal together by herself.

Usually, I had to pack a lunch for her and leave it by the door, or she forgot it altogether—but for once, those blue eyes seemed unusually alert as they homed in on me standing beside the screen door.

"There's mud on your shoes," she said, dropping a crisp, red apple into her bag along with the sandwich. "What did you do? Swim in that mud puddle on the McCoy farm?"

I flinched and glanced down. Sure enough, dark muck caked the sides of my sneakers.

"Yeah. I just went running," I lied, settling for her convenient explanation.

Dee just shrugged. "Well, since you're up early, mind giving me a ride to work? That damn piece of junk car won't start again."

"A…ride?" It took me a minute to realize why that simple request had me so uneasy. Then it hit me. Dee worked at the high school—a place frequented by one strange teenage girl with a habit of drawing disturbing pictures.

"No!" When Dee glanced at me sharply over her shoulder, I stammered, "I…I need to shower."

"It's just down the block, Kaydee," Dee scoffed with a roll of her eyes. "The upholstery doesn't care what you smell like. Besides, would you rather have me walk all the way downtown in these?"

She gestured to the bright-red stilettos on her feet.

"Uh…fine." I was in a daze as Dee grabbed her lunch from the counter and hastened me out the back door. I loved my aunt, but she could be as sharp as a fox when sniffing out secrets. I was surprised that she hadn't noticed that my "jogging" outfit consisted of the same jeans and sweatshirt I had worn yesterday—though, it seemed as though Deanna was preoccupied with other thoughts.

For one, despite those ridiculous shoes, her outfit was rather…modest. Or, modest for *Dee.* Her burgundy top barely revealed any cleavage and had been paired with a turquoise sweater. Her skirt even reached down past her knees.

"Did they finally give you a notice slip?" I managed to croak as I climbed into the driver's seat while Dee shimmied into the seat beside me.

"Hmmm? Oh, this?" She ran a hand down her relatively subdued brown skirt. "I have a private meeting with the principal later… Put some pedal to the metal, Kaydee! I want to get there today."

We didn't speak as I pulled out of the driveway and headed for the high school. It was raining. Huge, icy drops splattered the windshield as I turned onto Main Street. I was nearly halfway down the block when Dee suddenly pointed out the window.

"Kaydee! Stop!"

I slammed my foot on the brake and followed her gaze through the windshield. A lone figure stood on the street wearing a familiar brown jacket and a pair of jeans. They were mine from years ago, and yet they were still too big for the figure wearing them. In the chaos of last night, I'd still left those old clothes behind. Apparently, Renae had found them—and it was a good thing she had in weather like this. Rain had plastered that mane of dark hair flat against her back. She almost comically resembled a drowned cat—but, when a pair of hazel eyes found mine through the glass, I nearly jumped out of my skin.

"It's that Raven girl," Dee said, shaking her head. "Poor kid doesn't even have an umbrella. We should give her a ride—"

My jaw clenched while my foot jerked against the gas pedal. The car lurched forward, nearly zooming through a red light —only by sheer luck did the light switch to green at the last second.

"Kaydence Marie!" I saw Dee clutch her seatbelt from the corner of my eye. "What the hell is wrong with you?"

I couldn't speak. All I could do was stare straight ahead and keep driving until Renae Raven was nothing more than a drenched speck in the distance—and even that wasn't far enough away. The whole time, Dee verbally berated me in that sharp tone she only used when I thoroughly pissed her off.

"Are you insane? There's plenty of room. What the hell has gotten into you? Kaydee?"

I couldn't answer. In silence, I pulled into the high school's circular driveway, just as a bus rumbled up the hill with the first wave of students.

Deanna's disapproving gaze practically seared the back of my neck. I waited for a stern speech about how rude I was acting, but she didn't say a single word as she climbed out onto the curb—and somehow, that made me feel even worse.

I trembled when I peeled out of the parking lot. Nothing made sense. The world was twisting and curling into knots, with me trapped right in the middle.

Like a coward, I took the long way around, cutting through the back roads rather than going through Main Street and risking seeing Renae. With every passing second, the rain seemed to come down harder. Without an umbrella, the girl would have been soaked to the bone by the time she reached the school.

You're ridiculous, Kaydee, I mentally hissed to myself. *The girl's related to a murderer—who she accused of wanting to kill you, too!—and yet, you still feel bad for not letting her in your car.*

Hell, if I gave Renae a ride, it should have been right to the police station. Struck by the sudden thought, I wrenched on the steering wheel and cut through an alley, determined to put an end to this mess once and for all. The sheriff's station sat at the end of the next block, gleaming like an enormous stone beacon through the rain.

Only the red light up ahead kept me from heading straight for it. My hands gripped the steering wheel so tightly that my nails dug into the leather. *You can do this,* I tried to tell myself. *Just march into Sheriff Michaels' office and tell him the truth about that whole crazy Raven family.*

I don't think I'll ever know what made me glance out the window. A paranoid part of me wondered if the battered, old pickup truck had been waiting all along for my Beetle to drive past, choosing the second I came out of the alley to pull into the opposite lane. Sure enough, the passenger's-side window had already been lowered, and even through the rain, I had no trouble making out the driver's face.

Namely those eyes, darker than any brown I had ever seen.

"Your choice."

I shouldn't have been able to hear him above the rain pelting the hood of my car or the sound of his sputtering engine. I swear, the words echoed more inside my head than in my ears.

"Your choice," Liwai Raven repeated. "You could go to the sheriff. Or you could hear the truth."

He didn't give me a chance to think it over. The moment the light turned green, his truck made a sharp right turn past the sheriff's station and down another road.

Dazed, I watched him go, startled by the unspoken invitation. *Follow…if you dare.*

And I'd be damned if I wasn't the tiniest bit curious.

What the hell was wrong with me? Salvation was right *there*. All I had to do was ease up on the brake, go a few short feet, and turn into the parking lot. Confronting Sheriff Michaels with the truth was the smart thing to do—the *right* thing to do.

The argument reverberated in my brain as a line started forming behind me. Someone honked. Shouted. I couldn't move. My entire body tensed as I eyed the brick building a few yards ahead and tried to tell myself that I had every intention of heading straight for it.

Really, I did. As if to prove it, my foot eased off the brake and dutifully moved to the gas pedal. But right when I would have crossed the center of the intersection, my hands suddenly seemed to have a mind of their own. They wrenched on the wheel—hard. Before I could react, the car lurched into motion, and nothing could stop me from making a sharp right turn.

My name is Kaydee Blanchett.

My favorite movie is Beauty and the Beast.

The worst grade I have ever gotten in my entire life was a C.

It felt important to tell myself those things and remember the person I had been before this mess started. Good, ol' dependable Kaydee. The mantra was all I had to hold onto, as I blindly followed a pickup truck down an empty, country road—a truck driven by a man who, supposedly, wanted me dead.

I should have gone to the damned sheriff's station. Instead, all I seemed capable of was clutching the steering wheel and trying to breathe. It was a struggle just to suck in air—let alone ignore that my foot was tapping the gas pedal against my will. That I couldn't control my hands. Couldn't hit the brake. I couldn't even glance back at the town I was leaving behind.

A naïve part of me just wanted to pretend that this was nothing more than a regular trip out of town and that I was completely in control. But, when Liwai's truck turned off the main road, I had no choice but to follow.

Beneath me, the seat pitched like a mechanical bull ride, as my tires crunched over branches and loose rock. What little daylight there was faded beneath the shadow of the trees. Up ahead, Liwai switched on his rear lights, and the reddish glow washed over me, as though I were in my own, tiny sliver of hell.

The ghoulish imagery merely cemented that there was no space to turn back. The forest enclosed me on all sides, and I was trapped, forced to continue forward.

The road snaked along an incline, depositing us at the edge of a sheer drop. Altogether the entire drive must have lasted ten minutes—though it felt like a hundred years. I didn't recognize this section of Kittywatt—if we were even still within the town limits. There was nothing but wild and overgrown greenery and leagues of forest stretching for miles below.

The sight was beautiful, in a twisted way. From this height, one good slip and fragments would have been all that remained of my body.

I gulped at the thought—especially when Liwai's truck stopped on a nearby patch of grass. I held my breath as he climbed out, black hair fanning out in an arch as he turned to face me. There was nothing standing between me, him, and what had to be a thousand-foot drop.

Run! I told myself. *Fight! Escape!*

The only move I made was to switch gears into park. My pulse thrummed erratically in my ears. I couldn't keep my eyes from drifting up—seemingly on their own—to meet a dark gaze through the windshield. The next second, my hand was on the handle of the door.

There was no hesitation before I pulled it open.

Liwai leaned against his truck, as though he were just waiting for me to cross the distance between us on my own.

And—damn it—I *was*. My feet seemed to move on their own accord, one after the other. I tried to push the fear out of my mind and think logically. With Sheriff Michaels already on his trail, Liwai Raven wouldn't be so bold as to murder me in broad daylight—even if he was a dangerous criminal. Right…?

Though, as I crept closer, a part of me whispered, *what kind of idiot goes off with a man she was warned to stay away from only a day earlier? A man who, allegedly, wanted her dead?*

My palms were slick with icy sweat. I couldn't breathe. Try as I might, I couldn't avoid those eyes either. They narrowed as though he was aware of every thought running through my mind—the crazy suspicions I could never voice out loud.

Unwavering, his gaze held mine, until I finally came to a halt nearly ten paces away. *Still far enough to run,* I told myself, but there was no conviction in that thought. I was too cold and exhausted and wanted nothing more than to curl into a ball, resigned to my fate. Liwai stood back as if expecting me to do that very thing.

It wasn't fair that he still took my breath away. I hated how I could admit he was beautiful, even as terror formed a painful ball in my chest.

Seconds passed. Minutes.

The rain kept falling until my toes were numb in my soaked sneakers. Moisture glued my hair flat to my forehead, and a misty blur obscured my glasses—but I was almost thankful that I couldn't see him clearly. He was just a tall, dark, indistinguishable shape that I could easily write off as a nightmare—minus the eyes that stood out like jewels.

"Why did you bring me out here?" My words echoed back to me. *Why? Why? WHY?*

I knew that he could hear me, but he didn't respond. I wasn't sure if he was drawing out the silence on purpose... *Or,* a part of me suspected, *maybe he just doesn't know what to say?*

I sure as hell didn't, but it felt important to babble anyway, to keep talking.

"I don't *want* to be here," I blurted. It sounded so stupid when said out loud, but even now, I couldn't make myself move to turn around. Hell, I hadn't even taken my keys out of the ignition. It would be too easy for Liwai to drive my car off a cliff once he disposed of my body…

"You want answers."

Some things never change, I supposed—because even while my heart skipped a beat, I had to admit that it wasn't from fear. More like…primal recognition. I could still hear that very same voice calling me back from the brink, and…for the briefest, most insane moments, the previous night didn't matter.

Just the fact that he was *there,* standing so close that all I would have to do was stagger a few steps forward to touch him. And I wanted to. God help me, I *wanted* to.

"You want answers," he repeated, gruffer this time. It was almost as though he could sense what I was feeling— thinking—and it irritated him almost as much as it did me.

Without warning, he moved, displaying agility I could only envy. He circled the truck and came to the passenger's side. A quiet pop echoed through the clearing as he wrenched open the door.

"But can you handle them?"

I jumped at the unspoken threat. *Can you handle the truth, Kaydence Blanchett?*

"Why bring me here, if you just wanted to talk?" I countered. Talk. My palms ached as if to contradict that theory, and my lips tingled in a way that had nothing to do with the icy rain. Puffs of white breath painted the air in rapid succession. *Huff. Huff. Huff.* "We could have done plenty of that at the sheriff's station—"

"It's not safe." I flinched as his voice easily sliced through mine. "Being out here in the open." He nodded to the sheer drop below as though the woods were teeming with lurking ears eager to listen in.

"My mama always told me not to get into cars with strangers," I retorted. It was such a dumbass thing to say. My cheeks instantly flamed with shame—but it was the truth. If Marie Blanchett could see me now, she'd fix me with one of those trademark frowns—eyebrow raised, blue eyes sharp. *"You know this isn't a good idea, sweetie pie."*

I wished she were there so fiercely my chest ached, willing to make Liwai Raven disappear as easily as she used to vanquish the imagined monsters hiding in my closet.

"I don't have long." The crisp words snapped me back to the present. I blinked, once again focusing on Liwai. His fingers tightened on the door, pulling it open wider. The message was clear. *Get in.*

Warily, I took a step forward, then another. I could feel his eyes on me the whole time, observing every move I made. The look in his gaze wasn't heartless, as I figured a murderer's would be. All I saw in them was raw, all-consuming exhaustion that took my breath away.

"Get in," he urged, and I managed to close the distance and haul myself into the passenger's seat. He closed the door behind me, and the thuds of falling raindrops counted the seconds as he crossed over to the driver's side.

I stared straight ahead while he settled into the seat beside me. There wasn't much decoration in the cabin. No cute knickknacks stuck to the dashboard. Nothing hanging from the rearview mirror, not even a funny bumper sticker or decal in the window.

The interior smelled like him, however—a wild, dangerous musk.

I refused to look at him and huddled in my soaked sweater, praying that I could muster the strength to bolt from the truck if he decided to pull a knife from the glove box. As if to spite me, he reached for the knob that controlled the heat and switched it to full blast.

"What now?" I croaked without taking my eyes off the glove compartment. *You kill me?*

Suddenly, the engine roared to life, and I jumped.

"It's not far." Something in his tone kept me from panicking as he switched the truck into drive. He sounded so tired, as if he didn't give a damn whether or not I believed him. "Your car couldn't make the distance. Not on this terrain."

I glanced back forlornly at my Beetle, still there alongside the cliff. I imagined it watching me with disapproving eyes as the truck lurched into motion and Liwai turned onto another narrow path—this one even more overgrown than the first.

"What's not far?" I asked.

The whirr of the engine and the patter of raindrops hitting the windshield were my only response. Liwai seemed more focused on navigating the winding, bumpy road than humoring me—and I had to admit he was right. There was no way in hell my Beetle could have hacked this wild terrain.

The thought didn't comfort me in the slightest. I was truly trapped now, with no way out. No way home.

"Here."

I flinched as the truck came to a sudden halt, and I was thrown forward, forced to brace my hands against the dashboard just to get my bearings.

All around—in every which direction—I only saw mist. Thick, impenetrable, and white. The wind stirred the fog just enough for me to make out snatches of the surrounding landscape through it all—trees, rock, and a drop so steep that I could only see shapeless carpeting of emerald green down below.

"We can talk here," Liwai announced, switching the gearshift into park. He turned to face me, and suddenly the vehicle seemed about as small as a thimble. He dominated the entire space, and for a moment, I couldn't tell where he ended and where I began.

Get a hold of yourself, Kaydee! Snap out of it! I tried every reassuring phrase I could think of. The most inane wishful thinking. Nothing brought back my sanity.

"Talk about what?" I rasped, wrenching my gaze down to the console. "Maybe about the fact that you saved my life? Brought me back from the dead? Or that you and Renae…"

I couldn't say it.

"I didn't mean for you to hear that."

Something in my stomach twisted into knots as his gaze met mine—for the briefest of seconds—before I chickened out and wrenched my head around to stare out the window.

"Well, I did," I snapped. "And you have about two seconds to tell me why I shouldn't go straight to Sheriff Michaels." The fact that he had brought me to the middle of nowhere, aside.

"I didn't save your life that night," Liwai grunted, "in the bar."

"I'm not insane," I insisted, though current events certainly put that into doubt. "I know what I saw. I know what I heard. Don't try to convince me that I'm crazy, because I'm not…"

At least when I'm not around him, I'm not. The thought taunted me until Liwai finally spoke again.

"I didn't save your life," he repeated. Before I could argue, he slammed one hand on the dashboard. The resounding *thud!* echoed like a gunshot. "If anything…I should have let you die."

The venom in his tone seeped into my veins, paralyzing me.

"I should have let you die."

I thought of myself, lying on the bar floor, bleeding out. I thought of Mari, Sheriff Michaels, and Dee. My aunt could barely make her own lunch in the morning. How could she survive without me there? And what kind of a person did Liwai Raven think I was to *deserve* to die like that?

I didn't even realize that my hand was on the door handle—lo and behold, I could control my limbs again—until his voice rang out behind me.

"I didn't mean it like that—"

"Well, h-how then?" It was impossible to speak with him so close. His right hand rested on the console between us, mere inches away, but he never attempted to grab me.

Undeterred, I tugged on the door handle, but it wouldn't budge. With an icy sense of clarity, I understood why—he had engaged the automatic locks when I wasn't watching.

"It's too dangerous to run off at this altitude," Liwai explained, his calm cutting through my building panic. "At least wait until we're back at the base level, and I've said what I need to say."

"What do you need to say in a locked car that you couldn't say back in town?" I countered, hoping that my voice would come out sounding brave—but it trembled. Fear mangled my drawl like nothing else, and *car* cracked into two bleating syllables.

"Everything." Again his eyes bore into mine, rendering me immobile. "But are you willing to listen to me?"

"Just say it!" I snapped. "Tell me. Why do you seem to hate me so much? What the hell did I ever do to you?"

"Nothing. You didn't do *anything* to me," Liwai insisted, "but, because of me…your entire life has been—" He broke off, but I didn't miss the hitch in his tone. *Guilt.*

Your entire life… It sounded as though he was referring to a lot more than just that night at the bar. Sheriff Michaels' words marched through my mind as if to bolster that thought. *He's dangerous, Kaydence.*

"What have you done to me?" I rasped, not sure if I really wanted to know the answer. "I don't even know you."

He nodded. "You don't. But I know *you*..." Before I could question him, he sighed. "What do you remember from that night—at the bar?"

I shrugged. "Not much. Just noise, and falling, and…your voice." I could still hear him inside my head. *Come back.*

Besides, we had both seen the bullet.

"What did you do to me?"

His jaw tightened, and I half-expected for him to rattle off that same, tired line—*nothing.* "I healed you."

He healed me. When said inside my head, it all had made sense—Liwai *must* have saved me, because I couldn't have imagined that darkness—something that felt so real, it haunted me at night. I couldn't have. But now that he was all but admitting it out loud…

A million realizations hit me then, all at once. I had been shot. I had died. Liwai Raven had brought me back to life.

"How?" I croaked. It seemed to be the only question worth asking. "CPR? First-aid?"

The corner of his jaw tightened, and I got the drift—*I'll answer your questions—but on my terms.*

"You were following me," I said, changing the subject. "Even before that night."

He didn't try to deny it. "Yes."

"Because of Renae's drawing?" It sounded like a question, but I didn't need to see Liwai's slow nod to know the real answer.

"I knew that something would happen," he said, pausing after every word. "But not *when.*"

"You *knew* that I would be shot." I could barely get the words out. "But why save me if you wish you hadn't—"

"It's not like that," he hissed. "Saving you just made things complicated for us both."

"What things?" My mind was spinning. It felt like he was speaking too quickly and too slowly at the same time.

"My life. Yours. There is so much that you won't understand —that you *can't* understand."

"Try me." Desperate for a distraction, I tore my glasses off and rubbed at the lenses with the hem of my shirt. When I replaced them, he was still watching me, his expression blank.

"By saving your life, I just placed you in even more danger," he confessed.

"How?"

Liwai didn't speak for so long that I was worried he wouldn't. In the end, all he said was, "Because one way or another…you'll still die. Not by my hand—" Those last four words kept me from panicking. "But I won't be able to stop them—stop *it.*"

The way he spoke… I had never heard anyone sound so helpless. It was as if my life and *death* meant everything to him, though I couldn't even begin to fathom why.

All I could ask him was, "Why do I have to die?"

He flinched and shook his head. "I don't want to hurt you. Never. But I can't stop it. If they find out…I won't be able to protect you."

"If *who* finds out?"

He held my gaze for so long that some of the dampness in my clothing had dried by the time he finally spoke. "Let me ask you a question. While you don't know the whole truth, what little you do know should have you running in fear. Nothing that I could say should have stopped you from going to the sheriff if you truly feared for your life. So why are you here?"

My mouth opened…but not a word came out. There *was* no explanation—no sane rationale anyway. Liwai nodded as though he were right there inside my mind with me, puzzling over the complicated thoughts, like the fact that I felt drawn to him in ways I couldn't explain.

Repelled.

Enticed.

Confused.

"I'll tell you why," he began, in a guttural tone that had me shivering before the next words left his mouth. "We are cursed, Kaydence Blanchett. Cursed."

I flinched as his hand came from nowhere to cup my chin. He barely touched me, and yet explosive sensations raced through my skin regardless. He was so warm. In an instant, the chill and numbness in my bones eked away. I craved more.

"I'll tell you why," he repeated, daring me to listen. "Honestly, you shouldn't even be…you weren't—" He broke off and tried a different tactic. "Your mother's maiden name was Blanchett?"

It was a strange question, but I forced myself to nod. "Yes."

"And your father's was Dewitt."

I nodded again.

"That's impossible." Liwai chuckled, but he wasn't amused. His lips were pursed like a man recently told the sky wasn't blue and that he had to guess the real color. "It doesn't make sense. You shouldn't be… I guess it doesn't matter either way. You're drawn to me, and that's why…"

I didn't realize I'd been holding my breath until he trailed off. "Why what?" I sounded hoarse. My hands were shaking, and I couldn't keep my eyes from darting down to his thick fingers still holding my chin.

"And that's why, some say the right thing for me to do, would be to rip your throat out here and now."

Every cell in my body went on high alert as I jerked back. "You're crazy!" I lunged for the door handle, forgetting that the locks had been engaged. As if reading my mind, he casually hit a button to unlock them.

"Then run," he told me in an icy tone. "Get out. Go home. Call the sheriff."

I wrestled the door open, prepared to do just that.

"But you *can't*," he said as I remained in my seat. "Just like I couldn't stay away from you. Renae had foreseen the inevitable. I wouldn't have had to lift a finger, just let fate happen, and…"

My mind filled in what he wouldn't say—*me, a bullet wound, dead.* Poor Mari and Dee and even Miller, the idiot—no one should have to be responsible for murdering someone else.

"It would have been simple," he said after a long pause. "Nothing should have been easier than just staying away from you…but I couldn't. I went the first night Renae showed me that damn drawing—just to make sure. She's been wrong before." He paused, and I swore that I could feel his breath on the back of my neck. My hand was still on the door, holding it open. Icy air ruffled my damp hair, but it wasn't enough to cut through Liwai's heat. "So I went," he continued. "And when you didn't die, I tried to convince myself that she had made a mistake, but then…"

"You came back," I croaked, picturing him there, watching me from his corner of the bar.

"I came back," he echoed. "And then the next night. And the next. I told myself that it was only to see you die in person. But then, it happened. You were shot, and I…I didn't think. I couldn't leave you there."

"What did you do to me?"

"I…" He took a breath. "I strengthened our connection. With blood. I couldn't just leave you there—"

"What?" Did he just say blood?

"I should have walked away."

There it was again—the statement that should have had me running, but all I could do was just sit there and listen.

"I should have," he repeated, almost as though he were trying to believe it himself. "But I couldn't. For the same reason that you can't leave this truck. Why you came to me that night. Why, even now, you aren't afraid of me."

It was true, in a twisted sense of the word. I *wasn't* afraid. His voice, echoing in my head, was the only thing in the world that seemed to matter.

"Are you…some kind of magic?" I croaked, desperate to have some shred of explanation to cling to.

He laughed, but the sound came out tortured, and I found myself turning to watch him.

"What do you think?" He sounded genuinely curious even as my blood ran cold at the blunt questioning. He should have called me insane for even suggesting such a thing.

"I think you're crazy," I said, trying and failing to sound brave. "I think you're dangerous and psychotic. I think that I need to leave." That last part was more directed at myself than him—that stubborn part of me that seemed to disobey my mind's frantic commands to escape. "I think that…"

"Kiss me."

I flinched back against the partially opened door and had to wrestle it shut at the last minute or fall out of the truck altogether. "W-What?"

"I'll prove it." He leaned forward so that his mane of dark hair flared out around his head, shrouding his expression in shadow. "If you don't believe me, then kiss me." His tone dipped as if daring my heart to skip a beat—which it did.

I could barely find the breath to speak. "What?"

He nodded as if that question alone had proved his point. "Even at the mere suggestion, any other woman would have gone running. But you're still here. So why is that?"

"Stop making it seem like this is *my* fault," I hissed, crossing my arms over my chest.

And yet, I *wasn't* running.

"I don't want to kiss you," I whispered, but I couldn't ignore the tremble in my voice, the telltale hitch of a lie. He was so close... My eyes drifted down to his mouth before I could help it. His lips were pink—almost too pink.

I remembered how they looked dotted with blood—my blood. God, the image didn't disgust me. It just intrigued me.

"You bit me," I blurted, merely to hear the statement out loud. "Is that what you really meant instead of kiss?"

He didn't even flinch. "If that's what it will take for you to understand..."

He lunged, and I had no time to react. The next instant, his mouth was on mine.

And the rest of the world vanished.

The effect of his nearness was instant and overwhelming. The fear disappeared. The confusion, too. The ache. Everything disintegrated beneath a desire so raw it burned—and it felt *damn* good to give in and forget.

"You can feel it, can't you?" Liwai asked.

Insistent, his lips nudged mine apart, making way for his tongue, and I couldn't keep him out. My hands were in his hair, and *his* were on my waist, dragging me closer until I couldn't tell where he ended, and I began.

"Kaydence…"

Calloused fingers raked the bare skin beneath my sweater, and I greedily arched into them, allowing his thumb to drift to the waistband of my jeans.

My heart skipped a beat, though he never went any further than to drag a finger along the side of my hip, and my eyelids fluttered. Sparks prickled down my spine. I swore I could hear his voice inside my head—*Kaydence*—but different from his usual tone. The same husky, desperate cadence had called me back from the brink. *Do you see?*

The voice grew louder, more insistent, but I couldn't think, couldn't focus on anything else. Not when he was *everywhere, everything. Mine.* His mouth opened, inviting me deeper, even as that familiar tenor ran across my mind again. *We should stop…*

The words were like the buzzing of an insect I couldn't swat. I didn't *want* to stop. I had never been surer of anything else in my life—this was right. Perfect.

I'm his…

He's mine.

My nostrils flared, dragging his scent deep into my lungs as I lunged against him, trying to squeeze out every ounce of air between us. I would've pushed my way inside his skin if I had to. *Mine.*

Suddenly, Liwai broke the kiss—but it wasn't until an odd noise reached my ears that I understood why. It was the same eerie sound as someone running their nails down a chalkboard, only very *sharp* nails down a metallic board. My eyes flew open while my heart seized in my chest.

Don't look, something inside me warned—but I turned anyway, staring through the windshield…and right into a pair of yellow eyes. It took my mind one full second to process the sight in front of me—a canine body so large it nearly spanned the entire width of the truck. Fangs peeking from a triangular mouth that fanned hot breath across the windshield. Those few, simple details added up to one inescapable truth—there was a wolf crouched on the hood of the truck.

The damn thing was massive—nearly twice the size of the timber wolves at our local zoo. Coiled muscle made up the bulk of a stocky body covered in a pelt of thick, gray fur. I blinked, convinced that I was hallucinating—but its yellow gaze seemed too real and brimmed with more anger than any animal should have been capable of.

"Don't move." As he spoke, Liwai sat forward, shrugging me off. His face was hard, his narrowed eyes unreadable. Tension thickened the air as he stared the creature down without an ounce of fear.

I didn't know what I expected him to do. Shout? Jam his foot on the gas? Scream? He spoke instead. Just one single word that rippled with authority. "Leave."

Through the glass, I saw the wolf snarl as if in response—*Hell no.*

"M-Maybe it escaped from the reserve?" I sounded ridiculous, but for some reason, I couldn't stop trying to rationalize this. "Maybe—"

"Kaydence." Liwai never took his eyes off the wolf. "I need you to trust me. Put your head down."

I sank in my seat, feeling my sweater rise as I curled partially beneath the dashboard. One second crawled past. Another.

"Hold on."

For what? I didn't get the chance to ask. The next second, his foot slammed down on the gas, and I could only grab hold of the door handle before the truck spun in a violent arch, tires squealing. *Thump!* Something heavy bounced over the hood. A split second later, a low, animalistic sound tore through the patter of rain, raising every hair on the back of my neck. There weren't too many creatures in the world that could have made a sound like that—no wolf, bear, or even dog that I knew of. Nothing natural. Nothing…*normal.*

A single word tore from my throat, choked with fear, "Drive!"

Luckily, Liwai didn't need any prompting from me. My heart pounded against the wall of my chest like a sledge-hammer as the truck sped down the overgrown path. I climbed back into my seat, clutching my seatbelt, but my hands trembled too badly to fasten it.

"What the hell was that?"

Liwai ignored me and kept driving, eyes narrowed, fixed straight ahead while my brain spiraled with a million real-izations. Wolf. On. Truck. Were there even wolves near Kittywatt? All I knew of was a wildlife reserve a few hours outside of town. Maybe an animal really had escaped from it? Maybe there were more out there? Maybe—

Wham!

The tires squealed as Liwai wrenched on the steering wheel, sending the truck into a sharp spin that threw me forward. My head struck glass, and a million tiny stars danced across my vision.

"Damn!" Liwai hissed. I glanced up as his fist slammed against the dashboard hard enough to jostle a piece of gray plastic loose. It was only then that I realized that we weren't moving.

"What…what's going on?" My head ached, my thoughts fizzling out. Every instinct in my body was on red alert. *Run!*

"Come on." Liwai wrenched open his door, reaching back for me. Without waiting for me to get my bearings, he tore off my seatbelt and tugged me over the driver's seat, out onto the muddy earth after him.

"What are we doing?" I croaked. "Why did you stop?"

We were maybe halfway down the path, surrounded by thick, overgrown pines. Mud churned into a thick soup at my feet. If Liwai wasn't holding me upright, I would have fallen. The thought of that *thing* had me glancing around frantically, convinced that it would lunge from the shadows at any moment.

"Why did you stop?" I pressed again.

Liwai inclined his head toward a shadowy thicket of trees ahead—*come on*. I took a hesitant step after him while glancing over my shoulder, and my heart sank right through the soles of my sneakers. A few feet ahead, a tree had fallen—blocking the only path large enough for the truck to have taken. At first glance, the wreckage could have just been a casualty of the storm, but the base of the tree was too far away from the path, and the wood had splintered. Almost as though something massive had snapped it off, right at the bottom, and dragged it into place.

"Come on." Liwai continued to marshal me after him as the horrific reality set in—someone had trapped us there on purpose.

Up this high, the rain battered down like bullets. The lenses of my glasses quickly became distorted by mist. I couldn't see anything but smudges of color. Green. Gray. Black. Liwai's hand was like a tether, steering me through the swaths of emerald that I guessed to be trees. It was almost as though he knew these woods like the back of his hand—but even he wasn't fast enough to outrun whatever chased us.

I heard it first—a low, dangerous sound that reverberated in my bones. I stupidly wanted to believe that another truck had just pulled up the path after us, filled with innocent people who might have been able to help, but then Liwai turned and shattered that theory by picking up speed. I didn't have a chance in hell of keeping pace. My foot slipped, and then everything seemed to happen in slow motion.

My slick fingers lost his grip, and then I was falling, rolling through mud and earth and over sharp rocks. When I finally came to a stop, my glasses were gone—I couldn't see

—but I could still hear as two distinct male voices filled the air rather than growls.

"What are you doing here?"

"It's *her*, isn't it?" The voice was familiar, though I couldn't place a name to it. "You bastard. I *knew* it—you found her."

My mind struggled to make sense of the words as I rolled over, testing my limbs as much as I dared. Nothing felt broken, thank God, but every part of me throbbed in a way that promised fresh bruises.

"Stay out of this," a second man growled, and my entire body tensed with recognition. *Liwai.* "Just walk away, Cody. This has nothing to do with you—"

"Bullshit. This has everything to do with me," Cody hissed in reply. "With *us*. What do you think Kahil will say when he finds out? When he learns the truth—that you've been lying to your pack all this fucking time?"

Even I could tell that the words were a threat.

"How long have you known, huh? How long have you pined after her, too much of a coward to do your duty?"

If Liwai replied, he spoke too softly for me to hear while I focused my attention on standing. I pulled my knees underneath me and tested my weight, sighing with relief that my legs seemed fine. I must have rolled down a hill of some kind, but I couldn't make out anything at all or even tell which direction the voices came from—but one thing didn't make sense. Cody was one of the boys from the house. What the hell was he doing out here?

"Just stay out of this," Liwai said. He sounded closer this time. "I'll handle it—"

"The same way you 'handle' Renae?" Cody released a harsh bark of laughter that echoed in the wind. "I don't think so…"

I scrambled to my feet, feeling my way blindly through the muck in search of my glasses, and came up short. I could only pray that I wasn't close to the cliff.

"Stay out of this." Liwai's voice drifted down to me. I figured that he and Cody were both somewhere higher up the slope. "Go near *her* or Renae, and I'll—"

"What?"

An icy sensation trickled down my spine as I froze, too terrified to even breathe—oh, God, he sounded closer. They both did. I could hear slow, stealthy footsteps as though one was herding the other in my direction.

"I will kill you," Liwai swore in a voice that cracked like thunder. "I swear on my life, I will *kill* you."

Cody laughed again. "I doubt it," he scoffed. "Not even you would be stupid enough to kill one of your own kind. You know the price. No…I figure you just need some *incentive…*"

Run, Kaydence. Liwai's voice slithered across my consciousness—real or imagined—it didn't really matter. *Go!* I took off in a random direction while praying to God that I didn't run into a tree. Raindrops pelted me as an icy wind lashed at my skin like a whip. Then, all at once, everything fell silent. Eerie. *The calm before the storm,* an ominous part of me whispered.

The sound of my heartbeat surged through my ears as I staggered toward a blobby green smear that I hoped led back to the main road. Mud slicked beneath my sneakers. The ground felt unsteady—ragged. I could barely go a step without tripping over something unseen.

Crunch!

Panic built in my chest, choking me. Someone was following me. They were fast, and they were close, and…I knew deep down that there was no way in hell I would ever be able to outrun them.

I sprinted, not caring that I could have been heading straight for that damn cliff. My shoulders smacked off the trunks of trees. Low branches snagged at my skin and hair like loose fingers, desperate to slow me down.

Oh, God. I chanted the mantra mentally, unable to focus on anything else but those two simple words as I tried to find some semblance of familiar territory. *Oh, God. Oh, God.* The green splotches thinned until the only thing I could see looming before me was an endless, terrifying gray. I took another step, and…

Wham!

One minute I had been upright, and the next, I simply wasn't. I almost thought I had run right off that sheer drop —I was *dead*—until a sound rippled all around me like a crack of thunder, so loud my eardrums ached. Then I felt the heat—thick, hot breath fanning against the back of my neck. There was something on top of me. Something so heavy I couldn't breathe. My bones throbbed beneath the weight, my lungs straining for air. I struggled for purchase, nails raking through the mud. I couldn't see anything but gray and the darkness…

I'm dead.

Dead…

A bright light filled my vision, and I waited for the sound of angels or bells or whatever it was you heard or saw when you died. Instead, the only thing to greet me was a low, raspy growl.

In an instant, the suffocating pressure evaporated. While coughing up mud, I wasn't even able to get my bearings before a harsh grip seized my collar and pulled me to my feet.

"Run!" My hands flew blindly out, barely catching my balance against a nearby tree. Urgency ran down my spine in a single, instinctive impulse—*get away, get away*—but I could only glance over my shoulder, my eyes straining to make out anything through the rain.

Two dark shapes loomed over the emerald background of the forest. I recognized one as the wolf, its sleek body glowing like silver. The other was taller—*human?* They moved, circling each other with an eerie, predatory grace. *Not natural,* something told me. Even the man-sized figure closest to me—with gleaming, golden skin—didn't seem *normal.*

My body reacted to him anyway. *Liwai.*

I had no idea where Cody had gone—or if I'd simply imagined him. Either way, the present danger was real enough.

Low, vicious sounds tore at the air. *Snarls.* I wanted to run. I tried to move, but my body wouldn't cooperate. My muscles had turned to liquid. The bones in my legs were mush. I could only cling to the trunk of the tree—nails splitting the bark—and stare, transfixed by the scene unfolding in front of me.

It happened so damn fast…

The wolf lunged, knocking the man to the ground in a spray of mud.

There was a growl.

A shout.

Then a long, painful second of silence before a single, violent sound ended the skirmish in an instant. *Snap!*

"No!" Terror unlike anything I'd ever felt washed over me— so real that it clogged my throat, filled my veins, and then everything inside of me shattered.

No, this broken, pathetic voice inside me cried. *Not Liwai…*

Suddenly, one of the figures rose, shrugging off the other—a *body resting* limply on the ground.

There were no growls.

No snarls.

Just a *voice,* one that I could hear inside my head rather than out loud.

"It's alright," Liwai rasped. *"It's alright..."*

I HAD no idea how in the hell he managed to find my glasses.

Or how he managed to carry me down the slope, back to my car—and he *must* have, because when I finally had enough sense to get my bearings, I was leaning against the passenger seat of my Beetle, and I could see again. Someone had drawn the spare jacket I kept in the trunk around my shoulders, tucking it under my chin. The side of my face was pressed against the window, allowing me to watch as empty fields blurred past.

When I finally turned his way, I found Liwai huddled over the steering wheel, eyes firmly on the road.

He looked horrible. Mud streaked his face and coated his hands. Rain plastered his hair flat against his shoulders, and there was a hole in his T-shirt. A hole, I realized, that was edged in blood.

"You're bleeding." I barely recognized my own voice. It sounded garbled, as though I were talking with my mouth full. "You're hurt."

He didn't even glance in my direction. Gravel crunched beneath the tires as the car came to a stop. Without a word, Liwai climbed out, leaving the keys in the ignition. I could only stare blankly as he circled the car and came to my side.

He pulled open the door without waiting for me to do it myself. I felt so dead tired that I couldn't have moved regardless—his steadying grip on my shoulder was the only thing keeping me from falling right out of my seat.

Within an instant, I was in his arms, shrouded in warmth, and I couldn't even muster the strength to feel afraid.

"You're bleeding," I repeated, eyeing the wound on his collar.

His jaw clenched, but he stared straight ahead rather than respond.

The rain had stopped. Now a bitter chill had sunk into the atmosphere. It nipped at me, even wrapped within my jacket. Overhead, the sky was an inky shade of gray. Hours must have passed—night was already falling.

A million concerns gnawed at me.

Dee had to be worried sick if she wasn't still angry with me. I didn't even know when Mari wanted me to return to work. So many thoughts and fears raced through my mind, demanding my attention—but somehow, I found my gaze drifting right back down to Liwai's shoulder as though nothing else in the world mattered but the fact that he was hurt.

"You should get stitches…" I was leaning against him, my forehead resting against his arm as though I'd known him my whole life, and the intimacy was perfectly normal. Lost in a drowsy daze, it was a solid minute before I realized he was carrying me somewhere.

And it wasn't up the porch steps to the house I shared with Dee. *Or* to the sheriff's station. Instead, he headed for a small, gray trailer with peeling metal siding. *His* trailer.

Something in me twitched at the thought of being taken inside his home. Should I have been afraid? Uneasy? Wary?

I still hadn't decided by the time he wrenched open the screen door with one hand and carried me inside. The narrow kitchen was in shambles. A half-eaten sandwich sat on the rickety table by the window. Piles of dishes cluttered the sink. Random pieces of clothing littered nearly every available surface—but Liwai didn't seem surprised by the mess.

I imagined someone pacing the narrow space, too distracted to even eat. They had probably fixed a mug of coffee and set it down before leaving in too much of a hurry to even close the front door.

I wondered what kind of dilemma could have tormented someone to that point—even though a part of me hissed the answer. *You.*

Liwai carried me through the kitchen and past a small living room with nothing more than a couch and an old-fashioned television. At the end of the hall was a door that he nudged open with his hip. The small room beyond it must have been his. The walls were gray with black curtains shielding the only window, and there wasn't much else apart from a bed and a wooden dresser in the corner.

"I need to go home," I croaked as Liwai headed for the mattress. Suddenly, I wasn't so tired anymore. Every cell in my body flared on high alert as he sat me down on the edge of the bed and stood back.

He wouldn't...

I watched him carefully, noticing every little detail—like the fact that he was dripping blood onto the floor—and every trace of fear vanished.

"Jesus Christ!" I rarely took the Lord's name in vain, but "Gee whiz" didn't seem to cut it this time. I stood, reaching for him with a trembling hand. "You need help—"

"No." His voice was soft, but there was an unmistakable command in it that had me plopping right back down.

Ignoring me, he wrenched his shirt over his head with barely a wince of pain. Blood and rainwater speckled the carpet as he tossed it onto the floor.

My eyes flew up, taking him in...and I was struck dumb. Even injured, the man was beautiful—every inch of his body seemed to have been carved out of pure, hard muscle. Traces of rain still clung to his skin, making him almost glow in the dim lighting. I didn't know how long I stared before his eyes found mine.

"Take off your clothes."

I blinked. "W-What—"

In two steps, he was in front of me, hands seizing my jacket by the collar. A scream formed and died in my throat as he gingerly pulled the edges apart, easing the fabric from my shoulders more gently than someone undressing a fragile porcelain doll.

The jacket, he tossed aside. Then his fingers were sliding under my sweater, lifting it up…

The air clung to the inside of my lungs as his hands brushed the skin of my stomach. Trying to remember how to breathe, to think, was impossible. Especially as he stared into my eyes while easing the fabric over my head.

Cool air tickled my bare skin as I sat only in my bra and pants. With a grunt, Liwai crumbled my sweater in one hand and tossed it aside to join my jacket.

His eyes drifted down to my jeans next. "Stand up."

Oh, God. I knew that I should have been feeling something —fear, terror. *Something.*

But nothing seemed to matter other than doing what he wanted.

Rather than undo the clasp, he waited until I reached for the zipper. Clumsily I pulled, wiggling my hips as best as I could to loosen the damp fabric. I went painfully slow, though I wasn't sure if I was doing it purposefully or if I was just too damn tired.

After twenty-plus years of life, I had never fully undressed in front of anyone—ever. Not Dee, or Mama, or even Nora, my old friend from high school…

And I seriously doubted that I would have felt the same way in front of any of them that I did now.

My entire body burned. Seared. I shouldn't have wanted him to see me half-naked and soaked to the bone—but some dark, unknown part of me did. Needed to.

A part of me came alive, and the only words I had to describe it were stark, biological ones. My nipples stiffened, my belly quivered, and I drew my thighs tighter together, painfully aware of a pulsating ache building between them.

He's a stranger, the last, logical voice in my head insisted. Sheriff Michaels' words echoed as if to bolster that fact. *He's dangerous, Kaydence!*

And if I hadn't been convinced before, then what had just happened in the woods should have reinforced it. How many men could fend off a wolf with their bare hands with hardly a mark to show for it?

"Are you hurt anywhere else?" I shivered as his warm breath ghosted my shoulder, snapping me back to the present. "Tell me the truth."

"N-No." Honestly, I couldn't feel *anything* with him so close.

"Good." He was magnetic. My body swayed in his direction. Every beat of my heart seemed to be in tune with the way his hands held my hips securely, keeping me upright.

God, I wanted him to pull away. Move closer. Let go. Hold on. Kiss me. With my jeans pooled around my ankles, and his hands dangerously close to the hem of my blue polka dot undies, all I could think was…

God, don't ever let him stop touching me.

"I can't..." Something in his tone snapped through the drowsy, heady daze taking root in my limbs. He was angry —it was funny how I hadn't realized it until now. He frowned as he sank down on one knee and started to ease me out of my jeans, ankle by ankle. I stared, entranced by the way his muscles rippled with every movement.

"You saved my life." I had no idea what made me say it.

Liwai just went still, dark hair shielding his face. When he finally spoke, it was only two terse words. "Lie down."

I staggered back automatically, climbing onto the mattress. It was as though the sound of his voice alone was enough to snap me into action. My heart thudded in my chest as I settled over the dark comforter. All the while, my greedy eyes clung to him, watching as he gathered up my wet clothes in a single fist.

I didn't know what would happen next, and some hidden part of me didn't really give a damn. Just as long as he stayed there. Suddenly, he turned to the dresser and snatched something from the top of it.

"Put this on—" I blinked as a gray shirt landed on my lap a second later.

I moved stiffly, carefully pulling it on over my head so that I didn't jostle my glasses. It was too big on me and fell almost down to my knees—but his scent hit me full in the nose, so rich it made my stomach churn into knots.

What now? I wondered, too tired to ask out loud.

There was a dangerous and probably *mutated*, from the size of it, wolf running loose. Liwai had saved my life, again—only after, of course, claiming multiple times that he should have ended it. And Cody…

The remnants of the argument from the woods taunted me, threatening to drive me insane. My mind spun until I ran my fingers through my hair as though I could smooth the thoughts into submission. *Renae. Kill. Kill. Kill.*

"Cody," I blurted. Suddenly, I knew that I hadn't imagined him. His voice had been too real. That anger—the hatred. "He's still out there with that thing. We need to call the sheriff. Someone needs to do something—"

"Kaydence."

"We need to help him. That thing was—"

"*Kaydence.*"

God, he sounded so damn gentle. It was unnerving. *Terrifying*—because this stupid crazy thought kept running through my head, and I couldn't silence it. Something so dangerous and *insane* that I could never say it out loud.

I couldn't.

I wouldn't.

"Cody," I croaked, my voice cracking as the severity of everything sank in like a punch. "*He* was the wolf."

TWELVE

I wished he would have laughed or shaken his head in pity and urged me to lie down again.

Cody was the wolf. It sounded crazy—but so was the fact that I had seen a wolf in the forest at all. According to local ordinances, overhunting wiped out the wild population years ago, and the nearby preserve was the only place where they thrived. I knew, because I had been bored enough to read the town archives back during a month when Dee had forgotten to put up her share of the rent, and our cable had gotten cut off.

"Y-You can tell me that I'm crazy now," I blurted when Liwai remained silent. I huddled like a child beneath the weight of his gaze, drawing my knees up to my chin. "It's alright… You can say it—"

"What do you remember?" His tone was carefully unreadable, almost as though a curtain had been drawn over his emotions, locking them up tight.

My mouth opened as a few fuzzy memories returned in snatches—*the wolf, the chase, him…*

Liwai sighed and took a step toward the bed. Then another. Another—and I backed up all the while, digging my nails into the comforter as though the sheets might have been a useful weapon.

"Kaydence—"

"I…I want to go home now." I lurched from the mattress, but my knees gave out a second later. His grip on my shoulder was the only thing keeping me upright.

"Just—"

"No!" I wrenched my arm away from him, but even as I stumbled for the door, something inside me protested. *Go back. Listen to him. Stay.* "Just leave me alone!"

I barely made it into the hall and nearly collapsed again. My body felt so heavy. I had to cling to the walls, my eyes glued frantically to the screen door.

"Kaydence."

Despite every instinct warning me not to, I glanced over my shoulder and found Liwai standing in the center of the room. He watched me for a second before uttering three terrifying words. "You can't leave."

"Why?" My heart sank to the pit of my stomach. *Does it matter?* a part of me hissed. *He's psychotic. Stay here a second longer, and you'll just end up like that wolf.*

The massive wolf that I, for some reason, wanted to believe was also a teenage boy. A beast that he had killed. *Snap. Snap. Snap.* That final spine-chilling sound had been more than just a random twig breaking.

I whirled around and lurched toward the front door. Sweat dribbled down my spine. With every step I took, the trailer seemed to lengthen, growing a mile long. Endless.

I didn't know what made me glance down to where someone had left a pot out to dry beside the sink. My first thought was that the woman staring back at me from the metal surface was proof of how damn exhausted I was—a horrible figment of my imagination.

She was a ghost, with skin so pale it *glowed* and haunted blue eyes. Whatever part of her face wasn't white almost appeared painted instead—a deep, vibrant shade of purple. It was a solid minute before I realized what the splotches really were. Bruises.

"You *can't* go home." A warm hand snaked around my waist, and I found myself easily lifted off my feet. "Not tonight."

I was too stunned to even ask why the distinction—*tonight.* With my face looking like I'd been put through the shredder, I couldn't go home for *days*—not without raising questions that I couldn't even begin to answer.

I didn't say a single word as Liwai brought me back into the bedroom and set me down on the mattress. Only then was I aware of the pain. The ache whenever I blinked. How my shoulders throbbed as well. I was too scared to peek beneath his borrowed shirt and see what waited underneath. *Claw marks?* The memory of that immovable weight pinning me down threatened to shatter what little sanity I had left.

"Not tonight," Liwai repeated. I shivered as his thumb trailed across my lower lip, raising goosebumps.

"My aunt will be worried about me," I rasped in that husky, unfamiliar voice—only now I understood why I sounded so funny—my lower lip was swollen, and my tongue stung. "She'll call the sheriff if I don't go home."

He didn't seem threatened by that prospect. Instead, he reached down and pulled back the edge of the dark comforter. Without prompting, I weakly crawled onto the sliver of space, allowing him to drag the blanket over the top of me.

God help me, I couldn't explain why. A million admonishments ran through my mind. *You're in a stranger's bed. You're in a stranger's bed half-naked. You're in a stranger's bed wearing his shirt!*

I wanted to demand that he call the sheriff, Mari, or *someone* who could take me home. But I was tired, and my head hurt, and the blankets were so warm...

My head felt weightless against a soft pillow. His scent was in the sheets. Hell, it was everywhere, wrapping me in heavy, thick musk.

Creak. The mattress shifted, and genuine fear sank in as I sensed Liwai lying down beside me, spreading out amid the sinewy pop of muscle.

Oh, God.

I should have fought. Tried to run. Not…

Greedily leeched off his warmth. It was as though I had been freezing my entire life—only I hadn't known until right *then*, when he was there to take the ache away.

My eyes drifted shut, and my body shifted closer to his, until only a breadth of space separated us—a dangerous predicament to be in with a stranger. He was closer to me now than I figured anyone else had ever been. My last boyfriend hadn't even kissed me more than once before the relationship ended.

And Liwai Raven had already seen me in my underwear.

"I'm a virgin."

I had no idea where the hell the words came from. Had I been in a better state of mind, I would have probably died from sheer embarrassment. Thankfully, the concept of my virtue seemed to be the last thing on Liwai's mind.

He grunted, "Sleep," but his arm went over my waist as if to tether me to reality. "Sleep," he whispered again, and for the briefest of seconds…

I almost believed that I was safe.

My dream became a nightmare—and the nightmare began as a story.

Once upon a time, there was a girl with frizzy hair and glasses. She lived in a world where monsters belonged in fairy tales, and good girls didn't do things like impulsively kissing strangers on the sides of roads.

Then one day, she met a man with dark eyes and a sense of mystery that infected everything he touched like poison. There was something between them. Not *love*, exactly, but something darker. Violent. More dangerous.

They were cursed, you see, and as long as they stayed together—as long as they even *tried* to coexist—both of their worlds would be torn apart...

GROWLS CHASED me from the remnants of the dream, and I bolted awake, scrambling from underneath the covers. My heart pounded. I couldn't get any air to go into my chest— but it took only two seconds of glancing around the darkened bedroom before I realized that there was nothing lurking but shadow. That and an orange glow illuminating the only window that doesn't disappear when I adjust my glasses.

"What the hell..."

I staggered toward it, peering through the glass. It was dark out. The sky was an inky shade of black—but light blazed from only a few feet away. After spending summers on my uncle's farm, I knew instantly what the source of it was. A bonfire.

The fire was small, but burned hot—standing before it, feeding the flames, was a tall, brooding shape I knew all too well. When I turned away from the window, I had to feel along the wall for the doorknob. The rest of the trailer was dark as well, forcing me to pick my way through the shadow to reach the screen door. The heavy scent of smoke irritated my nostrils before I even opened it.

It was freezing out. Barefoot and wearing only an oversized shirt, my teeth were chattering within seconds—but I hadn't even gone a step from the trailer before a towering figure appeared at my side.

"You should be asleep."

I had to swallow a laugh even as my entire body reacted to Liwai's nearness. *Should be.* There were many things that I *should* have been doing—and not a single damn one dealt with sleeping.

I should have called Dee or maybe the sheriff.

I should have gone home.

I *needed*…to ensure I didn't have a damn concussion. Everything was coming back to me like pieces of some distorted slide show.

Wolf, Liwai, wolf, Cody, Liwai, wolf, wolf, snap!

The clarity was terrifying, and I almost wished for the exhausted delirium again. The blackness that came from not remembering.

"I need to go home," I said, spying my car in the driveway. "I need to—" My words ended with a gasp as he reached down to cradle my chin in the palm of his hand.

"Better," I thought I heard him mutter as his eyes scanned my face, reminding me of my bruised, battered reflection.

He released me, and I staggered back against the screen door. The bonfire was still burning. My gaze seemed drawn to it, and I finally understood just what Liwai had been feeding to the flames.

There were random piles of brightly colored cloth scattered on the grass. *Clothing?* Two items I recognized instantly—a battered pair of tennis shoes.

"Are those my sneakers?" I lurched forward, stumbling over icy earth. The closer I came, the easier it was to make out the other items. A pair of jeans. A green sweater. All mine. And there, already smoldering atop a pile of wood, was a hunk of fabric in the same lime-green color as my jacket.

A terrifying realization hit me all at once—he was setting my clothes on fire. Was I next?

THIRTEEN

True terror shatters you like glass. It's ruthless, crushing your fragile defenses, until your body is a suffocating prison that you can't escape.

I couldn't breathe. Couldn't move. I could only stare, transfixed by the oddly beautiful glow of embers sparking from the remains of my jacket. Within seconds, the neon-green polyester blend disintegrated into ash. It felt like ages before I regained control of my limbs enough just to take a shaky step forward—I had no idea what I planned to do—but Liwai's hand was like a vice on my shoulder, yanking me back mere feet from the blaze.

"No."

He shoved his way past me and snatched one of my sneakers from the pile. As if it was just a piece of kindling, he tossed it onto the flames.

Then the other.

Followed by my sweater.

And my jeans.

Bit by bit, I watched as every garment that I had been wearing—save for my underwear—was thrown into the blaze and gobbled by fire.

"W-What the hell are you doing?" My voice cracked. An icy sweat traveled down my spine, and I couldn't escape the horrible, crazy thought that he wasn't burning my clothes because of a little water damage. Or even just for the hell of it.

It was something else.

The way he moved was methodical. The bonfire wasn't your average, cozy fire pit either—the wood had been stacked just the right way to allow things to be piled in the center.

As I watched, Liwai reached for something else that sat close to the flames. It took a full second for my brain to put a name to the bright-red bottle of liquid—the same kind that Dee had made me lug from the garage last summer when she had an insane impulse to fire up the grill. *Lighter fluid.*

Liwai squeezed, swinging his arm out toward the fire. Clear liquid sprayed from the opening in an almost beautiful arch before meeting the flames in a violent burst of heat. *Whoosh!* Within seconds, my clothes were little more than black hunks clinging to burning wood.

I didn't know how long I stood there, at the mercy of a wind that tore through my hair. I had fallen asleep wearing my glasses, and the frames dug into the bridge of my nose.

Oddly enough, the pain was like an anchor tethering me to reality—reinforcing the inescapable.

This was no dream…

"Why?" I croaked, when the roar of the fire had died down to a low crackle. "Why? Why?"

I sounded like a broken record. Or one of those horrible little dolls from childhood that said the same phrase over and over once the little string in its back had been pulled.

I might as well have been nothing more than a toy, for all the attention Liwai paid me. His shoulders were tense, his gaze focused solely on the flames. He had changed into a gray T-shirt that clung to his body, making every inch of him seem lethal. Hard.

"Answer me!" I didn't even recognize the voice that tore from my throat. "*Please.* What the hell are you doing—"

He was in front of me in an instant—way too fast for me to escape. I staggered back, unable to avoid him, when he reached for my forearm. His grip was firm but not painfully so. If anything, it was more steadying, keeping me from pitching over onto the grass.

"Kaydence…"

The sound of his voice affected me like nothing else. My eyes drifted up to meet his before I could fight it. It was impulsive. Instinctive. Darkness swallowed me whole as his gaze took me in. He was frowning. Tan nostrils flared as if testing the air…then the frown deepened, and his free hand slid down to my waist, cinching the hem of my T-shirt in a single fist.

A shiver rippled through me as he slowly lifted the hem, baring my thigh to the cold.

I tried to scream. I *wanted* to—but only air came out. My entire body seemed determined to defy me. I was utterly frozen, locked in place, as he yanked—just once—and a violent *rip* echoed through the clearing.

You're naked, a part of me announced even though the hem of my shirt drifted back down to my knees—but Liwai held a wad of blue fabric in his fist, which he promptly hurtled into the flames.

My breath caught as he turned back to me. There was no expression on his face.

My heart faltered as if knowing where his hands would travel next. So softly that I barely felt them, his fingers found the overly large sleeves of the shirt and slid inside, drifting up to my shoulders. *Snap! Snap!* My bra was ripped away as easily as though it had been toilet paper.

A second later, my plain, white push-up found itself engulfed in the fire as well—and then there was nothing at all shielding me but a thin sheet of cotton.

My voice was barely a rasp above the crackle of the flames greedily devouring my clothes. "Why are you doing this?"

If I expected some kind of creepy, morbid, serial killer-esque speech, I didn't receive it. He merely looked me over for the second time and then turned, pulling me after him by my wrist as though it were a leash—and I was the wayward puppy.

Words wouldn't come as he headed for the trailer, and I had no choice but to stagger inside after him.

He moved in a direction opposite the bedroom, past the kitchen, and propped open another door with his hip. Casually, he flicked a switch, and light flooded the narrow room. Bit by bit, my eyes took in the modest surroundings —a shower stall in the corner. A small toilet. A counter and sink.

I couldn't understand why he'd brought me into the bathroom. Without bothering to explain, he brushed past me to turn the dial of the shower.

The sound of the water rushing from the showerhead snapped something awake inside of me. *Fear.*

This is bad, Kaydee.

Very. Very. Bad.

I shifted, eyeing the doorway, desperate for an escape. Before I could take a step, he caught me by my shoulder and spun me around to face him. God, he was so tall. I had to crane my neck just to see his face, along with the grim, determined expression that crossed over it.

No! My jaw clenched as if stubbornly fighting down the words I needed to say. *Let me go! Take me home!*

I could only stand there, gaping as Liwai reached for the hem of my shirt again—only this time, he wrenched it up fearlessly. Against my will, my arms rose to assist him, and then…

I was butt naked, and there was nothing left to shield me from him. The man was inside my head—God, I swore I could hear him. Not words exactly, but this deep, calming murmur reminded me of the way my grandmother used to comfort me during a nasty storm, before I could even begin to feel afraid.

"Hush now, darling," she'd coo. *"Everything's gonna be alright."*

He never said a word out loud. It was all in the way he gingerly folded my shirt and then draped it over a towel rack hanging from the wall. How he took a cautious step closer, his eyes never leaving my face for an instant. Gently, he reached forward and removed my glasses, setting them down on the counter. Then he shifted and urged me into the shower stall, guiding me with every step.

I felt like one of those little lambs on some program on the Discovery Channel. A poor, innocent, stupid creature with no idea that the hungry predator was lurking within the shadows until…

Snap!

I waited for that moment to happen now. For Liwai to change into a monster and for this nightmare to take a whole new, morbid twist, but when the water hit me, I found myself gasping instead. I had been freezing without realizing it, and the water was just the right temperature to make my muscles turn to mush.

For three seconds, I forgot where I was. Forgot that I was in the home of a stranger who'd stripped me naked, burned my clothes, and killed a wolf and…

Smelled nice. God, his scent hit me like a wave. I inhaled through my mouth, hating how my stomach curled into knots at the taste of him—but I didn't even realize until it was too late that the wall of heat encasing me was way more intense than just the water coming out of the showerhead.

He was behind me.

All I could do was stare at a wall of cracked, gray tiles and count. It was a nervous habit—something I had done in the hospital the night my mother had died. Dee had cried, and I had paced the hallways of the wing, counting every single damn tile—one thousand, two hundred and six, to be exact.

One, two…

A muscular arm reached over my head to snatch a bottle from the shower rack. He squeezed the substance into the palm of his hand and worked it into a lather. I could hear every wet stroke of his fingers churning the liquid, and something in me flickered. Heated up.

Three…four.

The shushing murmurs in my mind were deafening. I couldn't make out individual words, but my tired brain managed to come up with some anyway. *Hush, Kaydence. I won't hurt you. I'd never hurt you. Ever, ever, ever, ever…*

Then he touched me, and my entire body jerked as though his fingers were a live wire, charged with a million volts.

Inside I screamed, waiting for the violent assault I knew had to be coming—but his fingers, slick with soap, only slid down my shoulders.

Around my neck.

Along my collar.

It seemed he concentrated most of his attention on the sore, throbbing skin that had taken the brunt of the wolf's assault.

Knowing that didn't keep a smoldering heat from creeping through my body, though.

"It's alright." It wasn't until his breath ghosted my shoulder that I realized I was shaking. His hands froze, and, for a second, he seemed unsure of what to do. How to react. Finally, he pulled back, allowing the water to wash away all traces of his touch.

"I won't hurt you. I will *never* hurt you."

Five.

I stopped counting and stood there, struggling to breathe as the water continued to pour down, and Liwai remained behind me. The strange part was…I didn't feel so weak with him this close. With every second, more fire seared through my veins, desperate to feed off his warmth.

The murmuring sounds inside my head deepened into something else. A low, reassuring purr that I could feel resonating in my bones—everywhere. The sound chased away the last dregs of fear, and when Liwai shifted closer again, I knew that I was entirely in control of my body this time.

And I stayed.

I'm naked, I told myself, as though that might help it to sink in. *I'm naked in a shower with a man, and...*

I'm not terrified by his nearness.

A man who brushed his fingers along my spine with an intimacy that took my breath away. Gently, he started to slather me in soap. My back. My hips. Lower... Modesty didn't seem to matter in this instance. My fears were smothered by the firm, slightly calloused sensation of his fingers over bare skin.

"This isn't right," I whispered into the spray, clinging to the small part of me that felt uneasy. "This isn't right. Not right..."

The murmuring in my head slowed to a trickle and became two words I could finally understand. *Yes.*

Mine.

"Why?" I asked out loud, feeling like a child demanding an answer to an impossible question. "I feel... I feel like I'm going insane—"

"You're not," Liwai said. "You just... You just need me."

I don't know who moved first, but he was even closer. His thumb traced the curve of my wrist, drifting up... over...higher...

My heart sped up, anticipating his next move before my mind comprehended the flood of sensations crashing through my veins. He still wore his jeans—I could feel the roughness of denim against the back of my thighs. But his shirt was gone. Firm, sculpted muscle met the skin of my back.

What are you doing, Kaydee? Are you insane? He's a psycho!

It was as though none of his *actual* actions mattered. I couldn't understand it. Every trace of rational fear was gone. Even the little voices in my head that should have warned me to run were...

Silent. The murmuring returned again—only this time, it was actual words, spoken out loud.

"I'm sorry." His voice was thick as his fingers slid to my waist, barely touching. "I'm so sorry..."

"Why?"

I couldn't even remember what he had to be sorry for. He stiffened as my fingers ghosted his calloused one. He was so thick. Every inch of him oozed a sense of strength that I knew could easily break me. Into pieces.

"Because this is my fault," he said in a low voice. "All of it. I'm the reason why... Why you can't stop thinking about me touching you. Why you *need* me to." His hand shifted, palm pressing into my skin, and there was no more hesitation on my part. Delicious heat darted down my spine, chasing all the fear away.

The water disappeared.

The shower faded.

In this moment, it was just me and Liwai and nothing else. No one else.

"It will get worse," Liwai went on, sounding way too serious for this moment. Cold, again. "You'll need me until you can't stand it. You'll ache."

Unease stirred to life at the back of my mind, but then he touched me, fingers rising up to my stomach. Higher. I held my breath as they inched closer to my breasts—those parts of me that boys seemed so interested in and I could never be bothered with…

Until now.

It felt like there were a million nerves I hadn't been aware of. A billion terrifying sensations prickled in anticipation of his touch, as though some dead part of me was slowly coming back to life. Inch by inch. Piece by piece.

"I feel it too. Damn it, it's taking everything I fucking have to keep from—" he broke off, moving to face me. Even without my glasses, I had no trouble deciphering his expression. *Fear. Confusion*…something else that made my heart seize.

"I won't take advantage of you by going too far. But I can make the ache go away. For now." He leaned closer, and my bare chest met his. Closer until I couldn't breathe without drinking him in. "Just until we end this."

How? He didn't say, but as his hand swept down my abdomen, I couldn't care anymore.

He had used the word ache to describe the feeling building beneath my skin, and it seemed to describe it perfectly. Muscle and bone throbbed, and only his touch relieved the heavy, suffocating pressure. In my hips. Along my spine. Lower.

I stiffened as his palm pressed between my legs, urging them apart before I could even process what was happening. I had only a basic grasp of that intimate part of my body, but I somehow knew that he knew exactly how to touch me— with no hesitation.

A thick, calloused finger caressed those delicate folds of skin, and I shivered, my eyelids fluttering. It felt…good. No, beyond that. It felt so darn right I couldn't stand it. I needed more and arched my hips, desperate to find it. Feel more.

A low sound resonated in Liwai's throat as he lurched, pressing me into the side of the shower stall with a loud thud. Within seconds, he fully supported my weight while angling his head to meet my gaze.

A rare glimpse of the cautious man lurking behind his cold exterior peeked at me from behind those dark irises. My heart panged. It should have been impossible for one man to be so darn beautiful. So haunted.

His gaze flicked down to rest on my lips, and he groaned as if the sight physically pained him. At the same time, his tongue traced his own lower lip as if he were starving and the only sustenance capable of sustaining him was…

Me.

The thought had barely entered my head when he moved in, brushing his mouth over mine with an experimental nudge. Then harder, with more pressure, until his tongue was easing my lips apart for further exploration.

My eyes fluttered shut as my brain overloaded with the sensation of him. His taste. His warmth. I felt like I'd been jolted with a million volts of electricity—only for that surge of power to suddenly dissipate as he withdrew. A series of featherlight touches traced a cautious path across my cheek and toward my neck. Tentatively, he grasped my flesh between his teeth, vibrating with what must be restraint, before gently pulling back, scraping as he released me. I hadn't even processed the sensation, when he dove back in, nuzzling that very spot. With every ragged breath he exhaled, I shivered, reminded of that moment in the woods when…

"I won't hurt you," Liwai insisted, smoothing a hand over my damp cheek. Our eyes met, and more of his stoic façade cracked, exposing what lurked beneath—a range of emotions I couldn't even begin to decipher. Something different than attraction or even lust. Something…hungry that made him seize his bottom lip between his teeth and bite down while my belly dipped in response.

"Damn." His voice was so thick I could barely understand what he said. When his hand slid higher up my inner thigh, however, I could feel the intention in every trembling finger. "I need to feel you. I need—"

"Liwai!"

The shout shattered the daze, and reality returned like a punch. His finger was mere inches from slipping inside me. Around us, the water had turned cold.

And there we were—him half-naked and me in nothing but a thin layer of soap.

FOURTEEN

L iwai recovered first.

With one hand, he switched off the water. The other darted out of the shower stall to snag something from the counter and press whatever it was into my hand. *My glasses.*

I was too stunned to put them on. Too terrified by the thoughts circling my own brain.

Mine, mine, mine.

The aftermath of having him so close decimated my senses, until I had to cling to the wall for balance. My mind was still stuck somewhere between the water and the feel of his skin.

Thankfully, the shouting cut through the din and snapped me back to reality.

"Liwai! Liwai!" It was a female's voice, high-pitched with fear. I was too dizzy to put a name to it—but Liwai was gone in an instant, barreling straight for the bathroom door. He threw it open, and while I couldn't see the figure standing on the other end, a girl's face popped into my head even before he said her name.

"Renae—"

I shivered. *Oh, God.* My arms went around my chest, shielding what little I could—though I assumed she couldn't see me anyway, not with Liwai blocking the doorway.

"What is it?"

"Cody's missing." Her voice broke. *Missing.* "Braden and James can't sense him anywhere. He didn't show up to go hunting. Liwai, I'm scared. You know what happens if he doesn't—"

"Slow down." Liwai's tone was gentle but firm enough to make Renae break off. "You know him. He's probably out sulking—"

"No. No! They'll blame me. They'll blame *me*…"

The sheer terror in her tone made my stomach sink—something was wrong.

Liwai picked up on it too. I could sense him tense—it was as though all the air was suddenly sucked out of the room as he inhaled. "Who will blame you? For what?"

I could hear Renae swallow, voice hitching on a sob. The sound echoed around the bathroom, dragging me into her fear.

"I didn't go to school today," she began. Her voice was flat —dead. "I didn't want to be late. I tried to take a shortcut through the field, but…Cody… He was there waiting for me."

My entire body went cold as I pictured her, standing on the sidewalk, drenched in rain.

And you left her there.

"What?" Anger drifted from Liwai, every bit as intense as his heat. "Did he—"

"He asked me…if I wanted to play a 'game.'" Renae's cold, detached tone revealed the true horror of that statement. Cody had alluded to that himself. *Come out, come out, little owl…*

I knew in the pit of my stomach that there had been nothing playful at all about his proposed *game.*

"I tried to run," Renae went on. She sounded farther away, and I realized that Liwai had steered her into the main part of the trailer without me even noticing.

For some reason—call it plain old nosiness—I found myself shuffling out of the shower and onto a bare, brown throw rug. The room was so damn cold in comparison to Liwai's heat. After settling my glasses on the ridge of my nose, I snatched the first towel I saw and draped it over me.

It smelled like him, and the scent filled my lungs as I crept over to the doorway and peered out.

"He chased me," Renae said.

They sat at the kitchen table. Renae had her back to me, and from over her head, Liwai's eyes met mine just once.

"And?" he prompted, returning his attention to the girl after a long, searing minute.

She sucked in a breath that made her entire body quake. "He followed me," she said. "I knew that I couldn't outrun him—not if he shifted—"

Shifted. Something in me seized on the word, stealing it away to mull over later.

"I was scared. So I…led him somewhere where I knew I could get away."

"Where?"

My mind had already started to envision a place, even before Renae rasped out a name. "Settler's Point."

I had never heard of it. The area around Kittywatt had all kinds of random hills with odd names, but I had a sneaking suspicion that Settler's Point overlooked a particular sheer drop in the middle of the forest. One so remote that you'd need a truck with four-wheel-drive just to reach it.

"Why there?" Liwai's lower jaw clenched. His hands were pressed flat against the table, and tension coiled his body so tightly that I could count every rope of muscle flexing in his forearms.

Renae shrugged. Her long hair shrouded her like a blanket, hanging down over the sides of her seat. I could tell that underneath, all she wore was a thin, ratty sundress and an old pair of pink flip-flops.

"I know that sometimes…Mark Fisher and his buddies like to go hunting up there. I knew it was a long shot, but I *had* to get away from him."

Liwai sucked in a breath and then swallowed. When he spoke again, his tone was sharp enough to slice through concrete.

"What happened?"

"It was too hard to climb the slope in the rain, so I had to circle around," Renae said, panting for breath. "I knew he was behind me…but then… I heard trucks coming. I saw headlights, and I took off. When I looked behind me, Cody wasn't there anymore—"

Abruptly, Liwai stood. "Go home, Renae."

It was only then that I realized he was still dripping wet. Droplets of water hit the linoleum as he headed for the screen door. Each sound echoed, oddly loud in my ears—like a gunshot.

"Liwai!" Renae shook her head, sending waves of dark hair whipping out around her. "What if they were hunters?" she croaked. "What if they found Cody, and he couldn't fight them off? What if—"

"Go home."

"You know what happens," she continued in a rush as if he hadn't even spoken. "You *know* the price for k-killing your own kind—"

"Renae."

"He's *dead,*" she shouted over him. "It's my fault! I killed him. They'll kill me—"

"Stop it!"

In two strides, Liwai was beside her, pulling her harshly to her feet. Within a second, he had her crushed against his chest, face buried in the crook of his shoulder.

"It's going to be alright," he insisted.

His eyes found mine again, and I got the sense that the words were directed at me as well.

"Everything's going to be alright."

"No, it's not." Renae sounded muffled, and Liwai loosened his grip enough so that she could pull back to stare at him. "It's *not* alright! Cody's dead."

She stressed the word. *Dead.* Final. Done.

Liwai's expression was guarded. "You don't know that."

Without explaining, Renae reached into a ratty pocket on the side of her dress and withdrew a crumbled piece of notebook paper. Her fingers were shaking too badly to unfold it herself, so Liwai did it for her and placed the page flat on the kitchen table.

"It's not okay," she croaked, gazing down with wide, haunted eyes. "It's not okay."

Even from my position in the doorway, I had no trouble making out the image on the page. It was a drawing. Or more like a series of random sketches, each overlapping the next.

There was a startlingly detailed sketch of a row of trees that overlooked a steep cliff. Drawn over top of that was a boy's face, stern and cold with mean eyes. *Cody.* And beside that...covering the rest of the page was the crumpled, broken body of a wolf.

"I drew that a month ago," Renae said in a strained whisper. "Only I didn't know what it meant...until now."

FIFTEEN

Liwai's expression hardened. I had never seen anyone look so cold before. So distant.

"Why didn't you show this to me before?"

Renae flinched. "I... I didn't think it mattered. And you know that sometimes…they don't always come true—"

"They *always* come true," Liwai growled, cutting over her. "Recently, anyway. Damn it…"

He snatched the page from the table and tore it in half so violently the loose edges snapped in the air like whips. He crumbled both halves in his fists, which he slammed down onto the counter. *Bang!*

Renae shrank. Suddenly she seemed to be two inches tall in Liwai's shadow. "I'm *sorry.*"

"Rae." He broke off, exhaled, and when he spoke again, I could tell he had worked to make his voice softer. "Who else knows about this?"

"No one." Renae shook her head, her eyes glistening. "I didn't tell the others. He…he grabbed me…" She held out her arm, and I gasped in sympathy. A dark, vicious bruise encircled her forearm like a manacle—or a handprint. "I was afraid his scent was on me, so I threw my old clothes in the river. Then I hid out in the woods until school was over."

Her words rush over me in a blur. *I threw my clothes in the river. I hid. He chased me. I ran. He's dead.* All of it circled back to *me*—every damn thing that had happened was on my shoulders. All because I had been too spiteful to give her a damn ride…

"This is my fault…"

Both Liwai and Renae whirled around to face me.

At the sight of me, Liwai's face became utterly blank, and the line of his jaw went rigid like steel.

Renae only blinked. Her massive eyes took me in, starting with my bruised face, before noticing that all I wore was her brother's—or whoever he was to her—towel around my soaking wet body.

But rather than looking alarmed or frightened or even *surprised*, she seemed…relieved instead.

"I'm sorry," she spoke in a rush, body swaying as though the words had been weighing her down. "I'm sorry I showed you the drawing. I'm sorry. I'm sorry—"

"It's okay."

If anyone should have been sorry, it was me. Liwai had made it seem like I was the bane of his existence—in not so many words—and only *now* was I beginning to see why—it seemed as though merely being around me had caused him nothing but bad luck.

"Wait here, Renae." He turned and disappeared into the bedroom. When he returned a minute later, he held a gray sweatshirt clenched in one hand that he tossed to Renae. In the other was what seemed to be another long, oversized T-shirt.

"Here." He came just close enough to hold out the shirt to me. Slowly, I took it and jerked back into the bathroom, closing the door impulsively.

What are you doing? The logical part of me—no longer muffled—flared up with a vengeance. *You should be jumping from the window! Running for the sheriff! At least barricade yourself until they call the police!*

Instead, I shimmied out of his towel and gingerly placed it on the rack. Without hesitating, I pulled the new shirt on over my head. It didn't smell like him. It was funny how I noticed that first. The cotton smelled crisp as if brand-new —with none of his masculine, husky undertones—and I wasn't sure why that fact disappointed me.

I turned back to the door and reached for the knob. Hesitated. Then, before common sense could finally steal my nerve, I pulled the door open and staggered into the kitchen.

Liwai and Renae had already moved into the living room.

They both sat on a worn couch. Renae was wrapped in the sweatshirt with her head resting on Liwai's shoulder. That long hair pooled at her waist, and he had one arm thrown around her, holding her close. It was such an intimate embrace, like a father and daughter.

I felt like a gaping, unwanted trespasser witnessing something tender that I had no business seeing. I wanted to turn and run from that trailer right then—but before I could so much as twitch in the direction of the door, Liwai's eyes met mine through the shadows. He inclined his head just once. *Come.* Useless admonishments ran through my mind, even as I crossed the room over to him. *Stay away! Run! Leave!*

There was space beside him on the couch, and I settled into it. I couldn't explain why—my body didn't seem to give a damn about the "logical" part of me whining about fear. Oddly enough…it didn't feel strange to sit down next to him either.

It felt nice. This close to him, I felt safe and warm, and all those dangerous things a girl like me shouldn't have felt around a stranger. Carefully, his arm settled around me. I sat back, drawing my knees up to my chin as his scent filled my nose.

I felt safe.

I shouldn't have rested against him. Or closed my eyes. Or…for the second time that day, drifted off into thick, black sleep without a shred of rational fear.

"Kaydence Marie Blanchett!"

The racket yanked me from a dreamless sleep. I groaned and tried to burrow under the covers—but the assault was ruthless.

"Kaydee!" *Bang!* "Open this door!" *Bang, bang!* "You've been asleep all damn day!" *Smack!* "Damn it, Kaydee! If you don't open this door—"

"What?" With a sigh, I tore back the covers. The moment I peeled my eyes open, a million realizations hit me, one right after the next. For one, I was in my own room—my own house. Gone were the plain, white walls of a trailer I had expected to find instead. Even still…a heavy, masculine scent lingered in the air, real enough to taste.

"Kaydee!"

I had to blink several times before the contents of my bedroom came into full focus. Bright sunshine spilled through the window, stinging my eyes. Dee was right. It looked to be late afternoon—way longer than I usually slept.

"I was making sure you weren't dead, for one." My aunt harrumphed from behind the door. "Now, are you gonna open this damn door, or do I have to knock it down?"

I stood, fumbling for my glasses. I had already staggered to the door, prepared to open it, when something caught my eye. A piece of paper had been taped to the back of it, right over my solar system calendar. The message written across it was simple. *Check mirror.*

My entire body went cold as Dee continued to grumble from the other side of the door.

"Damn it, Kaydee, don't make me go grab the screwdriver!"

"You don't even know where it is," I croaked, responding to her banter out of habit—but I didn't even recognize my own voice—the throaty whisper belonged to a stranger. *The mirror…*

I turned and headed for the one beside my closet. It was an antique heirloom that had belonged to my great-grandmother. In it, I could usually see my entire body when angled right. That day, I hardly recognized the person I saw staring back at me. The girl *looked* like me, just a worndown version. A plain T-shirt hung down to her knees. Her red hair was a dry, crunchy mess of curls—but beneath the familiar blue eyes was a faint, splotchy shadow that wouldn't go away no matter how hard I rubbed at it. The skin was tender, and I hissed through my teeth the moment I realized what it was—a bruise.

Still…something told me that it was nowhere near as vibrant as it *should* have been. An image popped into my head—my reflection, seen from a metal surface. *Pale, battered face. Haunted blue eyes…*

"Kaydee? Are you really gonna make me go get that damn screwdriver? You know I'm afraid of tools."

"Uh…coming." On impulse, I stumbled to my closet and snatched a sweatshirt from a hanger. I threw it on, drawing the hood low over the right side of my face.

My heart pounded so fiercely that I could feel my pulse beating through my eardrums. When I finally opened the door, Dee looked ready to stab me with said "terrifying" screwdriver. Her eyes were caked in dark eye shadow, making the bright blue irises seem extra piercing, though her outfit—a cross between a stripper and a librarian—kept her from seeming too threatening overall. The moment she saw me, her irritated expression softened.

"Aww, honey…" She glanced me over with a frown. "If you were having one of your 'ugly' days, all you had to do was say so." Before I had the chance to get a word in edgewise, she shoved something in my direction. "Here—"

I blinked to find several crisp pieces of notebook paper, all neatly stapled together. "A Story by Renae Raven" was written across the front in neat handwriting, and stuck to the front page was a sticky note that read—*For Kaydence.*

"I just wanted to give this to ya, is all," Dee explained. "I found that in my mailbox this morning."

"What is it?"

Dee shrugged and flicked a stray curl behind her ear. "I thought it would be hate mail for being so *rude* yesterday —" She glared at me. "But it seems like it's just an assignment for Maxine Archer's creative writing class. It's beautiful, actually, if a little morbid."

"A story? From Renae? Why?" The questions flew out, one right after the other.

Dee shrugged again. "I have no idea. The assignment's not even due for two more weeks. Poor kid. I figured, she'd gotten a head start on it and didn't want it to go to waste. I've already shown it to Maxine, and she said it would have been A-plus work."

Would have been?

"Did Ms. Archer change the assignment or something?" I wondered as I absently flipped through the pages. There were ten of them, all filled with the same, deliberate handwriting. From the first line, I could tell that it wasn't something along the lines of "The day I was left in the rain by a spiteful bitch." Rather, the opening was simple: "Once there were three brothers..."

"No," Dee said in answer to my question. "But there won't be any use in grading it *now*, would there?"

"Why not?"

"Well..." She gave me an odd look. "Considering that the Ravens just picked up and left town with barely any notice, it's not like they'd bother to care what kind of grades Renae finished the semester with."

It took a full minute for the words to sink in. *Picked up and left town...*

"What?"

The corner of Dee's mouth quirked up, and I knew the real reason why she'd all but battered down my door—gossip. "*Well,* Liwai Raven came into the high school this morning and withdrew Renae. Just like that—" She snapped her fingers for emphasis. "So, of course, when I went to the Ravenswood gas station after work, Barney Puckett was furious. He said that Liwai had just strolled in and quit. Out of darn nowhere."

I stood there as the words slowly began to register.

Liwai had quit his job.

He had pulled Renae out of school.

They were gone…

"And, now, don't get mad, Kaydee, but I didn't hear you come in last night, and with all the rumors, I almost thought…" She laughed without voicing just what exactly she had thought. "It doesn't matter. Anyway, I guess what everyone's been saying about those Ravens turned out to be true, after all. I just wonder what drove them out of town this time… Kaydee?"

I didn't even realize that I was moving until I found myself staggering down the stairs. I didn't grab my shoes. Not even a coat from the hook by the door. Barefoot and wearing only my sweatshirt, I staggered out of the house and down the porch steps.

It was a shock to find my Beetle sitting in the driveway, though I don't know why—when it came to Liwai, nothing should have surprised me anymore. The keys were waiting for me in the front seat. Nothing seemed out of place, but the moment I opened the door, a heavy, musky scent filled my nose.

I couldn't breathe. I barely registered placing Renae's paper in the pocket of my sweatshirt or even starting the engine.

The next thing I knew, I was standing before the battered screen door of a gray trailer as if waiting for someone to appear on the other end—but the windows were dark. A certain pick-up truck was absent from the driveway…

He's not here, a part of me whispered even as I formed a trembling fist and knocked just once. The sound echoed, and then there was only silence. Slowly, I sank down on the concrete step before the door. I was freezing, but for some reason, I couldn't bring myself to go back to my car—or even move at all.

My toes had gone numb by the time I had enough sense to wiggle them to prevent frostbite. I huddled, sticking my hands within the front pocket of my sweatshirt, only to feel something crunch beneath my fingers. Renae's assignment. Dread weighed heavily on my chest as I settled the pages on my lap.

Don't! a part of me hissed as the paper crinkled beneath my fingertips. Burning it would have been the smart course of action. The remains of Liwai's bonfire scorched the earth nearly ten feet away, beckoning me to destroy the pages. I had this horrible sense that, once I started reading, there would be no going back. Though it wasn't like I had any other truth to fall back on. With a sigh, I reached up to adjust my glasses and then scanned the first line.

Once there were three brothers.

Their father, a powerful god, had grown lonely in the heavens. Even though he lived amongst the bright and beautiful stars, the universe felt empty. So, from his own heart, the god formed the earth, and he used his eyes to create the moon and the sun to always watch over his beloved creation. To enjoy his new world, the god created three brothers born of himself to live in it.

The oldest brother, formed from the moon, was as swift and mysterious as darkness itself. The second, shaped from the sun, was as bright and fleeting as daylight. Together, they would rule his world during the night and the day so it would never be empty. The third brother, however, was different—for when the god attempted to create him from the belly of the earth, she resisted.

Beautiful and unyielding, the earth demanded that the being created from her was to be the strongest of all, unrivaled by any other. For her, the god consented and bestowed upon the last brother a drop of his own blood, allowing him to take the physical form of the god himself—a monstrous beast to strike fear into the heart of even the bravest hunter. For the third brother, the earth also bestowed her own gift—a dark, rich oasis for him to live in, hidden from the children of the light and the moon.

Despite these differences, all three brothers lived in harmony within their own corners of the world. The eldest and his descendants dwelled in the night and shadow. The middle brother and his children claimed the day, while the youngest and his kind ruled the forest realm the earth had created for them.

For many years, they lived at peace with the old ways—but over time, the children of the earth grew arrogant and began to resent the children of the light and the shadow. The forest home their mother had given them was not enough, and with their strength and speed, they were not content to merely share the whole world with lesser beings.

They wanted it all.

So they crept into the shadows and into the realm of the day-dwellers, taking any land, food, or woman they saw fit. When confronted with their selfish actions, the earth-children declared that as long as they possessed the protection of their mother, nothing could stop their terrible reign.

Distraught, the earth watched and wept, knowing that the great gifts she herself had given her children had only enabled their cruelty. Overcome with grief, she could think of only one solution that could temper their power once and for all.

She cursed them, so that every man born of the god's blood was destined to be bound to only one woman, born of the lesser races, living on the land that she herself had created. This woman would hold their power and heart, and he would love her more than any other—but the cost of such a union would be that any child he bore to this woman would be weaker than the father. And its children would be weaker still, and so on, until the original vanity of the earth was nothing more than a memory.

Infuriated, the leader of the god-blood pack shunned the earth and declared that he would resist her curse. He hunted down his promised woman, born to a brother of the light, and killed her—even though, in doing so, he felt as though he had slayed a part of himself.

When he returned to his pack of brothers, he commanded that they, too, seek out their cursed women and destroy them, protecting the divine blood they had been blessed with. Only those strong enough to resist the curse could rejoin his pack and take their true wives, daughters of the earth.

While many disagreed and left the pack land, the children they bore eventually lost touch with their divine gifts just as the earth had intended—save for the children of the first leader. They continued their cruel existence, seeking out their own earth woman born on their ancestral lands and destroying her for the good of the pack.

They called this woman "Luna"—named for the mother goddess who had utterly betrayed them. And they swore to continue this painful resistance until the end of time itself.

SIXTEEN

The distant sound of paper crinkling pulled me back to reality. An icy rain had started, coating the top of my head and seeping through my sweatshirt. I could only blink to a hazy vision of green trees as a mixture of confusion and something that could have been pain settled in my stomach.

Renae Raven had done it again, living up to her bizarre talent of terrifying me. If it wasn't for what Liwai had said…

No. I shook my head before my mind even went there. None of the Ravens' strange theories or superstitions made sense. They couldn't be real. The story in my hands was nothing more than that, a *story*—and, as Dee said, it was a morbid one at that. It didn't matter that this tiny voice at the back of my mind challenged that theory. Absently, I scanned each page, running my fingers over the neatly penned words until the ink began to rub off. On the tenth pass, I noticed something written on the back of the last page, just as the rain came down harder, nearly obscuring the hastily scribbled note. Renae must have written it afterward, leaving this message in pencil rather than pen. "A List of the Cursed Families," she'd titled the passage. Underneath was a series of last names that I vaguely recognized. *James, Brown, Williams, Michaels, Cavanaugh, Hawthorne, Peake.* There were roughly thirty last names of most of the families in town—namely, the ones with long ties to the area—but Blanchett wasn't on that list. Neither was my father's last name. Scribbled beside it was the name of a town several hours outside Kittywatt. *Chambersburg.*

Tucking the pages into the pocket of my sweatshirt, I couldn't understand the significance of the list. If I even wanted to believe her crazy story, my family wasn't one of the "cursed" ones. Therefore, the Ravens were all criminally insane.

But one of those names kept echoing through my thoughts, refusing to be drowned out even by the sputtering sound of my Beetle's engine once I climbed inside and stuck the key in the ignition. One name resonated within this small part of me that had always suspected a truth too painful to name inside my head.

It couldn't be—*I* couldn't be...

I went home first and somehow managed to make it inside without running into Dee. After throwing on a pair of jeans, I returned to my car and drove aimlessly, turning the wheel without even understanding which direction I was headed. Eventually, I found myself in front of the sheriff's station, and my rebellious body stubbornly put my vehicle in park. The rain had stopped by the time I forced myself to enter the building. This late, the receptionist's desk was devoid of the usual secretary, but Burt Michaels himself stood hunched over it, shuffling through papers with one hand while cradling a steaming mug of coffee in the other.

"Kaydence," he greeted, glancing up. A frown tugged at the corner of his mouth, but he did his best to hide it while sticking out his hand for me to shake. "What brings you by? Are...are you okay?"

I was dripping rainwater all over the floor of the lobby. My clothes were soaked, my hair a tangled mess. I wasn't okay, but he had the power to make me feel a tad bit saner—all he had to do was say the right thing.

"I need to ask you something..." My heart thumped in my chest as I warily took a step closer. My eyes scanned his face before I could help it, tallying up the little details I'd never noticed before. Burt had blue eyes. Stubborn freckles dotted his chin, and his nose had a familiar shape. Too familiar. We had the same lanky build. Similar facial expressions, like the involuntary furrowing of the eyebrows when someone caught us off guard.

"Um...sure, Kaydence. What about?"

There wasn't a suitable combination of words in existence to bring up this sort of topic. For a minute, I could only stand there, watching him, before my lips seemed to move of their own accord. "I need to ask you something about my mom," I heard myself say. "This may sound crazy, but..."

Something funny happened the moment I mentioned my mother. His face flushed. His nostrils flared, and for the first time since knowing him, Burt Michaels refused to meet my gaze.

"Kaydence, I—"

"You knew." His expression alone cemented a reality I would have never considered only a few hours ago. Marie Blanchett may have been a lot of things, but a liar wasn't one of them. While she may have been guilty of being too strict or overly protective, my mother would never lead me to believe that the wrong man was my father my entire life. Or so I thought.

"Kaydence, wait—" I didn't even realize I was halfway to the door until Burt's hand fell over my shoulder. Just as quickly, he pulled away, uneasily clenching his fingers at his sides. "Marie…she didn't—"

"How long?"

If he had said any time frame within the past few months, that might have lessened the sting. Maybe my mother revealed the truth in some cryptic message after her death. Maybe the man I spent twenty-two years believing to be my father had spilled the beans during one of his few and far between visits from the city. Maybe. I wished more than anything that was the case—it might have lessened the pain tearing through my chest.

"For a long time," Burt said finally. The lack of a time frame revealed the truth—since the day I was born. "It was a bad time, Kaydence. I was going through a rough patch, and your mother…she only ever wanted to protect you."

Protect me. I didn't feel very protected now, caught in the web of an insane legend spun by people who believed they could turn into wolves at will. I didn't feel very protected standing face to face with a man I'd always thought was a charming, though meddlesome family friend. My life was fracturing around me, and the only ounce of substance I had left seemed to be a stack of stapled notebook paper and the words written by a teenage girl who had no reason to lie.

"Kaydence, wait!" Burt's voice chased me through the main entrance of the station and out onto the street. "We should talk about this—where are you going?"

Even I didn't know the answer to that question. By the time I reached my Beetle, I only seemed capable of climbing inside and palming the steering wheel with one hand while pulling Renae's story from my pocket with the other. *Chambersburg*—the same place Sheriff Michaels mentioned. It was all I had to go on—and who knew if Renae and Liwai were even headed there—but at the moment, that jagged name written in pencil seemed like the only link to answers…

Whether or not Liwai wanted me to find them was another story.

SEVENTEEN

After realizing how far away Chambersburg was, and the late hour, I decided to head home to get rest before continuing my quest. I don't know why I thought I'd be able to sleep—I couldn't stop thinking about Liwai and Renae. As morning approached, I was resigned to the crippling exhaustion that had my eyes burning and my resolve breaking. At least I had the sense of mind to wait to get up until Dee left for work to avoid the interrogation that was sure to come.

The universe had a cruel sense of humor. I spent most of my teenage years dreaming of what life would be like once I was finally able to leave this God-forsaken town. Fast forward to my senior year when, despite being armed with a full-ride scholarship, I couldn't drive past the town limits without dissolving into a panic attack.

That moment cemented the grim reality of who I was at my core—a coward who could only dream, but never put her plans into action. I'd felt so pathetic then.

But now? While the allure of college hadn't done the trick, blindly chasing a man who didn't want me? Rejection, it seemed, was a strong enough motivator to help me finally put that crumbling Kittywatt sign in my rearview mirror.

And what a terrifying sight it was.

I'd spent so long, trapped by the weight of small-town expectations and big-city fears, but when I finally turned onto the highway, I couldn't characterize the emotion constricting my chest as relief.

It was something far more insidious. Doubt? Maybe that, mixed with a tiny bit of panic and desperation to find the one person who could give me answers.

Then it hit me sometime between the drive from Kittywatt to Chambersburg—Liwai Raven had been in town since I was old enough to drive to the Ravenswood Gas Station. Six years, perhaps seven tops.

He'd always been there, and so had I, stuck working at Bardee's once my college dreams fell through. I'd thought my fear was some kind of genetic flaw. Only now could I finally face another explanation, perhaps one more selfish and fantastical, but it took the blame off me—it was *his* fault.

Through whatever voodoo mojo Liwai Raven believed in, he'd kept me in that town close to him. I could only leave when he did so first.

Bravery wasn't the source of my newfound independence. Just fear. The man stalking me from afar had finally turned his back for the first time in seven years.

Damn him to hell.

Anger was an emotion preferable to shame, and I latched onto it, letting it help me devise my next course of action. As it turned out, Liwai wasn't my only source for answers.

There were other avenues I could take, starting with finding if there was any basis in the tales of the Ravens being psychopathic murderers.

I wouldn't go crawling after a stranger like some sex-crazed groupie.

I'd make sure he and his creepy band of outlaws couldn't hurt, confuse, or maul anyone else while under their delusions.

The plan sounded good in my head. It was only three hours later—as I neared the boundary of Chambersburg—once I sat parked outside of the local police station, that I realized it might do me some good to come up with a better angle other than—*the man stalking me might belong to a pack of serial killers.*

Instead of repeating the truth verbatim, I decided to wing it.

Chambersburg was roughly twice the size of Kittywatt, meaning their police station operated out of a detached building in the heart of a bustling downtown rather than a renovated warehouse. One step inside the spacious, modern interior nearly stole my resolve.

I'd become so accustomed to marching into our P.D. and getting an audience with Burt Michaels by request. I had no clue what the proper protocol was.

"Can I help you?" The woman at the receptionist's desk seemed friendly enough, with warm brown eyes peering from behind wire-rimmed glasses.

Stealing myself with a deep breath, I approached her and attempted to come up with a believable cover.

"I was wondering if I could have information on a murder case that happened a few years ago. The murder of a young girl?"

The woman's eyes narrowed. "I'm sorry, sweetie, but I can't reveal confidential information related to an active investigation."

I stiffened. The term "investigation" sounded so much more serious than rumors and gossip. Active meant there were still officers on the case and evidence being collected. Evidence that led to more crimes involving the Ravens?

"I..." A telltale hitch in my throat was my only warning before my eyes began burning. Blinking alone couldn't keep the tears back, and they fell in rivulets down my cheeks as the secretary watched on, horrified.

"Sweetheart, is something wrong?" She scrambled for a nearby tissue box and offered it to me. "You can tell me."

"I know you can't tell me everything with confidentiality," I managed to blubber. "But I just... There was this guy, and Sheriff Michaels told me that I should be careful, but I don't know what to be careful about, and the victim was from—"

"Is Burt Michaels your sheriff, sweetie pie?" the woman asked, an eyebrow raised.

When I nodded, her entire expression lit up as if I'd said the right word to some secret riddle.

"Oh, then I think I know what this is about. Come with me." She stood and hurried down a hall, dodging an array of officers meandering in our path. Her eventual destination was a small room crammed with bookshelves of binders and a tiny desk sporting an outdated computer system probably a decade older than me.

"I don't normally do this," the woman said while settling onto the seat before the dusty computer monitor. "But in this case, I'm willing to make a teensy exception. Burt Michaels is one of the best men around, and if he mentioned this case to you, then it must have been for a good reason. I know this one more than any other still haunts him, what with the victim being his sister and all—"

"Who?" I felt my eyes go bug wide, but I had enough sense to smother my shock. Burt Michaels had a sister? One who died under mysterious circumstances, it seemed—but somehow, I don't think this is what he meant for me to find. "This happened fourteen years ago?"

"Oh no!" The woman gave me an odd look. "This was about twenty or so, but I'm sure this is what Burt wanted you to ask about. Here, take a look."

As the woman finally stood back to reveal the screen, my heart dropped as so many puzzle pieces fell into place all at once. The headline of a blurry newspaper image displayed on the screen, explained it all. Why Burt Michaels had been so wary of the Ravens, and why I had every right to be as well.

LOCAL GIRL DEAD IN SUSPECTED ANIMAL ATTACK

A chilling detail was that this murder had nothing to do with Chambersburg, instead taking place further up north near the mountains, about another hour's drive away.

"This old thing doesn't have any sensitive case information on it," the woman explained with a sigh. "Just supplemental stuff like newspaper clippings and the like. We rarely use it nowadays with all this newfangled internet technology and such. So... If I were to let you poke around it for a bit and claim that you were from the high school paper doing an assignment, I don't think anyone would have a problem." She winked at me and tiptoed back into the hall. "Take your time, sweetheart, and send Burt my best."

As she left, closing the door behind her, a cold sense of dread settled into my chest, growing heavier the more I read.

Her name was Beatrice. Beatrice Michaels, a young nature enthusiast barely eighteen years old when parts of her were found scattered over Ridgley Mountain, where she gave hiking tours as a part-time job.

It's chilling how much of yourself you can find in a stranger, gleaned through only a few keywords. Beatrice was described in the same way I figured many would describe me. She was "*charming*," according to a quote in one article. "*The sweetest, kindest girl you ever knew.*"

The only lead the police publicly acknowledged was evidence of an animal playing a role in her disappearance and suspected death. They didn't say what exactly, but I could guess.

Wolves. They ripped her clean apart hours after a tour she gave over twenty years ago—when I had been a toddler. Her death left behind a grieving set of parents and a half-brother who lived three towns away and had been the star of the high school football team.

Burt Michaels.

Only a few months later, he would have a publicized downfall and a decade-long descent into chronic alcoholism while my mother married another man and went on to live a seemingly perfect life.

Until said life was cut short by a drunk driver, leaving everyone else to buckle beneath the weight of her lies. It felt like a twisted irony that, in the end, the Michaels' family trauma would come full circle.

And any twisted mixture of guilt and shame I felt toward Liwai Raven became loathing. Disgust. Hate.

He and his family of psychopaths thought they had every right to galivant across the country, wreaking havoc wherever they went. Women like the girl from Chambersburg and Beatrice Michaels were fun toys, left scattered behind for their families to pick up the broken pieces.

And, when pressed, he couldn't even tell me the truth himself. He merely hid behind riddles and lies like a coward. Well, no more. I wouldn't let myself become just another victim to be whispered about years after my death.

I would take the reins of my own life into my *hands*, whether Liwai Raven, Burt Michaels, or anyone else liked it or not.

EIGHTEEN

Ridgley Mountain wasn't the sweet, charming hill I'd pictured after reading about Beatrice Michaels.

In reality, it was a vast, wild bit of jagged rock threatening to pierce the sky, shrouded in forest that distorted the landscape north of Chambersburg. I had never even heard of it, meaning that it probably wasn't a preferred camping spot or scenic location where families spent their weekends exploring.

As I drove up in my shitty little Beetle, it looked…

Hungry. A ravenous maw composed of gnarled branches and emerald-green shadows, waiting to swallow me whole.

Before I even gathered the nerve to park somewhere, doubt began to creep in. What was I doing here? Alone? Even if I managed to find some piece of evidence that two decades of active police investigation had missed, it wouldn't mean much in the long run.

Just that, the Ravens had a string of victims—perhaps Liwai himself did. He preyed on innocent young women trapped in small towns, trying to make a living any way they could. He teased them with the hint of something far larger and then led them to the woods to be murdered.

Violently murdered, according to the information available on Beatrice Michaels.

The sobfest I'd managed to thwart at the police station returned in full force. I bawled, slumped against the steering wheel, hearing my own cries echo back to me on an endless loop. I barely noticed the knock at first.

The culprit had to bang louder on my passenger window before I finally jolted to awareness and whipped around to find a stranger staring at me.

They weren't Liwai Raven or even Renae. Something that might have been disappointment washed over me before a stronger sense of embarrassment overrode it.

Forcing a grin, I swiped a hand across my face and rushed to roll down my window to address the poor woman gaping at me.

Going off her modest clothing, I assumed she lived somewhere nearby. She wore a straw hat that covered most of her face and a long, blue sundress paired with an oversized green sweater. On her feet was a pair of ratty flip-flops that had seen better days—shoes I desperately tried to keep my attention on rather than her face.

It wasn't polite to stare. I went out of my way to avoid gawking at Old Tom, who came to Bardee's every third Sunday and had lost his arm in the war. Tom, however, didn't give a damn if anyone stared at him, or not once he was well into his third beer.

This woman, however, had tried her best to arrange her long brown hair to cover the left side of her face. Though, it would take a lot more to fully obscure the vicious scarring distorting her left eye and cheek.

I didn't even want to imagine what kind of accident could have caused it. In fact, I had done enough investigating for the day.

"You can't park here," the woman said. Her voice was soft and gentle, barely rivaling the wind ripping through the trees behind her. "The camping is on the far side of the mountain, a few hours' drive away. It's all rocks on this end and far too dangerous."

"Thanks," I said before rolling up my window.

In a sense, the woman was right in more ways than one. This wild goose chase was far too dangerous. People like me didn't hunt psycho murderers on a whim.

We stayed in our small towns well past our expiration dates and wilted away behind the counter of the local bar, counting down the days until something exciting happened.

After wiping the rest of my tears, I turned around and headed back down the mountain. Maybe I'd stop in Chambersburg—and ask about the *other* murder Liwai was supposedly linked to—before heading home, if only to prolong the inevitable.

Mari could probably use me tonight, and I could only avoid Sheriff Michaels for so long. Sooner or later, I'd have to face him and Dee and put the Ravens far behind me.

I was fully determined to do just that right until the second my gaze fell over a sign up ahead. It was triangular and brightly painted by someone who loved color. In a million shades of blue, yellow, red, and purple, they'd decorated a sign displaying "Luna Ridge" in varying forms of wildlife and plant forms.

Its quirky beauty alone might have been why it drew my notice. Until I read the name three times. Then something clicked.

Luna. The same word from Renae's story. Coincidence? Probably.

Knowing that didn't stop me from parking near it, though, and eyeing my tennis shoes skeptically. They weren't fit for running down the street, let alone traipsing down the side of a mountain—not that I would go far. Just a peek to fulfill the savage curiosity that wouldn't leave me be.

Foolish or not, a part of me needed to traverse the uneven, gravel-strewn path if only to hammer in how much of an idiot I was being. How selfish. How stupid. How...human.

Twenty years ago, Beatrice Michaels had been in a similar position. A harmless girl just trying to live her life and walk home after a shift earning honest money. She probably enjoyed the sensation of being surrounded by the vast wilderness, accompanied only by the sound of nature...

And the chilling feeling of being watched.

It started as a prickle along the back of my neck before quickly blossoming into full-blown paranoia. I'd gone only a few paces from my car—it was still in view, beside the sign. Yet, an invisible tension grew stronger, weighing down my limbs until I couldn't take another step forward.

Go back, a tiny voice in my head warned. *Not safe. Go back. Go back...*

"It isn't safe."

I jumped, choking down a scream as a figure stepped from a shadowy grove up ahead. Belatedly, I recognized the blue dress and green sweater as belonging to the woman who had stopped me earlier. She now had a wicker basket tucked under one arm, and her hat was skewed at an awkward angle that revealed more of her face.

One look at her resonated with the traumatized part of me still grappling with the reality that I'd sported claw marks on my shoulders. Nothing else had that same jagged, vicious appearance. As if the flesh had been ripped through by something impossibly sharp, designed to tear. Destroy.

Staring at her—breaking that unspoken social rule—an insane thought came to mind, one so improbable that I felt the need to blurt it out loud. Only then could I rationalize how stupid and impossible an idea it was.

My throat went dry as I voiced just one name, watching how the woman reacted. "Beatrice?"

Contrary to my expectations, she didn't wrinkle her nose in confusion. She didn't laugh or ask me to repeat myself.

The color of the unblemished part of her face went white. Then she turned on her heel and ran away.

"Wait!" I chased her, surging off the path and through the wild underbrush.

She was fast. I merely caught a glimpse of her between a swath of swaying branches before she vanished completely. Panting, I ventured as far from the path as possible without losing sight of the entrance.

"Beatrice?" I called out, hopeless. My voice echoed back to me, increasing in pitch until it faded into a distant, shrill cry.

I could have imagined her—deep down, a part of me wanted to believe that and head back home.

Instead, when I got in my car, the first place I drove to was a camping supply store just outside of town. Luckily, this area seemed to sport one on every corner. With only the slightest bit of apprehension, I bought a pair of hiking shoes, a switchblade, a heavy jacket, and a few packs of trail mix, paid for with the hundred-dollar bill I kept in my glove box for emergencies.

Why? I knew those items alone weren't anywhere near what one would need on a serious hike. Maybe it was just a cover for what, in essence, was stalking.

If the vision on the trail was real, I needed to find her. Beatrice Michaels, a woman thought dead for the past twenty years. How had she survived this long undetected? By living in those mountains?

And why?

An answer came to me as I returned to the driver's seat of my car. Even thinking of it made my fingers shake, and it was harder to draw in any air. I forced myself to consider it anyway.

Beatrice was afraid. So afraid, she'd spent these past years living in hiding, sporting vicious wounds that bolstered the rumors that she'd been attacked by an animal.

Because of Liwai Raven?

The need to find out more was like an itch I couldn't scratch, growing more irritating with every passing second. Instinctive. I needed to know—to the point that wandering the wilderness as night fell was preferable to being in the figurative dark.

Minutes later, I was back on Ridgley Mountain, following the Luna trail aided only by a cheap flashlight and desperation. In daylight, this stretch of forest was intimidating. As the sun set, it seemed downright hostile. With every step taken, the wind blew past as if whistling a bevy of insults meant for me alone.

Idiot. Go back. Go back!

I kept inching forward, alarmed as the moon climbed higher in the sky, a faint silvery crescent. In lieu of any other noise apart from nature, Renae Raven's ghost story echoed ceaselessly in my mind, taunting me with every inch gained.

He hunted down his promised woman, born to a brother of the light, and killed her—even though, in doing so, he felt as though he had slayed a part of himself...

At least part of that was a lie if Liwai was responsible for what happened to Beatrice, and the girl in Chambersburg. That's two women beyond the supposed limit allotted by the curse. The thought should have comforted me.

It didn't.

Soon, it became too dark to see my own hand in front of my face, and I reluctantly turned back, huddled inside my car with the doors locked and the windows rolled up. If I'd truly seen Beatrice, or any other figure on the mountain, they hadn't decided to stick around and make introductions.

I blamed pure exhaustion for why I cried again, but this time the tears weren't of shame or even fear. Just confusion. My brain kept replaying that moment in Liwai's trailer over and over, in increasingly explicit detail. Did I merely imagine the intensity of his touch? The hungry way his mouth rasped over mine? The pain in his voice...?

Pity was the last thing I should have felt toward him. It didn't matter if he seemed to genuinely mean his insistence that harming me was the last thing he wanted. Or how dutifully he cared for Renae. Or the fact that he had spent six-plus years working at the Ravenswood gas station without so much as a tardy slip to his name.

A man like that didn't fit the image of a vicious, remorseless killer. Cody, on the other hand? He more than fit that bill, and his age was the sole reason I didn't slot him in as the culprit in both disappearances I knew of.

When I wasn't thinking of the Raven men, I thought of Renae. The poor girl seemed so haunted, even if she was as delusional as the rest of her family seemed to be. *Stay away,* she told me. *Please. Maybe he won't…*

The endless looping thoughts didn't let up long enough for me to sleep. By the time faint rays of sunlight scratched at my windshield, I doubted I'd closed my eyes for longer than a handful of minutes at a time. After driving down the trail searching for a public restroom, I headed straight back to Luna Ridge and waited.

For what?

I had no damn idea. By being here, I was merely prolonging the inevitable, and I guess that was the point. Chasing ghosts gave me an excuse to avoid work, my nosy Aunt Deanna, and a father who'd spent my entire life lying to me.

But, with a sigh, I realized that confronting those dilemmas might give me another avenue to tread rather than wandering the wilderness.

Before I finally drove off, I fished out the last few pages of Renae's story from my pocket and stuck them to the sign with a wad of gum from my glove compartment.

Was it stupid? Yes.

Even so, I left my cell scribbled at the bottom of the page and hoped that ghosts had access to a telephone.

Four hours later, I arrived back in Kittywatt before the evening rush.

Work was the safest of my options. It was a weekday, so Deanna wasn't home by the time I snuck in through the back door and showered. Dressed in my uniform, I hustled over to Bardee's, and Mari was so swamped she didn't even mention "time off to recover from trauma" before ushering me behind the counter to help out with the evening shift.

After less than a week away, even working a typical closing shift felt foreign. It was a typical day—before seeing a certain rugged fixture every day had become typical. The regular patrons were sweet and friendly, and everyone handled me with kid gloves.

By the time I got off, my cell phone held just one sweet message from Dee telling me that she'd left food in the microwave for me and that she was a terrible cow of an aunt. Sheriff Michaels steered clear of this part of town, and all in all, I couldn't have asked for a better day to lay low.

Yet, when I reached my car, I felt an irrational, desperate, pathetic desire to go anywhere but home.

NINETEEN

I just drove, once again leaving the town boundary without so much as a panic attack.

This time, I kept it local, heading toward Settler's Point. Why? Masochism might have explained it. My throat tightened as the familiar landscape passed by, bathed in shadow. Cloud cover obscured the moon tonight, rendering everything beneath it in near pitch-blackness.

Attempting to traverse the winding, jagged roads in the daytime was a stretch. Doing so at night could be classified only as suicidal. Not far up the trail, I parked anyway and exited the car, inhaling the fresh air while trying to remember…

Something. Some minor detail to prove that all of this was merely in my head. Liwai and his family weren't wolves, just psychos. I had made up the supernatural aspect to rationalize a series of very twisted coincidences. Nothing more.

If I followed the hillside to where I'd been attacked, all I would find was dirt, gravel, and the hard truth that there was no grim conspiracy. I'd merely been rejected by a man too mysterious for his own good.

Acknowledging that brought more relief to me than believing in serial killers, at least. A genuine smile shaped my lips as I shook my head at how insane I'd been the past few days.

Of course, werewolves didn't exist.

Though wild animals *did*—especially in the woods around Kittywatt. Mainly reports of coyotes and bears, one of those creatures was certainly large enough to be responsible for the snapping branches I heard shatter the quiet nearby.

I whipped around, straining my eyes through the dark in the direction of the noise, just paces from the path.

A wild animal was big enough to make such a sound.

But not the low, unsettling laugh that echoed next.

Run! The thought ripped through my skull as I pivoted toward my car. The headlights were still on, painting a swath of light through the shadows. Plenty of light to illuminate the figure bounding toward me from the direction of the trees.

Not Liwai, a part of me sensed. There was something primal in how my body reacted to him, even from a distance. An instinctive knowledge of him.

But this figure was recognizable for another reason. His laugh and his cocky swagger brought an identity to mind even before he came close enough for me to make out his angular features and cold grin.

Cody.

"It's about time the bastard came back." He continued to advance, allowing more of himself to catch the light.

My cheeks flamed as I realized he was naked. Then any awkwardness turned to fear as I noted the dark streaks painting his skin. His teeth were bared, and his eyes were an unholy hue of amber, blazing through the darkness.

"Did he finally realize he didn't finish the job?" He laughed, the sound unsteady. Broken. "Poor little Liwai. He knows the penalty for killing one of his own kind. And let me guess? You're the bait."

Run, Kaydee…

I took a step, but he was already crossing the space between me and my car. I'd have to run to reach it, but one look at him warned me that an escape route was the least of my worries.

My mama used to say that some people had bad energy. Like Jeb, the creepy mailman who got arrested for child pornography in my junior year of high school. They gave off an aura that wasn't right, translating to goosebumps and unpleasant feelings.

Or, in the case of Cody, downright terror. It was as if my conscience had split in two. One sounded like the familiar inner voice I'd been subjected to my whole life. Like me. This newer murmur resonating through my brain sounded different and yet eerily familiar. Like Liwai Raven.

Run, he said. *Don't talk to him. Don't let him get closer. Scream and run.*

My lips parted, but only a breathless gasp came out as I took off down the path.

Don't go far, that disembodied voice warned. *Turn around. Now!*

I did, only to find that my car was still in view, but Cody wasn't.

Because wolves prefer to hunt from the shadows. I must have read that once, and only now did that particular fact choose to resurface, along with another mental warning.

Get into your car and drive. Now!

With every step I took, a million more seemed to echo in my wake. Then another sound pierced the quiet far louder than my panting breaths.

A growl.

Panicked, I grabbed for the door handle, but before my fingers could make purchase, a force slammed into me from behind, throwing me forward.

Pain shot up my spine as I hit the ground on my knees, feeling my left shoulder glance off the car door. A flicker of movement drew my attention to my right, but it was already too late.

A hand fisted through my hair, using the grip as leverage to wrench me back.

"I know he's out there," Cody snarled. He must have been behind me, heading ruthlessly off the trail and deeper within the tree cover.

My heart dropped, and for a second, I was trapped in that horrific sensation of trying to scream but hearing nothing come out. Just air.

In the resulting silence, that familiar inner voice returned, more guttural than ever.

Don't let him drag you far. Fight!

All I could do was lift one of my arms and fling it back, striking what felt like a solid thigh. Another chilling laugh ran down my spine in response.

"Where is he?" he demanded. "I know he couldn't have gone far. Where?"

A vicious tug on my hair flung me onto my back. Blinking, I stared into a pair of searing, orange eyes and blindingly white teeth.

I jerked, kicking out with both feet. One connected, giving me the leverage to roll onto my side and scramble upright.

Mocking laughter echoed after me. The teasing, manic cadence of someone fully enjoying a fun game. Sadistic.

Don't worry about that, Liwai's voice warned. *Your life is the only thing that matters. Just move. Get away from him!*

I tried to run, lunging between two close-set trees.

The laughter fell silent. In its place, heavy footsteps rang out. Then harsh breathing, edged by a low, unsettling tone.

There wasn't time to think or plan. The only course of action seemed to be the obvious one—scream. This time my cries rang out in startling clarity, but I knew deep down there was no one around this late.

No one would be stupid enough to attempt climbing this ridge in the dark.

Just me.

I tripped over a stray root just as the road came into view. My car still idled, headlights blaring.

But I wouldn't be fast enough.

For a second, it was as if someone else had taken control of my body, making me plunge my hand into the pocket of my jeans. I'd nearly forgotten about buying the small switchblade earlier. It fit my palm perfectly as I withdrew it and braced for the inevitable.

"What did he tell you?" Cody called after me. He sounded mere paces away, but I didn't have the heart to look back. "That he'd always protect you? Shun the pack? Leave it all behind? They tell you dumb bitches that the first few times. Makes it easier to gain your trust. That way, what happens next can't be traced back to us."

His cold tone tugged at some desperate part of me that just wanted answers. Even if I had to beg a monster for them.

"Why?" I croaked, adjusting my grip on the blade to keep it hidden in my fist. At the same time, I inched a few steps closer to my car, but I turned so that he was in my view, standing boldly amid the brambles, his eyes gleaming. "Why me—"

"Because you're damned like the rest of us," he spat. "That's why. Where is he? It isn't like him to make a dramatic entrance. Liwai!" He raised his voice, shouting across the hill. "Come out, come out, and play!"

"How many others?" I asked, latching onto that tidbit of information. Beatrice and the Chambersburg girl made three, including me.

"Hundreds," Cody said, though his attention was focused on the swaying branches around us and the figure he seemed to think lurked among them. "And there will be hundreds more. When I find my Luna, I won't hesitate."

He advanced a step, and I scrambled back two more, tightening my grip on the knife.

And yet, that strange, itching impulse wouldn't let me shut up. I needed to know more.

"What happens after?" I choked out. "When you... Do you get a prize or something?"

He scoffed at the phrasing and whipped his attention back to me. "We go home, where we belong. With the pack. With our own kind. Liwai's been out the longest, and all this time, they thought the bastard just got lucky. It skipped a generation or some shit. All along, he's been taking us for a fucking ride."

He came closer, his eyes narrowed, and I felt my pulse surge like mad, hammering through my chest.

"I won't do his dirty work, though," Cody added. "By the time he finds you, he'll have no choice but to put you out of your misery—"

Kaydence, now!

With Cody mid-word, I turned on my heel and sprinted for my car. I doubted I'd ever run so fast in my life. My lungs burned as my legs pounded the earth to drive me several feet in mere seconds.

Even so, I just wasn't fast enough.

"No, I don't think so!"

A hand slammed into my shoulder, shoving me forward. Bang! The world went dark for a second. As my vision returned, a faint ringing resonated through my eardrums.

"He healed you, didn't he?" Cody said, his breath on my shoulder. "Well, let's see him heal this—"

A growl swallowed the words as his weight pinned me to the ground. It was as if he'd grown ten times as large in a heartbeat. Massive. Furry...

Kaydence, run! That voice echoed weakly inside my head as I saw a dark shape come for my skull. Fire. I tasted blood as flames lanced at my left cheek.

Ignoring the agony, I lashed out with the switchblade and used every ounce of strength I had left to lurch forward and grasp the handle of my car door.

Somehow, I managed to open it and climb onto the seat. In a panicked rush, I locked the doors, put the gear out of park, and slammed on the gas.

A tiny papercut wouldn't hold Cody for long. Especially if he managed to survive his fight with Liwai in the first place. There went my "they're only human" theory.

God, there was no place to outrun something like that. I couldn't go home and bring a wolf to Deanna's doorstep. Sheriff Michaels couldn't help me.

So, I just drove, only partly surprised—as I regained my senses—to find that I'd passed an exit for Chambersburg.

Cody's "answers" had only left me more confused than before. Loneliness wasn't something I felt often—not physically, anyway. Mentally, on the other hand, there were days when I felt like the only soul desperate to leave Kittywatt but with no way out.

I'd been selfish then. Being alone meant having the open road at your disposal but no one to run to. No safe harbor. No clarity.

Just a bunch of goddamn rumors and literal ghosts to chase.

And the man who plunged me into this chaos was nowhere to be seen. He'd left. Did he know Cody was still out there? I wanted to believe that he didn't. Even Renae seemed to think the worst. They should have called the police to be sure, not that the Ravens seemed to be fond of law enforcement.

Which, in all honesty, should have been the first place I'd head to. The Kittywatt P.D. Every ounce of common sense I had should have been warning me to turn back.

Not…

Wait. Kaydence, wait. Slow down. WAIT FOR ME!

"No!" I was being irrational by imagining the voice of my stalker in my head, let alone responding to him. Still, I felt the need to, if only to keep myself from slamming on the brake in the middle of the highway. Waiting…

"I don't need anyone but myself," I said out loud. "I don't need the Sheriff, and I certainly don't need Liwai Raven. I just need…"

To think. To have someone tell me that I wasn't insane and give me the answers I so desperately needed. Someone who wouldn't run without giving me what I craved so badly I felt the urge to scream. I just wanted to talk.

But as I finally stopped my car, I found myself in silence again, alone at the base of yet another jagged mountain. This one was far larger than the range outside of Kittywatt, and as dawn breached the horizon, I realized that I wasn't alone after all.

TWENTY

She stood by the comically decorated sign. Dressed in gray, she resembled a specter in comparison, with her straw hat the only vibrant part of her against the dark backdrop of the forest. At a glance, I noticed the paper I'd left behind was gone, but the woman held nothing in her hands. She merely inclined her head as I rolled my window down and tried to come up with something to say.

"You look like you could use a cup of tea," she said, beating me to the punch. "Follow me in your car. My place isn't far. But just know…" She seemed to stop herself from saying more and shook her head instead. "Come on. I'm surprised you made it out here with a wound like that. You could have a concussion."

Her quiet observation made me glance in the mirror, and my heart nearly stopped.

"Oh my God."

The left side of my face was covered in dried blood. It was a miracle I'd driven this far, and no passerby had thought to call the police. A nasty gash was the source of the liquid, slicing down my forehead vertically, nearly down to my jaw.

It looked bad. Real bad.

"It seems superficial. You won't scar," the woman called, as if reading my mind. "But you should get some rest."

The longer I looked at myself in the mirror, the more I realized her warning might have been prescient. I felt dizzy. My stomach lurched, and a concussion seemed the least of my worries.

I felt liable to pass out.

Pain wasn't the source of it. Just… Fear. An overwhelming, consuming, suffocating fear. Not of Cody, but of the increasingly persistent voice in my head.

Kaydence! Where are you? Kaydence!

"Come."

Something in her tone goaded me forward. Slowly I drove behind her in my car, following her down the path and around a bend. With every passing moment, the shouting in my head intensified.

Kaydence.

KAYDENCE.

WHERE ARE YOU—

All at once, my thoughts went mercifully quiet. It was as if a switch had been flipped as I got closer to her home, silencing everything but my own tired observations. There, safely tucked within a swath of trees, was a small, homey cabin with a bicycle propped against a bright-yellow fence.

"Come in," the woman said. "I'll try to find you something to wear. Don't mind the mess."

I exited the car on trembling legs and waited as I got my bearings.

"Come inside." The woman stood in the doorway. In her arms was a bundle of cloth I assumed was clothing. Just how long had I stood here, clinging to my car door?

"Come. I think you'll feel better once you sit down."

Belatedly, I realized that I'd entered a narrow hallway, and the strange woman was beckoning me into a brightly decorated living room.

Every color that ever existed had to be represented in the modest, but beautifully crafted décor. There were beaded pillows in rainbow hues, and the couch seemed hand-painted with matching polka dots.

It was an overwhelming visual assault, yet at the same time, there was something undeniably homey about the neat, clean interior.

"Have a seat," the woman said, though I'd already collapsed onto the surprisingly comfortable couch. "I'll make you some tea."

She removed her hat and propped it on a hook near a doorway that I presumed led into the kitchen. As she stood there, bathed in the glow of dawn, the familiarity of her soft blue eyes struck a resemblance that was undeniable.

"You're Beatrice Michaels," I said, but this time I was sure of it.

She didn't react to the accusation other than to enter the kitchen with her back to me. Still, her voice reached me a second later, no sign of alarm concealed within the gentle tones. "And you… I'm afraid I don't know who you are or who you could possibly be."

She must have already had the kettle boiling because she reentered the room with two steaming mugs , not even a second later. One was a brilliant blue that she set on the coffee table within my reach, keeping a yellow mug for herself.

"And I don't mean that lightly," she added, frowning. She pursed her lips as if weighing a question on her mind. With a sigh, she seemed to settle on a course of action that had her crossing the room to a small bookcase filled to bursting with plastic binders. "You see, I've had every paper from every surrounding county, every day for the past… twenty or so years, I think. Every birth. Every death. Every graduating student. Everyone who attended the town bake sales. Countless names."

"I don't understand," I said, my voice rasping. "I've lived in Kittywatt all my life."

"Kittywatt, ah!" The woman nodded. "That should have been a likely area for one of us to appear. But, in all my studies, I have never come across someone your age who fits the required criteria. You seem twenty…twenty-three at the most, I presume?"

"Twenty-two," I admitted. "Why does that matter?"

Beatrice raised an eyebrow, but only the uninjured side of her face displayed any emotion. "Because, my dear, you yourself had the list of names. I'm sure you understand exactly what I mean."

Apparently, she'd found Renae's story, after all, only she found far more substance in the names scribbled at the bottom than I wanted to believe.

"James, Brown, Williams, Michaels, Cavanaugh, etcetera. Etcetera. None of those families have born a girl who could be your age. There are other cells, of course, throughout the country, but I can't imagine why you'd come all the way out here to find me."

"What… Are we?" I could barely get the words out.

Beatrice sighed and took a seat on a painted chaise across from me. For several seconds, she stared into her tea. Finally, she raised her head and met my gaze directly. "We are plain, simple human women—that's what we are. We haven't done anything to anyone. Let me get you cleaned up." She stood and retreated down a hallway. This time she returned with a damp washrag, and she brought the pile of clothing closer to me. "The bathroom is down the hall," she prompted with a nod in that direction.

I obeyed, squeezing into the minuscule space painted a bright shade of light blue. I couldn't even bring myself to look in the mirror—so I didn't and got dressed while eyeing the floor.

Beatrice was roughly my size. The brown sweater and yellow sun dress resembled what must have been her chosen style. The garments seemed worn but meticulously cared for, with several neat rows of stitching in varying colors of thread denoting where she'd patched up holes over the years.

Wearing them, I felt… Safe and warm, a feeling that had eluded me these past few days. I couldn't resist sniffing the end of one sleeve and sensed a calming scent of lavender.

Belatedly, I realized I should clean off my face before potentially staining the borrowed clothing. In the end, I just used a rag and dragged it over my forehead until it came away clean.

When I returned to Beatrice, she was still seated on the chair, but a pile of open binders surrounded her, forming an impenetrable fortress of old newspaper clippings and handwritten note pages.

"What is your name, sweetheart?" she asked without looking up. I noted that her nails were also painted, each a different color, and they sparkled as she absently tucked a strand of long brown hair behind her ear.

"Kaydence Blanchett," I said while sitting on the couch.

Her head shot up, and confusion flitted across her expression. "Blanchett? But… That name isn't on the list. I don't understand. Why look for me if you aren't—"

"My name isn't on that list, because I spent my entire life believing my father was someone else," I admitted. A yawn, of all things, escaped me next. It was as if everything I'd experienced over the past week decided to hit at full force. My eyelids fluttered, and keeping them open was a struggle and a half. Still, part of the exhaustion might have been chalked up to plain old relief. It felt good to finally say the truth out loud to someone who'd listen. "I think my real father might be Sheriff Burt Michaels."

I watched her carefully, noting every nuance of her reaction. Surprisingly, shock wasn't all I found. Just an all-encompassing sadness that sucked the joy and color from the room.

"Oh… Oh, honey." Her delicate voice broke into a sob, and she slumped forward, face in her hands. "I didn't want this to happen. Oh, sweetheart. Your mother was supposed to take you far, far away from here. I thought… I guess I'd been wrong. Oh, God."

It was as if someone had dumped ice water over my head. All traces of exhaustion vanished, and I sat forward, as alert as if I'd been electrocuted. "You knew?"

That hoarse question contained so many unspoken ones. You knew my mother. You knew about me. You knew about this curse?

Renae Raven wasn't an overly-imaginative girl, after all.

"Yes," Beatrice said, eyeing me through gaps in her trembling fingers. "I knew that Burtie's girlfriend at the time—Marie, I think her name was. I didn't know her last name. I knew she had a little girl who might have been his, so I told her… Oh, goodness, the things I told her. I knew she wouldn't believe the truth, so I made up a horrible lie. I wanted to scare her so badly that no one would ever know that you could possibly be a Michaels. I thought that alone would be enough." She shook her head and buried her face in both hands while my mind conjured up several horror stories she could have told my mother. Surprisingly, I already knew the gist of a few potential options—that he was a dangerous drunk, from a family of drunks, and sooner or later, he'd drink himself to death.

Beatrice didn't reveal the full story, however. She just sighed again and shrugged. "I thought I'd never forgive myself for hurting him, but I thought it was for the best. Poor Burtie…"

"He doesn't know?" I asked, picking that one detail, among the many more volatile ones, to focus on.

"No. Not a thing. Not even that I'm still alive…" Beatrice lowered her hands and sat upright. The unscarred side of her face was contorted in agony, while the other side remained eerily still. "He can't know—no one can. It was the only way. The only way to keep them safe."

"From what?" My heartbeat stuttered even before she finally met my stare head-on.

When she finally spoke, her voice was distant. "The truth. When I was fifteen, a man came to me," she said. "He was more beautiful than anyone or anything I'd ever seen. Flawless. He was older than I was—uncomfortably older, but… Talking to him was like talking to a part of myself I never knew existed before."

She sat back, and her face transformed. A shadow of the girl she used to be appeared for an instant before overwhelming sadness banished her again.

"I think I fell in love with him instantly that very day. There was no choice. Do you understand that, Kaydence?" She held my gaze with an intensity that took my breath away and made the little hairs on the back of my neck stand on end. "No choice. No rhyme or reason. I saw him, and the entire world ceased to matter if he wasn't in it. Do you understand that feeling?"

No. I wanted to deny ever feeling such a strange concept. Shake my head. What she described was nowhere near the confusing mixture of curiosity and alarm I felt toward Liwai Raven. In the end, I couldn't do either.

Some part of me reacted to her words and ignited. She was right, able to adequately describe the feeling haunting me since the very day I saw him at the gas station years ago.

"It isn't natural," Beatrice went on. "I need you to understand that. It isn't natural, and it isn't right. We have no say, and it's wrong. It's not fair. It's…!" She threw her hands up in exasperation and stood. Rapidly, she began to pace, and her dark hair flew out behind her with every step, forming a tangible shadow that morphed with her movements. "It's a curse. I knew it from that very moment, and I believed everything he's told me ever since. The beautiful man I met that day was both my savior and my doom. To his credit, he didn't encourage me," she said, frowning. "He never once tried to indulge in the attraction I knew we both felt. That very day he told me the truth, and I cannot fault him for that. Despite all the pain that came later..." She brought her hand to the ruined side of her face, cradling the damaged cheek. "He never once lied to me. He told me then and there what he was. What I am. Why he..."

An uncomfortable feeling of déjà vu washed over me. I think I already knew exactly what she'd stopped herself from saying. Still, I needed to hear it voiced by someone other than Liwai Raven or me. "What did he say?"

She stopped short, and her hands fell weakly to her sides. "He said that he needed to kill me. For the good of his people and for mine. Because if he didn't, they would come and rip the entire town apart in retribution."

TWENTY-ONE

I didn't make a sound. Didn't gasp or scream in horror. Bravery wasn't the reason. Internally I was too lost for her statement to resonate much.

The words merely served as a hammer on the nail of what my subconscious was already wrestling with. Of course, there had to be more to it. More than a silly curse or a legend penned by a fourteen-year-old girl. A risk surmountable enough that Liwai felt the need to attack Cody and then run to prevent it.

"They've carried out the practice for centuries," Beatrice said. Her soft voice was a gently ruthless backdrop to the chaos of my thoughts. "Countless women. Countless years. All in the same territory throughout the ages. I think they believe they must, though Jerome never explained it to me in full—"

"Jerome," I echoed, eyeing her more closely. It wasn't the name itself that caught my attention but how she said it.

Softly, uttered with both reverence and aversion. "Was that...*his* name?"

She nodded and began to pace again, averting her gaze from mine. "Believe it or not, there is some predictability to it. Always a girl from one of the families, at an age past puberty. Her counterpart is usually older, already lying in wait for her to come of age. I think it has something to do with hormones. When he comes of age, it triggers a change in her that doesn't take effect until she does as well... They need to act then, you see. The moment they sense she's reached puberty. Any longer, and it becomes harder. The bond is too strong, and they can no longer resist..."

She trailed off and spun to face me. Her eyes were saucer wide, and I couldn't stop myself from self-consciously swiping at my face, afraid I'd missed a spot of blood.

"How old are you, dear? Twenty-two, you said?"

"Yes."

"Oh, dear." She sank onto the chaise and stared blankly at the wall. I could almost hear the gears in her brain turning. It was a familiar scene, only I'd never witnessed it from the outside before. I assume this was how I looked when I went off on one of my tangents, and Dee would always tease me that it was like I'd left my body for a moment to rummage through some mental library.

"Twenty-two. Far too old. Far, far too old. He should have been able to find you the second you reached puberty. Fifteen, sixteen, seventeen at most—"

"Why does that matter?" I croaked, stunned by the prospect. At sixteen years old, I'd been reeling from my mother's death. How much more complicated would my life have been if some stranger came out of the woodwork, professing a need to kill me? "Either way, he wants to kill me, so I doubt the age matters much."

"Oh, yes, it does," Beatrice insisted. Then she cocked her head, an eyebrow raised. "Tell me something… You hear him, don't you? In your head, almost like a faint voice speaking. You might ignore it at first. Write it off as a trick of your imagination."

I could barely speak. "I don't understand… That sounds insane."

"You have," Beatrice surmised, an eyebrow raised. "You'll be able to feel him, too. An instinctive drive. It's kept you near him always, even when you wanted to leave. Even when you needed to. You couldn't, and you didn't know why, but it was him."

"You're scaring me." The picture she painted didn't, surprisingly—but the genuine honesty in her voice. This insanity she described… She believed every last word of it.

That scared me.

"He can feel you too, you know. Everything…" She captured her right wrist with her left hand and ran a finger along the width of it. "He will know you better than you know yourself. He's had over five years to adjust to you. Five years of your thoughts and emotions—"

"That's insane," I retorted. Though, the concept—as strange as it was—didn't horrify me. No... But the thought that someone could know me so intimately and still leave me so woefully in the dark...?

That made my throat constrict and my eyes well up.

"I don't care about him," I managed to rasp. "I just need to know how to make it stop. Whatever this is, I want it to go away."

"You can't." Beatrice didn't sound exasperated or even amused by my obstinance. Just matter-of-fact. The sky is blue. Liwai Raven will always have some weird vendetta against me. The world will continue to go around.

"He can't ignore it either," she went on. Her eyes flitted to my forehead with renewed interest. "Did he... Was that him?"

I winced as the scratch decided to throb at full force. "No. He didn't hurt me."

If anything, he'd gone out of his way to do the opposite. He brought me back after I was shot—a feat that I was beginning to realize may have had more significance than him being a concerned Samaritan.

Not that his motives mattered one damn bit. Liwai Raven had thrown my life into turmoil. He wasn't the one who required sympathy.

"Either way, no one will be able to harm you here." Beatrice sent a wary glance at the window. "For reasons I won't explain right now. Just know that you are safe. I think you should get some sleep."

A refusal was on my lips, but I never managed to voice it. This woman, despite her apparent relation to me, was also a stranger. I should have been focused on going home and checking in with Dee or something...

As it turned out, my body had other plans. My eyes were closed before I even finished processing the many, many reasons why sleeping was a bad idea.

And I barely heard the front door open, and shut.

TWENTY-TWO

My head was throbbing. Forming a coherent thought at all took considerable effort, but my first true recollection was that it was dark.

I could only see a few inches in front of me—courtesy of a stream of moonlight drifting in through the nearby window. Blinking, I let my eyes adjust, too comfortable to move.

I was on a couch. Someone had draped a woolen blanket over me, and I huddled beneath its warmth against the overall chill in the room. I think I might have drifted back to sleep if it weren't for the shouting.

"Bringing an outsider through the boundary. Showing your face? What the hell were you thinking?" The voice was male —guttural enough to have me lurching upright before I fully got my bearings.

I stumbled off the couch, swaying on my feet as the world pitched unsteadily beneath me. The window drew my notice—there, bathed in the silvery glow of moonlight, stood two figures. One towered over the other, presumably the source of the deeper voice.

Whoever he was, he seemed agitated, pacing back and forth with his hands gesturing wildly in the air. "I've warned you to lay low. Keep your head down. If anyone catches wind of you—"

"She's my niece," a woman murmured. Beatrice? "I could sense it even before she told me. Somehow... I knew she needed help. What else was I supposed to do?"

"How did she even find you? Were you in the town—"

"No, I wasn't." While soft, I couldn't sense any fear in her voice. Just a quiet, stubborn determination. "I don't know how. But I think you didn't understand exactly what I just said. Jerome, she is my *niece,* born of Michaels' blood."

The man slowed to a stop, his back facing my direction. "They found her," he said, raking a hand through his dark hair. "Damn it, Bea—"

"Don't Bea, me," Beatrice snapped, crossing her arms. Her hair was unbound, but she somehow seemed intimidating, even in the shadow of someone so much larger. "They found her, but something is wrong. She's over twenty years old. She claims he didn't hurt her, but she's been attacked. It will take me days to get the blood out of my couch."

"Damn it... Did they follow her here?" Jerome asked, his concern evident. "Bea, do you know what they will do to you if they find you?"

"Maybe they'll see the error in their ways," she retorted wryly. "I've been here all this time, and you were still able to return and marry and create plenty of children of your kind. The only life destroyed in the end, was mine. A fair trade—"

"Beatrice..." The man sighed and raked a hand through his hair. It was a shade dark enough to stand out in stark contrast to the shadowy forest behind him. "I didn't come here for a fight."

"No," she agreed. "You came here because I asked you to, and this time, you couldn't refuse. Can you help her?"

"I don't know how. I can't exactly reveal what happened with you, now can I?"

"You could reach out to the boy," Beatrice insisted. "See if you can see what his intentions are. What he's planning to do. Maybe... Maybe he is like you—"

"Did she give you a name?" Jerome asked.

"No. But he would have to have been gone a while, given her age."

"I don't... Wait. There is someone..." Jerome sighed again and faced Beatrice directly. "But if it is him... Damn it, then there is no way out."

"Who?"

"Liwai Raven has been out the longest of anyone in the area. Some thought it odd, but the records always backed him up. There seemed to be no one else who fit the criteria.

Now, if I were to come clean, the consequences would rock the pack to its core. The damage would be long-lasting and would extend generations. But Liwai? If he turned his back on our ways, there would be no pack to salvage. They wouldn't overlook it. They couldn't, not with his family name on the line. His brother is Bartow's heir. That makes him next in the order of succession. Should Liwai falter, the entire council would venture here themselves to ensure he carried it out."

"Why?" Beatrice asked, voicing the same question I had.

"Because Liwai is a Raven. A direct descendant of our founding ancestor. His brother is the future leader of the pack. No way in hell would they let him revolt against the binding tradition."

"You did," Beatrice said. "Perhaps he could leave her here with me and spend the next few decades living a lie, creating children with a woman he doesn't love and pretending to uphold the very tradition he couldn't uphold himself."

Jerome seemed to flinch. "Bea..."

"But if you *were* to suggest such a thing, I would tell her what I wish someone would have told me. To run. To throw herself into the nearest lake and never look back. Death is far better than being forced to live a lie."

For a moment, the two said nothing, but a mournful tension filled the air, thick and inescapable. Finally, Beatrice gestured toward the house.

"She'll be waking up soon. You should go."

"Take this," Jerome said, extending his hand. "It isn't much, but I can arrange for a new couch."

"Good. I'll use it to buy more flowers. I could use more color out here. Anything to break up the monotony of endless green." Her tone was so cutting that even I winced.

"Bea—"

"Goodbye. Thank you for the money."

Both figures wandered out of view, each heading in a different direction. A second later, the front door to the cabin opened, and Beatrice hurried inside.

Bathed in shadow, I couldn't tell from her expression alone if she was surprised to find me awake or not. All she did was shuffle into the kitchen, and a rush of running water made me suspect she was in the process of refilling her kettle.

"You heard that?" she asked, her back to me.

"That was Jerome," I said, avoiding the question. "How? I don't understand—"

"He didn't kill me," she explained while setting the kettle on the stove. "He tried to, of course. In the end, he couldn't, so we concocted a lie to fool his clan and my own family while he hid me here in these woods. For so long, I lived that lie. Sometimes I even fool myself into thinking it was told for my benefit. Most days, though, I can face the truth."

She turned to me and wiped her hands on the skirt of her gray dress.

"The day I agreed to live here was the day I died in spirit, if not in body. The woman you see before you now? She is a ghost. A specter of lost dreams and unfulfilled fantasies. It isn't Jerome's fault either," she added with a wistful sigh. "I can feel his pain. It's no easier for him, and yet that somehow makes it worse. There isn't a day that goes by when I don't crave a change. A break from this relentless, shadowed existence. I tried once—" She held up her left wrist, and in the dim lighting, a silvery scar stood out prominently. It was slender, evoking a chilling meaning behind it. "He stopped me. He will always stop me."

She advanced and placed her slender hands on my shoulders.

"If you want my advice, Kaydence, it is this—go home. Live your life, and don't let anyone distract you from it. The things you love. Your hobbies. Enjoy them. Cherish them. His choice is his choice. You have no say in it, but you didn't choose him either. Go home. Give my brother all my love, though I know I don't have to explain why he can't know where I am. But Kaydence? If you change your mind, I am here. He can't touch you while you are on my land, and I know enough about his kind to keep you safe. What they fear, anyway. Come back if you ever need help, and I will do what I can."

She returned to the kitchen without another word, but not long after, the kettle began to whistle.

And the sound echoed like a chilling, foreboding scream, warning me of what was to come.

TWENTY-THREE

I made it to my car before the waterworks began anew. The tears fell in a torrent, far too fierce to stop. All I could do was breathe through the onslaught and try to refocus my thoughts.

On the one hand, I'd gotten the answers I'd been begging for. On the other…

Everything was more of a mess than it had been the moment I stared up at Liwai Raven with a supposed bullet hole in my stomach.

Him wanting to kill me hadn't been a mere figure of speech. According to whatever twisted rules his family lived by, he *had* to. Otherwise, my future consisted of lurking in the shadows, dead to everyone in my life who mattered.

Always at his whim.

But he wasn't here now. I told myself that over and over as I choked back the remaining sobs and wiped my eyes. Liwai Raven and his issues were his issues to deal with. Not mine.

I needed to go home, talk to Dee. Talk to Sheriff Michaels, even. I needed to assess my life without a psychopath waiting in the wings.

And, God, I needed to sleep. For real, in my own bed without fear of wolves weighing on my mind.

With that hope as my focus, I started my car and faced the windshield—only to spy Beatrice watching from the doorway of her cabin. She lifted one hand in a simple wave, but I didn't have the heart to return the gesture.

Only an hour into my drive to Kittywatt did I have the sense of mind to call Dee and check-in. My phone was off. I turned it on and threw it onto the passenger's seat as it booted up.

Not even a heartbeat later, the thing exploded with a near-constant stream of pings and nearly vibrated off the seat. Deanna must have been worried, but she usually wasn't the type to panic if I didn't come home on time.

Warily, I pulled over and scanned the first few messages.

Kaydee, where are you?

Kaydee, please call me back.

KAYDEE, EARTH TO KAYDEE.

I'm getting worried, kiddo.

There were ten more messages following along those same lines, until, finally, she simply wrote:

Liwai Raven is here.

Oh, God. The color drained from my face. A million different reasons for such a message darted through my mind all at once. It could have been a trick utilized by Deanna as a means to make me respond faster.

But, though Dee was many things, she wasn't a liar and wasn't prone to reckless stunts either.

The other possibilities, however, made my heart sink. Frantic, I scrambled to call her directly.

"It's about damn time, Kaydence Marie," Dee snapped the second she picked up. "Do you have any idea how worried I've been? Blowing in and out of town like a goddamn twister. Not bothering to say hello. And to top it off, you have strange men corner me in my own damn kitchen demanding your whereabouts as if you're in danger or something—"

"Dee…" I couldn't breathe, paralyzed by the thought that Liwai would use her to get to me. "Is he still there?"

"No," she said, oblivious to my audible sigh of relief. "He left about an hour ago, like a bat out of hell."

"Did he hurt you?"

She paused, and I gripped the steering wheel with my free hand, prepared to drive like hell to reach her if he'd so much as laid a hand on her.

"Not unless you count proving how horrible a hostess I am as hurting me," she quipped. "He asked where you were, cut the grass while he waited. He even made me coffee this morning. He's polite, if a bit obsessive, Kaydee. I think I approve, though he seemed upset, like you two had a fight or something—"

"Dee, lock the doors."

"What are you talking about?"

"Lock the doors!" I shouted, slamming my hand on the steering wheel for emphasis. "Now, and if he comes back, you don't let him in no matter what. You wait for me, okay? Or you call Sheriff Michaels."

"Okay, Kaydee, but I didn't think it was a big deal. Besides, I thought you'd called him first, given the way he ran off…"

Called him first. Left an hour ago.

Vaguely, I remembered what Beatrice had said as the phone slipped from my grasp and the call disconnected. *No one can find you here.*

But I wasn't on her property anymore…

And as if the thought were his cue to appear, a lone figure stepped from the trees bordering the side of the road.

"We need to talk." His voice was deep enough to penetrate the car's interior even with the windows rolled up—but that wasn't why I heard him so clearly.

Each word resonated inside my head as if spoken there, only for me to hear.

"No." My foot twitched over the gas, revving the engine as it remained in park. "I'm leaving."

"Just hear me out."

His voice was so darn insistent, creeping into my skull and going to war with my common sense. *Listen to him,* a part of me whispered. *Hear him out.*

"No!" I grabbed the gear shift, intending to put my car into drive instead.

I never even saw him move.

The next second, he was at my door, his hand on the handle. "Let me in."

"So, you want to add kidnapping to your impending charge of attempted murder?" I croaked. "Was that your plan all along? Let your friend Cody do your dirty work?"

His eyes flashed, and I broke off mid-word. I couldn't help it. The entire world seemed to dim in the wake of his frown, as if even the wind held its breath. At the mere mention of Cody's name, something changed in him, glinting at the back of those fathomlessly dark eyes. Something primal.

And Renae's legend held more substance. Mainly the part mentioning wolves.

"He hurt you." He seemed to notice my forehead for the first time, and he tugged on the door so hard the entire vehicle rocked in protest. "Let me in. What happened?"

"No…" My refusal was decidedly softer. His concern threw me off. His voice dipped a few octaves. He sounded…serious. Worried. For me?

I doubted he felt such sentiments toward Cody.

"Of course, I'm worried about you—" He broke off, hissing through his teeth. In a lower tone, he tried again. "You wanted to talk? Well, I'm here. Are you willing to listen or not?"

I was still reeling over the fact that he seemed to finish a thought right out of my own head. Maybe I was being paranoid. To distract from the suspicion, I risked taking my eyes off his face to scan the rest of him.

He didn't look too worse for wear despite being virtually on the run for the past few days with Renae. His hair was slicked back into a low ponytail, and his black shirt and jeans looked clean enough. He hadn't suffered. He hadn't spent every damn night tossing and turning in the midst of nightmares, or run himself ragged chasing down leads in the hopes of finding someone—anyone—to give him answers about the mess his life had become.

"I'm leaving." I wrenched the gear shift into drive and moved to slam my foot on the gas.

"You don't really want to know why?"

Don't listen, a part of me warned. *No. Don't. Stop!*

Regardless, my foot stilled inches from the gas pedal.

"Why you've stayed in that town despite wanting nothing more than to leave? Why you've felt so lost in your own damn skin. Why… Why I know everything about you. Everything."

I forced out a scoff even as I panicked internally. He was lying—and Beatrice had exaggerated. No one could read minds, sense feelings, or whatever nonsense he claimed. Right?

"Nice try—"

"You're skeptical. Intelligent. You won't believe me if I don't give specifics, so I don't have a choice. Your last name is hyphenated," he said before I could argue. "Blanchett-Dewitt, but you go by your mother's maiden name only. You don't hate the man you thought was your father, but you don't trust him. When he left, you took it as him turning his back on you, so you turned your back on him. You don't trust easily. In fact, you don't trust anyone at all. It's why you have few friends outside of your family or work. Your isolative nature isn't my fault—but you can blame me if you want."

I blinked. Then I somehow managed to choke out, "So what? You're an expert in daddy issues? That doesn't mean anything—"

"You've always wanted to be a writer," he continued, stepping back from the car, his hands in the air. "Always. From the moment you first held a pen and realized what words could be used to convey. Even though you sucked at grammar. You applied to every college within a hundred-mile radius and hoped you'd get accepted into the one that was the furthest away. And you did. Then you packed up your car and couldn't even make it past the town boundary. Do you want to know why?"

God help me, the answer was obvious—I was a coward, too chicken to take her chances outside of the safe harbor of her hometown. But for the past two days, I'd known that explanation didn't fly.

Since childhood, when I watched my supposed dad take off for the city, I'd craved more than anything to leave Kittywatt. As it turned out, the only time I ever could was on a wild goose chase concerning the subject of the murderous Ravens. Beatrice herself had alluded to it. "*I tried to find a way out. He stopped me. He will always stop me...*"

"I knew if you left, I'd follow you," Liwai said. He lowered his hands to his sides, his expression so grave that I shivered. "Maybe because of the curse. Maybe because... It doesn't matter. I would leave behind Renae and the others—I wouldn't think twice. I would follow you, and by doing so, I would only put your life in danger."

He fell silent, almost as if daring me to roll down the window to hear him better. With my ears as well as inside my head.

No, a part of me warned. *Don't...*

Even fear wasn't strong enough to banish whatever impulse I felt. My hand flew out for the console before I could stop myself, and I struck the button to lower my window a fraction of an inch.

"You don't understand the hell I've been in for seven damn years," he said, advancing a step. The wind fanned out his ponytail, highlighting the sharp planes of his face and the beauty one wouldn't expect to find in someone like him. A monster. A would-be murderer. A liar.

He still had the power to compel me to listen, no matter how insane the words coming out of his mouth were.

"I've watched you," he said, his tone gruff. "Learned you. Thought about the many ways I would have to hurt you. I would *always* have to hurt you—there was no other option —I need you to understand that."

I reached for the console again, sending my window up.

"Until that night," he went on, undeterred. "I knew then I couldn't watch you die—and not just because of the bond."

I held my breath, unsure of how to interpret the raw pain in his voice. It hurt him to admit that to me, but why?

"Then what?" I asked.

He shook his head. "It doesn't matter. The point is, I couldn't watch you suffer. Not then. Not now. My cowardice puts you in more danger than you realize. Give me a chance to explain."

"Why?" I countered, though I didn't have the heart to voice the arguments racing through my mind. So, he could leave me again with no warning? So, he could hide me away like Beatrice?

He shouldn't have heard that last thought—he couldn't. Nonetheless, his eyes widened and narrowed as if he'd processed something new.

"Kaydence, you can't outrun me." His inflection dipped to a dangerous octave, and a shudder ran down my spine. "It's taking everything I have in me not to rip the door off your car and drag you out. You know I'm capable of it. Don't you?"

And somehow… I did. An image filled my mind of him doing just that—and how easy it would be for him—but I didn't put it there. It wasn't *mine*.

"When you're in pain, I can feel it," he added, coming closer. His hands flexed in and out of fists, and for the first time, I noticed just how large they were. Massive, sufficiently capable of ripping both my car *and* me apart. "I feel it now. You're hurting, and I'm sorry for that. You're scared. It's driving me fucking crazy, so I'm asking you… Begging you. Let me in."

I had every right to run. To drive off even if I had to run over him. This man didn't own me. He had no right to dictate my life in any way.

"I know you're angry," he said, displaying that uncanny ability to sense my thoughts. "One day." He came closer and reached for the door handle again. "Give me one day to explain, and then you can do whatever the hell you want. I won't stop you. I swear it. But Kaydence… I'm not asking—"

He began to tug, rocking my poor Beetle, and I reached out impulsively, striking the button that controlled the locks.

The door popped open in his grasp, still connected to the vehicle.

He was so damn big. Effortlessly, his body towered over mine, and he utilized his strength to make me scramble into the passenger's seat while he claimed mine for himself. Then he slammed the door after him and grabbed the wheel.

"We will talk," he insisted. "Somewhere neutral, where you can feel safe—"

"What about Chambersburg?" I spat. "The site of your last murder?"

If the accusation bothered him, his face revealed nothing.

"Fine," he said before pulling off the shoulder, back onto the highway. "Chambersburg it is."

TWENTY-FOUR

It is strange how so many things can hinge on timing. Perhaps a day ago, I would have accepted Liwai's return out of the blue if only to hear what he had to say. An explanation for all of this. Clarity.

But now?

Seated beside him in my shitty, narrow car, I couldn't find it within myself to say a damn thing. Not a word.

I watched him instead. It took him at least five straight minutes of adjusting my seat to find a position that suited him. As a result, he towered over the steering wheel, and I found myself holding my breath, as if his presence alone displaced the amount of air the cabin contained.

Finally, a question came to me as my attention turned from him to another player in this nightmare who wasn't in view.

"Where is Renae?"

"Safe," he replied, but I sensed he held something back. Out of reluctance or perhaps mistrust? Despite all his talk, he didn't trust me.

"Where?" I demanded, trying again. My voice sounded brave enough, but I couldn't stop wringing my fingers, digging my nails into the tender flesh.

"A campsite west of here," he said, his voice low. "Where she's been by herself for going on two days because I've been too damn busy chasing after you—" He cut his eyes from the road, meeting my gaze directly. "Satisfied?"

"No," I said. "I want to know why."

"Why?" A muscle in his jaw twitched as if the words were being ripped from his throat. "Because she's safer there on unmarked territory. Kittywatt is too dangerous now."

A strange way of describing a campsite, but I ignored it for the time being.

"No. I want to know why… Why now? Why me? Why did Cody seem so angry to learn that you'd 'found' me?"

Or why my heart sped up at his nearness, and all I could taste on my tongue was him. The remnants, anyway. Our last kiss echoed ceaselessly in my brain as if someone had left a clip playing on repeat.

But there was one other question that overshadowed my hormone's instinctive reaction to him.

"Why wait so long to find me?"

He himself had mentioned a timeframe—seven years.

"Because…" He sighed and sat back in my poor seat, straining the hinges. "It was selfish, really. The longer I avoided you, the longer I could stay out on the rim."

"Away from the pack." My tongue stumbled over the strange word choice, borrowed from Cody.

He shot me an inquiring look I didn't have the heart to return. I stared from the window instead, watching the trees race by. What had been thick forest was becoming less dense the closer we came to civilization.

"Alright, let's do this the fair and honest way," Liwai suggested. "You ask a question. I'll answer it, and in return, you answer one of mine. Where did you go?"

Alarm ran down my spine. Beatrice had seemed terrified of anyone knowing her whereabouts—and perhaps for a good reason. What might Liwai and his creepy family do if they knew she was alive? Hurt her?

Though, it seems they would have to hurt Jerome as well.

"Jerome," Liwai said, making me jump. "What do you know about him?"

His tone was decidedly hostile, but I was too startled to care why.

"How did you…"

Know. Because he had read my mind, some way, somehow. Panicked, I tried thinking of bunnies. Of Deanna's hair balls that clogged the shower drain. Of anything but what I'd learned.

"You don't need to hide from me, Kaydence." I couldn't tell from his tone whether my efforts were working or not.

Bunnies…clumps of red hair…imminent doom if he took me out into the middle of nowhere and hurt me.

"I won't hurt you—"

"Stop doing that!" I slammed my hands over my ears though I knew the action was futile. I still needed to do something. Though, I really should have opened the door of this moving car and jumped from it.

Click went the sound of the locks engaging without me having to move a muscle.

"Fine," Liwai snapped, his eyes on the road. "Back to the question-and-answer method. Be honest with me, and I'll be honest with you."

"Then why did you bail and leave me alone looking like a gosh darn crazy person!" The vitriol in my voice startled me.

At least he had the decency to wince.

"I thought it would be easier," he admitted, his jaw clenched. "You were afraid. You'd stay away, and I would have time to go on the run with Renae before anyone else caught on."

"On the run." It sounded more serious than a weekend camping trip. "From what?"

He hissed out a conflicted sound through his teeth and adjusted his grip on the steering wheel. Despite his unease, we traveled at a steady rate, just below the speed limit.

"Renae isn't safe here," he said finally. "Not without me. You want to know why I didn't approach you sooner? Because of her. She needs me on the outside, and the longer I avoided you, the longer I could stay."

"On the outside?"

"We're from a place that isn't open to strangers," he said after an awkward pause. "Somewhere far from here, and we can't return until… Until a certain task is fulfilled. At least that stipulation applies to me and the others, but Renae can never go back. She will always have to live out here on her own."

The pain in his voice ripped through me. Almost as if…I could feel it, mingling with my own desperate mixture of confusion and exhaustion.

"Is she your daughter?" I asked, the only relation I could think of to cause such conflicted agony in his voice.

He shook his head. "No, but I wish she were. I would have a say over her, then. She wouldn't have to fear a damn thing, and there is no way in hell I'd leave her out here to rot."

"Where are her parents?"

He stiffened, and something that could have been anger flitted across his controlled expression before vanishing.

"She has no parents. All she has is me, but I can't protect her alone, and if I go back… It will be open season on her among the vagrants out here. They'll rip her to pieces, but if it gets out that I found you… She'll be the least of my problems."

"How so?"

Even as I asked the question, I remembered something Jerome had said. *If he turned his back on our ways, there would be no pack to salvage. They wouldn't overlook it. They couldn't. The entire council would venture here themselves to ensure he carried it out.*

"How in the *hell* do you know of Jerome?" Liwai snarled, once again breaking his promise. "I can't fucking help it," he added in answer to the thought. Rattled, I watched as the speed gauge ticked higher and higher. "I spent so damn long trying to keep you out. When you were in pain… I opened myself up to it, and it's like trying to shut off a broken faucet."

He groaned and pressed a hand to his forehead. It trembled as his breaths echoed in rapid succession. Gradually, they slowed, as did the car. Soon both it and his breathing were under control.

"Jerome has no real status, but if he's out this far, it can only mean trouble." His words were stilted. I sensed he was trying his hardest to convey something to me in terms he thought I'd understand. "This is bad, Kaydence. If he's here, it's only a matter of time before they send more—"

"I don't think he'll tell anyone," I croaked, picturing the stern yet submissive way he'd dealt with Beatrice. As though he'd do anything to keep her hidden away and maintain his double life. "He won't tell."

Did Liwai already know the reason why? Perhaps he was trying to uphold his promise not to pry into my head because his expression gave nothing away.

"Will you tell me where you were?" he asked.

"First, you tell me something." I fished for the right wording, but quickly realized that there wasn't a pretty way to say what was on my mind. "Are you going to kill me so that you can return to the pack or your family or whatever it is—"

"No!" He sounded emphatic enough.

Maybe I believed him, at least in the most basic sense. There were other things he could have been planning to do to me —such as lock me away on a mountain for twenty years, away from my family, and with little access to the outside world.

"There is no plan," he insisted, his tone hoarse. "Not yet. You can believe that, at least. This whole thing is a damn mess."

That sounded genuine, too.

"How many of you are there?" I asked while eyeing the road, though I wasn't sure exactly what I was referring to. How many family members he had in total? How many were just psycho killers?

He took his time replying, and we passed the exit sign for Chambersburg when he finally sighed and parted his lips. "Nine on the outside, myself included," he said. "Ten if you count Renae. Five on this side of the mountain range and five on the other. We stick close to our ancestral territory and cycle through periodically, depending on certain… factors. Some of those factors led to Kittywatt. For that reason, we were allowed to set up a makeshift outpost of sorts, but it isn't common."

"Because you aren't supposed to stay by your victims long," I surmised.

"Victim," he echoed, but I couldn't tell if he was amused by the term or insulted by it. "Our goal is to return as quickly as possible. Most stay out only a year or two, if that."

"Like Jerome?" I wished I'd stayed longer to ask Beatrice more questions about him.

"Jerome Grayhale was out for eighteen and a half months," Liwai recited with obvious disgust. "They trade their times the way you humans trade championship records or batting averages. We aren't encouraged to 'dawdle.' We come, fulfill our purpose, and go home. The longer you remain on the outside, the more suspicion you bring upon yourself. No one wants my record, that's for damn sure."

His mocking scoff intrigued me. "Because you've been out the longest?"

He inclined his head to shoot me a searching look that left me squirming. Suddenly, the world beyond the windows blurred—we were speeding again.

"I've been out the longest." He didn't seem to regret that distinction. His gaze was fixed, determined. "And I know better than anyone the danger I've put you in."

"Because you aren't like the others," I said, again utilizing the information I'd overheard at Beatrice's.

He sighed and returned his gaze to the road. "I'm not."

"Your brother is the leader."

Or the heir to one, anyway. I struggled to remember the name Jerome had mentioned. Bartow. Their father?

"I think it's time I ask a question of my own." He took a deep breath as though to steel himself against showing any sign of irritation. I had a mental image of the stress balls Dee would maul whenever she tried to quit smoking. She'd lost interest in them after a week, and I sensed Liwai's calm in this instance was a lot more fragile. "How do you know Jerome Grayhale?"

"I don't," I admitted. "Not personally. He didn't know I was listening in—"

"Where?" His tone was a fraction higher, but still passable for calm. "The territory is a full day's trek from here—via our travel methods. By car, it's double that. If he saw you, it could be dangerous. I need to know if I should be prepared for an attack."

Our travel methods? I was humbled enough by his fear of an attack to bite back a snarky question regarding if he could fly.

"We can't fly," he said, but I wasn't sure if he had read my mind or sensed the direction my thoughts had taken. "Our way is just as fast."

"Because you can turn into wolves."

It was his turn to play coy. He eyed the road and followed every traffic guideline as he left the highway for the sleepy outskirts of Chambersburg. For the first time, it struck me that I had no idea where we were going. Thankfully, the presence of a mini-mart and Taco King ruled out the "bury me in the wilderness" theory.

"We can do many different things," he said. "Becoming a wolf is merely one. Maybe I should explain it to you. So that you can understand the pressure I'm under. The expectation. To walk away from that life would be like you walking away from more than Kittywatt. Walking away from your humanity. Your essence. Your soul. It's more than never talking to your aunt or your friends again. It's having them pretend you never existed. That you were never there. It is death in everything but the long sleep."

I kept it to myself that it sounded a lot like what Beatrice Michaels had been forced to endure. Loneliness beyond description. A deathlike isolation.

"It hasn't been easy for me," Liwai continued. "But not all of that is on you. I would have done it anyway."

For her. Renae, a girl he loved as if she were his very own.

"Can Renae…do what you do?" I asked, though I think I knew the answer even before I saw him shake his head. She'd said so herself—another instance of my eavesdropping. *I can't shift.*

"No. She's physically weaker than any girl her age back home," Liwai admitted. I was alarmed to see that we were in the middle of nowhere again, though scattered farmhouses dotted the roving hillside landscape. "She can't turn the way we can. She isn't fast. Objectively, one could say that she isn't like us at all."

"But?" It was strange how quickly I was picking up on his social quirks. He wasn't comfortable with talking for long stretches like this. He felt awkward when stringing sentences together. As a result, he liked to test the listener to make sure they were following. He craved clarity more than anything.

"*But* anyone who spends time with her will quickly learn that Renae isn't normal. She is brilliant—has a mind like a whip. Give her a book on anything, and she'll become an expert on it in a week, if that. One day, a few years ago, she picked up a pencil and drew a picture so real… It was like a photograph. Then a few months later, what she drew came true."

His eyes were downcast for a heartbeat, his knuckles white against the wheel.

"You're afraid of her," I blurted.

Could I blame him, after what I'd seen of her "talents"?

"No. No, never." He emphatically shook his head. "I'm afraid *for* her. She's smart, but she's trusting and so damn naïve. Without me, she won't last a second with the vagrants. They'd tear her apart."

"Vagrants. You mean Cody and those other boys."

He grunted in agreement. "Cody."

"He seemed like a psychopath," I admitted.

"No." Liwai shook his head, sending more of his hair spilling from his ponytail. "Even I can admit that Cody is a reckless, cruel, twisted piece of shit, but he isn't crazy. He's too damn smart for his own good. There is a rule for those of us on the outside—while out on the rim, status doesn't matter. Your family's name or your bloodline is insignificant. On the outside, everyone is equal, and there is no discussion of the past. Not a word. He tormented Renae, but only I know why."

"Why?"

"Because she's a threat to him," he said. "You want to know what happens to those who stray from our ways? I'll show you."

He parked alongside a gravel road, seemingly in the middle of an empty field. Though on second glance, the neatly tended plots weren't vacant at all.

It was a graveyard.

TWENTY-FIVE

I had barely taken in the eerie, morbid landscape before my door was opened from the outside, and Liwai extended a hand in my direction.

"Come on," he prompted.

I avoided him and staggered out on my own. My head spun. I was still dizzy. Everything seemed fluffy around the edges—though it could have been due to a low rolling fog that shrouded most of the area in mist.

"Where are we going?"

"It isn't far." He took the hint and let his hand fall, moving into step ahead of me. With every yard gained, I couldn't help but feel as if bringing me here was his silent way of warning me—no matter what he'd promised, this was my inevitable end.

In the dirt beneath a metal plate sporting my name and date of birth.

And death.

"Here." Suddenly he crouched and wiped a layer of grime from a modest, raised tombstone. On it was a name that made me do a double take.

Laurie Ann Palmer. The date of death was fourteen years ago, and going off her date of birth, she'd only been seventeen.

Oh. A wave of understanding slammed into me, and I felt the need to crouch beside him and do my best to swipe at the dirt coating the stone. Liwai accepted my help, and once the stone was finally clean, we both observed it in silence.

I was the one who spoke first. "She was Renae's mother. Wasn't she?"

If I surprised him, I couldn't tell.

"She'll never know more than her name," he said. "I can't even find a picture of her for Rae. She might as well have come from thin air."

The desecration of Laurie's memory angered him. Were we still in the car, I think he'd be going well above the speed limit.

"She has her necklace," I pointed out.

"That." He frowned. "It was the one thing they couldn't take from her. I won't let them."

"How did it happen?" I gathered up the nerve to ask.

He shot me an odd look, his eyebrow cocked. "It's complicated," he said, returning his focus to the tombstone. "Though I think you can guess well enough."

After my meeting with Beatrice, he had a point.

"But Cody knew?" I asked.

He inclined his head toward me, but I wasn't prepared for the scrutiny of his gaze. The man was like a laser, eyeing me with deliberate focus. To tell just how much I knew?

But he didn't need to stare at me for that. He could just take the answers from my mind.

"Cody knew," he said finally. "He hates her for a multitude of reasons."

Hate was a strong word choice that I sensed he didn't use lightly.

"But I don't understand. Renae is fourteen—" And Dee had told me that all of the Raven "boys" were over eighteen. "How could Cody be her brother if—"

"Not by blood," Liwai said, rising to his feet. "Just know that he is dangerous. I pity the poor soul destined for him. When it comes down to it, he won't hesitate."

"Do you pity me?" I don't know where the question came from, but suddenly I wanted an answer to it. Needed one.

Jerome had seemed to pity Beatrice, enduring her obvious frustration with relentlessly gentle patience. Was that our future? For me to resent him for stopping me from hurting myself?

"It's harder to stay out of your mind when your emotions flare," he said, his tone verging on scolding. His ponytail whipped out as he turned away and headed for the car.

How much had he managed to glean? He didn't say.

"Why isn't it reciprocal?" I demanded, watching him retreat. "Why can't I read your thoughts, but you can read mine?"

"Because you haven't tried," he tossed back. "You haven't opened yourself to it. Even now, I can feel you resisting the connection. You don't trust me."

"Why the hell would I?" I blurted out.

"Why?" He stopped. Slowly, he turned his head and took me in with an impassive sweep of those dark eyes. "Because you don't have a choice. Every second I spend with you puts us both in danger. You want a way out of this? I need you to trust me. Open yourself up to the connection and tell me how you know about Jerome."

His restrained calm was fracturing. I could feel it, like a fragile glass vase slipping from my grasp. Sooner or later, it would shatter, but the resulting mess could be dangerous for both him and me.

"You've alluded that it's tradition," I said, forcing the words past my thickening throat. "That the men 'back home' have all done it. Killed the one 'meant' for them. But what if they're all just hypocrites?"

Or at least one of them, anyway.

"Explain." His tone was sharp, reminding me of the way he ordered around Renae and the other vagrants. I hadn't realized, but until now, he'd utilized kid gloves with me. His real nature was far more domineering.

"I know Jerome Grayhale didn't kill the woman destined for him. I know it for a fact."

And he didn't. His confusion couldn't be faked. His eyes widened, and I felt an echo of emotion run through me. Fear? His?

"How?" He was before me in an instant, his hands on my shoulders. "How do you know that?"

"Because I spoke to her," I snapped, pulling away. "Don't ask me any more than that—I won't tell you."

But he could steal the information without my permission. I could see the impulse glinting in his eye. He wasn't used to this—negotiating on equal terms with someone. He preferred to do things alone. To abide by his own judgment.

It was a stubbornness I don't think I'd witnessed in anyone else before. An almost inhuman doggedness—pun intended.

"That's not possible," he continued in a firmer tone. "You were mistaken."

"What?" I raised an eyebrow. "That those people who want you to kill innocent women might have lied to you?"

Instantly, I knew I'd made a mistake. His expression darkened, his lips a hard, flat line.

"Don't insult me," he warned. "What sounds like a fantasy to you is my life. My world. Not a game."

"Good," I countered. "Because I'm not having fun."

He was closer. His hot breath nudged my lower lip, and it was all I could do to hold my position without running away. He scared me. He did. Beneath the beautiful exterior was something dark and primal. I could feel it. Sense it.

And I knew that sooner or later, it would hurt me.

As if to counter that fear, his eyes lost their hardened edge, and he backed away. "I will never hurt you." The tension left his body with a heavy sigh, and he turned away, tilting his head toward the graying sky. "If you don't believe me, ask yourself this—could you stab yourself without hesitation? Strangle yourself? Maul yourself? Harming you would be the equivalent for me. Painful. Excruciating."

"Jerome hurt Beatrice," I countered in a whisper.

"Beatrice." He whipped around again, and I berated myself. *Stupid!* I'd revealed her name.

"Don't hurt her—"

"Beatrice Michaels." He raked a hand through his hair, destroying the thinning ponytail. Freed, the strands fell down his shoulders in a thick stream of ebony. "Still alive? That doesn't make any damn sense—"

"What? That he didn't kill her?"

"No." His eyes met mine, and any need to challenge him left me in a heartbeat. "It isn't like collecting a Boy Scout badge," he added with a firm shake of his head. "They verify it. Every time one of us 'fulfills our duty,' they triple check that it's been done. There is no room for error, and our methods are far more thorough than any you can think of. There is no way to circumvent them. Unless..." He frowned, and I felt a glimmer of confusion flit across the periphery of my conscience. A heartbeat later, a grim understanding replaced it, and Liwai growled a reply through clenched teeth, "Talia."

Hearing another woman's name come from his lips shouldn't have inspired the defensive range of emotions that it did.

Talia, voiced with a mixture of reverence, alarm, and respect. Who was she to him?

"Another 'destined' woman I should know about?" I even choked out a laugh, though I couldn't reconcile the uncomfortable pinch I felt in my stomach. Jealousy?

"No." He seemed startled by my reaction. So was I. "Just a powerful woman I hope you never meet. This Beatrice must live somewhere protected, unable to be sensed by anyone without permission. When you shut me out, it was like you had disappeared completely. I couldn't feel you. Only a skilled clanswoman could cloak an entire region so expertly."

Cloak?

"So, you thought I'd vanished. Is that why you scared my aunt half to death?"

"Jerome couldn't arrange that kind of protection on his own," he went on, ignoring me. "He's had help from someone else. Someone who should know better than getting involved in such a stupid scheme, but the point remains. He could see you as a threat. For all we know, he could be arranging an attack of his own—"

"I don't think he'd want to," I admit, picturing that terse conversation in the woods. "Not if it risks Beatrice."

"Hers isn't the only life he's put at risk," Liwai grumbled. Was he referring to Talia? I wasn't brave enough to ask. In the resulting silence, he inspected me for so long that my legs felt numb when he finally turned away.

"I need to get back to Rae," he said.

"And what should I do?" I asked, once again sounding more irritated than I wanted to acknowledge feeling. "Wait back home for the man who claims to have singlehandedly ruined my life to come back when he feels like it?"

"No." He extended his hand to me with the palm facing upward. "You can come with me."

I stared at his tanned fingers, feeling my heart threaten to jump up my throat.

"Why? So, you can try to convince me to live in secret for the rest of my life?"

"No." He didn't bother explaining what he did have in mind—something I suspected was by design.

A test with only one aim.

To see if I could trust him.

TWENTY-SIX

He drove for at least an hour, though it could have been longer. My poor baby was only a few licks of gas short of empty, forcing us to stop halfway through the trip to whatever destination he had in mind. There, he got what had to be enough snacks to feed a small army—or a fourteen-year-old girl—and a few cases of water.

"You really left her alone for two whole days?" I asked. Only now could I comprehend how recklessly irresponsible that sounded—and he didn't seem like the type.

"She's fine," he said, though I wondered if he were trying to convince himself more than me. "She isn't as strong as one of us, but against a human, she's no lightweight, either. She'll be fine."

"What was your plan?" I asked while absently rummaging through a plastic bag he'd placed on my lap. Inside was an assortment of snack cakes and sweets that I suspected appealed more to Renae's tastes than his. "Hide out with her, and then what?"

"And then…" He exhaled raggedly and made a motion that might have been a shrug. "I'll regroup. Come up with another plan. Even if you weren't…an issue, I still wouldn't go back. Not until I know she'd be taken care of."

"But you said she can never go back to where you're from."

"So, she'd live out here," he said. "Once she's eighteen, she's considered an adult in this part of the world. She'll be able to find work. She won't need me anymore."

"And you think that would be easier for her? To be without you and the only family she's ever known."

"She can create her own family," he countered. "One that won't deem her *unworthy* of life. It's a better shot than the one she has now."

"And you? Once she's old enough, will you go back?"

I didn't mean it as a cruel jab, but he seemed to take it that way. He winced as if I'd stabbed him, and for a second…

Maybe I even got a glimpse inside his mind. Anger was what I found. A swirling, dizzying, ravenous rage. It scared me, but beneath it, all was a more terrifying emotion I couldn't grasp in full. It was too vast, like trying to guess the depth of an ocean by merely glimpsing the surface. Whatever it was, I sensed it was directed toward me, my own monster of sentiment writhing inside of him. Hate? Or something else. Something even he didn't understand…

"Stay out of my head." The command lacked any energy. I think it might have been a joke under different circumstances. As it was, I flinched back and tore my gaze to the window. "It's a lot to take in, I know," he said, his tone softer. "You'll get the hang of it."

"If you know so much about me, then I'm sure you know that nothing like this has ever happened before. Dee was nearly disowned when she bought a pack of tarot cards. The weirdest thing we've had to deal with is a shooting, and I think werewolves would be quite the stretch—"

"We aren't werewolves," he corrected, frowning at the term. "Thinking of it that way is a bit too limiting. It's more like… We are stewards of nature, unrestrained by it as you humans are. There is more to our range than howling at the moon, in any case."

"Like what?"

"Like tradition. Honoring the land. Respecting the old ways. Living as one tribe, one people. I know, it sounds a bit idyllic." He wrinkled his nose, and for a second, he almost seemed…normal. A regular man explaining his culture in basic terms. "To us, it's not an identity that can easily be summed up by our affinity toward shifting into one creature or another."

"You miss it, don't you? Your home?"

Another flash of emotion assaulted me without warning, taking my breath away. Pain. So much pain my eyes watered instantly at a mere taste of it. I could only compare it to what it might feel like to walk around with a knife embedded in my chest.

"How can you ask me that? Would you miss Kittywatt if there was a chance you might never see it again?"

I'd angered him, but as I deciphered his statement, I wasn't sure if I agreed.

"I've honestly never gotten to know what it feels like," I admitted. "I've never left. I've never known what it feels like to miss a home that's fallen apart around me, regardless. My father left. My mother died. My real father watched me grow up from the sidelines, and I couldn't even follow through on the one damn goal I ever had."

A fact that he'd claimed responsibility for, but blaming him would be taking the easy way out.

I never really had it in me to leave. So no, I couldn't understand the pain he felt.

"To be honest," I croaked, "my home's been falling away from me since I was ten years old."

He didn't argue with my assessment. Instead, he turned off the main road and began to navigate my Beetle down a bumpy, gravel-strewn path down a sloping hillside. I sat up straighter, inspecting our surroundings. Another forest… somewhere. It didn't seem as wild as where Beatrice dwelled, though.

Up ahead, a battered trailer idled near an empty picnic table.

"Wait here," Liwai ordered before parking a few yards from the campsite. The second he exited the car, a tiny figure bounded from the trailer and raced in our direction.

"You're back!"

For once, Renae wasn't wearing a nightgown, but an oversized shirt—which I suspected belonged to Liwai—paired with denim shorts.

Liwai held out his arms, prepared to scoop her into a hug, but she darted past him and raced to my window.

"You're here! You're okay. I was so worried. I thought that it might happen, but it hasn't. You're—"

"Let her breathe, Rae," Liwai scolded, but his tone was more playful than parental.

Renae was too busy opening my door to listen. Her eyes scanned me intently from head to toe. As she neared my forehead, she gasped and took a step back.

"You're hurt." She turned to Liwai, reminding me of a child looking to a parent for guidance. "How?"

"We haven't gotten to that part," Liwai admitted, but his tone was cold. The sensation of cracking restraint returned —only the glass had finally shattered, and I was in danger of stepping over the minefield with bare feet. "Rae, why don't you go find Kaydence some clean clothes and make her a place to sleep?"

"She's staying?" Renae sounded a mixture of excited and horrified, her eyes comically wide.

"She needs a place to sleep if she does," Liwai replied. "I brought some food, too. It's in the car."

"Good, because I'm sick of chips," Renae grumbled, but she raced off, her hair flying out behind her.

"Come." Liwai beckoned me after him with a nod before stalking off toward a distant part of the field.

I bristled at that. Wasn't he the more animalistic one between the two of us? If anyone should have been commanded like a dog, it certainly wasn't me.

"You are so damn stubborn."

I wasn't meant to hear that, but I did. His voice was gruffer than the tone he used with me. Perhaps another glimpse of the real Liwai.

A man who didn't like being challenged.

"Maybe it's proof that you got it wrong," I called out to his retreating back. Even though a part of me wanted to rebel, I'd started to follow him, traipsing through the brambles on exhausted legs. "I'm not your 'destined' woman, after all. I'm just…"

"Kaydence."

He said my name like it physically pained him to, and I stopped with one foot held midair.

He stood with his back to me near two tall, winding trees whose branches had tangled within each other. Years ago, when those seeds were planted, who's to say they knew which direction they'd grow in—until there was no choice. No way of stopping what nature had intended.

They had to adapt, even as branches contorted and snapped between their joining.

"There are so many things I need to tell you. So much that I can't," he admitted. "But if you choose to doubt anything, don't let it be the fact that I give a damn about what happens to you. More than a damn. I can't… It's…"

A suffocating emotion he didn't have the vocabulary to voice. Something wrenching and twisted and utterly broken.

"I would rather die than hurt you," he said, stressing each word. "Believe that."

"What if… What if I don't want this?" I asked him. "I'd always thought I'd marry… Oh, I don't know."

Perhaps someone like Boyd Thomson should he deign to settle down with some country hick like me.

Never! The thought wasn't my own, and it didn't even feel like one of his—not the usual, careful, calculating thoughts he preferred to think. It was primal. An instinctive part of him that railed against the mere prospect of any other man entering my life.

Stubbornly, I soldiered on, picturing my future with this imaginary Boyd. Together, we'd find a white picket fence somewhere and pop out two beautiful children and the matching family dog. A normal, peaceful existence—but even that was apparently too good for me. My mother was denied the same dream in the end. Only her future was cut short by a drunk driver with no warning.

Who could say my life wouldn't end the same way?

It won't. Images flooded my mind, too quickly to make sense of right away. Glimpses of my limbs entwined with those of someone bigger. Darker. He would taste like honey, and his voice would resonate through my body with the impact of thunder heralding one hell of a storm. His love would be the storm, drowning me in safety and protection to the extent that I never felt scared or lonely again…

But I can't. His thought echoed inside my mind so clearly that I gasped aloud and realized that he had moved sometime during this mental exchange. His mouth was against my temple, his hands on my shoulders.

Feeling him pull away from my mind this time physically hurt. I winced—and a dangerous thought came to me. I wouldn't have to worry about this level of mental anguish with Boyd.

Suddenly, my mind went blank as a dangerous heat assaulted my mouth, swallowing me whole. The kiss shocked us both—it startled me into letting my guard down, and for a split second, I sensed him do the same. I felt sympathy for my self-pitying whining that took my breath away. Never in my entire life had I felt so understood without having to say a word. Liwai saw me.

In a way no one else ever will, his voice warned. The words haunted me as he drew back and ran a finger along his bottom lip, tracing the remnants of me.

Watching him made my heart pang with something that might have been jealousy. Destiny had ripped so much away from my life already. This was just one more thing added to the list. My own future was predetermined, and I had no say.

"There's another way to look at it," Liwai suggested, his voice low. His unbound hair cast jagged shadows across his face—it was already nearing sunset, rendering the landscape marginally more hostile.

"How?"

"We do have a choice." He advanced one step at a time, giving me plenty of room to run. "Both of us, whether we want to face it or not. We could run. Hide. Deny it."

Or… That part I heard only in my head, convinced his lips didn't move.

"We exist," he said, coming to tower over me. "No expectations. No rules and no traditions to uphold. We exist and whatever happens, happens."

"You spent a three-hour drive telling me that you don't have a choice," I pointed out.

He pressed a single finger to my lips, sealing them shut. "Damn what I said."

"Why the change of heart?" I asked around his finger.

He lowered his hand and turned his head. I was beginning to notice that he did that a lot when I caught him off guard.

Like he needed a second to compose himself. Think. Hide his real reaction from me.

He didn't want to say. I could feel it through whatever tenuous connection may or may not have existed between us. He didn't think I could handle the full truth. *Not yet.*

"I want to know—"

"Renae," he said, his brow furrowed. "I've never seen her that damn relaxed. Never."

And that mattered to him more than any doubts he may have harbored. In a sense, it mattered to him more than my life, more than his. Renae.

"She knows what it means if I go back," he continued, his gaze on the woods. "I think she's always known, though I tried to keep it from her."

I remembered what she'd said to him. "*You're not like them!*"

"The only good damn thing to come of this mess is that if Cody attacked you, it means he isn't dead. That's good. He won't have the balls to call them back out here himself. He'll try to track us down alone, and I can handle him."

"Cody."

He went still, waiting for me to continue.

Voice shaking, I told him everything, minus Beatrice. About driving up Settler's Point and being attacked.

"Cocky son of a bitch," Liwai snarled, curling his hands into fists. "He's gonna get himself or someone else killed.

He has no sense of restraint. No fucking clue the danger he'll put us all in."

"Why won't he tell them? Your family?" My teeth were chattering. It was freezing out, and maybe I was still lightheaded from hitting my head.

All at once, Liwai moved. I didn't even have the chance to resist the embrace he pulled me into. It was stiff and awkward, with my forehead pressed to his chest and his arms held out at my sides. Still, I couldn't deny that it felt…

Strange and oddly thrilling all at once to be in the arms of someone other than my aunt or the sheriff. He smelled so darn good. Like musk and woodsmoke and other intangible things that made my belly twist into knots. I almost forgot why I shouldn't have submitted to his embrace.

Then he spoke. "Cody knows the law," he said, referring to the latter's supposed silence. "He won't risk drawing attention to himself out here, and he won't risk bringing attention to Renae. She's an open secret, but one that isn't spoken about. If he attacks her directly, it opens him up to certain…accusations. Nothing that would risk punishment, of course."

And that bothered him.

"He'll keep his mouth shut, but he will come after us. We need to clear the area as soon as we can. Up north, he'll have a harder time tracking us down. Only when he senses we're gone for good will the others be called in. By then, we'll be well beyond their reach."

I couldn't shake the feeling that he didn't sound confident. Not in the slightest. He sounded worried. He *was* worried. The lie was for my benefit, but I could sense what lurked underneath. The truth he didn't want to face, at least not out loud.

So, I said it for him. "But not for long. They'll find you eventually, sooner or later. Then… They'll want you to kill me, and you won't have a choice."

It sounded like bullshit when spoken, but I could sense the underlying tension that bellied that statement. Images filled my head—of me ripped to pieces. Broken. Torn. Abused.

"They'll take pleasure in making me do it," Liwai said. "Jerome Grayhale can live in secret and maintain the lie, but I can't—"

"Because of who your family is," I surmised.

"There is more to it," he admitted. "Cody… When he goes back, he'll have a simple choice to make. An alliance to fall into. His life path is rigid, but not like mine. My life has been decided for the past decade. There are others… People whose futures rely on me returning. The longer I stay out, the more I put them at risk."

Was his "promised woman" one of those people?

"I won't lie to you," Liwai admitted. "It isn't easy to consider just walking away."

He was alluding to something he didn't have the heart to say. I could sense it, evading my attempts to suss it out.

Finally, I took a stab in the dark and pulled back to hold his gaze.

"Who is Talia?"

Something strange happened. He grimaced, displaying an uncharacteristic discomfort. "She is—"

"I made dinner!" The gleeful announcement came from Renae, who faced us from across the field, waving her arms wildly in the air. "Come get it! I'll set the places."

She skipped back into the trailer, radiating boundless energy that made me do a double take. If I wasn't mistaken, she almost resembled a normal, hyperactive teenage girl.

Liwai sighed again though I suspected it was more tentative than annoyed. "Let's go."

He led the way to the picnic table, where Renae eagerly flitted around, plating her meal. Canned tuna formed a lump on three plastic plates. Arranged around the entre was a semi-circle of potato chips, carrot sticks, and Cheetos.

"Eat up," Renae declared before munching from her own plate. "These are all my favorites. And then we can have dessert!"

"Dessert?" Liwai asked, inclining his head her way. Despite his obvious skepticism, he took his seat dutifully and picked up a chip.

"Snack cakes and ketchup packets. It sounds gross, but trust me, it rocks." She beamed at me around a mouthful of tuna, and I forced myself to grin in return.

Her newfound joy was such a stark contrast to the meek, timid girl I'd witnessed at the Raven house. Every impish grin she flashed was infectious, and the mood somehow lightened even as the sky grew grayer and stormier with the threat of rain.

After Renae served us our "dessert," she sprawled out on the bench beside me while Liwai watched on, his plate partially untouched.

"You're in a good mood today," he said. He spoke to her in a way I couldn't pinpoint. Like he was always on guard, but not out of fear. Maybe respect? Every reaction he gave was carefully tailored, as if he knew one wrong word might upset her.

"Yep," she chirped, eyeing him from her resting place as her bare feet kicked in the air. "A very good mood."

"Can I ask why?"

She hesitated for a split second as her large eyes darted to me.

"It's okay," Liwai murmured. "You can speak freely around her."

She beamed and threw her hands into the air. "Cody isn't dead! I was wrong! I was wrong, and the world is okay, and all is well!"

She giggled, and I felt my lips twitch into another smile, but Liwai… He frowned.

"What do you mean?"

"It didn't come true," Renae went on, her voice rising in pitch. "My vision. It didn't come true, and we can all run away. Run, run, run, and they won't find us!" She lurched to her feet and grabbed my hand, pulling me from the table.

With the breathtaking grace of a ballerina, she began to dance, urging me to twirl with her.

"We're free! We're free, and Cody isn't dead!"

"You might change your mind if he catches our trail," Liwai warned.

Renae's beautiful smile didn't even waver. "He's so grumpy! So grumpy! I told you, we're free!" She twirled and twirled until I had to break away, violently dizzy.

The world spun no matter how hard I tried to stand unmoving. In the end, a solid surface caught me from behind, and gradually, my senses returned.

"I think you could really have a concussion," Liwai growled into my ear. Raising his voice, he said, "Rae, she needs to rest. Let's get ready for bed."

"Okay!" Giggling, she spun around and collapsed onto the grass. "Can I sleep outside with the radio on? Please! I never get to listen back home. They always keep it on the Rock channel."

"It might rain," Liwai warned.

Renae shook her head, her expression serious. "It won't. Can I? Please?"

"Okay, but you stay where I can see you. If so much as a drop of rain falls, you come inside?"

"Yeah!" She darted inside the trailer. Not even a second later, a staticky radio blared through the speakers, though not loud enough to be heard from far away. Renae bounced outside with a flannel blanket and a pillow tucked under her arm. "Goodnight!"

"Where I can see you," Liwai reminded. Then he guided me toward the trailer.

Near the steps leading inside, I hesitated. Was this a particularly smart course of action? Probably not. Though "smart" wasn't a word I'd apply to anything I'd done as of late.

"You can let me take a look at you, or we can head over to the regional hospital. Your choice."

"You don't own me," I felt the need to point out.

His reply came after a heartbeat of silence. "I don't."

For some reason, hearing him confirm that small detail was what I needed to finally cross the threshold and enter the tiny dwelling.

It looked a lot like his place in Kittywatt, small and modestly furnished. The only difference, perhaps, were the scattered items that very obviously belonged to a young girl. A hairbrush on the kitchen counter. A neatly-folded set of pink shirts on the dining table. Liwai released an audible sigh once he spotted a pair of pink underwear tucked amongst the pile.

"Rae…" Clutter bothered him. As I sat down on the small couch built into the wall, he set about tidying up the mess with ruthless efficiency.

More than neatness, he craved order. Structure. Serenity. All things that were the antithesis of someone intending to take on the chaos that came with raising a teenage girl.

"I've raised her out here better than anyone else could," he said out loud with his back to me as he tucked Renae's clothing into a gray duffle bag resting on the floor near the bathroom. "I at least give a damn. That has to count for something."

Because he'd beaten himself up repeatedly over the logistics of this plan. I could feel it. Maybe a bit of guilt was the reason I didn't panic at the realization he'd read my thoughts once again.

"It's harder with you close by," he explained while zipping the duffle. "Like trying to keep out a tornado with a wall of tissue paper. You can't blame me for that."

"There's a lot of things I could blame you for," I countered. "You yourself told me that."

"I did…" He set the duffle aside and spun to face me. In such a small, cramped interior, he looked entirely too massive. A towering wall of muscle and scrutiny.

"Wait here. Let's get you cleaned up."

I didn't like how easily he seemed to take responsibility for me. My chest felt heavier every time he did. A sense of foreboding, maybe?

No one should be able to assert themselves in my life so easily. Even Burt Michael's hadn't been able to.

"The sheriff," Liwai called from the bathroom. He wasn't even trying to be subtle about breaking his promise anymore. "He is your biological father."

"*Biological* being the key word," I sniped back. "I'd grown up only knowing what it was like to have a deadbeat dad, but at least my fake one had the decency to live in another state. I wonder if that was why he left in the first place."

He always knew that I wasn't his. Rather than tell me as much, he left. Maybe that's preferable to living down the block from me in a big, beautiful home that had been in his prominent family for generations. I'd heard so many damn stories about Burt Michaels and his glorious heyday. Perhaps that was what made it sting so badly? I was the product of a bona fide American love story, and I never even knew. A love story that shattered to pieces like so many things left in Kittywatt.

Was I next?

"Here." Liwai emerged from the bathroom armed with a first-aid kit and a damp washcloth. "You should clean that off."

He approached as if he had every intention of letting me handle it myself. At the last second, he pivoted and settled onto the cushion beside me. With all the sternness of a moody, distant clinician, he captured my chin in one hand and dabbed at my face with the other. At his touch, my heart raced like mad.

I think it was the first time he truly let himself inspect my wounds. His assessment was made clear when he hissed a curse through clenched teeth.

"I'll kill that son of a bitch."

It wasn't idle talk. An undercurrent of lethal intent reinforced his words. He meant them, every last one.

But the most chilling part of hearing him say it was that I wasn't as afraid as I should have been.

He was a puzzle, Liwai Raven. A glorious mix of contradicting contradictions and muddled motivations. By threatening Cody, I sensed that he'd meant it—and yet, he had no intention of actually carrying it out.

"It won't scar, at least," he said while wiping the area clean.

Was that a good thing? No. I pictured Beatrice's face, and a chill ran down my spine. How long before I wound up like her? Especially if I remained in the orbit of the mysterious Ravens.

That thought, however, Liwai didn't feel the need to refute. He just smeared some ointment along my forehead and covered the wound with gauze and medical tape.

By the time he finished, the entire space was nearly pitch dark. Only the soft hum of cheerful pop music broke the silence, and through one of the windows, I could see Renae lying on top of the picnic table, her eyes on the stars.

"You should get some sleep." Liwai stood and ambled toward the front of the cabin. "I'll keep watch from the truck."

"You think someone might find you out here?" I asked. Though, considering that he'd left Renae out here alone for nearly two days, he obviously didn't take the threat all too seriously.

"I think it's better to be waiting than to be caught off guard," he countered. "Stay here. You'll have the place to yourself unless it rains."

He started to head out, and I stood, feeling slightly steadier on my feet than before. When I began to follow him, I sensed that he wanted nothing more than to command me to stay.

By sheer force of will, he said nothing.

"I thought you said there was no hierarchy among the 'vagrants'?" I directed the question at his back as I followed him outside and climbed into the passenger seat of the truck.

A moment later, he claimed the driver's side, his expression less than pleased.

"There isn't."

"But you call the shots." It wasn't a question, merely a statement of fact.

But that characterization bothered him. He frowned and raked a hand through his hair. "I'm the oldest. In our clan, we defer to our elders for everything from guidance to pairing of the bloodlines, to—"

"Pairing of the bloodlines." As I mimicked him, it didn't take rocket science or a psychic connection to gauge his reaction. Utter loathing and disgust. "What does it mean?"

He leaned back and drummed his fingers against the steering wheel, subconsciously following the beat of the current pop song, crooned by an upbeat girl singing about her newfound crush.

"Love has no purpose in my culture," he said finally. His grim tone was a startling contrast to the bubbly music. "Love between mates, in any case. Every male is cast out as soon as he comes of age, and the women remain behind, typically for their entire lives. There is no room for courtship or 'dating'," he uttered it as though it were a foreign word. "The day you leave the pack, you are presented with the woman who will be waiting upon your return."

"Were you?"

The question made him squirm in his seat and send both hands tearing through his hair.

"We all are assigned our—"

"Assigned," I snapped. "Assigned a woman by destiny. *Assigned* a mate by the 'elders'. Do your people not have a say in anything?"

"No." His tone became harsher as that quiet anger returned. I swallowed hard. Though his vague wording might have been frustrating, I didn't want to anger him. Or insult him.

And I had just done both.

"Tell me," I pleaded rather than launch into a self-righteous speech about freedom of choice. "I'll listen."

He inclined his head, and more of the man beneath the façade became clear to me. Just a snippet. He wasn't used to being encouraged to verbalize his thoughts out loud. Someone as careful and calculated as him... He took his time compiling his thoughts, and I gave him every second he needed.

"Humans can afford 'freedom of choice' because your numbers vary into the billions. You aren't in danger of dying out with every new generation—" He broke off, seeming to grapple for control. "You don't understand the fear of scarcity. Every life matters. Each member of the clan can't afford selfishness or to think only of themselves. We must only think of the good of the clan. Of future generations. Of continuing our bloodlines for years to come. Emotions are not a factor."

"You don't believe that." I wasn't trying to needle him. I could feel it. A part of him, deep down, grappled with the philosophy I suspected had been fed to him since birth.

He didn't matter against the backdrop of his people. He was merely a tool for procreation.

"It doesn't matter if I believe it," he said. "The council believes it. A few thousand clan members believe it. They will die following that belief, and they can't afford for a single follower to go astray. My opinion means nothing in the face of a few thousand years of control."

"Talia is the woman meant for you," I said, voicing another suspicion that had blossomed as he spoke. He said her name with the same pained reverence he'd referred to the clan.

"Talia Grayhale," he said. "Jerome's twin sister, to be exact. The match wasn't for political reasons, as the Grayhales have no real prominent position on the council, but they are a strong bloodline, known for siring strong descendants. We would have had many viable, healthy children."

"Would have?" Did it bother me to hear him speak so casually about a future with another woman? Maybe, though, I really didn't have any right to be upset. Even now, that could have very well been his future. From Beatrice and Jerome's conversation, I gathered that he had done just that, despite leaving her alive.

He'd gone back and had children with the woman assigned to him.

"It's not as draconian as it sounds," Liwai said. His head was tilted thoughtfully, his gaze on the darkening expanse of sky viewed beyond the windshield. Yet, I sensed that he felt obliged to say as much. He didn't necessarily believe it. "The practice ensures our bloodline goes on. I wouldn't be here without it."

"But…" I didn't know what I was trying to say. Clumsily, I soldiered onward and made it up as I went along—I wasn't as careful as he was. "Are the men really happy when they come back after having… Killed someone?"

It sounded like an impossible concept, but Liwai nodded.

"I used to think so, anyway. When one of us returns, it is a glorious celebration. Festivals for days and plenty of celebrating. Every birth is met with raucous joy, as if we feel the need to overcompensate. To convince everyone that what we do is fine and for the greater good. I'm sure some of them believe that."

"But?"

His brows creased, his gaze distant. "I saw firsthand that most of it is a façade. A crock of bullshit. They live with the pain of their actions, and there is no recovery from it. No happy ending, and the resulting children merely carry that burden, whether they realize it or not. They're born angry. Bitter. They spend their lives learning to deny themselves pleasure because it's expected. Sacrifice is our only purpose. But what point is living a life if your only purpose is to throw it away for the good of everyone else? And the people you make that sacrifice for are just as miserable. The misery breeds misery, and this is what you get—" He gestured half-heartedly toward my end of the truck, but he wasn't referring to me.

He was pointing toward Renae, who slept on her side, blissfully unaware of the conversation taking place.

"A beautiful girl any family should be proud of. Any father should be lucky to have. A girl who doesn't give a damn about anything but ponies and flowers. She's made to be an outcast, and someone like Cody has his darkest, most vile impulses encouraged. You can't tell me it's a fair trade-off for either of them."

It was such a strange way of looking at it, but one that made so much sense my mind was blown in the face of it. Renae and Cody weren't victim and perpetrator as he saw it. They were both just creatures formed by the decisions that shaped their conception. Nothing more.

Did I feel the same?

Probably not. Cody was an asshole, and some people were just born that way.

"If I weren't around, he would hurt her," Liwai said, as if to show he agreed with me in some small way. "I know exactly what he would do to her, because he's been taught to hate her and what she stands for. He tells himself that he was only doing it for the good of the clan. And when the dust settled and the wounds he inflicted healed, there would be no relief to be found. No peace. He'd find someone else to harm, and the cycle would continue. What kind of life is that?"

"You feel responsible for her, Renae," I said, picking up on what he'd clearly demonstrated all this time. Yet, there was something unspoken in his concern. A wall he kept up.

"I am," he said cryptically. "I owe her that much."

"Owe her?"

He angled his face away from me. "Because a monster took her mother away and plunged her into this mess. They killed her."

He wasn't talking of Cody anymore, and my belly flipped. Was he the person in the figurative tale? A monster forced to harm people in an endless cycle of violence?

I couldn't tell. He was closed off, and there was an uncanny sense that I was alone in my skull. Just me, my thoughts, and my feelings. It felt...

Unsettling.

Maybe I was pathetic for wanting to extend that fragile connection to him. At least, for a second, I hadn't felt like a crazy person.

"Do you still talk to Talia?" I asked, hoping to broach a somewhat neutral topic.

Instead, I tripped over a landmine.

He stiffened, and I sensed a wave of emotion that I knew wasn't my own. Unease, riddled with disjointed images—a woman with piercing eyes, her chin tilted defiantly. *You're a selfish bastard, you know that?* She'd told him, her voice hauntingly beautiful.

And those words had hurt him deeply.

Just as quickly as it came, however, the brief insight vanished.

"Get some sleep." He cocked his head back and closed his eyes, revealing his intentions to stay up all night.

I reached for the door handle, intending to enter the RV like he so obviously wanted.

In the end, my hand fell without ever opening the door, and I just sat in silence beside him, chewing over every word. Every bit of expression he couldn't smother. Every intention he'd consciously or not made clear.

He was a complicated man, Liwai Raven.

Complicated and dangerous in more ways than one.

TWENTY-SEVEN

I did a bad thing, and I took full responsibility. It was my fault for tossing and turning, trying to get comfortable in that stiff, gosh darn front seat. Only one position brought me relief and finally allowed me to drift off.

It wasn't until I peeled my eyes open to the stinging light of dawn that I realized that position happened to be with my head resting on Liwai's shoulder, my hand inches from his thigh.

He was already awake, staring blankly ahead, enduring the contact. Not out of a desire to share the embrace. He merely wanted me to sleep for as long as I could.

And realizing that made it worse. Our thoughts were mingling again, and this time I could clearly make the distinction.

My thoughts were fragile and furtive, but his…

They rumbled like thunder, coloring my perception with his unique, primal point of view.

It was as if my brain had a front door, and I'd left it open, allowing any old thought to fly in and out. Who knew what he might have learned just through me being asleep—and that was assuming I hadn't sleep talked the whole night.

"We'll need to leave soon," he said, rather than divulge what secrets he might have garnered. "It isn't safe to stay here long. In another hour, I'll wake up Rae and—"

"Liwai!" An ear-splitting scream had us lunging from the truck. Within seconds, Liwai was tearing across the field to where Renae stood, radio in hand.

Her expression made my heart sink, and I scanned the woods, sure that Cody or another threat had arrived, ready to attack.

"What is it?" Liwai demanded as he crouched before her, smoothing his hands along her shoulders. "Honey, what is it?"

She said nothing. She merely pointed to the radio, and I strained my ears as fragments of sound finally reached me. The crisp, masculine speaker was most likely citing a news report.

"...found yesterday morning on Settler's Point. Police are asking for leads and anyone who might have been in the area between eleven p.m. and five a.m. to call..."

"It's Cody," Renae said between gasping sobs. "He's dead. He's dead..."

Her swollen, bloodshot eyes met mine, and I don't think I'd ever been more terrified.

"We all are."

TWENTY-EIGHT

I stood outside a rest station bathroom off the highway and desperately tried to get cell service. After contorting myself in a pretzel for twenty minutes, I finally got a hold of Dee.

"Kaydee?" She yawned, and I suspected she was on her way out the door. "Where are you?"

A simple question with no simple answer. The truth—that I was miles from Kittywatt, living out of an RV with a man who wanted to kill me because I may have accidentally murdered someone—wouldn't fly.

"I needed a break," I croaked into the receiver while scanning the busy parking lot. A few cars away, Liwai Raven stood beside his truck, his arms crossed, watching me. Deciphering his expression alone would take a day and a half, but I had a secret method.

Somehow, I knew exactly what he was feeling—he was worried. Did he think I'd spill the beans and demand Dee send over the sheriff? Perhaps I might have if I didn't have my own baggage with Burt Michaels.

"I decided to take a little road trip," I lied. "You know, after everything that happened at the bar… I'll be back in a few days."

"You… Take a road trip?" I couldn't tell if the dramatic pauses were due to the spotty connection, or Dee's genuine surprise at the prospect. "Kaydee, you don't do impromptu stuff like that. What's really going on?"

"Nothing's going on," I stammered—an understatement if there ever was one. "I'll be back home soon. Can you cover with Mari for me?"

"Well, I guess. But, Kaydee, at least check-in every day, ya hear? I don't know if you've heard, but they found someone dead on Settler's Point yesterday morning. You know I'm close to Delroy Jenkins, over at the sheriff's station? Well, they haven't released the details yet, but they're deeming it foul play. An actual homicide here in Kittywatt. Can you believe it?"

"No," I said hoarsely as all the blood drained from my face. "That's awful."

Suddenly, a thought intruded into my mind, but it wasn't my own. It carried a distinct, foreign wave of emotions I didn't want to decipher. The gist, however, was easy enough to gauge.

Come on. We need to go.

"I have to go. I'll talk to you later, Dee."

"Bye, honey, but if you're with that Liwai Raven, don't forget to use protection—"

I hung up, but my hands were shaking so badly I couldn't put my phone in my pocket. I could barely maintain my grip on it as I crossed the parking lot, dodging an oncoming minivan, and made it to Liwai's side.

He said nothing before claiming the driver's seat. As I followed him inside, the darkening storm clouds on the horizon seemed to convey what he couldn't voice. This was a mess. A raging, disastrous, messy mess, and no one would escape the oncoming downpour.

Ten minutes later, we returned to the campsite and found Renae inside the RV. Slumped against the couch built into the wall, she seemed practically catatonic.

"Honey?" Liwai stroked the hair from her face and crouched on one knee, bringing his face closer to hers. "Talk to me, Rae."

"It's all my fault." Her large eyes welled with tears, and she rolled over, turning her back to us. Her slender shoulders trembled, and her sobs echoed off the walls, each one more heart-wrenching than the last.

"We can't say here," Liwai said to me, rising to his feet. "I'll hook up the truck, and we'll head out."

Before stopping at the rest station, we'd gone to a local supply store and gotten enough camping gear to last a week on the road.

Why I included myself in that scenario? I had no idea. The right thing to do would be to get in my car and head straight to the police station to turn myself in.

"You don't know anything yet," Liwai said from the doorway. "We aren't doing anything rash until we get more information."

"And how do you plan on doing that, huh?" I asked above Renae's cries. "Waltz right onto the mountain and ask for details of an ongoing murder investigation?"

"No," he said, relentlessly calm. "I have my own methods, but you need to trust me."

Trust. He made it sound as simple as a handshake. Could I extend something like that to a man who had upended my life overnight?

Surprisingly... Yes. In this instance, I had no one else to turn to.

"Okay," I rasped.

"Good. See if you can get Renae into your car. Then follow behind me." He stormed out and began circling the RV and the truck, preparing to hitch the two.

"Renae?" I turned to her and placed one hand on her shoulder.

She sniffled and quieted down, though she didn't face me. "Honey, you should ride with me. You can have free rein over the radio."

I forced a grin, but she seemed to hunch in on herself, her face shrouded by a curtain of black hair. Awkwardly, I stood there, with the quiet broken only by the rev of the truck's engine as Liwai backed toward the RV.

"Renae, please. We have to go. I… I'm scared too. I have no idea what the hell we're going to do. If I…" I broke off, horrified. The world started spinning, pressing in on all sides. I might have killed someone, even if in self-defense. If Liwai Raven didn't kill me, my future was headed toward a dead end, anyway.

Suddenly, someone brushed my hand with theirs—Renae. Her face was red, her eyes bloodshot and swollen. Still, she stood and followed me out to my car. Not long after, I was in my car with Renae seated beside me. Up ahead, Liwai navigated the RV along the winding path.

"It's not your fault," she said, her voice hoarse. "It isn't. I should have done something. I should have—"

"Honey, it's not your fault, either," I insisted. "You couldn't have known."

"I *did* know," Renae said softly. "I did, and I saw it, and I tried to ignore it. I saw him dead, and I know what will happen next."

The certainty in her voice sent a chill down my spine. "What will happen, honey?"

She turned to gaze from the window, her expression constricted. I couldn't take my attention off the road long enough to decipher it. But I could guess.

"Honey, you didn't cause anything bad to happen," I said, trying a new tact.

"I did." Her tone was quiet but insistent. "It's my fault. If I… If I never led him to Settler's Point, he would have never known where to find you. Liwai wouldn't have made us leave. It's my fault."

"Why don't we put on some music, huh?" I reached over and turned the dial to the radio. "You can pick the station."

I settled on one blaring upbeat pop music, but Renae didn't seem interested.

"If she comes, we'll know," she murmured, her eyes wide. "If she comes… Everything will go wrong."

"If who comes?" I asked.

She didn't reply. I could only assume she meant Deanna, barging into whatever campsite we settled in next, wielding a rolling pin, her hair in curlers. It was only a matter of time before she caught on. My half-assed lies couldn't placate her forever.

I stewed over the logistics while following Liwai deeper into the territory north of the valley where Kittywatt and Chambersburg rested. I'd never been up this way. The gently sloping landscape became rugged. Huge slabs of sheer rock pierced the jagged hillsides, overgrown with lush greenery and towering trees.

It might have been beautiful when viewed under different circumstances. The perfect place to camp without the accusation of murder hanging overhead—or to fish in the glimmering lake nearby.

The body of water seemed to be Liwai's destination. It was remote, with only a handful of campsites scattered nearby, each one in disrepair. He navigated the RV as far down the winding path as possible before stopping at a site close to the water's edge.

My heart panged at the scenic beauty, bathed in the darkening storm clouds. It would have been the perfect place for a Kaydee in an alternate reality to retreat for a weekend getaway, perhaps with a boyfriend.

Not him.

The man in question was already waiting as I parked nearby, and he headed straight to the passenger's seat. Renae had stopped crying, at least, and she allowed him to lead her from the car and straight into the RV.

I pictured him comforting her and settling her to sleep in the one bedroom. A few minutes later, he reemerged alone, his eyes narrowed, focused inward.

"We need to talk," he called to me. Then he beckoned with a nod of his chin.

I hesitated. If he had changed his mind about killing me, this would be the perfect place to do so—out in the wilderness with no one around to hear me scream. Apart from Renae.

"If I wanted to hurt you, I could have run you off the road." Liwai was watching me, his arms crossed, head cocked.

With the glistening water as a backdrop, he seemed more feral than I previously gave him credit. He hinted that his abilities extended beyond turning into a wolf, and for the first time, I believed him. Though that brought to mind what else lurked beneath that muscular form. A lion? A tiger? A bear?

"Kaydence, I can't… If you want me to play the role of a villain, I can," he warned. "I don't want to, but now that Renae is involved? I won't let anything happen to her."

He meant that. Every last word—and that hadn't been a threat, but a promise.

"Okay," I croaked, following him up a beaten trail. From there, we could still see the RV, but were most likely out of Renae's line of sight.

Liwai seemed to realize that, and I suspected that was his reason for leading me here in the first place. His shoulders slumped, and the careful mask of calm he maintained shattered. He was worried.

Tearing his hands through his hair, he began to pace back and forth, his jaw clenched, eyes flashing.

"I need you to tell me exactly what happened."

"Can't you just…know?" I asked. Snark wasn't the motive behind the question. I just didn't think I had it in me to recite what happened.

All at once, Liwai pivoted toward me, placing his hands on my shoulders. "Try."

I looked up into the face of a man I didn't recognize. He was sterner beneath his mask, with nothing to soften the harshness of his features. His eyes were darker than ever, and I sensed the control he fought so hard to maintain was fracturing.

"Tell me."

"I went to Settler's Point," I said, my voice monotone. "He was there. He thought you were with me. He attacked me… And I had a switchblade in my hand. I can't remember stabbing him or anything close to it. Still, somehow I must have. Oh, God… What have I done?" The tears came hot and fast. Before I knew it, I was hunched over, hands on my knees, gasping for breath. It was as if someone were squeezing my chest in a vice. No matter how hard I tried, I couldn't get enough air.

Not until a pair of sturdy hands caught my forearms, pulling me against a body that served as an anchor against the pain and the fear. Everything. He felt so damn strong. I couldn't fathom possessing such radiating strength.

I felt so damn helpless.

Oddly enough, Liwai didn't feel the need to comfort me with gentle words of encouragement. He merely let me cry, holding me against his chest while I sniffled and gasped to regain control of my breathing.

Only then did he speak.

"I shouldn't have left. Not until I knew for sure that he wasn't a threat." His tone was soft but cutting. Beneath my own pain and horror, I recognized a foreign emotion that might have belonged to him. Guilt?

"You didn't. You didn't know," I pointed out. "What he would do."

"But I did." His arms stiffened around me, and I looked up, scanning his expression. He wasn't gloating over that fact. His eyes were stormy and downcast, displaying a wealth of emotions I couldn't decipher. "I knew exactly what he wanted to do. I should have put him down."

Put him down. The word choice chilled me to the core, and I stood back, horrified. "You wanted to kill him."

"Yes," he admitted. "He was a threat, to both you and Renae. You don't understand the inner workings of the clan. Our laws are far more primitive than the ones you live by. Think of it as this?" He extended a hand out to me, his smooth palm upright. "Hit me."

I shook my head, confused. "No—"

"Do it." His tone was more than insistent. I could feel a tendril of emotion lurking beneath the calm exterior. He was desperate to convey something to me. I needed to listen.

"Fine." I smacked his hand as hard as I dared, which wasn't hard at all.

He didn't react other than to keep his hand extended, displaying the delicate series of interconnected lines etched into the flesh.

"Were we both in clan territory, your transgression against me would give me the right to return the blow twofold. It doesn't matter that you are a woman, or even if you were a child. Our law is equal and reciprocal. No one stands above it, and no one is unrestrained by it. Now let's say that you didn't merely slap my hand. You stabbed me. Do you see where I'm going with this?"

Slowly, I nodded. "An eye for an eye."

"Only if you cut out one of my eyes, I would be owed two of yours. And let's just say you only had one eye to begin with. Then I could take my retribution from the person deemed closest to you. Your Aunt. Your friend. Anyone I choose."

My throat tightened. "That sounds…"

Barbaric, though I had enough tact not to say as much.

He nodded, presumably reading my mind. "It is our way. By attacking you, Cody gave me every right to seek retribution in any way I see fit."

"But," I pointed out. "I'm not one of you."

He frowned as if realizing that the second I said it. "Either way, I should have dealt with the threat he presented head-on. It's the only language we understand—"

"No." I steeled myself with a deep breath and squared my shoulders. "I know how to deal with this."

In the only way I realistically knew how.

"I can call Sheriff Michaels, tell him the truth, and turn myself in."

If I killed Cody, I was the one who needed to face judgment for it. No one else.

"No."

My head whipped up at Liwai's tone. It was hard. Stern. A voice that warned he wasn't in the mood to be challenged.

"You will let me handle this. This doesn't involve you—"

"What do you mean?" My voice broke. "You aren't the one with your switchblade in his chest. You didn't kill him, and you have no right to dictate what I should do about it!"

"Can't I?" He inclined his head, those eyes piercing. "Kaydence, I'm not trying to insult you, but you need to let me handle this. You should go with Renae. Wait for me to return, and we'll go from there."

"Return?" Something about the way he said that word made my breathing hitch. He sounded too calm. Too careful. "Where are you going?"

Rather than meet my gaze head-on, he angled his face away from me, obscuring his expression. "First, I need to contact the other vagrants and confirm that Cody isn't with them. If he isn't… We'll go from there."

"You don't know where they are?"

He looked away, staring out over the water. "We split up. I sent them south and went north with Rae. They can handle their own under Braden's guidance. He's the oldest among them and more reasonable than Cody. By the time they realized I'd gone, he would lead them to set up roots in another town."

Another town, where some other girl from a "cursed" family might live, blissfully unaware of the horror her mere identity had plunged her into.

I tried not to think about that.

"And if you find them and Cody *is* missing?"

He inched closer toward the water's edge, leaving me to follow. The darkening sky cast shadows over his features, making him resemble more a creature cut from stone than a living being.

"If Cody is missing, that will be the least of our problems," he finally said from over his shoulder. "I told you before— our kind have ways of confirming deaths that don't rely on human means. The clan will know soon enough. They'll send out an elder to make inquiries—something that isn't done lightly. If they learn that a human was involved, they'll demand retribution. Who you are won't matter to them."

I picked up on his nonverbal unease and shivered. He was so direct compared to most people I was used to. He didn't soften things to coddle my feelings. I doubt if he had a daughter wandering around in the same damn town as him, it wouldn't take him twenty-two years to make himself known.

"We need to talk about that," Liwai warned. "When I return. Among many other things."

"You're being cryptic again," I croaked. Unsurprisingly, his vagueness was more disarming than his blunt statement of facts.

"I need you to trust me. I know this is hard for you, but I need you to give me this one thing. Stay with Renae, and let me handle this. I won't let anything happen to you."

"Can you be so sure?" I countered. "If Cody is gone and the body is his, then what next? We're back at the same position we're in now."

"I'll handle it."

The same way he'd handled everything up until now? I had enough tact not to say that, at least. Strangely enough, I didn't want to fight with him.

"Poor Renae." I looked back to where the RV was barely visible through the trees. "Does she get like this often?"

"Often enough," Liwai replied with a heavy sigh. "And this is one area that I can't help her in. Were she accepted in the clan, she would have a mentor. The other women would take her under their wing and help her to hone her gifts."

The phrasing caught my attention. "You mean... Is that a common trait? Reading the future?"

We were treading over the rocky shore lining the lake, our footsteps crunching over loose stones with every step.

"Among the women, yes," he said. "Men are inclined toward physical prowess, while the women are typically more prone to other skills. Healing. Shielding. Foretelling."

It sounded oddly misogynistic though he shrugged off the thought the second it entered my head.

"Every gift is equal in importance," he explained. "Foretelling is one of the most revered, and it's far more nuanced than staring into a crystal ball or reading tea leaves. Without proper guidance… It can be dangerous. Typically, it takes over a dozen women with years of training under their belt to home in on a clear, trustworthy vision. What Renae can do… It's unprecedented."

He sounded so grave that I suspected there was more he wasn't saying. More than a fourteen-year-old girl capable of drawing the future.

"It takes a toll on her." He hissed through his teeth in exasperation, his hands clenched at his sides. "Her trances get stronger with each new vision. If she can't learn to control it…"

"Do they know?"

He laughed, but it was a violent, cold sound. "I tried to tell them. I thought they might at least send someone to test her. 'Worthy' of our blood or not, she's too powerful to go unnoticed on the outside for long if she can't control it."

"And they said no?"

His laugh verged on something far more primal. A growl?

"They said *nothing*. Didn't even bother to respond to my plea. If Cody is dead and you… There is no reasoning with their small-minded beliefs. They won't let you turn yourself into Sheriff Michaels and live out your days in mortal prison, Kaydence." He turned to face me, his gaze so cold I flinched. "They'll rip you to pieces and make the entire clan watch. That is the retribution they will believe they're owed. I won't let that happen."

There was nothing I could say. He didn't strike me as the dramatic type, nor one to over-exaggerate.

"Give me a day," he said. "Please. A day to do this my way. Can you give me that?"

"I… I can try," I rasped.

"Good." He nodded, and some tension left his shoulders, rendering him slightly more approachable.

A few wayward steps brought me to his side before I realized it. Awkwardly, I stood there, wringing my hands together as the sky grew grayer overhead, wrought with more ominous clouds.

A subtle tension tinged the air, much like the heaviness that thickened the atmosphere before a storm. All that was needed was a roll of thunder and a burst of lightning to herald the rain and get it over with.

"Why did you?" I asked, feeling the need to say something without touching one of the more dangerous topics lurking between us. Though, it wasn't safer by much. "Why did you save me that night?"

I wasn't taunting him, either, or trying to play semantics. Deep down, some part of me needed to hear him say it.

"I couldn't," he said simply, with a halfhearted shrug. His gaze ruthlessly scanned the water as if hunting for an answer among the lapping waves. "Some might say that makes me weak."

Did it? If I wanted to be brutally honest, perhaps it would have saved us a hell of a lot of trouble. But that didn't mean no one would have to deal with the aftermath—mainly Dee and Sheriff Michaels and anyone else who happened to be in Bardee's that night.

"And now you answer a question of mine," Liwai said, pouncing when I least expected him to. He grabbed my hand, rooting me in place, not that I was inclined to run.

A gasp escaped my lips before I could help it. He felt electric. Volatile. Like fire and lightning trapped within a fragile vessel, dangerous if let loose.

"What?" I could barely get the word out.

He reached out, stroking a wild piece of hair from my face. A shudder ran down my spine in response. "Do you think I'd lock you away somewhere and pretend you didn't exist? Even if I don't want the bond... That would be cruel. Do you hear me?"

The conviction in his voice caught me off guard, but...

I thought of Beatrice and her obvious pain. It made me shudder to even consider living like that. Not because of the isolation, but the agony of always wondering, what if?

"You are not that woman, and I am not Jerome," Liwai said. "Don't punish me for the choices they made. I won't make the same."

Oh. Apparently, he didn't have a plan to hide me away in a forest for two decades. Somehow, that didn't seem like the peace offering he thought it was. "And what about Laurie?"

It was a low blow. I almost regretted bringing it up—but a stubborn sense of desperation quashed the guilt. I needed to know.

"Do you regret what happened to *her?*"

He didn't react with anger. His touch remained gentle, playing over my cheekbones before roving down to the base of my throat. His thumb settled there, tracing the racing pulse humming beneath my skin. "I was supposed to protect her," he said, his voice thicker than I'd ever heard.

"From what?" I felt tempted to ask.

A shadow fell over his expression. A tendril of foreign emotion brushed along my consciousness—regret, guilt, anger. Overall was a single, distant thought. *It's not my story to tell.*

"All that matters is that I failed her," he said out loud. "So yes, every day I regret it. Not one second goes by when I don't wish I could go back and change what happened. But I can't, and neither can you. Renae doesn't need me to spend my time dwelling on the past. She needs me to protect her here in the present. I can't afford a distraction, even if it's deserved."

Fair enough. He had a strange way of framing things, no doubt a side effect of his analytical, concise nature. I'd never met anyone so… Infuriating. So different. His mind was a minefield of secrets and shadows, and I knew better than to traipse around it unguarded.

"One day," he reiterated, circling back to his original request. "I want you to promise me."

Because he knew that otherwise, I'd try to rationalize a way around it. With every passing second, I felt more unnerved by the thought of him shouldering every burden without so much as a complaint from me. It felt dirty. Weak.

"Can you at least tell me what you're planning?"

His lip twitched in a way that made my heart stammer. Was that a smile? A fleeting one anyway.

"I will. When I return."

I sensed the promise was a carrot, and he was readying to apply the stick designed to make me comply.

He didn't do so right away. With a curt nod, he gestured for me to follow him back to the RV. By the time we reached it, Renae was asleep on the bench across from the kitchenette, her dark hair shielding her like an ebony blanket.

"I should go while she's asleep," Liwai murmured as we tiptoed outside. "It might upset her otherwise."

"Because she knows what really should be done," I surmised. "This isn't your problem to handle."

His eyes glinted, but he merely headed toward the hitch connecting the RV and the truck. Too quickly for me to follow, he began unhooking the two.

I watched as he drove the truck free of the trailer and parked toward the main road. Rather than drive off then and there, he surprised me by climbing out and waiting for me to approach, his head cocked.

I swallowed hard before advancing, coming close enough to touch him if I wanted. Though I didn't.

"I want that promise now."

My heart jumped.

Without warning, he grabbed my hand again and said, "Give me this..."

Though that wasn't quite what happened. He reached out for my fingers, and they lurched toward him as if he were magnetic. I had no control over it. I couldn't stop myself. I felt that prickling, electric sensation again when our hands finally connected. There was lightning between us, just as violent and lethal as anything that might shoot from the sky.

I must have stumbled closer because then our lips met. What started as an accidental peck became a longer chaste kiss—until his mouth opened and his tongue battered mine into submission, triggering a rush of emotion that had me grasping fistfuls of his shirt for leverage.

Suddenly, he pulled back, leaving me standing on trembling legs. My head swam, and I barely heard him say, "…and you can have the answers you crave in return."

It shouldn't have been enough to tempt me. If anything, I had every right to demand more. More answers, right then and there.

His gaze, however, rendered me speechless with raw emotion. I had never been needed by anyone—I was always the one being pampered and cared for, even by Sheriff Michaels. Nobody ever treated my decisions like they were life or death. As if my choice alone could tip the balance.

In any case, he did.

"I need you to trust me, Kaydence."

These words were more than idle remarks. Despite my apprehension, I nodded, and he ruffled the ends of my hair while he sighed.

"Good. I'll be back by tomorrow night, but if for whatever reason I'm not…"

I went still as his hand came for my face. All he did was run a thumb along my lower lip, still tender from what happened mere minutes ago. Every second of contact made my stomach flip and my heart twist. Only when he withdrew could I find the breath to speak, "If you aren't back, then what?"

"You head north," he said. "You take Renae, get into your car, and follow the mountains until you can't go any further. I'll find you." He reentered the truck and revved the engine.

I'm not sure what I expected, or perhaps wanted... A wave? Another kiss?

Instead, the only sign to mark him leaving was a spray of mud and the sight of his retreating truck vanishing within the woods. Deep down, however, a part of me recognized that emotional gestures weren't natural to him. The fact that he had gone out of his way to reassure me left a bad taste in my mouth.

It didn't feel like the action of a man going on a casual errand.

It felt like a goodbye.

TWENTY-NINE

Renae wasn't quite as emotional as Liwai made her seem. When she woke up an hour after he'd left, all she did was ask for a bottle of juice which she sipped from as I explained his directives.

Stay at the campsite.

Wait for him until nightfall tomorrow.

I selectively left out the part about what would happen if he didn't show up, not that Renae seemed interested either way. Her gaze was distant, and I got the feeling she was barely listening to me. Her mind was elsewhere.

Finished with her drink, she set the bottle on the floor of the RV and crossed her arms.

"Can we put on some music?" Her big, upturned eyes fixated on mine, and I rushed to do her bidding.

After about three hours of pop tunes, she faced me from her position cross-legged on the floor of the kitchenette while absently toying with the ends of her hair.

"Liwai's bossy," she said, her quiet voice far softer than usual. Devoid of the chirpy cadence, she sounded monotone. "It's not his fault. He thinks he has to be. If he were back in the clan… He'd be the leader for sure."

I didn't know what to say. Oddly enough, I suspected she sensed the gist of my sentiments, anyway. He was bossy, but so was I. Barely halfway into his self-imposed deadline, and I was already berating myself for going along with such an infuriating plan anyway—especially with so few details given on his part.

Cody, however twisted, deserved justice. I should have been on my way to Kittywatt to see to that. After going along with this crazy ride, it was the least I could have done for sanity's sake.

"He's been on his own for too long," Renae went on with a wistful sigh. "He doesn't know how to talk to people. He thinks it's better to keep us in the dark about things. Not because he's mean. He just cares too much."

I noticed that she'd started to fiddle with her necklace.

"We?" I gently prodded.

Renae met my gaze head-on as if to say, "*What do you think?*"

"I'm not afraid of their secrets," she muttered instead. "You can ask me stuff. I'll tell you the truth. What do you want to know?"

I wasn't sure whether to be alarmed or eager. Though, how much could a teenager tell me?

"I'm not sure Liwai would want me to bother you with my silly ol' questions," I said with a forced laugh.

"Did he tell you what he is? Really?"

I felt so awkward, unsure of what terminology to even use around her. "I know he doesn't like to be called a werewolf," I said.

"No. Not that." Renae didn't crack a smile in reply. "I meant that he is my uncle," she said, reaching up to play with more of her hair. "He thinks I don't know, but I always have. His brother is my father, though I'm not allowed to call him that. Kahil. That's his name."

Ah. So many things clicked into place, and I wondered how I hadn't put the puzzle pieces together myself. It explained his protectiveness over Renae, and the mixture of anger and tension in his voice whenever he referred to the clan. Not to mention that it revealed a new suspect in the death of Renae's mother.

"I've never met him. Kahil," Renae continued, now inspecting her small, bitten nails. From the stubborn tilt to her mouth, I think she liked saying his name as a small measure of defiance. He might deny her, but she wouldn't play along by refusing to acknowledge him in return. "He doesn't want me, but they won't let Liwai have me, either."

"They?" I asked, copying her by sinking to the floor, extending my legs before me.

"The clan." She whispered the word as though it were sacred. Both a curse and a hallowed term demanding respect. "It's their rules. Outsiders can't be accepted unless another member is willing to fight on their behalf. If they win, not even the elders can dispute it. It wouldn't matter what I am. If Liwai was willing to fight for the right to claim me, I'd be his daughter. I'd be one of them."

The rebellious tilt became a full-blown frown. Then a wave of sadness gradually washed it away. God, I had a horrible suspicion that Liwai had refused to do so—but that didn't seem like him. Not with how fiercely he protected her until now.

"They won't let him," she said, her voice so faint I barely heard her. Seated on the floor, she looked so small and childlike. It made my heart ache just to watch her. "In the eyes of the clan, I still belong to my father by blood."

"I'm sorry," I said hoarsely, unsure of how else to respond. No wonder Liwai seemed so conflicted. Yet, unease gnawed at me. He made it seem as though Renae had no options. None. If there was a way to adopt her as his own, why wouldn't he take it, no matter how dangerous?

"*Kahil* won't let him," Renae insisted, eyeing her dirt-streaked toes as she spread her legs out before her. A terrible suspicion that she could read my brain as well crept across my mind, but the haunted misery in her gaze banished it. This story wasn't being told for my benefit. I wondered if she'd ever been allowed to discuss it freely before.

"What do you mean?"

"It's their stupid rules." She sighed and rubbed the tile floor with the flat of her hand. Back and forth. Forth and back. "He hasn't disowned me. He won't. Until he does, I don't exist. I'm just a ghost."

My breath caught. Being ignored by her father was one thing, but to be denied a guardian who truly cared for her? That was downright cruel.

"Liwai's tried many times to make him release me," Renae added, her tone less mournful, more wistful. "He never told me that. He hates reaching out to them, but he has every year since I was born. Only for me." The shadow of a smile shaped her lips, betraying her age—a young girl, happy that someone wanted her.

"How do you know that?" Again, the prospect of her reading minds arose. Though, was it that much of a leap from psychic visions?

She looked up with an impish grin as if sensing the direction my thoughts had taken. "The boys. I listen in when they hunt. They think I'm too stupid to hear them while in the ancestral form—but I can. Liwai never hunts with them, so it's the only time they break the rules."

"Because they aren't allowed to talk about the clan while on the outside," I recited, recalling what Liwai had said. It

seemed he'd forgotten what it was like to be a teenager—
every rule was merely an opportunity ripe for exploitation.

"They don't talk about any juicy stuff," Renae went on with
a conspiratorial smile. "Just gossip. Like a bunch of girls."
She giggled, but the fleeting sound was quickly cut short.
Her expression fell, reflective once more. "They talk about
me. Cody said he wished Kahil would let me go. Then he
could challenge Liwai to 'right the wrong,' so he could kill
me, and no one could do anything about it."

Horror made my eyes widen. "He said that to you?"
Presumably, far out of Liwai's earshot. Given my anger at
hearing the insult, I suspected his reaction would be far
worse. Beneath the steely calm, the man was a raging
inferno. I shivered at the thought of what his temper might
look like unleashed.

"Not to me," Renae said sadly, drawing her knees up to her
chin while letting her head rest against a nearby cabinet.
"He thinks I can't hear, remember? But I can hear everything. And…" She raised her eyes to mine, and I went cold
all over at the expression I found lurking in them. "I know
Liwai isn't coming back."

Liar. The thought lanced through me with the bitter ache of
betrayal. He'd lied right to my face, and like a fool, I
believed him. Common sense prevailed before I rose to my
feet and stormed from the RV, destination Kittywatt.

Instead, I tried to slow down. Think rationally.

"What do you mean?"

"He didn't go to find Braden and James," Renae said. "He went to the clan."

I felt as though I'd been dunked into ice water. My chest tightened, and all the air in my lungs turned to ice. I couldn't breathe. Somehow, I still had the space of mind to ask, "Why? What does that mean?"

A part of me came up with an explanation on the spot—he went back to reveal me as his promised woman. Then barter my life in exchange for his return to the clan. An idiot couldn't miss the aching longing in his voice whenever he spoke of his home.

"He's going to claim responsibility for Cody," Renae said, exposing another facet of this nightmare I had yet to delve into. "He'll open himself up to retribution, and they'll kill him."

I lurched to my feet. "He's a fool. He can't!" My heart ached at the thought though I wasn't entirely sure why. He was a stranger. His choices shouldn't have made a difference to me either way—but they did. I couldn't sit around and let him clean up my mess for me. It wasn't his fault, and I was no one's burden.

Not anymore.

"It's all cloudy from there," Renae said, still seated on the floor.

I stopped short and realized I was already near the door, ready to head out. During our conversation, the promised rain had started to fall, blanketing everything in thick sheets of soupy, blinding rain. Even if I wanted to stop Liwai's suicide mission, I would be signing up for my own accidental death if I attempted to drive in such a violent storm. Besides…

I'd promised him I'd look after Renae. Maybe to another man, that wouldn't seem so monumental a request, but I had seen into his mind directly. I knew how important her safety was to him—and that he wouldn't entrust it to me lightly. For her, at least, he would return for a proper goodbye. Right?

"I can't see what happens next. It keeps changing." I looked back to find Renae curled onto her side, cradling her head between her hands. "I don't know which way it will go. I just know that if she comes… *She* is a bad omen."

"Who?" I crept over to her and crouched to place a hand on her shoulder. She was trembling, her voice hitching with smothered sobs. "Who, Renae?"

She shook her head. "I can't see it. It's all blurry. I'm tired."

"Okay." I stood and took in a steadying breath. Liwai and his self-destructive crusade would have to wait. Renae needed me before I could focus on anything else.

When it came to caring for someone else, I ironically only had one prime example to fall back on. What would Dee do?

Step one would be to make a terrible pot of black coffee and utter some tasteless joke about penises. I opted for performing just the first part.

Minutes later, the rich smell flooded the RV's interior, coaxing Renae from her fetal position. I got her to sit at the table, and while she sipped from a chipped mug, I compiled a plate of food out of the "favorites" she'd served Liwai and me the day prior.

She ate woodenly, and when she finished, I ushered her into the bedroom and sighed the second I heard her lie down on the bed.

As I took up a vigil on the couch, I made a mental note to thank Dee for taking care of me all these years the second I got home. I'd never stopped to consider how stressful it must have been on her, shouldering the responsibility of caring for a child that wasn't hers.

I don't think I'd ever heard her complain once.

And here I was, itching for Liwai to come and for Renae's fears to be proven false. He wouldn't sign up for death, knowing he would leave her behind. Right? Or, more self-ishly, he wouldn't leave me here to pick up the pieces.

Though, in all honesty, I didn't know a darn thing about him other than his brooding nature and penchant for taking on problems that weren't his own.

By the time the sun came up, I comforted myself with having made it partially through Liwai's timeline. By sundown, he would return, and I could do what I should have done before letting myself be swayed by his dire talking points.

I even grabbed my cell phone and toyed with the idea of calling Sheriff Michaels, Liwai be damned—only to realize that I had several missed calls from the man already.

My heart sank. Realistically, it was only a matter of time before they made the connection between the tire tracks of my car and the proximity to Cody's body.

Apparently fed up with trying to call me, Sheriff Michaels had left a single voice message. I held my breath as I let it play.

"…Kaydence." He sounded so old. So tired. "I know things between us are… Just give me a call when you get this, please. I know you've been up around Settler's Point—"

This was it. Tears stung my eyes, and I braced for the inevitable.

"But it isn't safe to be out there right now. Your Aunt said you went on a camping trip. Why you'd do something like that in the middle of damn fall, I don't—never mind. The point is, they found a dead hiker the other night. They think the poor bastard fell off a cliff—the body was damaged beyond all recognition, but they want to ship it out to some specialist for testing. That's the last thing we fucking need. You keep that detail to yourself. They don't want it getting out just yet and causing a panic," he added as all the air left my lungs. I couldn't breathe, let alone speak. "God, Kaydence… I just need to know you're safe. Come by the station when you get the chance. We'll talk. Bye."

With that, he'd hung up, and my mind was left reeling with several realizations that battled for control. One lone thought was the first to shake loose.

A dead hiker. A part of me wanted to feel relieved. It could have been the poor, average rock climber, not Cody. Just a freak accident.

Yes. I struggled to convince myself that all was well. I wasn't a murderer, and Liwai Raven was off being a gallant hero for no reason. Hopefully, he realized that before he took the credit for a death that never happened.

I must have zoned out, overwhelmed by the potential terror unleashed on Kittywatt. I didn't notice Renae was awake until she padded into my line of sight and gingerly took a bottle of juice from the fridge. She cracked it open and sipped slowly, turning her large eyes on me.

"Hey honey," I said. "You can sleep in if you want. Liwai won't be back until later tonight."

I strived to keep the fear from my voice, even as my mind raced ahead to the inevitable. If Cody was dead, Liwai couldn't protect me. He would take Renae and leave, this time for good.

Could I even blame him?

Renae shrugged, still guzzling her juice. Once she'd drained the bottle, she set it aside and sat at the kitchen table facing me. "Maybe I heard the news wrong," she said, biting her lower lip. Then, she propped her chin in both hands, appearing deep in thought.

After a few seconds, she lifted her shoulder in defeat. "Nothing's changed. It's all still as blurry as it was before. I can't see what's happening. Ugh!" She curled her hands into fists and released an exasperated groan. "I can't make anything out. If it doesn't come to me all at once, I'm useless."

My heart panged. She sounded so dejected. A young girl, who, like Liwai, had taken way too much on her tiny shoulders. I could wallow in my own despair or push it aside for her sake. Once again, my mantra came in handy. What would Dee do? She wasn't much of a role model, but she had her methods for lightening tension.

"You know what I think?" I asked her while rising to my feet. "You should pick a music station for us to listen to while we clean up and get dressed. Then you can show me some dance moves so I can dream of one day not embarrassing myself during Bardee's rodeo barn dance nights."

She beamed.

We cleaned.

For a handful of precious hours, things felt almost… Normal. Like the days after my mother died when Dee bent over backward to distract me with *I Love Lucy* reruns and way too much caffeine. Once or twice, I might have been guilty of considering her immature and silly, but now I knew the truth she'd had the tact to never let on to.

Even if she were being silly or careless, I could think of whatever dish she'd broken or meal she'd burnt that day— not my mom. She'd done her job to the extent that she'd gotten me to focus on anything else. Looking back, I can't blame her for that.

It's a harder skill to master than I could have imagined—especially when my attention was being pulled in two drastically different directions. The harder I tried to be in the moment for Renae, the more a part of me envisioned a future in which I had killed someone in cold blood.

No amount of dancing and giggles could change that, though I certainly tried, and Renae didn't seem any the wiser.

Long after we'd collapsed, exhausted from dancing around the RV, I fixed lunch, and then we resorted to staring in silence, avoiding the subject we both seemed anxious to acknowledge. Liwai was due to return at sundown.

By the time evening fell, I couldn't deny a strange sense of relief. My unofficial guardian duties had come to an end. He would pick up where I left off and devise some new brooding, self-righteous plan that would leave me on the outside and probably conclude with him and Renae on the run.

I was preparing myself for it. That way, it would be easier to face the rejection head-on. After all, I'd done it before. The day my fake father picked up and left, all I'd done was help carry one of his bags to the car. We didn't even say goodbye. After that, I developed a brisk, businesslike efficiency when it came to people leaving me.

But when Daddy left, I didn't go on a multi-town rampage and cajole innocent secretaries into giving me anything that might help me find his whereabouts, either. That one detail set Liwai Raven apart from the other men in my life who'd disappointed me.

I hadn't been able to let him leave. Not without a fight. Clarity. Closure?

The idea bothered me. A lot. I wasn't used to craving contact with people, let alone a virtual stranger. My stomach felt tangled into knots. I wasn't hungry, but as dinner time rolled around, I figured it was either put a meal together or dwell.

I fixed Renae some tuna and found her at the kitchen table, kicking her feet out and twisting strands of black hair around her fingers.

"It's getting late," she said, voicing an observation I'd already made.

He said nightfall, and the sun was already setting, ushering in a berth of dark storm clouds. Sooner or later, it was going to rain again. I just hoped I could be on the road home before it did.

Against the backdrop of her preferred music, I ate alongside Renae, and then we settled into silence, gazing from the window with furtive glances.

Nightfall, he said. But as darkness descended, there wasn't a hint of yellow headlights to herald the arrival of a vehicle on the road. Neither did my cell phone buzz with an incoming message from an unknown number. Either he was okay with blowing past his own unofficial deadline or...

"He's late," Renae declared as the darkness outside gradually became pitch-black. "He's never late. Never. Something's wrong."

I picked up on her fear, feeling my stomach twist into knots. Perhaps the supposed elder had already been sent from the pack. What if Liwai really did try to take responsibility for my mistake?

I had to dig my nails into my forearm just to keep my breathing steady.

"He probably just got held up in traffic, honey," I said, trying to make my voice soothing. I must have failed because she winced and shook her head before spinning to face the window directly.

"He's never late," she repeated. "Something's wrong."

And I didn't know what to do. This wasn't included in the Dee Blanchett child-rearing manual. When my mother died, there wasn't a possibility of her returning, and my father had more or less made it clear that he wasn't coming back. How to deal with such a wrench in the anticipated timeline?

I tried to improvise.

"It's stuffy in here," I said, heading for the door. "Why don't you and I go out and star gaze?"

In my mind, it was a good pretext to get her closer to my car without scaring her. Liwai's warning rang clear in my mind. *Get Renae and go north until you can't go any further.*

Running away with a minor was the last thing I wanted to do, but there didn't seem to be any other options.

"It's going to rain more," Renae said without moving. "It will be harder for him to track us. What if he can't find the others? What if he went to turn himself in. What if…"

They'd already killed him, and he sacrificed himself. I was thinking it, too. I just hadn't been brave enough to voice the fear out loud.

"Let's not panic yet," I suggested. "How about you think of something we can do to take our minds off everything? We could listen to some music in my car?"

I wasn't sure yet whether or not to reveal Liwai's warning should he fail to return. The prospect loomed overhead like an ugly cloud I didn't want to acknowledge just yet. In fact, I wanted more than anything for Renae to happily go along with my plan to forget and spend more hours dancing on bare feet.

But, while she may have been young, Renae apparently wasn't stupid.

"You know something," she said, her tone soft but no less accusatory. "What is it?"

I could have lied to her. I think I had it in me if I wrote it off as being for the greater good. As it turned out, I didn't share Liwai's knack for hiding under secrets and mystery.

With little fanfare, I told her the truth, but she took it all in with a reflective frown rather than alarm.

"I don't think the clan is north," she said, though I wasn't sure why she felt the need to make that distinction. "I still can't see. It's all blurry."

"We can wait a little longer," I suggested.

However, Liwai failed to appear by ten o'clock, and it was too late to ignore his absence. As the adult in the equation, I needed to act. But how?

For starters, I fished my car keys from my pocket and held them up for Renae to see.

"He's probably fine," I said to preface the suggestion, "but if you think we should follow his advice, I'm ready when you are."

She nodded solemnly and went over to her duffle. After rummaging through the RV for various items, she stowed them in her bag and followed me.

An uneasy feeling tainted the air. It was probably just my imagination running haywire, but the shadows seemed to… move. Each time the wind blew, they flickered and morphed into recognizable shapes. Tree branches. Leaves. Limbs.

It seemed the forest was watching us go—or trying to chase us out.

I found the keys to the RV hanging on a hook near the door and locked it before Renae, and I finally clambered into my Beetle, and I strained my eyes to find the road.

It was a slow, silent trek with only my headlights illuminating the narrow road leading out. Renae served as my quiet copilot, scanning the landscape intently for any sign of Liwai.

Unsurprisingly, he didn't come jumping out of the bushes when I finally hit the main road. He wasn't there to elaborate on his terse instructions, either. *North.* Several towns could have fit that distinction, but I decided the safest bet was to hit the highway and just keep going.

Within an hour, that method quickly lost appeal when I realized that, within a full day of driving, I could reach the northern border without knowing where to go or what to do next. A safer bet would be to go home. Beg Sheriff Michaels for advice, murder or not. He could track down Liwai before he did something foolish.

Or, I could make things worse.

Having egg on my face seemed slightly better than running out of gas on the highway miles from home. I started to turn around.

"Wait," Renae said, sitting bolt upright, her gaze fixed ahead. "Keep going," she continued.

I hesitated. "Honey, we could just be driving in circles—"

"Please." Her voice was firmer than I'd ever heard, so persistent the hairs on the back of my neck stood on end. "Keep going."

I drove, assuming that she meant for me to follow Liwai's vague instruction to the very end—only, just a few miles later, she pointed to a sign for an exit that would take us further east.

"There."

"Honey, I don't—"

"There! Please. We need to go that way."

In the end, I had no idea what made me listen. Maybe it was the pleading note in her voice. She seemed so used to rejection and being ignored. I didn't have the heart to add my name to the list of adults who'd failed her.

So, I took the exit and tried to smother my growing dread. I'd never been this way before, and I had no frame of reference for the towns scattered across the next few signs we saw. Coxwhatain, Bidtyntee, Harmon.

"Do you know someone who lives out this way?" I asked in the halfhearted hope that she knew where we were headed.

She shook her head, her eyes riveted to the road. "Keep going."

Twenty miles later, she slammed her hand on the dashboard. "Go right."

Right led to yet another exit, and this time I had no idea in hell where it could lead. North? South?

"Renae, I don't think—"

"Please," Renae insisted.

She seemed so intent, as if she were watching a scene unfold miles away. Whatever she saw drove her to lead me on a wild goose chase. Where would it lead?

I had no damn idea.

Because I hadn't a clue how to get home, I had no other option.

As I moved to take the requested exit, Renae came alive and sprouted off a series of directions. Right here. Left. Go down this road.

I drove until the time trickled into the hours of early dawn, and my eyes were burning so much, I could barely see straight. Finally, Renae gasped and uttered, "Here. Stop! Here!"

Here being the side of the road overlooking a glistening body of water, much like the lake we left behind. The second I slowed the car, Renae scrambled out of the passenger's seat and took off across the road and through a field.

"Honey, wait!"

I chased after her, relieved that the road was mostly deserted. By the time I reached Renae, she was circling the same patch of earth over and over, scanning the surrounding landscape as if searching for something.

Or someone.

"Is this where Liwai went?" I asked.

In the darkness, I saw her shake her head. The storm clouds had let up, allowing a tendril of dawn to illuminate everything in an ethereal, blue glow. Bathed in the lighting, Renae resembled a fairy in an oversized T-shirt, or perhaps some horribly lost woodland goddess.

She kept pacing, kept searching…

And I took my chance to creep away from her far enough to pull out my cell phone and do the one thing I should have done hours ago.

He may have been a deadbeat father, but Burt Michaels picked up on the third ring despite it being nearly five in the morning.

"Kaydence?" His voice was gruff with exhaustion. "Thank God. Are you okay?"

"I'm fine," I replied, deciding it wasn't a total lie. Physically, I was. "I just, got lost, and a few exits later, I have no idea where I am."

He sighed. "What's the last exit?"

I wracked my brain. "Harmon, I think—"

"Harmon? What the hell are you doing all the way out there? Kaydence, there's just wilderness and bears out that far. Are you in some kind of trouble?"

I'd grown up most of my life without a father—so maybe that was why I felt so damn susceptible to the genuine concern in his tone? It made me want to confess that I was in trouble. That I needed his help. Guidance. Something.

"Kaydence?"

"N-No," I stammered. "I just…"

Didn't know. I think calling him was my brain's last-ditch effort to inject some kind of normalcy into this madness. Maybe the truth was I wanted him to yell at me? To force me to realize how foolish it was to run around at the whims of the Ravens. To make me come home and confess what I'd done.

"Look, to get home, just hop on the highway and head west toward Elkton," he said with a yawn. "You'll find the ramp for Kittywatt soon enough. When you get in, we can get breakfast somewhere and just talk. Okay?"

"Okay? Um… Thanks."

"Drive careful, Kaydence."

I hung up, oddly relieved and more confused than ever about the unaddressed questions looming overhead. I could worry about that later. For now, I could get Renae somewhere safe and figure out where to go from there.

When I turned back to find her, she wasn't there.

"Renae?" My heart sank, and I whirled in the direction of the car, wondering if she'd gone back to it. From here, the windows looked empty. "Renae?"

There weren't many places she could be, except a small section of the wooded forest a few yards away or…

The water's edge.

Oh, God. I ran like crazy, shouting her name as I went. Only my own echo answered back. I nearly reached the nearest trees when a single sound pierced the air and made my blood run cold.

A scream.

"Kaydee!"

"Renae!" I ran blindly in the direction of the sound, tripping over stray branches and brambles as I went. The blooming daylight didn't reach this far in, and twigs and thorns tore at my hair and any exposed skin.

"Renae! Where are you?"

"Kaydee! Kaydee—"

A rustling noise sounded close by. I turned toward it, feeling out blindly with both hands. "Renae?"

Warmth met my fingertips, encased within a surface that could have been flesh. A heartbeat later, the wind whistled near my ear.

Wham!

The world went black.

THIRTY

All I knew was a rustling, steady motion that jolted my body back and forth. I felt weightless, as though I were floating in the ether, untethered by mortal constraints.

Suddenly, everything came to an abrupt halt.

"Kaydence."

That voice. It tugged at me like a hook, forcing me to respond despite the wave of exhaustion attempting to knock me under. With a familiarity that resonated down my spine, the raspy baritone instilled a strange, overwhelming sense of comfort.

I knew the speaker's identity even before I opened my eyes and struggled to make them focus. Liwai.

"I'm taking you to the hospital," he warned, foregoing any niceties. "But I need you to tell me what the hell happened. Where is Renae?"

Renae? She was with me. Trying to recall the details made my heart ache, but a few snippets came tumbling out of the chaos. I remembered a forest, and then darkness and Renae screaming for me.

"You were struck over the head pretty hard," I heard Liwai say. His icy calm was back again, but quickly fracturing. He was a stone under enormous pressure, and the impossible seemed inevitable—he'd shatter.

"You could have a concussion," he went on. "You were out cold. It's a miracle no one came across you before I did… Damn it, Kaydence. Talk to me, please."

His control was such a relentless, stable facet of his personality—but when it wavered, his entire demeanor changed. Even though I couldn't see him, I sensed the shift in him. It was like the way my body would tense up at the zoo when near the lion's pen. The presence of a predator triggered an instinctive response I couldn't deny. Every nerve went on red alert, and the resulting adrenaline was enough to banish the remnants of pain or exhaustion.

I blinked, and gradually the world came into focus. I stared into a tanned, stained sky that I eventually realized was the ceiling of my Beetle. Someone had placed me in the back seat, lying face-up with what felt like a wad of fabric tucked beneath my head.

"Where…" My skull ached as I winced in agony.

"Somewhere on the east coast," Liwai said. "I sensed you were in pain, and I followed you. You had to be down for nearly an hour. What happened?"

"I'm not sure." Fragments of memory came back with the intensity of a wrecking ball. I'd failed. Renae was gone, and it was my fault. "Go back." I tried to sit up. My head felt as though it were held together with duct tape, but I managed to lift myself high enough to see him clearly. He was in the driver's seat, and the buildings whizzing past revealed we weren't near the remote area I last saw Renae.

"Where are you going? We need to find her—"

"Her scent was faded by the time I reached you," Liwai replied, each word terse and bitten off. "She's long gone. She'll be miles away by now if they're moving her by vehicle. If not… She'll be fine—"

"She's a fourteen-year-old girl," I rasped, horrified. "Who knows what monster took her? How can you just leave her there?"

At the back of my mind, I knew I had no right to berate him. Who knew what his plan was. I couldn't deny that it felt good to rage at someone anyway. Deep down, I was angry with him. So damn angry. Once again, he'd lied to me. He left me behind.

"I caught her scent near where you were assaulted, but there were no signs of blood or a struggle. Renae is stronger than you think. She can handle herself long enough for me to find her. You, on the other hand? Your pulse is racing, you've lost so much blood you're as white as a sheet. Your breathing is irregular. I wasn't sure if you would even wake up, so don't lecture me on who to administer aid to during a crisis. If I'd left you, and gone after Renae, you'd be dead by now."

I winced with every gruesome observation he listed. I knew he wasn't exaggerating. Not even a little.

"I… I'm sorry." Burning tears welled in my eyes and fell before I could stop them. "It's my fault. I'm so sorry. I took my eyes off her for one second. I…"

So many monsters in the world weren't encased in fur and armed with claws. My blood ran cold at the potential outcomes, and I envied his calm.

"There was something else," he admitted after a heartbeat. "I caught only one other scent nearby, but it was a woman's. She… Her scent wasn't entirely human."

The implications made my blood run cold. His cryptic warnings and Renae's obvious disdain had definitely colored my opinion of those Liwai considered "his kind." The clan. "But you said that no one from there leaves."

"They don't," he said. "This woman didn't smell like one of us. Once you're safe, I can track her down."

The hospital wasn't an idle threat.

"Just leave me here," I croaked. "I can call someone to get me. You take my car and find Renae—"

"I'm not leaving you."

I was astonished by his conviction. "Why not?"

"Because every second you're in pain, I feel it," he snarled. "In every pore, magnified by a million. You will lie down and let me take you to the hospital. I could heal you myself, but it could do more damage in the long run…" He sighed, seemingly torn by both arguments. Then he shook his head. "Enough arguing. You need rest."

"You can't order me around like I'm a child," I pointed out, though a fight with him wasn't what I wanted. I felt as though we were on the verge of a precipice. If I gave in now, I'd forever lose ground in whatever uncharted territory loomed between us. He would make up his mind that I had no say. No agency. No voice.

"What would you have me do?" he demanded. "Let you bleed out on the side of the road?"

But I had other options, including calling Sheriff Michaels.

"You can let me call someone to come and get me," I said, trying to mimic his unrelenting calm. "Or get me some Tylenol and take me with you to find Renae. I'll be fine."

And either way, I was willing to risk aggravating a head injury over letting a child stay with her kidnapper for even a moment more. And yet… A better question was why I didn't bring up the police? They should have been alerted in the first place and would have far more resources to find Renae.

"The police won't do much good," Liwai warned, reading my mind. "Whoever took her, knows how to cover their tracks in a way that most humans aren't accustomed to. I can find her. I just need…"

Time. He didn't need me to slow him down or wallow in guilt over having been responsible for her disappearance in the first place.

Groaning, I hauled myself into a sitting position and swung my legs off the back seat so I faced forward.

"I don't need a hospital," I reiterated. "We pick one of the options I laid out. I'm over eighteen. I can refuse to be seen if I want to."

It was a bluff, but I couldn't shake a foreboding feeling that warned me time was running out.

Liwai kept driving. When he finally pulled into a parking lot, I braced myself to find a sign for an emergency room entrance up ahead. Instead, I found a small, chain drug store. After leaving the car in a huff, Liwai returned moments later with a plastic shopping bag that he tossed onto my lap.

Inside it was a bottle of water, an over-the-counter pain reliever, a roll of gauze, and some antiseptic ointment.

"Sit up front so that I can keep an eye on you," he commanded, having already reclaimed his position at the wheel.

Walking was a task easier said than done. I had to cling to the car and hope I didn't collapse as my stomach roiled with every step I took. Somehow, I managed to make it onto the passenger's seat without puking all over myself.

Once I was beside him, Liwai snatched the bag from me and arranged the supplies on his lap. He was briskly efficient, pressing the water to my lips before dolling out exactly two pain pills. As I choked them down, he treated my newest head wound while I avoided facing myself in the rearview mirror.

"This one is going to leave a scar," he gruffly assessed. "You're lucky your skull didn't fracture. They must have used a stick."

My throbbing skull seconded that observation. A stick, or a barbell. Still, I made a show of shrugging him off and nodded toward the road. "Now drive back, and let's find her."

"Wait—" He snagged my fingers in a vice grip. Then he held them and didn't let go. "Just wait…"

Our eyes met, and a strange sensation washed over me. It was almost as if I did lose consciousness after all—but of the rest of the world. Any and everything but him. His gaze was turned inward, his expression as stern as always, but not for the first time—I managed to peek through the cracks in the façade to the real man lurking beneath.

Someone just as frantic as I was, though in a very different way. I tended to get impulsive when the pressure was on. Liwai, on the other hand… He became possessive. Perhaps the need was instinctive, bolstering the claims that his people could transform into wolves, among other things.

The strangest part was how vividly I could see into that corner of his mind where a foreign, primal thought process lurked. He needed to find Renae, far more desperately than I did—but one emotion was stronger. A need for me. To know I was safe. To ease the pain he could feel as though it were his own. He was just as panicked and frustrated as I was, but much better at hiding it.

Only when we were that close, physically touching, could I finally get some insight into him—and that glimpse terrified me. His thoughts were so alien, riddled with more emotions than logic. Anger. Frustration. Need.

And another base impulse so intense it took my breath away—longing. A craving—no, an ache. A painful need to mark what was his. Take it. Bite. Cement in blood the bond he felt in his soul...

Just a little, to ease her pain. It wouldn't make the bond any stronger than it already was. Just a little. A taste.

I shivered as a physical touch assaulted my body in real time—his other hand, running along the edge of my skull, finding a particularly sore spot. He prodded it once, then, with my head still infected with his thoughts...

He brought that finger to his mouth and brushed his tongue along the pad of it. From this angle, I could tell it was slick with a dark, red substance that vanished into his mouth.

And just like that, some of the pain in my skull eased up. Enough I could think clearly for myself—just one sentiment, though—What in the hell?

Suddenly, Liwai pulled away, robbing me of that strange insight. The next second, he started my car and veered toward the highway, inching slightly above the speed limit.

"Now can you tell me what the hell you were doing out this far?" he asked, his voice strained though controlled. His tense posture and stern expression all but begged me not to bring up what just happened. "I told you to go north, not east."

"It was Renae. She… It was like she was in a trance," I added, as the sheer idiocy of blaming a teenager for my driving sank in. Guilt banished even my shock at his strange penchant for drinking my blood. "I shouldn't have listened to her—"

"Describe it." His hand left the wheel and crossed over to mine, bridging the distance between us. Inches from making contact, he let it hover awkwardly in the air. "This trance. What was it like?"

I fished for the right words. "She told me where to go, almost as if she were hearing a voice in her head giving directions. Then she told me to stop at that specific location. She didn't say why."

He frowned, highlighting the wrinkles and worry lines etched into the skin around his mouth.

"Now, my turn." I eyed him warily, unsure of which tact to take. Angry? Or neutral as he had been. I settled for something in the middle. "Why were you late? We waited until almost midnight, and you never showed. Where were you?"

"Trying to get answers," he said, still manipulating the wheel one-handed. However, he avoided my hand, pressing his empty palm to his knee. "I caught up with the others. Cody wasn't with them—"

My heart sank, but Liwai's frown revealed he was concerned about far more than the vagrant he disliked.

"That isn't all. Something's happened at the clan. This situation just got far more serious than I'd thought."

"They think the body was a hiker who fell off a cliff," I added, praying that he could deduce more from that statement than I could. Was that a good sign?

Apparently not. He hissed through clenched teeth, causing me to stiffen in alarm. "I couldn't find anything definitive on my own. For now, we'll just have to rely on what we know."

That Cody had been stabbed by me.

Though, again, he seemed angrier than he had before. His shoulders were rigid, and he practically radiated tension.

"Did something happen?"

"The others," he said through clenched teeth. "I told them to go south when we left Kittywatt, but they headed west, toward the territory. That's why it took me longer than expected to track them down. Then they told me… They've been called back."

His voice rumbled, making the statement sound monumental. More than just a friendly visit.

"Back home?" I asked, struggling to understand.

"To the clan. It's never happened before," he added, his eyes narrowed. "Never. Not once. I thought perhaps due to Cody's disappearance, but there have been accidents before.

Other vagrants have died while on the outside. Usually, a ceremony is held to commemorate their death, but never has their group been called back. Never. I needed to find out more. I'd only just caught up to them when I felt you."

"Did they say anything?" I could barely get the words out.

"Nothing good," he admitted. "Apparently, they were summoned back just after we left Kittywatt. That night. I was still within the area. If the clan wanted me to know, they would have told me—the elders. They didn't. That was *before* your run-in with Cody."

Which meant that his death couldn't be the reason behind the request. Unease gathered in my chest, and I wasn't sure if it was his or mine. Maybe we both shared the same paranoid fear.

"This is my fault."

Predictably more guilt descended, but my aching skull couldn't contain it. My breathing hitched beneath the onslaught, and I did the only thing I could in the hopes of lessening it—I placed my hand over his, latching onto his unyielding calm.

While he let me establish contact, he didn't grab my hand in return. In any case, I felt marginally better, even if I couldn't explain why.

"I didn't have time to question the vagrants," he said, sounding agitated by that fact. "But I doubt they knew about Cody, at least. If they did, an elder would already be on their way. I would sense them."

But he was unnerved, regardless. Unnerved enough to risk breaking his own deadline hoping to find answers.

"For now, that doesn't matter. What does is finding Renae. Once we have her, we leave."

Which brought up a very good question.

"How? What if the clan elders have her? What can you do that the police can't?"

My mind went blank when I saw him smile. Words alone couldn't describe it. Despite his perpetual frown, I knew immediately that his beautiful features were designed to convey joy instead. The light in his eyes, and the radiance in his cheeks. I had never seen anything or anyone more breathtaking. However, a second later, the expression was gone.

"I have my ways," he said evasively. "And if the elders were in the area, I would know. They aren't exactly known for subtlety. You need to trust me. Tell me if there is anything you can remember. Anything at all."

There was one thing. "I called my... Burt Michaels, the sheriff," I admitted.

His eyes cut to slits. A new emotion leeched into our mental connection. Suspicion. "And?"

"I just told him where I was. He said there was nothing out that far but the coast and bears. My attention was off Renae for only a few minutes, but when I looked back, she was gone."

"They haven't taken her far," Liwai said.

"How do you know that?"

"Because I can smell her," he declared. "I've been aware of her scent this entire time, sensing the direction they're moving her in. It's been steady for the past hour, somewhere further east, about thirty miles away from where she was taken."

He sounded so sure, but what he was describing… It should have been impossible. Right?

"You can smell her from that distance?"

He nodded. "And more. I was wrong. There are two women with her, both seem young. Their scents are distinct. It's strange… It's like they haven't been near humans, but they don't smell like anyone from the clan."

"You think they're like you?"

He regarded me with a searching glance. "Perhaps," he said finally. "Though, it should be impossible. The clan doesn't tolerate outsiders. They monitor those on the outside and periodically check in with vagrants who have 'overstayed their exile.'"

Judging from his scathing tone, he had been the subject of one of those check-ins.

"Whoever they are, they've proven they're dangerous, if not to Renae, then to anyone else."

"How can you be sure she's okay?"

He sighed, though I don't think it was out of irritation. I questioned him, and he had to break out of his concrete thinking to find the right way to describe it. The way he thought was fascinating and complex to witness. His brain was prone to characterize things in more emotional terms. Wet. Dangerous. Harmless. Dry. Hot. Cold. Such simplicity didn't diminish him—not at all. It was a humble, efficient way of processing the world. It perplexed him to take the time to explain it in terms I could understand.

"I have her scent," he said carefully. "I can tell she's worried, but unharmed. There is no blood attached to her. No signs of injury."

I couldn't contain my curiosity. "Is that how you found me? By smell?"

Then I recalled the way he'd described the location he'd been in. First south, then further west than he'd intended. That put him over a hundred miles—not to mention a few hours—out of my range. Yet he'd been able to find me, according to him, in less than one.

"No," he said, confounding me further. "With you, it's different. I feel you. Your pain. Your fear. It's more than a scent."

The intensity in his voice sent a shudder through me. Along with his words, I got a smattering of images—*my throat, the way I'd felt nestled against his chest, my body glimpsed beneath a glistening layer of moisture in the shower.* In his eyes, I wasn't the awkward, innocent Kaydee I'd been my whole life. I was a body he craved to dominate, but it wouldn't be fair to take offense.

His perception was so alien, and even now, there was so much I didn't understand about this supposed connection between us. So much knowledge of me he possessed when I barely even knew his favorite color.

"I only enter your mind freely when I need to," he said without an ounce of guilt. "Or when your emotions are heightened. It's hard for me to control."

And yet, on my end, I only had insight into him during a few brief moments, none of them with full clarity.

Suddenly he inclined his head, his shoulders tense. "We're getting close."

I turned to the window. This area was similar to the one Renae led me to, though far vaster and wilder. There wasn't a house in sight, let alone anywhere a deviant kidnapper might hole up. His theory of them being other than human held more water. I doubted a normal person could last long out here without proper equipment and camping supplies.

"They aren't far." He turned off the road, driving my car straight onto a patch of overgrown grass and weeds. There, he parked, scanning our surroundings with his head cocked. Without warning, he climbed out of the car, and I scrambled after him.

"Stay here," he snapped to me. I had no intention of following him to confront these people, but I could make sure he wouldn't be ambushed like I was. Mustering all my strength, I grabbed the long, heavy scrapper I used to knock ice off the windows in winter. Then I copied him, surveying the landscape with a critical eye.

One of his assessments turned out to be accurate. There was no way in hell a grown man, even one half his size, could comfortably crouch among the rugged underbrush and low-lying vegetation. If they were nearby, our culprit had to be slight. Young. Small. Much like…

"Come out and face me," Liwai bellowed. "This is your only warning."

I jumped at his tone—it was feral, devoid of his usual stern warmth. I never wanted to be on the receiving end of it.

"You know what the law of retribution means. You harm one of mine—you harm *me*," he continued. "I can take the repayment however I choose. Face me now, and I might be charitable—"

"No harm!" A nearby bush shook with movement, and a small figure stood from behind it, her trembling hands raised above her head. Her size and her long, ratty brown hair were the only clues alluding to her sex and age. She wore a heavy, oversized jacket that looked like it was meant for a large man and had the hood drawn low over her face. Poking beneath the black leather, was a pair of filthy leggings that had once been a bright shade of bubblegum pink.

"Livvie didn't mean no harm," she said, stumbling over her words in her rush to speak. "Honest! I told her not to, but she was scared. We don't bother no one out here. No one!"

Liwai's posture shifted, and some of his primal intensity lessened, though not by much. "Who are you?" he demanded, his tone softer.

The girl shuffled forward and snatched back her hood. I couldn't silence a gasp. She was even younger than I thought, perhaps no older than Renae.

"Darcy Hillcox, Sir," she said, her accent as musical as the most rural of Kittywatt's citizens. Her large brown eyes were shaped like saucers, the easiest features to make out, considering the rest of her face was streaked with mud. "And we meant no harm, honest. Livvie didn't even mean to hurt her —" she nodded toward me. "We was just—"

"Savin' *her*."

The second voice was nearly identical to Darcy's but harsher and more thickly accented. It came from another bush further away, but the speaker remained low to the ground and out of view. "We was savin' the *tainter*. From you."

"We merely wanted to help someone we thought was in trouble," Darcy said, her expression earnest beneath the filth. "Honest!"

"Your kind doesn't want *tainters* anyway," the second voice replied. Livvie, I assumed, and I pictured her as young and small as the girl before us. "Go away!"

"Let me see Renae," Liwai said, his tone still level. From his stance, I couldn't tell if he was as alarmed by this scene as I was. In his world, wild young girls must have been a common occurrence. "I know she's close," he went on. "Let me make sure she's okay."

"No!" Livvie snarled.

"Maybe." Darcy lowered her hands to her sides, and her lips became pursed, her brows furrowed. "*Tainters* deserve freedom like anyone else," she said, brandishing her chin. Though she kept her head respectfully bowed, her hands began to curl into fists. "We won't let you hurt her—"

"I told you, Darc," Livvie called from behind her bush. "I told you! That's what they want. To take her back and rip out her throat. Like they did the others. She was a slave—"

"Slave?" I blurted, wincing at the word choice. "What do you mean?"

"That's what *they* do to those who aren't *pure*," Livvie growled with an unmistakable fury. "They chop us up or sell us off. We won't let anyone else get hurt. We aren't slaves—"

"Renae is my family," Liwai said, his eyes flashing. "If you don't show her to me right now, I'll find her on my own. I don't think you want that."

Darcy flinched, and her eyes cut in Livvie's direction. I sensed she was seconds from bolting, and even with his speed, the sheer makeup of the landscape could slow him down. Renae would be further out of reach.

"You can show her to me," I said, stepping forward. "I can't hurt her, can I? And if I tried to, you could hit me over the head again."

"Yes," Darcy blurted over Livvie's angry snarl, seeming desperate for a resolution. "She can see. I'll take her, and she can see, and then you go."

"I watch him," Livvie said without an ounce of fear.

"Kaydence…" Of the four of us, Liwai seemed the most disapproving of my plan.

"Trust me," I croaked back, the most convincing argument I could think of on the spot. I knew it was foolish, and I'd probably regret it later, but I couldn't justify any chance that Renae could stay hidden for even a moment longer.

Darcy pointed to me with a mud-caked finger. "Come. Come. I show."

"And he stays," Livvie snarled. For the first time, she crept from behind the bush, nearly identical in size and facial structure to Darcy. The only difference was her hair was white-blond instead of brown.

I inched forward before anyone could change their mind, myself included. I could feel the pain reliever kicking in, but I was still dizzy, and whatever Liwai had done in the car didn't seem to help much either. Every step was a game of maintaining my balance, and my stomach lurched as though I were on a seesaw.

Darcy, on the other hand, was fast, trudging over the hill-side at a pace that would have winded me were I at full health and well rested. As a result, I lost sight of her more than once, and my only clue of her direction was a stern, "Come," from somewhere up ahead.

There were no trees or dense forest, thank God, but the girl was slight enough that—clothed in her dark coat—she practically blended into the landscape, especially from a distance.

"Halt!"

The warning came as we neared a smattering of large rocks covered in moss and lichen. Standing at the crest of them, Darcy raised her hand. Then she darted out of view behind the makeshift structure. A few seconds later, she called out, "You may see. Come."

My heart sank at the thought of trying to climb the haphazard sack of boulders, but before I could take a step, Darcy appeared on the edge of the structure and waved me over.

The air gave off an untouched aura, and I suspected very few people regularly came out this far, if any. Only a child could make use of the rugged terrain so easily.

Around the rocks was a small gap that formed a makeshift cavern. Barely visible, lying on a dirty floor, was a tiny figure I recognized instantly.

"Renae?"

"She's tired," Darcy said solemnly. "Doesn't speak much. Livvie made her drink water, but she spit it out."

Fear stabbed down my spine. "Renae?" Pushing past Darcy, I squeezed myself through the narrow gap and crouched beside Renae's prone body. She faced upright, her eyes staring blankly ahead. Only one fact kept me from panicking—she'd looked this way before. Once after she heard the hiker's death on the radio and then briefly while she navigated our way east.

She was in a trance.

"We didn't hurt her," Darcy said. "Honest."

"We need to take her back," I said, injecting a fragment of Liwai's sternness into my voice. "Now."

Darcy hesitated, wringing her hands together, but when I slipped an arm around Renae's shoulders, she scrambled inside to help me.

"Ra-nae." The word stumbled off her tongue. "What does it mean?"

"It's her name," I said. "How long has she been like this?"

"A while," the girl replied. "But she has a name. Not *tainter*?"

I didn't even want to consider if people actually called these poor girls by that term. "I don't know what that is. Just help me get her out."

Together we managed to maneuver Renae through the narrow opening of the cavern and out into the fresh air. She still wore one of Liwai's shirts paired with her denim shorts. While her face was expressionless, she was able to stand on her own and walk with some guidance. She wasn't completely catatonic in any case.

Thank goodness.

"Has she said anything?" I asked the girl. Recalling my first few meetings with Renae, I could only hope she hadn't left any freaky, prophetic drawings around to spook the girls more than they already were.

Darcy looked at me with an expression that I recognized instantly—the same one I'm sure I sported the day I found a picture of myself with a bullet wound on my passenger seat.

"Tell me what happened," I prompted.

Darcy frowned. Then, cautiously, she angled her mouth toward my ear. "Livvie said she was being crazy, but…" Her expression became constricted, her lips pursed in a frown. "She said they were coming. The pure ones. A lot of them. That… She said they'd want a war. That we should hide before it started. Then the man came with you, and even Livvie got scared." Her wide eyes conveyed more fear than she'd let on before. Only God knew what Renae had *really* said—the poor thing was terrified by it.

"Liwai, the man with me? He's her uncle," I tried to explain. "He loves her very, very much. She belongs with him. He won't hurt her."

"With him," she echoed, her eyes wide at the concept. "We thought she was a tainter like us."

"What is a *tainter*?" I instantly hated the word with a fiery passion. It sounded just as bad as any racial slur I'd ever heard and knew better than to repeat.

Darcy's eyebrows shot up, and she scanned me intently with those unnerving eyes. Whatever observation she made softened her toward me enough that she said, "Tainter is a half-breed. Like Livvie and me. We're not moon called like the others. We get beaten and treated bad. Sometimes… Bad things happen to us. So we ran away to live out here. Free. Livvie smelled her first—" she nodded toward Renae. "We knew she was a tainter, and we wanted to make her free, too. We saved her."

"So, you hit me?"

Darcy winced. "Livvie got scared. She smelled the man on you. She thought you would lead him here. We can't be found out, and we won't go back." That subtle defiance returned, lifting her jaw rebelliously. "No, never! We won't ever go back."

"To the clan?"

Confusion flitted across her gaze as she shook her head. "Don't call it that. Not for a long, long time. We were with the Family. They live on the outside, but they are just as bad as the others. So, we got out."

So Liwai's suspicions were confirmed in any case. They weren't normal girls. There were other people like him, though why did I find the prospect so odd? After all, plenty of humans had migrated and split off from each other throughout the years. My mother's family was originally from Connecticut before moving south.

But Liwai's characterizations of his people made them seem stranger than even Yankees.

"Liwai isn't with the Family or any clan," I said, hoping my meaning came across. "It's just him and Renae."

"And you?" Darcy jerked her head toward me and wrinkled her nose. "You aren't like us. Not like him, either."

"I just want to get Renae safe," I said, a task easier said than done as we finally reached the clearing near the road where Liwai stood in what I suspect was the exact position we'd left him in.

Livvie, however, had moved closer to the road and brandished a large wooden walking stick she needed both hands to hold. Rather than a large, oversized coat, she wore only a muddied, hole-riddled tank top that had once been white and a pair of equally ratty jeans.

"Darc, what are you doing? You were to *show*."

"I did." Darcy left Renae's side and approached the girl I was certain had to be her sister. "They're not bad," she said, gesturing to me. "She's human."

"Human?" Livvie cut her eyes toward me.

"Yes," Darcy said. "He is her family."

"We have no family," Livvie snarled. "She's like us. No family either."

"She has me," Liwai interjected. "Let me take her home."

He didn't appear alarmed by Renae's appearance outright. He approached her slowly, giving Darcy plenty of time to back away. Then he crouched and cradled Renae's chin gently against this palm. "Rae. Honey. Can you hear me?"

Slowly, she nodded, and I couldn't silence a sigh of relief.

"Kaydence, take her to the car."

"Wait…" I kept my arm around her shoulder, but I couldn't stop myself from turning toward Darcy. "You live out here? Both of you? Alone?"

"Yes!" Darcy beamed at the characterization. "Alone, yes. We are self-sufficient and need no one else."

"What clan are you from?" Liwai asked, rising to his feet. "How long have you been on your own?"

"No clan," Livvie snarled. "We need no clan. We are free."

The sisters seemed pleased with their circumstances. I, on the other hand, was horrified.

"There must be someplace you can go. It isn't safe out here—"

"Nowhere to go, and we are safe," Livvie hissed, pointing her stick in my direction. I wondered if that was the culprit of my current headache. "Now, take your family and leave!"

"Let's go." Liwai took Renae's hand and gently led her to the car. "Kaydence."

I took a step, but something Darcy said wouldn't leave me alone. Bad men would come. Even Liwai seemed unwilling to completely write off Renae's premonitions. What if this one had been as accurate as her one about me?

"If you need something, you can find me," I told the two girls. "I live in Kittywatt," I added, speaking more to Darcy than her sister. "You can find me there. Kaydence Blanchett—"

"Let's go," Liwai commanded.

By the time I finally reached the car, he had Renae in the back seat, her expression still vacant. I didn't even have to look over to sense his simmering anger.

"Do you have to challenge me at every turn?" His tone was quiet, but the sentiment behind the question was anything but. "Can you trust, if only for a second, that I have your best interest at heart?"

I turned my focus to the windshield, unsurprised to find that the girls had vanished. I wasn't like him. Having grown up in, albeit rural, civilization, it just wasn't in my nature to ignore the obvious perils of two young girls living in the wilderness alone, or to take orders from a man who positioned himself as an authority just because he said so. My daddy left before I was old enough to start challenging the rules, and he sure as hell didn't have a say in teaching me to mind them, either.

"I don't want to dominate you," Liwai said, insulted by whatever he found in my thoughts to make him reach that conclusion. "My only aim—the one I feel in every fiber of my being—is to protect you."

"But not them?"

He had already pulled onto the main road, rendering the two girls a distant memory.

"You don't understand what it's like for us," he said by way of explanation. "They're not normal, sweet little girls. They're feral creatures, well-equipped for survival in a landscape far harsher than this one. Here they can hunt. They can find shelter. They'll last on their own long enough to decide whether to move on or return to their clan."

"And what if they're like Renae? Don't they need 'mentoring' too?" I pointed out, though I didn't know the first thing about how the abilities among his kind actually worked. Still, the question seemed to resonate with him. He sighed and raked a hand through his hair.

"Besides, I don't think they want to return," I pointed out. "They kept mentioning the word slave. Like they were mistreated. They'll have no resources on the outside. I doubt they even have birth certificates."

Liwai shook his head. "You don't understand. Boys far younger than them are turned out of the territory to survive on their own every year. I would have broken away if I were brave enough. Out here, away from anyone, they'll be fine."

"But you wouldn't let Renae live out there, would you?" I pointed out. "You're waiting until she's eighteen to leave her."

I didn't mean it so bluntly, but he winced as if I'd struck him.

"Renae is…different. She hasn't grown up having to rely on her instincts. For the first ten years of her life, she lived like a human. She can't change. She can't hunt. She's too trusting of others. She doesn't know the first damn thing about survival, or the clan."

Renae would probably beg to differ, but I didn't rush to challenge his argument. *She lived like a human.* I hadn't heard that part of the story before, but it made sense. Why the vagrants ostracized her, and why she seemed so thin and malnourished compared to the others. Wincing, I remembered something I'd heard her say once regarding Cody, "*He made me eat the entrails.*"

"I should have killed the bastard then," Liwai snarled, his teeth bared.

"What do you mean that Renae lived like a human?" I asked, turning the subject to a less volatile topic.

"She was born on the outside," he explained. "None of the elders even came to see her, let alone acknowledge her. For the first few years of her life, she lived with her maternal grandmother. When the woman died of a heart attack, the clan finally had to decide where she would go. Kahil wouldn't accept her, but he didn't cast her out of his family line, either. They didn't want to bring her to the territory, and by then, Renae was showing signs of her gifts. They couldn't take the risk of a human foster family catching on that their sweet little girl could see into the future. I was already on the outside, and let's just say I left them no choice but to place her with the vagrants. It wasn't ideal. They couldn't turn their backs on her completely, but they offered her no protection, either. A young girl left alone with young boys in the throes of puberty—"

The mixture of disgust and fear in his voice made me flinch. I couldn't begin to comprehend the terror he must have felt all these years, unable to let her out of his sight even for an instant.

"It was a nightmare waiting to happen," he added. "If she could survive on her own, I would have turned her out myself."

"This all just sound so…brutal."

I thought I might have insulted him, but he nodded in agreement. "You don't know the half of it. And with Cody missing? If an elder comes to investigate, it will be trouble. I need to stay one step ahead."

"So, you're leaving again." I leaned away from him to rest the uninjured side of my face against the window. The cool glass soothed some of the aches and pains, but the head wound wasn't what had my stomach twisting into knots. "If we're destined for each other, it seems like we've spent more time apart than together."

Maybe he had exaggerated the strength of the connection. After all, Jerome had been able to leave Beatrice for years, and even start another family despite finding her. Perhaps the extended absences were his way of easing me into that very fate.

"He could hurt someone else," Liwai growled. "I can't let that happen."

"Will the clan let him? Won't that bring attention to you?"

He didn't answer. For a long moment, he eyed the road, his jaw clenched. Finally, he sighed. "I won't go tonight. I'll settle Renae in first and leave tomorrow. You should come with us, at least until I figure out what to do about… When that mess is squared away, we'll figure out how to deal with the bond."

He made it sound so simple—but I hadn't forgotten his warning about how the laws in his clan operated—on vengeance.

"You can argue with me later," Liwai insisted. "This is the best plan to keep both you and Renae safe. The campsite isn't far now. Just try to get some sleep." His hand found mine though he didn't seem to realize it. I eyed our combined fingers as my eyes drifted shut. I couldn't help it. I was being sucked into his mind again. Instead of his anger or confusion, I found a new emotion to marvel over —his awe.

Physical touch was an anomaly to him. He preferred to verbalize his thoughts. This was an olive branch for my benefit. His attempt to reinforce one small aspect of our pseudo-relationship, if any.

And it intrigued him, the sensation of my skin on his, the way just being near me tested his restraint to the breaking point. He couldn't go any further than simply holding my hand, of course. For him, it was a monumental effort, and I didn't take that for granted.

I couldn't.

THIRTY-ONE

She tasted too damn decadent—better than any woman had any right to be. An image filled my skull to go along with the grated, feral thought—a slender, pale throat, quivering beneath a hard swallow. Damn. He ached to bite her there. Everywhere. Feel more than her blood on his tongue. It had been so much easier before—when he couldn't feel her arousal. Smell it.

Damn, he wanted all of her. Needed her. Craved the release of mating.

His entire body pulsated with the restraint it took just to sit beside her without pulling over and letting the instinct take over. He couldn't. If he mated with her in full, there would be no going back. He needed to keep his head clear and focus only on the present.

If the worst had truly come to pass back in the clan, there was already too much at stake. He had no choice but to act.

And, the woman beside him wouldn't be merely doomed to a bond she didn't understand by the end.

She would be forever bound to a killer—

"Kaydence. We're here."

I jolted to awareness, unsure whether what I'd experienced was a dream or… Thoughts. Physically, I felt marginally better but still exhausted. As I struggled to get my bearings, I glanced out of the window. Instead of the sleepy streets of Kittywatt, we were deep in the forest, with a glimmer of sparkling water in the distance—the campsite.

"Renae's inside." Liwai stood beside the open passenger's side door. In his gaze, I didn't sense any of the raw, hungry frustration I'd sensed in that dream. He was as stoic as ever. "You can get some more sleep. I'll stay in the truck."

"Wait." I gingerly sat upright. My head was no longer throbbing, and I could see clearly, at least. Enough to realize that we'd spent most of the day on the road. It was already nearing sunset.

"How is Renae?"

Liwai inclined his head. "Still out of it. Believe it or not, I've seen her worse. She just needs to sleep it off, and she'll be fine in the morning."

"Is this how she gets before a vision?"

No wonder he'd attempted to consult the elders of the clan.

He nodded. "The longer she's in this state, the more vivid it usually is. She'll be fine."

"What if she learns that Cody is really dead? That the elders, or whatever, are on their way? What then?"

He didn't have an answer for that. Instead, he helped me out of the car and guided me to the RV. His grip on my forearm held me steady, but it also served as a conduit to the wave of emotions he'd kept locked up tight. I'd been too tired to sense it before, but I could now.

He was hiding something.

"What aren't you telling me?" I pivoted to meet his gaze and hold it, watching the nuances of his expression shift as he wrestled with the decision of whether to tell me or not. His thoughts were still tightly controlled—I only got fragments. Confusion. Dread. Fear.

"You don't want to rest first?" he asked.

"No, thank you." I shook my head. "I want the truth."

When put so bluntly, he couldn't play semantics the way he usually did. I had him cornered. With a wary glance over his shoulder, he pulled away and headed toward the lake. "Not here."

I followed him, carefully picking my way through the uneven terrain. He led us further down the beach than before, but we still had a clear view of the RV and the path leading from it.

There, he faced the water, his hands at his sides and his gaze as stormy as the sky above. "I didn't tell you everything about why the others may have been called back. As I said before, Cody might not have anything to do with it—but we should both pray that he does."

I reacted to the tension in his tone and stumbled closer toward him without meaning to. A tendril of unease ripped through me, but it felt more like an echo rather than a genuine emotion of mine. Was it his?

"What's going on?"

"I don't know," he admitted with a helpless shrug. He'd changed since we'd returned, and the gray shirt and jeans made him stand out against the silvery backdrop of the lake and sky. "When we are children, before we are exiled, we are given a handful of reasons why we might be recalled—none of them good.

"Most are obsolete now—in times of extreme famine or war with rival clans. As far as I know, we own the largest territory in this part of the country. There are no other clans large enough to serve as a threat, if any exist at all—" Apparently, he doubted that Livvie and Darcy weren't from his territory. "But the most likely reason vagrants are called home? The death of the clan's elder."

I felt my eyes widen. "Your brother?"

"No," Liwai said with a harsh bark of laughter. "Kahil may think he runs things, but Bartow's ruled the clan for over thirty years. Usually, one of his male heirs would take over, but his only son, Raek, died years ago. Tradition called for Bartow to pick a successor to serve in his place. He chose Kahil…"

There was more to it that he wasn't saying. Frustration gnawed at me, tinged with a small, stabbing bit of guilt.

"Jerome made it seem like your family was important," I said, unsure what I was even getting at.

A certain part of that statement, however, made Liwai clench his teeth and hiss. "One could say that. We… The Ravens traditionally have led the clan, though not always. Rules state that the firstborn son or a chosen successor inherits. When my father died, that role passed onto me."

I swallowed at his tone. He didn't sound cocky or arrogant. He sounded pained instead, as if merely voicing that out loud hurt him more than anything. Still, that admission just confused me more.

"Not Kahil?"

Liwai shook his head. "Not Kahil. Only those who have returned from their task are eligible to lead, however. Which meant that Bartow assumed power, always with the assumption that he would stand aside when I returned. Instead, Kahil went back before I did. Because he is only the second born, Bartow was under no obligation to relinquish his leadership, but he made concessions to ensure Kahil is his successor anyway." With a heavy sigh, he tore both hands through his hair and eyed the sky. More tension flooded our tenuous connection, strengthening into two very distinct emotions. One was a greater, more potent sense of fear. The other? Anger.

"Was he close to you, Bartow?" I asked.

"Not particularly," he replied. "But he was steady. Reasonable. He maintained a fragile truce between tradition and violence. I'm sure it wasn't easy. Much of our laws and rules were enforced at his discretion. Our government isn't like yours—the clan leaders are entrusted with absolute power. The kind of power someone like Kahil should never have access to. Bartow didn't let zealous greed overrule logic."

"You're worried." And his unease drew me to him like a moth to flame. I couldn't help it. One of my hands ghosted his shoulder before settling against his forearm.

To my shock, he allowed the contact. I think he was too distracted to care.

"I'm cautious," he said. "Many things will change, and not for the better. I'm afraid Renae's safety could be one of the first things tested by his new leadership. Kahil wasn't *just* Bartow's successor. When Raek died, he had a wife and a son. By being named Bartow's successor, Kahil took them both as a sign of good faith. Repayment, you could say, for leading in our father's stead. Kahil became Bartow's son in name. In blood. It was an honor sacred enough to ignore the tradition of the promised woman, and the mate picked out for Kahil when he left was given to another. You can't even begin to understand the significance of that. The duty he had to undertake."

"The son... Was that Cody?" I asked, struggling to keep up.

He nodded. "Believe me, it's more complicated than you can imagine. In the eyes of the clan, Cody is—was—Kahil's son, his true heir, but Renae is still technically a part of his bloodline too. While Bartow was in power, she could be ignored. But if Cody is dead…"

More anger wafted from him, mingled with a helpless frustration that made my heart pang with sympathy.

"She isn't safe," I said, voicing what he couldn't.

"It was Bartow's word that granted her the ability to stay with the vagrants. That doesn't sound like much—and it isn't—but it was better than the alternative."

"You mean… You think Kahil will change that?"

"No. Worse." His tortured grimace proved that. "Rather than just disown her, the bastard wanted her cast out at birth. A death sentence. If he had his way now, she'd be hunted down and killed. I know it."

Horror washed over me. "But she's his daughter."

"He would kill you for saying that," Liwai snarled. "Because of the nature of her birth, he can't acknowledge her, but shame isn't what drives him. Revenge is. He sees her existence as a threat, and out of spite, he'll deny her any happiness. Any chance at a normal life. He'll take his anger out on a child. That is what cowards do."

"Why?" I thought I had daddy issues, but this was something far more sinister. I'd take my awkward situation with Burt Michaels any day. "Because of what happened to Laurie? Is that why you tried to take custody of her—"

He whirled to face me. "How do you know that?"

I hesitated, unsure of whether to reveal Renae's secret eaves-dropping. The second the thought entered my mind, his eyes narrowed.

"I told her to be careful around them," he snarled. "Damn it. It would be easier for her if she didn't know."

"Easier to think that no one cared for her?" I reached for him again, but this time I was fully in control as I braced my palm against his chest.

His eyes cut down to my fingers, noting how they trembled. How insubstantial they were against his bulk. He'd merely have to shrug to bat me away.

But he didn't.

He captured my hand instead, holding it captive against stronger fingers calloused with hard labor and age.

"Easier if she didn't take a side. She needs to stay neutral. If Kahil does take over… *When* he does—she needs to be far away from the territory."

"Because he'll use her as your retribution," I said, hating myself for putting him in such a position. My eyes burned, my chest tight. "But if you went back, wouldn't that make you the leader? You could stop him."

Suddenly, he was closer, his breath warm on my neck as he sighed. "There is another potential barrier to his ascension as the leader. He has to be anointed by the clan first. That process can take several days. Maybe there is someone bold enough to challenge him."

"How will you know?" I asked.

He pulled away and shrugged. "I won't. The only thing I can do is prepare for the worst-case scenario."

Prepare. I doubted he was referring to the ceremony.

"That's the real reason you're anxious to leave again," I surmised, resting my hand on his arm. "You want to go back to them, before your brother takes over. *You* want to be that barrier."

At the accusation, a thought crept into my head, but like always, it was primarily composed of images. Violence. Bloodshed. Then a snippet from my dream—*She'll be forever bound to a killer...*

Overwhelmed, I took a step back, though he said nothing out loud. I didn't have the heart to press him for more answers. I just stood beside him and watched the waning sunlight play off the rippling waves.

"We should get back," he said finally. "Before Renae wakes up."

"Wait. There's something else I want to know." I inhaled, bracing myself for his reaction. He could keep his secrets regarding his own personal relationships with the people from his past—but not when it came to me. "Why did you... *How* did you heal me?"

"You mean, why did I take your blood," he said, rephrasing my hesitant probing into a direct accusation. His posture shifted, losing its guarded stiffness. This was a topic he didn't mind discussing. "I don't have an odd fetish, if that's what you're thinking. It's instinct. A few drops can strengthen our connection without risking…more. Enough that you can heal."

Heal. He made it sound so simple, but it wasn't. Surviving a bullet wound without a scratch was no minor feat. It was a power I couldn't even begin to comprehend—one that lurked between the two of us, straining to be released in full.

"That's all?" I felt brave enough to prod.

Of course not. Newer images popped into my head, filling in the blanks of what he didn't say. Drinking blood was his last resort before pinning me down. Plunging his fingers inside me to taste another part of my body. I could see him imagining it, that moment in the shower. His hand between my legs. My body writhing. My gasps in his ear.

Every instinct in his body urged him to initiate the action. Only then would we be truly connected. And his aversion to doing so was *almost* as strong as his desire to fight for Renae. *We can't.*

"It's safer this way, Kaydence," he said out loud, snapping me back to the present.

Slowly, he turned to face me. As our eyes met, a sensation burned through my skin, reminiscent of an electric shock. It certainly didn't feel safe. It felt…

Suffocating. Like we both were holding our breath, desperate to resurface from this wave of hellish emotion we found ourselves submerged in. The only way out, however, was to give in to the impulse urging us closer, even as Liwai took a step back.

"You've always felt this," I said. It wasn't a question, but a recognition of what he himself had alluded to over and over. Only now was I beginning to understand. "Even when I was with someone else?"

The list wasn't long, of course, but the allusion to my past romances triggered an avalanche of responses within him. He stiffened, a grunt rasping in his throat. Fragmented thoughts tripped into my consciousness—*the others. Never let them get close enough. Drove them off. Couldn't help it.* A figure came to mind to go along with a burst of rage so intense I gasped out loud.

Boyd, laughing with me that night in the bar. Liwai's thoughts in that moment hadn't been his typical objective observations. Pure instinct drove him then. *Kill.*

Abruptly, the connection went dead, and I knew it was because Liwai was using all his effort to push me out. He didn't want me to see the depths of what the bond made him feel. Deep, simmering jealousy.

"I won't… I'm not going to hunt down any man who takes an interest in you," he said, his brows furrowed in frustration. He didn't like how those words came out. They sounded like lies. "Should you move on. You *need* to move on."

But he didn't believe that—he couldn't. And neither did I. Not because of the bond, either. That was all lust. Instinct. It wasn't the aspect of him that drew my notice the most— beneath all the heightened, violent sensations washing through him was a single thought that seemed trapped within the tempest like a twig in a rainstorm. Insignificant at first, but still powerful enough to puncture glass and kill someone with the right force and the right approach.

She's too damn smart. Too stubborn. Won't believe a lie. Can't tell her the truth, either—

"What truth?" I asked him.

His eyes narrowed. One moment, there was a respectful distance between us. The next, our faces were inches apart, his breath warm on my face.

He never said a word out loud, but whatever grasp he kept on his thoughts loosened for a split second, and I could see everything. All that he'd ever thought of me. *Too skinny at first. Too plain. Too weak. Glasses were a hindrance, a genetic flaw. The elders were right. Their way kept the bloodline pure. Humans were inferior.* Then as the years passed, his senti- ments changed.

She noticed too much. Saw too much. Thought too much— about every little thing. She was too isolative. So guarded. Watchful.

My thoughts intrigued him just as much as his confounded me, though back then, he'd only gotten snippets.

He thought I'd recoil at Renae and her odd behavior the same way most others did. She was an outcast at her school, always alone. Always. But I hadn't done that. I'd shown her kindness, and he was grateful for that. So damn grateful.

At the same time, he hated the connection growing between her and me. It would make it harder to run. He could deny himself everything—but he hated to deny Renae *anything*.

"I'm sorry," I blurted, struggling to disentangle my mind from his. "I didn't mean—"

With gentle but dizzying pressure, his lips settled over mine without warning. My brain went blank at the sensation, overwhelmed. It wasn't like before. Rather than mindlessly react to the impulse driving us closer, we simply *breathed* in and out before he nudged my lips further apart. The warm, wet velvet of his tongue was a shock. I froze, and he grunted in alarm as if he didn't realize what he was doing until it was far too late to stop.

He'd fantasized about tasting me, but this…

It was a teasing hint of a drug too potent to resist.

"Kaydence." He whispered my name, as if it were a prayer to some deity as vague and mysterious as him. Maybe a god of suffering and pain—that was what I meant to him, a burden he couldn't lift so easily. He had to destroy it piece by piece.

And some twisted part of me craved to submit myself to him. The desire was a wildfire, smothering all coherent thought in its wake. I arched into him, and he caught me by the waist. Rather than shove me away, he pulled me into him, and it felt good. Too good. I inhaled at the feeling of him—hard and sinewy muscle. Undeniably strong and yet lithe at the same time. Graceful. As he pressed in to deepen the kiss, I didn't resist.

I'd spent so much of my life cringing at normalcy. Hating the inherent protection that came with living in a small town and abiding by small-town rules. He changed that. With him, normal was creeping fingers and rasping breaths. A pounding heartbeat and a sensation I couldn't name pooled in my limbs, heading south to a part of me I'd never explored.

Not like this.

He made "normal" into a Band-Aid he ripped away, exposing the writhing, gaping wound beneath. I'd craved this for so long without realizing it. *This*—contact. Sensation. His hands on my hips, tugging my jeans down.

Right and wrong went out the window. All that mattered was experiencing more, and feeling all I could with him before he left.

Because he would leave me—everyone did.

Guilt stabbed through my chest, but it was only an echo of what he felt. *I'm sorry. So sorry…*

And he should have been. For taunting me with this— passion, lust, aching need. He owed me more than a sorry.

He owed me…something. Something to hold onto. A memory I could torture myself with when he finally left me—because I could feel it in my gut that he eventually would.

Can't cement the bond, came an answering thought. *But…*

Before disappointment could set in, he pivoted, guiding me off the path and against a nearby tree. The hard surface pressed into my back, allowing him to nudge my legs apart, all while still maneuvering his lips over mine.

My heart thudded like mad as he brushed a hand along my hip before tugging at the clasp of my pants. *Can't go further than touching*—he seemed to be chanting that reminder over and over in his mind.

For the time being, touching seemed more than enough. *Not for long,* I heard a part of him warn. Knowing that didn't seem to matter in the meantime. I felt desperate to return his kiss. Desperate to unhook my pants to let him feel the skin waiting beneath, and then what sat between them…

My breath caught as I rocked my hips against the palm of his hand. There were a million real-world concerns threatening to descend, but I managed to ignore them all. He presented a dichotomy with a single touch—rough and silky, hard and soft. Physical contact was just the beginning. In a way, our blurry connection had become a clear-glass window that allowed me to see into his heart.

He was so vast, his every thought process alien to me. Most men, I assumed, viewed sex as a conquest, their rite of passage, a boon to dating someone. To him, even a kiss was a blasphemous betrayal of his philosophy—to never waver, never falter, and never relent. Going any further was the last thing he wanted—and the only thing he could think about. I could see myself reflected in his mind, and his perception was so different from the lanky, gawky woman I knew. My hair was redder, my eyes were bolder, and my entire body cried out to him in a way that made my cheeks catch fire, along with everything else in me.

To him, my skin was alabaster, and every caress soothed an ache he hadn't been aware of for the past thirty-four years. I gasped at his age—but that was the least of his long list of reasons why this could never work for him.

The foremost among them?

He had already decided on a course of action that almost guaranteed his death, and nothing would change his mind. Not even me. With Kahil in power, there was only one way to end this…

Bloodshed.

"Stop—" I recoiled, wincing as my headache returned at full force. My knees buckled, and he rushed to hold me upright. All I could do to resist the contact was slam my palm against his chest—he didn't even flinch.

"You're going to challenge your brother," I croaked out, staggering for balance—but it was more than that. I couldn't garner the whole details, but I could guess the gist. Ranae's fears were cemented as well—he would take credit for Cody's death.

"You can't," I stammered, trying to put the pieces together, but it was like trying to navigate a maze in utter darkness. Whatever this entailed, he was willing to put his life on the line to see it through. He was willing to kill to enact it. Cody. Kahil. Anyone who got in his way. He would go to war. "You can't sacrifice yourself for me."

Liwai frowned, raising a dark eyebrow. "Now I know how you feel," he said in a deadpan tone. "It's invasive to have someone read your thoughts without permission."

I expected anger, not a dispassionate response that almost sounded like… Had that been a joke? He wasn't used to making light of a situation. The concept amused him, but he'd stolen it.

Right out of my own playbook.

"I've been on the outside almost as long as you've been alive," he said dryly. "My list of corny jokes is nothing compared to yours."

His upper lip quirked. A smile?

"How can you be so…calm?" I demanded.

It was more than a façade. Some of the tension coiled in his body since the moment he found me had eased. It was as if a weight had been lifted from him. He could breathe easy again, and even someone as stern as he was could make light of such a doomed situation.

He wanted to challenge Kahil and preempt any vengeance for Cody's death. Greed wasn't his reasoning or a desire to make a power grab. Only one person served as his motivation—Renae. There were other things, too, tucked away at the furthest reaches of his mind. A desire for freedom. A need to break away from the traditions he'd been bound to.

Maybe a little bit of selfish greed. He wanted to live his life on *his* terms, no one else's.

"If I challenge him outright, Kahil will have no choice but to accept my petition," Liwai said, his voice low. "You won't be his main focus, and he can't hold Renae's life over my head any longer."

"And if you lose?" I asked, though I already knew the answer.

Still, he didn't shy away from voicing it, his tone low. "I die. But if I do nothing…" He sighed, and images crept into my brain to describe what he didn't have the heart to verbalize.

If he did nothing, he would have to watch on helplessly as the clan tore her apart. Whether at the whim of hormonal vagrants or due to Kahil's decree, sooner or later, peril would find her.

And when it came down to it, his choice was simple. "I would rather die than do nothing."

"I know," I whispered. His reasoning showed brightly in my mind, stronger than any conviction I'd ever held before. To take offense would be ignorant, not to mention selfish. He knew his world far better than I did, and I doubted he'd undertake such a drastic action without good reason.

Still, the selfish thoughts lingered. Again, he planned on leaving, this time for good. So much for this vast, sacred connection between us. It only seemed to cause him an unwelcomed distraction, and for me, it meant pain.

"You're beginning to understand," Liwai said. His tone wasn't mocking that time. One of his hands bridged the gap between us and traced a path up my arm. "What I've had to live with these past few years."

His touch lingered—and he might as well have set me on fire. That prickling heat returned. A throbbing ache began to build in the pit of my stomach, between my legs…

Did he have to live with this, also? Constant, pulsing, mindless want.

With a grunt, Liwai withdrew his hand. "Let's get back before Renae wakes up."

I adjusted my rumpled clothing and trailed him up the path. Renae was still sleeping inside by the time we made it back. Liwai headed for the truck and fished out the mound of supplies he'd bought our first day on the run. I'd almost forgotten the tent and various other equipment he'd purchased.

For the time being, he set up two lawn chairs and began clearing the space for a fire. Absolutely useless with any survival skill beyond roasting marshmallows, I settled for watching him while trying not to replay what happened on the beach.

I failed.

The deft way he stoked newborn flames to life seemed to parallel the effect he had on me. I felt as easily manipulated as a pile of burning embers, dependent on his skill to grow them into a small, contained inferno—but even he couldn't control everything. Should one of those errant embers land in the right spot, it could turn into a much larger, more dangerous blaze, woefully out of his purview.

"You should eat something," he said once finished. If he'd heard the pity party taking place in my thoughts, he didn't say as much. He entered the RV and returned with a packet of hog dogs that he began to roast on metal skewers.

We ate in silence, and it almost felt like the normal camping trip I'd told Dee I was on. Until Liwai looked up and held my stare, that is.

"There is more," he said grimly, to preface yet another revelation. "If I die, you need to be ready."

He was referring to more than the potential emotional trauma aspect.

"I want you to take Renae and run," he added. "You can't let grief or pain stop you from doing that. You need to promise me."

For the time being, I decided to overlook the fact that he was asking me to take custody of a teenage girl in favor of another startling revelation. "Pain?"

"You'll feel it," he said thickly. "Everything I feel will resonate through you, times ten. You need to prepare your mind to withstand that. I've done what I can to keep the bond from reaching its full strength, but I don't think it will matter much in the long run."

"Is that the real reason you kept me alive?" I asked, facing him from the opposite end of the fire. "Because it hurt too much to let me die."

His dark eyes reflected the flames, seeming to dance with light and shadow. "If you want something to hate me for, then yes. Bearing the pain of a bullet wound to my abdomen was a bit beyond my threshold."

He was lying. I was starting to pick up on the nuances of his varying moods. He was the sternest when he had utter confidence that he was right, but when he felt there was no other choice to be made… He relied on dry, morbid humor to lighten the mood.

"Tell me the truth," I whispered, but my words were nearly swallowed by the crackling of the flames. "Why?"

He sat forward with his palms resting on either knee. Slowly, his expression shifted from thoughtful to grim. "Because I was weak," he said finally. "A coward. Hearing that hurts you, I know, but one day you'll realize that I was right. You need to be stronger than I was. Strong enough to let the inevitable take place and survive without wondering what might have been."

It was a convincing speech. I might have been swayed by the grit in his voice if it weren't for the subtle rustle of the RV door opening during the tirade.

Like a specter, Renae descended the metal steps and waited on him silently, bathed in shadow.

Liwai didn't even turn around, but he sighed. "Rae, wait—"

"You're a liar!" With that, Renae took off toward the lake, and he stood, hissing through his teeth.

"No," he snapped as I scrambled to my feet as well. "Let me talk to her alone."

He stormed off, his hulking shape moving at a fraction of the pace Renae's quick, sly frame was. Deep down, I knew he was right. They were family—I was just a voyeuristic outsider.

That didn't make being pushed to the boundaries of their dynamic sting any less. To take the edge off my embarrassment, I wandered in the opposite direction, never venturing further than the firelight reached.

This section of forest was beautiful, current circumstances aside. There was no reason I couldn't bask in what tiny shreds of enjoyment I could find on this "trip." The moon was beautiful and full up above, and with the whispering waves in the distance, it felt tranquil. Untouched. A place I should definitely return to with my real soulmate, who would be perfect, devoid of any baggage like curses, and shapeshifting, and…

Utter nonchalance when it came to death. Yes, sirree, my real future lover, would have none of those pesky cons to dim his shine. Yet, when I tried to envision him, all I saw was golden skin, dark eyes, and rich, long hair the color of midnight.

By the time I circled back around to the campsite, Liwai and Renae were still gone. Entering the RV without them just felt icky, so I retreated to my car instead—my bastion of isolation on this island of exile upon which I found myself. One might think I would have been used to being alone by now.

Despite the ache of rejection, I must have drifted off because a sudden knock on my windshield startled me awake. I came to disoriented, relieved to find that Liwai stood beside my door and not some stranger. His expression, however, was wary, and he placed a finger to his lips as I scrambled out to meet him.

Bringing his mouth to my ear, he said, "Something's wrong. Take Renae."

The girl stood beside him, and I grabbed her hand, pulling her to my side. Together, we watched as Liwai slowly began to pace the clearing, his eyes on the shadows, hunting for any swaying branch or bramble out of place. He must have made a complete circle three times before he finally stopped and beckoned us over with a jerk of his chin.

"It must have been a wild animal," he said, but I could feel his unease. He wasn't entirely sure the cause was truly that harmless. "When it gets lighter, we'll move out. You two can sleep inside."

I didn't argue with what was clearly an order more than a suggestion. I reached for Renae's hand and led her toward the RV.

We'd only gone a few steps when Liwai lunged in front of us.

From behind a tree, stepped a tall figure with dark hair and large green eyes that seemed to swallow what little light there was.

"I thought it would be hard to find you, but you were never one for subtlety," she said. Her voice was lilting, tinged with an accent I couldn't place. She certainly wasn't from around Kittywatt.

"And you aren't one for cryptic visits out of nowhere," Liwai replied, but his voice lacked the hostility he utilized around Cody. It was level, wrought with… Was that respect? It was so rare to see him defer to someone else. Only Renae seemed to bring that wry grin out of him. As quickly as it came, the expression fell. "What are you doing here, Talia?"

"Saving your ass, like always," the woman replied, advancing with confident strides. "My, my, my, Liwai. You've really fucked up this time."

She was beautiful, and I don't know why realizing that made my heart constrict and my chest ache. A chin-length haircut framed her angular cheekbones and delicate facial features. She was tall and slim, dressed in a perfect set of hiking attire— black boots, khaki shorts, and a loose-fitting plaid button-up left partially undone to reveal the black tank top underneath.

If I had to picture a woman who might look like a fitting counterpart to a man like Liwai Raven, she'd come close. Confident and bold and utterly unafraid of him.

"You're lucky I found you first," she added. "No longer are you just courting shame and embarrassment, Liwai. They're convening a council right now to discuss dispatching an elder, merely to deal with *you*—"

Alarm lanced through me, though I didn't recognize the term enough to react to it on my own. Liwai, however, did. His eyes narrowed, his posture stiff.

"And are you here to lead the way?"

"No." The woman shrugged. "I'm here, believe it or not, to *warn* you. Bartow's dead. Kahil is already stepping up to lead, tradition be damned, and you are his first order of business to see to. I'm sure you can guess why, considering your traveling companion." Her eyes flitted in my direction. "Ah, this must be—"

"No!" A blurred figure came from nowhere to slam into the woman before she made it across the camp. My initial fear was that a fox or a wolf had darted from the shadows, but no…. The creature lashing at the woman with her nails drawn was a compact, lithe figure that appeared entirely human. Renae.

"No! No! Get away!"

"Renae!" Liwai bellowed her name multiple times, but he had to hook his arm around her waist to drag her back. She kicked and flailed despite being restrained, her mouth fixed into a snarl.

"No! She's evil," she shrieked. "She's evil. Send her away! I hate her! No!"

She shouted a similar rant even as Liwai hauled her into the RV. His desperate glance in my direction was my only cue to follow. For once, I was needed, it seemed.

Still, I couldn't suppress a shudder as I raced past the woman and felt her large eyes on my neck. Talia. He'd mentioned her before, but with none of the open warmth he'd displayed in her presence. While he seemed disdainful of most things associated with the pack, he was different when it came to her. She meant something to him.

And I told myself that I had no reason to care.

Clearing my mind of everything but concern for Renae, I entered the RV and found Liwai in the process of wrestling her onto the bench at the kitchen table.

She fought him with every ounce of strength in her small body, shouting all the while. "She's bad! She's bad! Make her go away. Please, Liwai!"

He spotted me, his teeth bared in exasperation. "Think you can give me a hand, here?"

I rushed forward, but rather than help him pin her down, I placed a hand on her shoulder instead.

"Calm down, honey. If you want us to hear you, you need to talk clearly. Speak to me. I'm listening."

Sputtering, Renae went still, her eyes bloodshot and swollen with fresh tears.

"She's a bad person," she struggled to say. "I saw it. She does bad things. You can't let her stay with us, please. You can't!"

"What kind of things?" Liwai asked. From his tone, I could tell he believed her, and I could only wonder how many times he'd been in a similar position, prodding her for answers after one of her catatonic states.

Rather than explain, Renae shook her head and pursed her lips. Her gaze sought out mine, wrought with earnest desperation. "She's bad," she insisted. "Kaydee, you can't let her stay. I hate her—"

"Can I talk to her?" Liwai said with a sigh. "That's all. Let me at least find out what she wants—" He turned his attention to me. "Stay with her. I'm just going to talk to her. That's it."

"She's bad," Renae wailed mournfully. "She's a bad person. She's bad!"

Once Liwai left the RV, she clung to me and rested her head on my shoulder.

"You can't let her be with him," she said. "I don't want her to be. I want him to be with you."

Be with? That sounded far different than an imminent threat.

"Just calm down." I settled down beside her and did my best to comfort her in any way I could. In the end, I stroked the hair from her face. "Nothing bad is going to happen."

Though, given that I couldn't see into the future, my words rang hollow. Nonetheless, Renae quieted down, and her sobs became sniffles.

"I don't like her," she insisted. "She's one of *them*."

From the clan. One of the women whom Liwai claimed rarely left their territory—but not just anyone. Her.

I could feel his recognition of her seep through our connection. He was cautious, but maybe a little relieved? Then on guard. He knew Talia well—namely, when she was worried.

And when she was afraid.

Words entered my mind next, uttered in a feminine, lilting cadence.

"*...The council is in an uproar. Kahil is on the warpath, spreading rumors,*" Talia said, her voice hissed. "*He doesn't want to wait to be anointed. He'll move to strike you down and anyone else who gets in his way. It's not just your life on the line —so is mine. To counter him, you need the elders on your side. They won't even think of standing against him without knowing where your loyalty lies. You know what needs to be done, Liwai. Think of it as a mercy, for both your sakes—*"

"She's going to make him go back," Renae said in between gasping sobs, drawing my attention to her. "She wants him to return to the fold, and if he does, he'll kill you, Kaydence," she wailed, tears streaming down her face. "He'll do it this time for real. I've seen it. He thinks it will be the only way to save me."

And in her fragile, broken whisper, I knew she wasn't lying.

"The only way to stop it is to make him complete the bond," she went on, clawing at my hand to draw me closer.

"Make him do it, and no one can touch you..." She drew in a ragged sob and met my gaze, forcing me to hear the honesty in every word she would say next. "If you don't, he'll have no choice. He'll rip your throat out with his teeth. *She's* the start of it—" She gestured wildly to the window where Liwai stood, confronting the strange woman. "So, make her leave! If you tell him to, he'll listen."

"Renae..."

"Promise me! You have to promise! You'll make him be with you! Please!" She took both of my hands in hers, forcing me to meet her gaze.

But I froze, unsure of what in the world to do.

Which outcome would even be better in the long run?

To die?

Or tether myself to a man I barely knew on the whims of a teenager? *Liar,* a part of me whispered. Renae wouldn't be the only reason I'd pursue Liwai. Some deep-seated part of me needed to explore this bond in full. It felt more than a crush or a romantic whim.

It felt *vital.*

And this woman—Talia—was a threat I felt in the core of my being.

In any case, something told me that I wouldn't have long to decide. My life would change drastically whether I wanted it to or not.

Neither Liwai nor I could stop what was coming.

~ Liwai and Kaydee's story continues in Monster in My Heart ~

A Word from the Author

Hey there!

Thank you so much for reading! If you enjoyed the story, please leave a review and recommend the book to any friend you think would love this twisted world. You'd have my eternal gratitude. Even a short sentence goes a long way!

Then, come join the rest of us dark romance lovers in my Facebook Group where you can get snippets, sneak peeks of upcoming books and even help vote on aspects of future novels.

Come to the dark side:

https://www.facebook.com/groups/lanasbeautifulmonsters/

WANT MORE STUFF TO READ?

Join my newsletter and get a **free book**! Plus, you get to stay updated with any new releases, random giveaways and exclusive sneak peeks!

https://www.lanaskybooks.com/newsletter

Other Novels: https://lanaskybooks.com/

FREE BOOK - JOIN MY NEWSLETTER

DARK, TWISTED ROMANCE

Join my newsletter and get a **free book**! Plus, you get to stay updated with any new releases, random giveaways and exclusive sneak peeks!

https://www.lanaskybooks.com/newsletter

ABOUT THE AUTHOR

Lana Sky is a reclusive writer in the United States who spends most of her time daydreaming about complex male characters and parenting her Cockapoo Joey. She writes dark, twisted romance across several genres. Her titles include everything from mafia romance to vampires.

facebook.com/AuthorLanaSky

twitter.com/lanasky101

amazon.com/author/lanasky

pinterest.com/lanasky101

goodreads.com/lanasky

instagram.com/lanasky101

bookbub.com/authors/lana-sky

tiktok.com/@author_lana_sky

ALSO BY LANA SKY

For more titles by Lana Sky, please visit:

https://www.lanaskybooks.com